ordinary decent criminals

ordinary decent criminals

A Novel

Lionel Shriver

Previously published as
The Bleeding Heart

HARPER ● PERENNIAL

NEW YORK ● LONDON ● TORONTO ● SYDNEY ● NEW DELHI ● AUCKLAN

HARPER ● PERENNIAL

HarperCollins books may be purchased for educational, business, or sales promotional use. For information, please e-mail the Special Markets Department at SPsales@harpercollins.com.

Originally published as *The Bleeding Heart* in 1990 by Farrar, Straus and Giroux.

FIRST HARPER PERENNIAL EDITION 2015.

Designed by Liney Li

Library of Congress Cataloging-in-Publication Data has been applied for.

ISBN 978-0-06-239058-5

15 16 17 18 19   OV/RRD   10 9 8 7 6 5 4 3 2 1

To the Old Man:

Revenge is tribute

"Happiness is often presented as being very dull but, he thought, lying awake, that is because dull people are sometimes very happy and intelligent people can and do go around making themselves and everyone else miserable. He had never found happiness dull. It always seemed more exciting than any other thing, with promise of as great intensity as sorrow to those people who were capable of having it."

Ernest Hemingway,
Islands in the Stream

Contents

CONTENTS

In case of difficulty with acronyms,

jargon, and the morass of Irish history,

the reader is urged to consult

the Glossary of Troublesome Terms

at the back of this book.

ordinary decent criminals

1

Hot Black Bush

Between them, pure alcohol coiled from the turned-back lid; the air curled with its distortion. Vaporous, the face stretched longer and thinner than the pillar it began. The shimmer off the vat worried his expression, tortured his eyebrows in the heat, further emphasizing a figure already overdrawn: too wild, too skinny, too tall.

As she stood on tiptoe to lean over the wooden tub, on the other side the tall man saw only the dark tremble of a girl's unruly hair. He wondered at letting children tour a distillery. Then, why shouldn't they be confirmed early, sip at the chalice—Bushmills was the real Church of Ireland, after all. Later, he would catch sight of her down the walk toward bottling and not recognize the grown woman in black leather bouncing the red motorcycle helmet against her thigh. Though she was barely over five feet, at any distance her slight proportions created the optical illusion that she was not small, rather, farther away.

The man did not need to clutch the rim, but leaned at the waist to inhale. When the girl looked up he saw she was not ten or twelve but at least twenty. Their glances met; both took a deep breath. The man reared back again, snapping upright; the woman went flat on her feet. Tears rose and noses began to run. The fumes went straight to the center, acupuncture. The staves of the cavernous room warped cozily around them. The man could no longer remember what had so concerned him moments ago; for the first time in months he felt his face relax. Across the tub, she watched the lines lift from him and decided he was not fifty, as she'd first thought, but thirty-two or -three. In fact, if she'd asked him just then how old he was, he might have claimed yes, he was thirty-three, because the last ten years had been trying and he could not remember anything trying while breathing over a washback with this pretty girl. Christ, he missed whiskey.

"Better than shots," she admitted. "This is my second time through."

The alcohol evaporated from his head. He recalled what he'd been sorting out, and returned to *one and a half million paupers would never get a full vote in the EEC.* Her twang was unmistakable: bloody hell, she was American.

Their group had moved on; the two treated themselves to one more inhalation of the wort, which roiled between them like whipped cream gone off, Guinness on a stove. Its surface churned and kneaded into itself, a little sickening, too brown. The American let down the wooden flat regretfully. "We'll be missed." As her boots echoed down the washbacks, she passed a beefy man at the door.

"Farrell, lad. A wee five-minute tour and you're away."

Farrell. She remembered his name.

Farrell waited, not wanting to walk with her. He'd no desire to violate the intimacy of their brief debauch with the disappointing whine of an American tourist. His head cleared, the last two minutes had encapsulated his life: the giddy rise and fall of it. Excessive indulgence to excessive discipline, and that was substances, though women the same—the clasping of hands over tables, the grappling in the back of taxis, the sweaty riot in the hotel, so quickly giving way to veiled excuses, impossible schedules, the dread cold quiet of a woman's phone unrung. Increasingly, he had an eye outside the abandon, the desperate swings; all he could see was pattern, and in this way nothing changed. It was harder and harder to perceive anything at all as actually happening.

Estrin Lancaster was not the only American on this tour; the piping comments of just the couple she longed to escape had led her to bottling. The two were Northeasterners, though Estrin could no longer decode their accents into states. Abroad the better part of ten years now, Estrin was growing stupid about her own country, and had to admit that while she plowed her Moto Guzzi over the Middle East she hadn't a clue what was going on in Pennsylvania; and that this, like any ignorance, was no claim to fame. Rather, she'd made a trade-off, a real important trade-off, because there was a way you could know the place you were born that you never got a crack at anywhere else, and Estrin didn't have that chance anymore.

These years her access to U.S. news had been spotty, and lately, when Americans glommed onto her—a national characteristic—she didn't get their jokes. She was currently following the Birmingham Six appeal, with all the unlikelihood of a British reversal—the more miserable the evidence on which the six Irishmen were convicted, the more certain the decision would remain, for didn't people defend their weakest opinions with the most violence? Yet Estrin barely skimmed articles about presidential primaries in the States. She knew she was lost when in her *Irish Times* she no longer understood *Doonesbury*. The detachment had become disquieting.

"Did you notice all those *L*'s and *R*'s on people's cars, Dale? Do you suppose that means Loyalist and Republican?"

Estrin flinched. The stickers meant *Learner* and *Restricted*, and she saw locals look to each other and smile. No one corrected the woman's mistake. Estrin didn't either. Simply, she didn't want to be seen with them: sheer badness. Americans embarrassed her. They made no distinction between what came into their heads and what came out—an endless stream of petty desires and ill-examined impressions dribbling from a hole in the face, the affliction amounted to mental incontinence.

"Better you're not seen running after me, MacBride," said Farrell coldly to the man in the doorway.

"Only tourists. That was the idea."

"We were to run into each other. You're getting sloppy."

"Successful. Seen off with Farrell O'Phelan, I'll survive. You're such a chameleon, I paint you the color I like. More harm done you, I'd think."

"On the contrary, one of my accomplishments—"

"One of the *many*," said MacBride pleasantly.

"—is I can be seen with whomever I like."

"Everyone knows we were mates back."

"Everyone was everyone's mate back," said Farrell. "What makes this place so sordid."

"Quite a lolly passed me at the door," MacBride observed, moving on to more interesting business. "All that black leather, wouldn't have to dress her up, like."

"Young for you," said Farrell distractedly.

"Looks old enough to know how."

"Haven't you your hands full with—"

"Ah-ah." MacBride raised a finger as they drew within earshot of the group. "Now *that* is sloppy."

Estrin knew Bad Work, so she recognized the strain in their guide's patter. He injected his information with artificial enthusiasm, like pumping adrenaline into a corpse. If he kept the job he would have to give over, and not simply to boredom, for there are states far beyond that, where you no longer recognize that at 2:45 there is any alternative to repeating "Our water rises in peaty ground" one more time. It's relaxing, actually, a sacrifice to other forces. Minutes stretch out so wide and meaningless there is no more time, there are no more questions. Beyond interpretation or struggle, the advanced stages of Bad Work amount to a religious conversion. Also to being dead. She assessed the guide: Estrin would have quit by now.

She swung between the pot stills towering fifteen feet overhead, shining Hershey's Kisses. Bushmills kept the copper polished—now, that was the job she would keep. Estrin loved metal—its resistance, its arrogance, its hostility. She could see herself arriving weekly with chamois in every pocket, to rub down the curves, the stills now looking less like wrapped chocolate than firm upright breasts.

NO MATCHES OR NAKED FIRE.

It was the sign between them. Estrin, once more lost in her own world, which she was always mistaking for the world at large, had almost run into him. The tall man shot her a weary smile. He did not seem very interested in the distillery.

"We're honored, sir." The guide hustled over to Farrell's friend. "What brings you?"

"Tired of single-handedly supporting the shop short by short. Thought I'd save a few quid to come buy the lot of it."

The guide laughed. Farrell sighed.

Through the warehouse, where whiskeys married in boundless sherry casks, Estrin hung back to inhale. She tucked away stray jargon—*cooper, blend vat, spirit safe*—souvenir knickknacks. Pretty and useless, they packed well. Best of all she pocketed the smell, for Bushmills steeped the Antrim coast for miles around with a must of rising bread, liquor, and ripe manure, evoking pictures of a stout woman baking while her fagged-out husband rests his dung-crusted boots on the hearth and slowly gets pissed.

At the end of the tour, downstairs for her sample, Estrin felt sorry for the harried bartender and held back—the woman had to keep smiling and ask, "Hot, black, regular, or malt?" over and over in a happy voice, explaining slowly to Germans what goes into a toddy, fighting back disdain for Americans, who could easily afford a case, still so eager for their free drink. Estrin had the same problem in restaurants, where, whether or not her order was wrong or cold or late, she identified with the waiter rather than herself; in shops she sympathized with rattled salesmen, not clientele; in high-rises she allied herself with reception, janitors; and even in the restroom her heart went out to the lady with the towels. From a well-established Philadelphia family, Estrin Lancaster had downwardly mobile aspirations.

Farrell cast about the crowd, goaded by those sanctimonious poppies on every staff lapel. Thank God, it was Remembrance Day, after which the Somme would once more be over for another good eleven months. Farrell supposed dully that there was nothing wrong per se with mourning your war dead, though of course every gesture was subverted here and that wasn't what the poppies connoted at all. *Those are OUR wars. Those are OUR dead.* Take 'em, thought Farrell, childish bastards. Little matter that plenty of Catholics had died in both world wars; fact had never contaminated anyone's politics in Ireland. (The fiction was wick, since who needed it? We've got history.) No, ceremonies were divvied up and the Prods had picked Remembrance Day, the Twelfth, and probably Christmas, since they'd more cash. The Taigs got Easter, Internment Day, and for twenty years a whole smattering of, ah, unscheduled celebrations all across the calendar. Let the Prods have their sorry paper poppies and weepy parades to cenotaphs, it was only fair.

Don't get the wrong idea. This left Farrell in a conflicted position—Catholics didn't wear poppies and Prods did, but if Farrell were Protestant, being Farrell, he would refuse to wear a poppy, so to express this alienation in Catholic terms should he wear one instead? For *his own people* had excluded him as well, or he'd excluded himself; each had leapt to disown the other. Farrell despised groups of all kinds and made sure they despised him in return; then he needed the backs of crowds to feel wholly, spitefully himself. He was no different from the rest of this tip, where you loved your enemy all right, but not quite the way Christ had in mind—loved him precisely for being your enemy, for obliging you with something outside your own mirror to revile.

He was easy to locate, thick platinum hair curling over the crowd. The large crown and high forehead bent toward his boisterous companion. While Estrin found Irishmen a frumpy crew, given to bundling—they wore sweaters with their suits, jackets binding and short in the arm—Farrell's dark wool three-piece was impeccably tailored, European; his crimson tie, silk handkerchief, and long Dickensian overcoat suggested a kind of style she'd not seen on this island—that is: style.

And, she observed on the way over, he was a drinker, since in this deluge of a country whiskey was the only force of nature that gave the national complexion any color at all. So she was surprised on arriving at their corner to find his measure clear.

"Hot water," he explained.

"You don't drink?"

"Wine. After eight."

"A.m. or p.m.?"

"I sleep little enough to lose the distinction."

Estrin raised her malt. "I like to break my rules from time to time."

"You can afford to," he said severely. "You're still young."

"Not that young," said Estrin with a trace of irritation. "And I can't afford not to. Too many rules and too much obedience are just as dangerous as going off the deep end."

"Don't you worry now," said the heavier man, slapping his friend on the back. "Farrell O'Phelan's in no danger of being too obedient a boy, or too faint a drinker, either. Knows how to impress the ladies with a cup of hot water at tourist draws, is all." He laughed, though Farrell didn't, exactly, join in.

"You brought me here to torture me," said Farrell, and meant it; the smell was beginning to get to him. How happy it would make MacBride if he strode up to the bar and threw back a double. And how it firmed his resolution, to deny Angus that joy.

"Now, it was damned decent of Bushmills to open today. And I could hardly meet you at the cenotaph this morning," MacBride muttered. "Sure you'd hum 'The Battle of the Bog-side' all through the two minutes' silence."

Farrell was about to quip that he was more likely to hum Polish polkas than some whimper of Irish resistance, when he noticed the American's eyes had sharpened; most foreigners here were clueless, but he did not like the way she looked from one to the other and he did not like the way she looked at MacBride. He shut up. He did not want to be understood. That was the first thing women didn't understand.

"The fumes off that wort were something, what?" recalled the girl. "Ripped in thirty seconds. Like sniffing glue, and the end of the tube is six feet wide."

"You sniff glue?" asked Farrell.

"Putting together balsa Sopwith Camels at eight or nine? We breathed too much, they didn't fly so hot, but we'd had a good time. My life has had to do with airplanes from way back."

"How so?"

"I'm tempted to return-address envelopes, 'Window seat. Nonsmoking.' Though I don't send so many letters anymore . . . Lufthansa," she commended.

He clucked. "Free cocktails, but frozen salad."

"You travel much?"

"Same address, but on the aisle."

"Long legs."

"I like to be the first off the plane."

"I like to look out the window. Flying into Belfast I was pressed so close to the pane that the man next to me asked if this was my first flight."

"And you said?"

"*Always.* I never get bored with flying. Though I am sym-pathetic to the aisle seat," she noted. "My mother claims I used to stand in my crib and plead through the bars: *Ah wan ow*. She was impressed that I started talking in a whole sentence. But I'm impressed what it meant."

"Which was?"

"*I want out.*"

"And have you? Gotten out?"

She seemed to consider this more seriously than the facile question required. "Maybe not." Abruptly she accused him, "I have it on good authority that locals never touch this place. You don't even drink whiskey. What are you doing here?"

"Is this an interrogation?"

"Are you used to being interrogated?"

Farrell faltered, and wondered momentarily if she knew who he was—ridiculous. "Just—a diverting opening."

"You play chess?"

"Aye, and you?"

"No. I wouldn't have wanted to learn unless I was great. And I don't quite have that kind of brain. So instead of being second-rate, I just don't play."

"Then you do have that kind of brain," Farrell observed. "Abstention is a strategy."

"Never will forget that first game," MacBride nosed in again. "This sorry scarecrow teetering to the board. I shook his hand and nearly crushed it—a sickly sort, this one. But ten moves later, who'd have guessed he had it in him? Loopy, I thought, the boy's in a fever!"

"But I won." Farrell poked MacBride's chest in a gesture he realized too late was exactly like his own father's.

" 'Twas not a sound game, mate. Later that same afternoon I sat down to me own board and had you hammered three ways round."

"The gentleman at your right plays a sedulous game," Farrell explained. "Uses all the time on his clock. Knows all the books—"

"You could stand yourself—"

"Never! Never opened a page."

"Your man here considers learning a cheat."

"There seems little point in testing some other gobshite's wits when the idea's to test your own."

"I thought winning was all, Farrell. Why not read up, then, if it topples the other fellow's king?"

"I don't collaborate, at anything. I win."

"We might observe," said MacBride dryly, "that by that arrangement you get singular credit for falling on your arse."

"When you two play," asked the girl, "who does win, anyway?"

"Did," said MacBride.

"Oh, we still play," said Farrell softly.

At last MacBride had given up ogling the girl, because he couldn't resist looking at Farrell; funny, they were both showing off, for they had often used each other, or perhaps more accurately their relationship, to entice women. "I was trying to tell you, lass"—MacBride turned back to her—"the gawk here played reckless chess. Might seem a tame sport from the side, but your man conduct his pieces like commanding his crew into uncharted high seas. Could make you woozy to watch the board."

"And you," said Farrell, "never made an original move in your life."

"No such thing as an original move. That's your vanity, and your ignorance is vanity. It trips you, too. I always watched the larger game. You got too caught up in your flourishes, your flashy attacks. You wanted to impress me. It was the ruin of you."

"Fischer and Kasparov were both victorious."

"Aye, and where's Fischer now? Crawled off in a hole."

"Why did he quit?" asked the girl.

"Couldn't keep it up!" cried MacBride.

"No," said Farrell. "He was disgusted. Sick to death."

"Och, for you to fasten on to your man Kasparov and that, it's hubris of the first order. At least those lads had a clue. You, Farrell, just lit out. Never quite thought it through. You're impulsive, man."

"Yes," said Farrell. "And you're a bore."

"O'Phelan, you never have seen the difference between a hero and a fool."

"In my experience," the American ventured, "just as many cautious people get run over by buses as careless."

Farrell smiled.

As the trio trailed from the bar, the usual questions tumbled in: Where was she from in—, How long had she been—, How long was she planning—, Sure isn't her name—? Ten years of this conversation, how rarely she gave straight answers anymore.

"Esther Ingrid," she explained a bit through her teeth. "Little brother. It stuck." The shorthand was getting so clipped it was incoherent.

"So what do you do in the States?" asked Farrell.

"What I do everywhere," she leveled. "Leave."

"Does that pay?"

"Often."

"Yes," he agreed with a collusive smile. "Handsomely."

Both men were placated when she mentioned Belfast.

"And how might we look you up, now?" the lusty man inquired.

Estrin sighed, and glanced from one to the other. She had grown up with brothers on either side, and still attracted men in twos; the last cut was tense. And, she reminded herself, how frequently she had failed to keep *Maybe we'll run into each other sometime* poised on the tip of her tongue, letting a few digits trip off instead, because it's easier to give people what they want from you. But Estrin paid for laziness later, with the rude thud on her front door, a total stranger with flowers and expectations smoothing the tattered receipt where she'd scribbled an address only to get rid of the man. *Don't say anything dorky*: it was a new discipline. So she was about to toss off, "Put a note in a bottle and throw it in the North Channel," when some flicker in Farrell's eye seemed to catch her in her very thought, as if he knew she was pressed for her number often and saw these scenes purely as something to wriggle out of. *My dear*, read his expression,

don't switch on automatic, you might as well resign. Well enough, you're
harassed by plenty prats, and good luck to you turfing them aside. But
look harder now. You can't sell us all downriver, and you like men—
it comes off you like a smell. You look wildly young to me, but you're
no nun—you've that shine in your eyes as if you're always getting a
joke no one's told yet.

"The Green Door, Whiterock Road." Estrin flipped her club between them like a coin to beggars, turning to avoid their scuffle for the toss.

"Looks as if you're white this time," said MacBride to Farrell good-naturedly. "With that address."

"I thought you were so successful these territorial niceties didn't faze you anymore."

"Successful, not mental, kid. For all that leather, I'd not slop into the Green Door. Think of the laundrette bills to get out the smell."

"Laundrette? Mortuary."

Farrell never liked to win anything by luck, though he preferred luck to losing; his eyes followed his new chip. He'd no intention to cash in. The option was sweeter than any dreary discreet evening. Still, as he watched the small woman work on the thick gloves and dive into the red helmet with, he thought, a certain snail-like relief, Farrell had an unresolved sensation he hadn't felt in long enough that he didn't recognize what it was. The girl knew they were watching and hurried, switching the engine and failing to warm it long enough; the bike lurched and stalled. Feeling this wasn't a woman easily rattled, Farrell noted her fluster with satisfaction.

Finally the big red motorcycle pelted away; wind whipped the Union Jack down the road as she passed, the red, white, and blue curbside clouding with exhaust.

Their tour guide rasped up the drive toward MacBride. He was running, his face red with anticipation, as if he'd found the MP's umbrella and was savoring how obliged MacBride would feel at the trouble taken to return it. But the guide's hands were empty, and MacBride had his umbrella, and his hat.

"Your honor!" the little man panted. "Have you heard, sir? The radio—"

"Calm down, boyo, what's that?"

The guide gathered himself and pronounced, "*Enniskillen.*"

It was a test. Enniskillen? A small town. Prod, a wee orange bud in the otherwise deadly green slime of Fermanagh, choked on all sides, a lone flower in a pond gone to algae—or this was the image that sprang to MacBride's mind. Otherwise unremarkable; a fair concentration of security-force families, that was all.

However, the Bushmills tour guide did not say the name of Enniskillen like a small town, as no one in Northern Ireland would for years to come. Because Enniskillen was no longer a pit stop for lunch on your way to Galway, a Bally-Nowhere to be from. No, Enniskillen had been elevated beyond a dot on the map. Enniskillen was an atrocity.

The guide detailed the news grandly, taking his time. In the midst of Remembrance Day services, a bomb had gone off by the town cenotaph and blown out a gable wall. Nine, ten people dead, maybe more. Civilians every one. A bollocks. And injuries galore . . .

"Why, Angus," Farrell noted. "If it isn't a *mistake.*"

"Bleeding cretins," MacBride puffed. "Freaking Provo barbarians—"

"Come on," Farrell prodded. "Use *scum*. I know you save it for special occasions, but sure this counts as one."

There was much commiseration and head-shaking. They were both relieved when the guide was gone. All that indignation was exhausting.

Angus dropped the twisted brow when the guide turned the corner.

"Does it ever strike you," asked Farrell lightly, "that the Provisionals are quaint? Really. The Iranians blow three hundred air passengers with a briefcase. At current levels of technology, massacre by the dozen expresses considerable restraint."

"Grand," said MacBride. "I can see myself launching into

the BBC with that one. *I would just like to say that I thought Enniskillen was quaint.*"

"Handy, this," Farrell observed.

"Bastard of a thing," said MacBride. "Bastard."

As the two men whisked toward the Antrim Arms to find a TV, their step sprang, hands played with keys in pockets. Farrell began to whistle and stopped himself. Angus jostled against the taller man's shoulder and kicked schoolboy at stones, the mood of both gentlemen unquestionably bolstered.

2

Roisin Has Enthusiasms

"Why couldn't he nip in the back? Would he blink like a red light?"

"Blamed if I know, Roisin, you've never said who you're talking about."

"Lord, I can't, Con. It's not I don't trust you. But matters being as they are—"

"Spare me how matters are."

A little snippy, Roisin thought. "I'm only saying, so he was recognized, where's the harm? He might shake my hand and say how very much he enjoyed it and smile and only the two of us the wiser."

"Why risk it?"

"I want him to hear me read!"

"Then curl up in the coverlet and recite with your man on the next pillow. That way no one's the wiser."

Roisin bit her lip over the receiver. "Connie, you understand far better than you're letting on."

"So do you. You want your toy boy to see you all tarted up in that blue dress, in front of a whole crowd of eejits queuing for signed copies of *The Dumb and Frumpy Cows*—"

"That's *The Brave and Friendly Sheep*! And it's inhuman of me, when I see his own bake big as life on the telly every night?"

". . . On the telly, now?"

"Forget I said that."

"A fine way to get me to remember."

"Seems to me, just," Roisin went on nervously, "he might slip into one reading, who would point a finger."

"Such a TV star, why not? The English Lecture Theatre's hardly the King's Hall . . . What show might he be on, now?"

The biggest show in town. Roisin smiled. *The only show.* "I've name enough by now, he'd only display decent public relations, attending a do for a major Six County poet."

"A Republican poet."

"I'm not a Republican poet."

"Wise up! With your father and those brothers in the Maze, write a donkey's years about birdies and butterflies, or for that matter, join the UVF, burn your own house as a bonfire on the Twelfth, and go up with it, sure you'll still get your name engraved on the County Antrim Memorial, with a full IRA cortege strung out to Lenadoon."

"For years in my work I've tried to—"

"Doesn't matter a jot, Rose," Constance interrupted with the impatience that was beginning to characterize this entire call. "You are what they say."

"What has that got to do with Thursday?"

"He's a Prod, sure that's no secret."

"I never said that."

"Och, no! You're bumping the daylights out of Bill Cosby."

"Stop stirring me up! I said he was known, that's all—"

"And enough times."

To the injured silence on the other end, Constance continued. "I'm sorry, Roisin, but I can't hold with this carry-on month after month about your famous man this, your famous man that—it's a bit much, love. You've put the man terrible high up and there's your problem. He can't be as fancy as you figure, and if you could stare that down, maybe you wouldn't let him wipe his shoes on your face. There've been times if I'd not seen the marks I'd swear you were making him up."

"He's not a cruel man, and it was only those two times. And I'll not have you run him down or make out he's some wee Prod—"

"If you'd stop exaggerating to me, you might stop exaggerating to yourself! So he's some councilor or other—"

"*Angus MacBride is no councilor.*"

"You don't say," said Constance gravely.

"I haven't said." Roisin spoke with reserve, her dignity restored. "Now do you see why?"

"One of the bigger plums in the pie," Constance conceded. "And you're both better off he stays clear of the Thursday reading and every other."

"I'd not mind if it were only politics," said Roisin, already growing sullen, though with herself; her stomach felt glutinous, as if she'd eaten too much potato bread. "Truth is, he's not mad for poetry, even mine. Claims he doesn't understand it."

"Fair enough," said Constance. "You don't understand politics."

Roisin was too sickened now to rise to the charge. "I've to sort out my selection for tomorrow, so I'll ring off. But, Connie—"

"Don't worry, I'll keep quiet. All the same—" Constance paused. "You shouldn't have told me his name, love." The receiver clicked in Roisin's ear like a full stop at the end of any other simple, true declarative: The sky is blue.

It was, and it shouldn't have been; it should be bucketing. Roisin fidgeted from the phone and, to keep from ruining her well-kept nails, frantically hoovered the carpet. Well, obviously the only way to prove once and for all to Constance Trower just how big a secret she was keeping was to give it away.

The hoover was full of cat hair, and filled the room with pet smell; Angus hated the cat and despised the smell. She kicked off the machine.

Loose Talk Costs Lives.

She'd pinned the poster at the entrance to the bedroom not long after she'd first started up with MacBride.

> *In taxis*
> *On the phone*
> *In clubs and bars*
> *At football matches*
> *At home with friends*
> *Anywhere!*
> WHATEVER YOU SAY—
> SAY NOTHING.

While Seamus Heaney's advice was clearly lost on Roisin, every party in the Province followed the slogan to the letter.

"I have a story you'll like," Farrell announced, with that long stride she had learned to keep up with. "Enniskillen. Now, the way bombs are handled in the Provisionals now, one cell makes the device, those that plant it are different lads altogether, no one ever meets anyone, correct?"

"That's the conceit—but Fermanagh? Sure they're all first cousins and play on the same hurley team."

"Well, that's what the Prods think—that every Taig knows who did it and won't tell. But bear with me—"

Constance smiled. *The* Prods, not *you* Prods. After so many years she had earned herself out of her people. From Farrell, that was a compliment.

"—So the bomb was assembled weeks ahead of time. Now, it blew by the cenotaph smack in the middle of nurses and schoolteachers, and that's why it was a *mistake*, right?"

"Giant PR black eye. A real shiner."

"*They forgot about daylight saving time.*"

"I don't follow."

"One hour later, there would have been only soldiers by that cenotaph—everyone knows the ceremony, it's the same dirge every year. But the boyo who made the bomb set it to go off at 11:45 a.m. on November 8, and forgot that in the meantime the clocks would change!"

"Who told you this?"

"A little bird with a balaclava."

"I think it's a story *you* like."

"Well, yes. Perverse. Anarchic. Absurd. Their devices are so much more advanced than in my day—"

"It's not your day?" She sounded disappointed.

"I don't think I'd know where to begin with the contraptions they put together now. Microcircuitry, long-range radio control. But I could tell the bloody time."

"How is Enniskillen likely to affect your referendum? You figure it's really given the place a taste for reform and that? Enough is enough, let's get off our bum?"

They were crossing the Lagan on the Queen Elizabeth Bridge, and stopped to lean over the river. It was only 3:30, but in Ireland's stingy December already the sun was setting. Samson and Goliath, the two Harland and Wolff cranes, dipped the foreground, gold birds taking water. From here Belfast glowed, a vista never broadcast in news clips—a low city, its horizon stitched with spires. The light alchemized even Eastwood's Scrap Metal with its Midas touch; hulks of burned-out City Buses mounded the shore, pirate's treasure. Constance hoped the sunset was doing the same job on her face—projects of equal challenge, she supposed.

"I've been sniffing the wind, and it smells, as usual. The Prods are already getting resentful that the wet-nosed ecumenists have hijacked their tragedy. Pretty soon they'll want their atrocity back. And Gordon Wilson's getting to be a regular celeb—forgiveness as song and dance. There are churches in the States now that want to fly him, all expenses paid, to get up in front of their congregations and repeat for the umpteenth time, *I forgive the men who murdered my daughter.* So they can all feel warm and gooey. There's money in grace. The man should get an agent."

"You're one godawful cynic, Farrell O'Phelan."

"No, it's sad, really—I did rather admire him. I'd never be able to pull the line off with a straight face myself. But as soon as he's seen as successful he's dead. All Gordon needs is the Nobel Prize and the North will have him deported."

Constance sighed. "Poor Betty. She's in Florida now."

"I've tried to warn MacBride—if he does win that bauble, this mean-spirited backwater will have his head."

"But can't you use it, Enniskillen? Peace PR?"

"Not really. We're unlikely to get this referendum together for a year yet. I predict? Gordon Wilson jokes. In a year all of Fermanagh will detest him, even the Catholics—for not having the integrity to detest them back. And once the hand-clasping hoopla clears, the Prods will look around them and notice, *Bloody hell, those wankers took out eleven of our side.* They'll feel vengeful and persecuted, as always. Constance, how many times have you heard, these are the last caskets we will carry, now we're all going to be matey and damp-eyed? Now we will understand one another, albeit from separate schools and different sides of town? Of course you murdered my whole family last night, that's perfectly all right, you were just doing your job? The Peace People may have we-shall-overcomed the multitudes but without Taigs or Prods to bash were at each other's throats after six months; now the office barely limps from week to week with American volunteers. No, Enniskillen will have no effect on the North whatsoever. Like everything else in the last twenty years."

"Including you?"

"Oh, aye. Especially me."

"Then why are we working eighteen hours a day?"

"I do not believe anything I do will make the slightest difference. I do it anyway."

Then you understand me, thought Constance grimly. *Why I phone the same number hours on end until I get through because you said "imperative." Why I meet your planes on early Sunday mornings. Why I bring you cups of hot water and filled rolls you let dry out. Why I clip your piles of newspapers when you're finished not reading them, why I collect city council minutes from Derry and Strabane when normal women are shopping for pumps: I do not believe any of this will make the slightest difference. I do it anyway.*

She took his hand; that was permitted. They had sorted out the rules, even stretched them—he could put his arm around her, kiss her cheek. In tight spots with only a single available they had slept side by side in the same bed. He would curl against her. It was nice. She didn't even find it painful. And they often held hands.

"I have a story you're not going to like."

"Shoot." He did not sound nervous. Farrell preferred bad news to no news. He loved a turn of the wheel.

"You know Roisin St. Clair?"

"The name."

"Don't be coy. Why didn't you tell me she was doing the nasty with Angus MacBride?"

Farrell pulled up sharply. "Says who?"

"Says herself."

"You're right, I don't like this story."

"And I'm hardly her best friend, Farrell. Lord knows who else she's told. For all we know, she's leaking like a Divis tap."

Farrell dropped her hand and paced off the bridge. The sun ruddied his face; his eyebrows looked on fire. Now it was hard to keep up with him.

"I have warned and warned him!" Farrell railed. "How are

we to kick this place into shape if he's splayed in a two-page spread in the *Sunday World*? Look at Papandreou! Carrying on with that blonde is toppling his whole government!"

"You figure Unionists care that much about a wee bit of philandering?"

"Are you serious, it's all they care about! The North is 64 percent Protestant, 36 percent Catholic, 100 percent gossip. As MacBride knows perfectly well, and still the bugger gropes over Antrim as if he were on holiday in Hong Kong. You must have noticed, he even flirts with you!"

"Even me," said Constance. "Is the trouble that he's married, or that she's Catholic?"

"Either is dangerous, both are poison."

"Find yourself another softhearted Prod."

"No, I need the UUU behind this referendum, or it won't fly. Angus MacBride *is* the UUU. He's been coddling the party toward power-sharing for years. Half the lot will balk because they'll boycott any initiative unless the Agreement is scrapped. And when we're through lacing the proposition with Nationalist perks, there will be enough links with the South that the right-wingers in the UUU could easily label it an all-Ireland solution."

"Bye-bye, Border Poll."

"Better believe it. And it's Angus keeps that rabble together; they do as he says because they like him. But he's got to keep his nose clean. Bollocks—!"

"You're not overreacting?"

"I take my prediction back: a year from now Gordon will be old hat. Angus MacBride jokes in the back pages of *Fortnight* are passing before my eyes."

"Cross your fingers. Nothing's in public yet."

"When you have a leaky pipe, you don't turn up the radio and pretend everything's all right. People lose whole basements that way. No, the problem must be plumbed. Caulked tight."

"How is a woman like a kitchen sink?"

"That's the riddle, my dear. Now, tell me about Roisin St. Clair. What's she like? Pretty?"

Wouldn't that be the first question. "Rather. Well preserved, anyway. Thirty-five or so. Brilliant with clothes. Thin; I'd say from nerves. And if that lady ever hits the big time, some psychiatrist has it made."

"Because of her father?"

Constance shrugged. "That's the easiest answer. But it's the mother she whinges on about. Roisin's the only daughter. And the family is—old-fashioned."

"Low expectations?"

"Where have you been? *No* expectations. Considering, she's done well."

"She a good poet?"

"Lord, I couldn't say. I can't bear any of that palaver, you know that. But at least it's her one original interest, and she's followed through."

"In contrast to—?"

"Roisin St. Clair is one of those people with enthusiasms," Constance explained. "A bit of a dabbler. I met her when we were setting up that integrated entrepreneurial support scheme with Father Mahon. Och, she threw herself into it with a right frenzy—late nights helping Catholics stuff teddy bears, Prods bottle mayonnaise. Then one day she disappeared."

"What happened?"

"I suppose they broke up."

"With Father Mahon—!"

"No, no, she and whoever gave her the idea. Roisin goes through phases, so she does—"

"You mean men."

"I suppose the interest is genuine enough once it sparks. But your woman never lights her own fire."

"Romantic history?"

"Nightmarish, protracted. She takes a long time to get the message."

"Politics?"

"Reactive. Depends on whom she's browned off with—and sooner or later, that's everyone she's ever laid eyes on. I've wondered if she's carrying on with MacBride to spite her mother. She'd never tell her ma outright. But it might satisfy Roisin if the news slipped under the back door."

"Republican?"

"You're not getting the picture. Sure, stuck on the right boyfriend, she'd smuggle bazookas in her boot across the border with the best of them. With Angus I expect she's stitching Union Jacks for the Apprentice Boys."

"You don't seem to think much of Miss St. Clair."

"I'm getting catty. It isn't attractive, is it?"

"No, it's entertaining, but I'm beginning to wonder what MacBride sees in her besides the obvious. And the affair's been on for a couple of years."

"She is nice to look at. She's no dozer once you get her intrigued. And with all that resentment, well—she can get scrappy in a corner. I imagine Angus likes a good fight."

"As long as he can win."

"Exactly. Besides, there's a beguiling frailty to Roisin. One of those women who can spend all day in bed. I don't know if she gets migraines, but she should. She makes you want to take care of her."

"So far you've described a well-dressed rabbit."

"That's not fair," Constance insisted, with discipline. "Roisin can be fractious, but when you smooth her back down she is sweet. And to see her thrive on the merest tidbit, that you like her blouse or her sofa—her childhood must have been appalling."

"Aye," Farrell murmured. "What's sad is, she's still looking for what the rest of us gave up on long ago."

"Farrell O'Phelan, if you think you've given up on it, you're fooling yourself."

He put his arm around her shoulder, but absently. She liked it when he absorbed himself elsewhere so she could discreetly study his face. It never bored her. The eyes so deep-set, the nose so lumpy and Roman, those drastic bumps and hollows sculpture for the blind. She could see leading a pair of pale, unsighted hands to his head: *Now, this is a face. This is a real face.*

Because Farrell himself never bored her. And she knew everything—his distaste for red cabbage, his shirt size. Name a season and a year for the last forty-three and she could tell you precisely what he was doing and even when he got up in the morning—though a few years there were easy: at noon to drink till 5 a.m., like reporting for work. Yet there remained something insoluble about him; he was like Flann O'Brien's infinite bureaus within bureaus, so that every time when you thought you had drawn his very self out of his own drawer there was one more inscrutable bit inside; she would have to pick out the next speck with tweezers, and would shortly be found scuffling the floor, having dropped him, the part she didn't understand and there-fore the only part that mattered, the clue.

Farrell stirred. "You're cold," said Constance. "Let's head back. There's a powerful lot of phone calls to return. And two boys from Turf Lodge rang up, with word they're to be knee-capped. They want to spend the night in your office."

"Check their story; only the outer room; no beer."

"Then it's time for Oscar's, isn't it? I know the food is des-perate, but when you ignore them they're hurt. They miss you."

"What they miss is our sixty-quid checks. No, I've something on this evening."

"Oh." She did not know everything.

"I'll ring you when I get home," he offered.

"That would be lovely."

". . . We had dinner together last night," said Farrell.

"Yes."

". . . and the night before."

"Yes."

"And lunch! And probably will dine tomorrow night as well!"

"Of course, if you like," she said graciously. "If you've noth-ing else planned."

"What do you bloody want, then?"

"I didn't say anything."

"You didn't have to!"

Farrell scowled into the collar of his overcoat. They did not hold hands.

3

The Green Door,
or Everybody Likes Lancaster

The Green Door had no such thing. Caged across the front, the club was coiled with razor wire; even the little neon sign, burned out, was fenced in. The entrance wasn't green but brown, its peephole rheumy.

"O'Phelan," the guard at the door grunted. "Trouble himself."

"I've gotten as many pillocks out of trouble as in. A good record, for this town."

"Right you are, our own Captain Marvel. Though I hear tell, you don't muck in as you used. Keep the nails clean and that."

"Excuse me, but at eight o'clock," Farrell towered, "I have a date in there with a curvaceous little glass of wine."

"For you, O'Phelan, the glass is sure only as wee as a mate could do laps in."

"I don't swim." Farrell made a move for the door.

"We've yet to explore," the guard said grandly, barring the way, "what makes you feel so comfortable in these parts."

"In the last ten years," said Farrell calmly, "I've been credited as a Provo, a Stickie, an Irp, and a legman for branches of the IPLO you haven't even heard of; as a propagandist for the UDA, eccentric fop for the SDLP, CIA agent, Special Branch hit man, British supergrass, and IDA occupational safety inspector. I imagine with those credentials I can waltz into any pub in town."

"Och, you think it's all a game, man."

"Yes."

After three separate grillings to get in, each more suspicious than the last, Farrell was bewildered why he bothered. He hated catering to their self-importance.

Inside Farrell shook his head—a whole city full of warm, intimate bars, the Crown, the Morning Star, the Rotterdam, and West Belfast crammed into these grotty drinking clubs. By what poor guidance or misfortune did the American drink here? For the Green Door was the worst: bare bulbs overhead, long, laminated tables, crumbling ceiling tiles. A wooden Armalite mounted like a marlin over the bar; a collection of plastic bullets on the counter, long, round, heavy boles fondled gray, like merchandise from a secondhand sex shop. The usual Gerry Adams posters and H-block brouhaha covered the walls: REMEMBER BLOODY SUNDAY!; DON'T FRATERNIZE! THIS BRIT COULD BE STANDING BESIDE YOU—WATCH WHAT YOU SAY; SOLDIERS ARE WE, WHOSE LIVES ARE PLEDGED FOR IRELAND; BRIT THUGS OUT; SS RUC . . . but Farrell had read these so many times before that they faded into so much wallpaper. The best thing about propaganda is its short shelf life—successfully familiar, it disappears.

"Hulloo, Farrell!" Though they hadn't seen each other for five years, Duff hailed him as if that were just the other day—and in Duff's way of thinking, Farrell supposed, it was. Time was like everything else in Duff's life that he swallowed in quantity—Guinness, sausage rolls, other people's stories. "How are you keeping?" As he pressed Farrell's hand, Shearhoon's eyes squeezed tight. Strange, for such an expansive character he had a nervousness, a flinch. Then, Farrell had spent enough time around rapacious politicians to enjoy the more leisurely ambitions of Shearhoon tonight. He was one of those affable men out to take over the world simply by consuming it. Duff's steady advance on occupying space would make a pleasant low-budget horror film.

"Wasn't I talking you up the other day, just. Remembering back in '72 on the barricades, do you know? Brits lined up just outside the no-go all confused like, mothers and wains about, houses afire. Every wee soldier sure he's tomorrow's headline in the *Irish News* for shooting a toddler. *It's the lads!* your women all cry. *Make way for the lads!* And if Farrell O'Phelan doesn't climb on top of the burning bus like Moses, do you follow? Hair out to here and eyes out farther. Farrell, you missed your calling as a priest, so you did. You'd put the fear of hell in a bottle of Baby Cham."

"So were you one of the lads?"

Farrell turned and didn't recognize her at first: she was on the wrong side of the bar. Sweet Jesus, she worked here. Farrell felt immediately he'd made a mistake, and wondered why he'd come. Idle curiosity, he supposed, since this was the only plan for the evening whose sequence he couldn't quite foretell, while Shearhoon's tale here, for example, was strictly pub liturgy. He had liked that he couldn't write her lines. But now he could fill them in easily enough—she was another one of those NORAID bims from Boston with Irish ancestors. How exciting, working in a *Republican club* with the *hard men*—

Farrell rubbed his face. "No, my dear, I was not one of the lads. Disappointed?"

"Hardly."

Right answer; he would treat her at least to the story. "That was the day the British interned thirteen activists from the lead-ership of the PD. Dragged out of bed without time to wash their teeth. Searches all morning. The Falls was roiling. Whole families on the streets."

"Sounds like quite a party," said Estrin.

Of course it would to you, Farrell swiped, but had to admit, "It was. Though for me in '72 every day was a party."

"Meaning your youth, or the festivities?"

"Talisker!" cried Duff.

"Closer," Farrell explained, "to a premature old age."

Estrin shook her head. "A malt's a waste on a bender."

"Low as I ever sank, I never drank less. A matter of principle."

"Style," she corrected. "There's a difference. So what possessed you to climb on top of that bus?"

"To tell the mothers *not* to go inside."

"Why?"

"Strategy, my dear. Those soldiers had been trained for snipers, but were stymied by prams. They could plow up the barricade if it were manned by lads, but not if they were two years old. So I said, Bring up the prams! Best front line ever invented."

"What happened?"

"I fell off the bus."

"On a pram!" Shearhoon cried.

"You can imagine"—Farrell smiled—"this argued poorly for my strategy."

Through their laughter Estrin asked, "Was it really funny? At the time?"

"No," Farrell conceded. "Because if I'd been sober I could have changed what happened."

"You do think a lot of yourself."

"It doesn't matter what I think of myself," he dismissed impatiently. "The point is, I was right. The Provies moved in, swaggering like Charles Bronson, and everyone bloody well 'made way for the lads.' Prams—better than armored tanks!—pulled into the estates, and the Falls went empty save these yokels with Armalites, who braced on the hip and opened fire. You should have seen those soldiers' faces light up. They were delighted. Now they understood their parts: O.K. Corral. They burrowed down on the pavement and slipped behind buildings and trained their sights: hell, you'd seen this clip before, you could turn it off."

"And where were you?"

"Curled by the bus, just waking up, luckily on the Falls side, and desperate to take a piss. That, my girl, is the stuff of real history."

The club became crowded, and Estrin was busy at the taps. More of Farrell's acquaintances—he would consider them no better; in fact, he thought of himself as having no friends—rabbled to the bar, gripping his shoulder, blattering out tales. Their favorites were from his drinking days, extolling a fame that amounted to a medical achievement. "Aye, and I watched him myself knock back five brandy-and-ports the next morning, and then, steady as you please, strolls into the UDA and asks for a calendar!" Duff Shearhoon was in his element, for as most people will who prefer spinning yarns to living more of them, Duff maintained his old favorites in impeccable detail, like a man who, unable to afford new clothes, keeps his small wardrobe freshly laundered.

Farrell fought back a yawn. It struck him, amid the bawdy back-clapping, red faces leaning to his stool, how he might have longed for such a scene at seventeen—lonely and gangling, turning from the Church but with nothing to replace it, inward and socially inept, not even much of a drinker yet; full of ideas he could only put in exalted and therefore ridiculous form; to others, unpleasantly adult. No—Farrell looked around—this was adulthood: porter spilling on the floor, the laughter half relief there was something, anything, to say tonight. Back then he'd have lapped it up, and why had none of these big rowdy men gathered around him in the days he had bad acne? How reliably, even when you did get what you wanted, it was hopelessly belated—parts on order years ago arriving only once you'd sold the car.

Farrell's whole life was too late; he pictured Jesus rattling his screen door calling, "Mr. O'Phelan! Sir! We've your serenity in, so sorry for the delay!" and Farrell doesn't answer because he's dead.

Serenity, *uch*, just as well.

Estrin returned with his wine, though she could barely find room for the glass among the complimentary whiskeys he didn't want. Less arrogant, he might have prepared a look of embarrassment for when their eyes met, but Farrell being Farrell, he let his boredom show instead.

He followed her through the cracks in his retinue. The dogs-bodies were chatting her up. Most Americans weren't much at banter, so he enjoyed the easy reflex with which she kicked remarks back, a goalie defending against an inferior team. He wondered which of these willicks she was fucking.

Farrell ducked out of his party; they could tell Farrell O'Phelan stories better without him. The obligations of accuracy only rained on their parade.

"You seem quite popular here," he said in her ear.

"I know," she said with a funny despair. "Listen, I've got to wash up some of these pints, because we've run out again and I've told Kieran, just buy some more, but *no-o*—I swear I could run this bar by myself if they just laid in more glasses, but instead they hire a second bartender every night—typical false economy. Anyway, want to run back with me? Malcolm!" she shrilled over the crowd as only an American could. "Cover the bar!"

They were both relieved at the brief quiet of the back kitchen.

"You know it's funny, but I'm tired of people liking me? My boyfriend in Berlin, it drove him wild. We'd go to a party and he'd sulk in the back while I'd get on with his friends; they'd all switch to English just for me. Pretty soon he started thinking of excuses why we couldn't go. *Everybody likes Lancaster*—he used to say that all the time. More and more caustic. Dieter didn't like me himself; no, he detested me in the end . . ."

The rate at which she washed glasses was astounding, though this intimate a proximity to a dishrag made the sweat break out on Farrell's hands.

"You prefer to be detested?"

"It's more of an accomplishment. This liking business, it just seems a trick: make a few jokes, preferably at your own expense; be attentive, don't talk too long; confide only to the extent that you flatter, but never, never ask for sympathy, for *anything*; act as if you don't care if they like you, which is the key, but still just a gambit— Oh, there are plenty of methods, and—" She looked up from the sink. "I'm not employing any of them at the moment."

"No, if I'm to find you despicable, you'll have to do better than this."

"But have you any idea the number of people who've *liked* me now, all over the world? My God, I'm getting so when I take the train down to Dublin I try to take up the seats around me with my luggage, not because I don't want company exactly, but I don't want to compulsively ingratiate myself one more time. It's humiliating, it's obsequious, and then they want to keep in touch and everything. The pockets of my jackets are filled with ticket stubs scribbled with the addresses of strangers; I don't remember who half of them are. So I don't find likableness a particularly likable quality anymore. It's still an expression, if competent, of the desire to please. Me, I admire people who are obstreperous, inconsiderate, abusive, and nonplused. Card-carrying assholes."

"Spot on," said Farrell. "I'm your man."

"Not so far. You're fucking polite. Why don't you tell me to shut up?"

"You're amusing me."

"See," she went on, "I ask myself: How many of these fuckers would *like* me with running sores? Really, I ask that like a mantra now: *Who's going to like me with running sores?* I'm serious and you're laughing."

"I can see how you got this job."

"Why?"

"Because you *are* likable. It's sad, you can't help it." He put his hand on her arm. "*I* like you. And I hadn't intended to."

"Then why the hell did you come here?"

"Would you believe I needed a drink?"

"Frankly: no. You're a cut above this crowd, aren't you? Think I haven't sorted out that the Green Door is the pit of West Belfast? But I had to take what I could get. And let's not kid ourselves that I got the job because Kieran liked me. I got it because he wanted to fuck me. Which is, I'm afraid, how I get a lot of work."

"And do you? Sleep with them?"

"Christ, no. And Kieran's getting impatient, though by the time he figures out I'm a lost cause, he also won't be able to run this place without me: mission accomplished. But you certainly do not get what you want by giving the other person what he wants. If you ever come through, what are they to hold on for? So, in answer to your question, no, I am not a whore. Not exactly. Would you take these into Malcolm? Thanks."

The—the—*dishwater* was still damp on the glasses, and Farrell held them out from his coat.

"So don't tell me"—Farrell returned, toweling his hands—"you're writing a book."

"The last thing this place needs is another *book*. Besides, I abhor authors, painters, and architects—their lame little efforts to make their marks. Me, I go for leaving things behind and throwing them away. I don't mind losing stuff, even money, since that's one more opportunity to discover I can live without it. I happily prop up my beach chair to watch valuable coastland rinse into the sea. I prefer my antique china dropped on the floor. I appreciate totaled cars, one-way plane tickets, and old people. Entropy and red giants; big fires. I like topsoil erosion and natural disasters, and nothing makes my blood run like a country whose government is losing its grip."

"The North?"

"Not for a minute—here." Balancing two glass towers of Pisa,

Estrin handed him the shorter stack, and Farrell found himself trailing after her unpleasantly. "Mainland Britain may be more precarious, a race riot waiting to happen. This place is full of nice boys"—she smiled at the young bartender and handed him the jars—"who still buy flowers on Mother's Day. And children may go on about the Orangies, but they're incredibly well behaved."

"What have you done?" the boy directed to Farrell. "Don't get her started."

"I have too many opinions," Estrin admitted. "Which has turned into: one more opinion. No use."

"For opinions, you've come to the right part of town," Farrell suggested. "But West Belfast has a strict point of view. And they love to make ambassadors of Americans—"

"You say *they*," she noted. "Not *we*."

"I'm not sure I've used the first person plural in my life," said Farrell. "But I'm advising you to get out from time to time. This neighborhood can be too cozy."

"I told you before—the last thing I need to be reminded is to get out."

"If it isn't O'Phelan."

Farrell turned and he was still holding these bloody glasses; he foisted them on the boy.

"Hardly see you in these parts now," Michael Callaghan went on—a moist, pallid man who was forever pulling his trousers up over his belly. "Word's out you've changed, mate. Too fine for us now. Ordering wine, is it." He sauntered closer. "And take a geek at that suit, sure it's from London, or is it New York? Farrell O'Phelan wouldn't be caught out in Belfast rags, not even old Marks and Spark's. Why, look at that weave, look at the quality!" Callaghan fingered Farrell's lapel.

Farrell picked the man's hand off his jacket like a speck of lint. "Don't you dare touch my person again."

"Your person! Lads, we've a person here! In this herd of West Belfast animals. We may remember old Farrell a liter under, but Mr. O'Phelan's a star now, fancy! Seen him on our tellies, haven't we, all done up in three pieces, shoes shining like a wee boy's eyes on Christmas morning, hands crossed over his knee?"

Farrell let Callaghan go on, taking a seat impassively, for this was the first thing any of these gombeens had said all evening that actually interested him.

"You might explain to us, then," Callaghan proceeded, "why we're such sad wee folk, clinging all confused to some wet dream of a united Ireland, no longer able to think straight from the Brits bashing us too many times on the head. How we kick drogue bombs down the street 'cause we're on the dole and haven't a clue how else to spend our time? Then go on and explain how the UVF's just a charity relief fund and poor Reverend Paisley's merely got indigestion from a few too many Ulster fries—"

"If you're referring to *Panorama*," said Farrell calmly, "I don't believe I mentioned Paisley at all. I spoke of a united Ireland long ago having lost any practical political connotations. National aspiration has achieved the same qualities as faith in the Easter Bunny or Santa Claus—or perhaps something a bit more farfetched: the Catholic Church. Though don't forget, I gave you credit. I said this showed a capacity for abstract thought that from people of your caliber, Callaghan, is astonishing."

"You left out the part about how we're still in our nappies and that."

The club had gone quiet, the dynamic at the bar talk show: Farrell's legs were crossed, Callaghan's voice inquiring, mild.

"I said both Nationalism and Unionism, emotionally, are forms of arrested adolescence. *Pre*-adolescence. Unionists are still clutching on to mother's skirt. Nationalists seem more traditionally rebellious, but the rebellion is traditional and therefore not rebellion at all. Foreigners"—he nodded to Estrin—"often see Republicanism as a radical ideology, and Sinn Féin invites this misperception with its latching on to the ANC, its quotes in *An Phoblacht* from Camilo Torres and Castro. However, handed from father to son, it is more accurately conservative,

right-wing. Joining the Provisionals in West Belfast is the equivalent of working for Daddy's law firm in America. No one in
Ireland gets away from his parents; no one grows up.

"Furthermore—" The loathing in the club was narcotic. "So
convinced that Britain is in control, the Nationalist community
flatters the place: Britain is using the conflict to experiment with
espionage techniques, to train troops. You reveal a childlike faith
in order: there is a puppeteer; this is happening because someone
up there is making it happen. You lack the intellectual sophistication to conceive of ordinary bollocks. You are too terrified to
live in a world where no one is in control: there is no God;
Mother is an ordinary selfish woman the neighbors dislike; Father drinks and can't do your maths. In this world anything can
happen and there is no resort; you can't fix things by gaining
control yourself, because there's no such thing; you will be as
utterly at sea in a united Ireland as in a partitioned one. So these
proclamations about British might crushing the helpless Catholic
waif is, perversely, a belief in Britain, loyalty to the Crown. In
actual fact, Westminster is a tawdry has-been capital once victorious over the Spanish Armada, now reduced to claiming the
midget Falkland Islands as a serious military coup—bloody hell,
it makes you want to cry. Why, West Belfast is the last place on
earth where the British Empire still exists."

"But we're missing a wee bit here," said Callaghan, who
seemed satisfied with Farrell's performance. It was a regular
holiday to find a wally who'd string himself up of his own accord.
"That we're non-starters."

"Oh, aye," said Farrell pleasantly. "I did explore the culture
of victimhood, the culture of defeat. Your united Ireland Val-
halla, for example, only serves its religious, symbolic function
if it never comes to pass as a state. The South is obviously just
one more crumpled patch of map trying to sell cheese to the
EEC—which is why hard-line Republicanism has invalidated
the Dublin government: it is of this earth, and therefore squalid,
as any state has ever been. So you may aspire but you must not
arrive: in short, you must not succeed. That suits this island,

which is historically envious, resentful, and whiny. Likewise, the IRA can only exist so long as it fails. Fair play in '69, as an instinctive, as you said yourself, animal reaction to attack. But as an institution it is not in the long-term interests of the organization to meet its own goals: the lot would be out of a job. To put this in language you can understand, Michael: you're all witless gobshites."

Callaghan moosed closer. "If I was you, O'Phelan—"

"You wish."

"I'd steer clear of the Door. I hear your nine lives ran out about '79. Besides, we're a bit tatty for your tastes now. Try Whitewells. There you've lads to protect you when you say something ill-advised."

Farrell stood and straightened his lapel. "I'll go where I like, as I have my whole life." Farrell may have been taller, but Callaghan had two stone on him; Farrell had better scoot. He thanked himself, since with two more glasses of wine that wouldn't have glared nearly so apparent. Still, he needed one last slag, and his eyes panicked before finding an exit line. "Estrin"—Farrell's voice rang over the club, and his mouth felt strange—he had never, it seems, said her name before. "Dinner?"

"Tomorrow," she said. "Eight o'clock."

"Bedford Street, 44." As he turned, Farrell felt the bitterness glow behind him with all the tangible heat of a turf fire. It took restraint to keep from smiling.

"Sure you owe it to the girl to confess when you and Margaret be married!" shouted one of the boys, but it had taken him too long to come up with the quip, and Farrell was already out the door.

Estrin watched him go, wondering if he appreciated her collusion. She might jockey with them over politics, but she did have to contend with these customers five nights a week, and it was a queer choice to throw her lot in with the one character who clearly had it in him to alienate them to the man.

"They say he's always breezing off to British Air," said Callaghan, "reclining with a pile of papers full of waffle a mile high, white wine—and don't you know Maggie takes him shopping down Oxford Street, all kisses."

"What bleeding happened to the bugger?"

"Fuck all happened. He's been scarce and you've forgotten. O'Phelan was a weedy, hostile creature from day one."

Estrin would have chosen different adjectives, for in the last fifteen minutes Farrell had managed to be *obstreperous, inconsiderate, abusive,* and *nonplused.* It relieved her she was not the only one so consumed by the desire to please.

4

Women on and off the Wall

She had been waiting and pretending she was not, reading *The Use and Abuse of Emergency Legislation in Northern Ireland*, but she tired of these games with herself, as they no longer worked: she was waiting. All night; so she designed a reason she had to talk to him with that proficiency that characterized everything she did, and rang herself. No answer. And later, again, with only rugby and snooker and *Ulster Newstime* on TV—another bomb in the city center. Twice more; she wondered was he off on a tear. She knew it was not her affair. *Not her affair*. Words were always turning on Constance.

Finally she replaced the receiver for the last time. Her concoction was only so urgent; it was after midnight, and her excuse had just turned into a pumpkin.

* * *

Farrell kept a small office off the Lisburn Road with no sign on the door. It was a suite of two rooms and a reception area but no secretary, which Constance had long ceased to consider herself. Nowhere, not on his stationery nor on a single card in his wallet, was there a title or the name of an organization.

Constance Trower had no official position. He had never told her what hours to keep, paid her whatever she asked for, and gave her no itemized responsibilities, which of course meant that she would arrive early and stay late, ask for far too little money in return, and take responsibility for everything.

He'd bristled at an office, but later liked having another territory, another key. Farrell collected them; rings jangled every suit pocket. (Though he'd forgotten what the keys were to, he wouldn't throw them out. Farrell placed a high value on access.) "For security reasons" he didn't keep regular hours himself, though Farrell, like the British government, found "security" a convenient umbrella under which to protect a variety of idiosyncrasies.

He did not, for example, own a car, instead hiring taxis as far as Derry and Armagh. Yet Constance was convinced he was less terrified of gelly wired to his chassis than of insurance forms. Besides, he liked taxis. He liked making the driver go where he wanted, being conveyed. He liked privacy and scorned petty details like changing buses in Portadown; he deliberately had no sense of direction. Train schedules were an imposition; why, he might not want to go to Dublin *then*. The only organized transport he did not resist was the airplane. The atmosphere of hurry and importance made up for meeting the timetables, if barely—he liked nothing more than whisking onto international flights with the door closing on his coattails. Airports are the last refuge of urgency in this world.

His most aggravating "security measure" had to do with his own house—wherever that was. And if he didn't tell Constance where he lived, he clearly told no one. Farrell admitted parties here had probably found him out, but he was hardly going to make it easy for them by publishing in the directory. Once more, however, the nature of Belfast simply conformed to the nature of Farrell O'Phelan, as if he were not camouflaged for the city but the city for him. He would hardly be holding hoolies on his front yard every June if only he could afford to share his address with his many friends and neighbors, with their children and dogs.

As for the office, he had no interest in decor—and the number of things Farrell had no interest in by policy could grow irksome if you listed them out—and left the walls to Constance. Her original selection of, she thought, harmless travel posters underestimated the depth of Farrell's loathing for his island: the rolling hills of Kerry, the thatched byre houses in Tyrone—from which, he claimed, he could "smell the sheep from across the room," the craggy sprat fishermen of Antrim. ("Look at that face," he had cried, "twisted with fifty years of spite. You realize he's not fishing at all—which would be economically useful—but looking out for a boat of Kalashnikov AK-47s for the UDA!") After two days Farrell had had his fun, and Aer Lingus had to go.

Those intervening weeks had been frustrating; she wanted to please him. And Farrell did have an aesthetic, even if he wouldn't dirty his hands with carpet swatches. Whitewells and all that travel had refined him beyond Glengormley—he bought only the best in clothes, gadgets, presents when he remembered (with Constance, once). While the Best Of habit was lazy, the application of an easy rule that spared him individual decisions, inevitably he'd become rather starchy. No help, Farrell had less taste than distaste: he recognized what he *didn't* want. Had a Unionist streak in him, Farrell did.

When they next went to London, then, between setting up his interviews, she scuttled into the Museum Shop at the Tate. She turned her mind off entirely and just went by feel, flipping the racks of prints, art by Braille. What she unrolled back at the hotel surprised her.

For had anyone asked before the Tate how Farrell's preferences in art might run, she'd surely have answered the Futurists, full of tumult and flight; the nightmares of Surrealists, trapped in their own heads as he in his—contorted Dalís, absurd Magrittes; or dour Brueghels. She might have made a case for the Middle Ages, with the flat agony of those pigments, the gory, long-suffering crucifixions in which he'd recognize his own face, the plain, self-denying, racked penitence and flesh effacement of his childhood. Or perhaps, recognizing his stodgy side, she'd have said nothing modern—only classics, Da Vincis and Michelangelos, name brands, the way he bought everything, the Best. But none of these presentiments described what she spread on the bed that night.

Women. Not conflicted character portraits, either, but young, even virginal things, with red cheeks and languid fingers. Simple women, with water. Soft women—Whistler's *The Little White Girl*; seaside Seurat; Degas. Shapely, sway-hipped Tissots, splayed nineteenth-century picnics by a pool, languid bites into apples with a demitasse, bustles curved at a pleasure-boat rail. Inshaw's *The Badminton Game*, long hair in breeze, shuttlecock midair. *April Love*, the Lady of Shalott. Round women, drowsy women, beautiful women. And while some were dolorous—Matisse; *Ophelia*—the girls were never angry or scheming, filled with nothing so demanding as desire. No, these were guileless women, tender, and probably even stupid, not that he would value their stupidity, but what he would want from them had nothing to do with talk. Farrell might slop through every rank backroom in Belfast, but Farrell's women were innocent.

When she hung the prints late one night and waited for Farrell to walk in the office that morning, Constance jittered, only pretending to scan papers as he strode pensively from one painting to the next, all nicely framed. He said nothing. He studied each one a long time. He went to his own office and shut the door. He'd not mentioned them then or since, but neither did he insist they come down. And just as she knew to choose them, Constance knew not to bring them up. She was not hurt; he was, a little. The paintings were an intrusion. By accident or instinct she had found his neighborhood. Whistler's *Little White Girl* stuck to the wall by his desk like a pin on a map.

Having phoned until midnight the night before, Constance knew it was ridiculous to feel injured. So he hadn't rung himself, wouldn't he see her the next morning? At the office she was unusually efficient—which is to say immeasurably efficient, frightening, perfect—and, as Farrell swept in and out, a little cold. As evening drew he ducked in the loo and reappeared, face washed, hair combed, tie freshly knotted, and smelling of cologne, his kerchief perking from his pocket. With no mention of Oscar's, he kissed Constance officiously on the forehead and tripped, yes, ran, practically danced down the front stairs. Constance sat at her desk and typed an address. She didn't cry or confide on the phone or go on a bout of irrational cleaning. She finished the letter and locked up, relieved to be such a practical person.

Estrin could not remember when she had last actually planned ahead of time what to wear to dinner. She picked the black silk blouse with a thin strip of Bedouin embroidery, pleased that no one could tell from the outside it was her favorite shirt. Otherwise it was back to full leathers, to remain thick-skinned.

How often had she thrown on anything hurriedly without even bothering to check her reflection, already annoyed at having agreed to go, already waiting for the meal to be over? It had been a bad, dry fall, and as such seasons will, it eclipsed all others, as if she'd only known evenings that rose with a bottle of wine, and fell as she finally looked across the table: he was smitten; she was bored.

Yet tonight Estrin did check the mirror, with despair. Ideally she saw herself as a tall Russian heroine, unpredictable and desperate, hollowed and harrowing, with high cheekbones and wide, lethal eyes. The real Estrin was consumptive. The real

Estrin wore heavy hooded cloaks, under which she clutched a snickersnee; she had just done something dreadful. Estrin had read a lot of Dostoevsky when she was fifteen.

Instead, she was short. Her cheeks were round, her features even; if Tolstoy was correct, that a truly beautiful face always had something wrong with it, then Estrin was merely a pretty girl. And *girl* was the word, embarrassing at her age. The only aspect of her Russian heroine she sustained was the eyes: they crouched. They both took you in and threw you out. Estrin recognized that with satisfaction.

Otherwise there was a sweetness to her face she had tried to live down for years. No matter what she suffered, her face showed no trace of it. When she studied photos of Marla Hanson, the New York fashion model attacked by her landlord with a razor, the slash scars made Estrin envious. How much more fascinating Marla would look later, with the pencil of tragedy down her nose. Estrin looked *nice*. Of a full busload of passengers, Estrin was the one old ladies shook down for change. Panhandlers marked her from blocks away, crossing the street for her quarters; in India, "Baksheesh" could have been her name. And so long as she rode with an open visor, nowhere was this plaguesome Rebecca-of-Sunnybrook-Farmishness more apparent than at checkpoints.

That's right, even in Newry and Crossmaglen, when they were stopping every goddamned car, license, computer check, boot search, all soldiers ever did to Estrin was wave. Witness: Teeming the Guzzi to the city gates toward Bedford Street, Estrin slowed long enough for them to see that yes, that back compartment could pack enough Semtex to blow that new shopping center sky-high. But no. Three smiles and a "Happy Christmas."

Banking around City Hall, a banquet of a building whose Beaux Arts façade now blinked with reindeer, Estrin noted the BELFAST SAYS NO banner had been amended. The DoE had told the City Council it could not post such a patently Unionist response to the Anglo-Irish Agreement on public property. So the

Prods had soldered on an extra section of sign: -EL. Estrin laughed. She loved this fucking town.

"You look beautiful."

Estrin felt an wild compulsion to comb her hair.

As he took her jacket and asked for a back table, Farrell displayed that curiously grave quality which characterized all his minor moments; he attended forward neatly from the waist and ushered Estrin before him with precision, even delicacy. He was a formal man, deft and considerate in all the ways that didn't really matter—he would hold your chair out, pick up your napkin when you dropped it, pour your wine, and next week fail to show up altogether.

The gravity fell away as he began to chat about the assassination of George Seawright, when he became entirely light-hearted.

"Creepface!" recognized the waitress. "And here's another one! Don't I see him every week with one more lovely lass in tears."

Farrell glared.

"You'll pardon, but Mr. O'Phelan must be seated on the wall, eyes on all the windows and doors, isn't that right, love? Usually the lady's seat, but none seems to mind. Sure, she gets a handsome view whichever way she's facing!" She patted Farrell's cheek and delivered their menus.

"How lucky, Maire, we were seated in your section."

"Och, I asked, love, I switched! Like following *Coronation Street* and earning your keep at the same time."

She brought a bottle of Pouilly Fuissé without Farrell's asking. "Sure we can skip the charade of having you taste it," she announced, trickling Estrin's glass halfway and glugging Farrell's to the top. "Never known you to send a bottle back if it was turned enough to dress your salad. Now, should I bring the second right away, or would you like to wait and order it? A nice ceremony that, but as for the third, it's just from the case in the icebox. You'll have to hold your horses."

Estrin ordered seafood. She always ordered seafood. It was a rule; fish was light. Estrin ran courses like track. She followed precepts, and not because she wasn't a sensualist, but because she was and therefore couldn't be trusted. In Estrin's personal mythology, should she ever be set loose in a stocked kitchen to do as she really pleased, you would find her an hour later packed incoherent with raw beef and rolling on the floor in a melee of ice cream and apple pie.

As they had both ordered exactly the same thing, Estrin asked on an odd hunch, "Do you always order fish?"

"Or chicken."

"Dessert?"

"Never."

"Do you have a morbid fear of fried foods?"

He laughed. "I've never put it quite that way, but I avoid them."

She inclined an inch more forward. "When do you get up in the morning?"

"Seven. Exactly."

"Sundays, too," she filled in. "And go to bed?"

"When I am finished. Ideally before seven. Not always."

"When did you get up as a child? Say, twelve, thirteen?"

It was wonderful. His eyes whetted. "Five."

She nodded victoriously. "But when did you go to school?"

"Not until 7:30. Why?"

"It was still dark," said Estrin. "No one else was up. The house was yours. Most of the time you worked, read, wrote. But some mornings you got up only to think. For hours, watching the light gray out the windows. The birds here are exotic. And you still believed in God."

"Did you, at thirteen?"

"No, by then I was a violent agnostic. But my father was a minister, so that speeded things up. My most remarkable precocity was early disaffection."

"I meant, get up at five?"

"Naturally," she dismissed. "But I'm not finished. Exercise?"

His face clouded. "I don't have time now. I used to run—"

"All weather. All winter. Rain. In fact, you liked it when it rained. Other people were agog, when secretly the problem is keeping cool. The mizzle felt good on your face."

Farrell did look amused. "And how far did I go?"

She licked her lips. "Ten miles. Every day."

He laughed. "Only eight, and every odd. Still, you're very good!"

"I'm very like you."

The eyes unexpectedly brambled. "You know," he said, attacking his lettuce with no dressing at all, "I think it's time we had an ordinary conversation."

"So what are you doing here?"

"You asked me to dinner."

He would not dignify her with a response.

"All right." She put her hands flat on the table. "I travel. For the last ten years, I must have been out of the States for eight. I used to go back between trips; not anymore."

"Why not?"

"Because I was living a fairy tale: that my *real life* was in the U.S. Every time I flew into Philadelphia late afternoon, I knew better by nightfall. The best safeguard against the rude news that you can't go home again is to stop trying."

"Don't you miss your family?"

"Not precisely, though I am frightened my parents will die. Or get old, for that matter. I travel with an illusion of reverse relativity. I move at the speed of light and I age while everyone back home stays the same. In my head Philadelphia remains an impeccable diorama I can enter at will. But you know how you can leave for two weeks and come back and the furniture's rearranged, the mailboxes are repainted on your street? Try leaving for two years. Or twenty."

"So now it's twenty, is it?"

"Why not? I haven't been back for three. And my parents will die; I'll be in Pakistan. I'll have to decide whether to go to the funeral, and it will cost a lot of money."

"Would you? From Pakistan?"

"Right away," said Estrin, with a lack of hesitation that surprised her. "Burning my way though a dozen Glenfiddiches and staying horribly sober anyway and hating myself, continent after continent, coming back too late. Years too late, not just a few days. Because if I had any integrity I'd book Lufthansa tomorrow and throw myself into my mother's arms while I still have the chance."

"You get along with your mother?"

"I don't anything with my mother; we never see each other, thanks to me. She writes much more than I do. Chatty stuff, though sometimes— Well, my parents are liberal, urban, educated, but lately I get the same feeling from my mother that I would if she came from Dunmurry, you know? She's sad like any mother, in an ordinary way. I'm not married. I have no children. I don't even have a career. I have stories. Mothers don't care about stories. She feels sorry for me. And maybe she should."

"Meaning you feel sorry for yourself."

"Sometimes," she said defiantly. "Why not? Who else is going to?"

He tsk-tsked and leaned back. "Self-pity is indulgent."

"I can stand some indulgence. I'm a good enough little soldier. I'm hardly frolicking across the continents with Daddy's Visa card. It hasn't been easy."

Farrell gently flaked a forkful of sole and glanced up at her with a dance of a smile. "No, I'm sure it hasn't been. How have you managed to support yourself now?"

Estrin smoothed her napkin in her lap. "No, the work hasn't been that hard, or that's not what's been hard . . . I just keep going and going and I'm getting—"

"Tired."

"Yes," she said gratefully.

"I'd think you were beginning to run out of countries."

"There's something else you run out of well before countries," she warned. "Though it's been a good life. I've picked grapes in Champagne, lemons in Greece. I've made plastic ashtrays in Amsterdam, done interior carpentry in Ylivieska. I've bused trays in the Philippines under Marcos, manufactured waterproof boots in Israel, and counseled in a German drug-abuse clinic in West Berlin. Now I'm at the Green Door, and that's just a sampling— I swear I'm not off target and it could be the best of lives forever if I were perfect, but I'm not and something is going wrong . . ."

As she drifted off, he touched her hand, and the question was intent: "How old are you?"

"I'm sorry. I should have told you before. I'm thirty-two."

"That is—incredible."

"I know."

"Then you're past thumbing around Europe in patched jeans. What are you doing?"

"You mean, when am I going to settle down and *do* something? Product is slag. The only difference between my life and a foreign correspondent's is I don't write it down. Does that matter? Someone's sure to cover the fall of Marcos without my help. I am my product."

"You don't want to accomplish anything?"

Estrin folded her arms. "I'm not convinced you believe in accomplishing anything yourself."

"I try to keep my work—"

"Whatever that is."

"Safe from my nihilism."

"You mean you don't allow what you believe to affect what you do."

"I believe a number of things," he hedged. "They're not all comfortable sitting next to each other is all . . . Like certain women."

"It's called cognitive dissonance, and it's dangerous as all fuck."

"Suits me, then."

She sighed. "I may be just making excuses. I always was a no-frills talent. I made 'good grades,' but at nothing in particular."

"Are you running away?"

"From what? I didn't leave my family behind in Pennsylvania sliced up with an electric carving knife. I don't think I'm running away any more than I would in a Philadelphia condo with an answering machine and regular lunch dates. It doesn't matter where I am, Farrell. So I might as well go as stay. And I like other countries. You—you've got a lot of spark, but you have this morose side. My autobiography doesn't usually sound this depressing."

"I depress you?"

"No, I must think torment will impress you."

"I thought you didn't care if people liked you."

"I lied." They toasted. The crystal sang.

"Don't misunderstand me," she expanded. "I haven't lived for ten years out of a backpack. Especially for the last five, I've stayed places—I move into houses and buy dustpans. Right now I have a dynamite house on Springfield Road. I buy flowers, I have a whisk! Because you have to put together something to leave before you go."

"Is that what you're doing tonight?"

She didn't answer. She ordered brandy. Estrin had spilled out. This man had made her tense as no man had for months, but that was earlier, and now she felt herself break and spread over the restaurant like a neatly cracked egg, her eyes shining, double yolks. "So though I'm not ambitious, I do work hard, because I like the feeling. In Israel, I got up to pull boots at four, and it was loud and hot. I did overtime. Before I left Kiryat Shemona I ran the night shift, and was the only Gentile ever offered membership in that kibbutz. In Berlin, the clinic tried to send me to school in social work. In the Philippines, I was a hotel dishwasher, but when the head cook *disappeared* they put me in to pinch hit; found out I pickled a mean ceviche and kept me there. So I ran the kitchen for six months; while the busboys ambled in late afternoons the color of polished walnuts, I worked twelve, fourteen hours a day and turned the color of kiwi fruit."

"You're not complaining."

"No," she exhaled, remembering. "And today Kieran asked me to manage the Green Door."

"How did you pull that off?"

"Damned if I know! It's out of control! Everywhere I go I just want to be a schlemiel and somebody hands me a set of keys and the books, and before long I have employees and late hours and a lot of problems. It's the curse of the crudest possible intelligence. The fact is, if you tell a hundred people, *Put the chair in that corner*, fully seventy-five of them will promptly hang it from the chandelier. Did you know that most of the world is made of fruitcakes?"

He laughed. "You get more American when you drink."

"I can't help it. I was born this way."

"You don't like being American?"

"I've learned to get by with it, like any handicap—harelip, paraplegia. Do you like being Irish?"

"What do you think?"

She eyed him. "That you abhor it. In short, Ireland suits you perfectly."

She was getting swacked. Her voice was louder and higher; people were looking over at their table. She used her hands when she talked, and as her motions got wider Farrell eyed their tall goblets warily, though she always missed. Then, she knew her way around a landscape with glasses, that was clear. She had reached a phase he knew himself, marked not by sloppiness but by inordinate precision—her pronunciation was getting more rather than less correct. Her phrasing grew considered, her gestures semaphoric, crisp as air traffic control. When she rose to find the loo, he recognized the careful placement of her hand on the table, the excessively smooth ascent from her chair, the purposeful step-by-step glide around other diners—too exact, too concentrated. She had crossed the point where all these ordinary matters could be executed without thinking, and now to negotiate finding the ladies', asking Maire coherently, remembering the directions and being able to follow them, took the full application of her powers.

Farrell enjoyed her absence. He kneaded his forehead. He had to admit he'd no idea what to make of her. The boasting had been a bit much; though if she really had washed dishes in the Philippines and made plastic boots in Galilee, he supposed she deserved a little airtime over dinner for work that had surely been excruciating after the first half hour. Farrell was tired. That was it, she was tiring. He wished she would just quiet down. He was sick of words. This whole island never shut up, and he wondered at how much people said was in such reliably inverse proportion to how much they had to say. If Farrell chose to lose any of his senses, he decided he'd go deaf.

Yet when Estrin returned it was as if something had happened. She seemed sad. He felt sure he could make one mean remark and she would cry.

"Are you married?" she asked straight up.

"You know when I woke up at thirteen, but you can't tell if I'm that much of a shite?"

"That's right," she said calmly. "Only the incidentals of your life are apparent."

When the bill came and Farrell went for his wallet, Estrin crumpled into her pocket for a wad of pound notes. "No, no." He put a hand over her fist of cash. He flicked a card to Maire, allowing Estrin to catch that it was platinum.

Farrell gave her a hand up, pressed gently at her waist between tables; opening the door, he slipped his fingers under a shock of hair still beneath the jacket and pulled it free; she paused to let him finish, and a little longer still for the back of his hand to rest at her collar. As a result, by the time they were outside they had run through all the routine moves of the gambit like speed chess. Then, she was thirty-two, he forty-three; openings had become so easy. Perhaps the very definition of adulthood is a fascination with the middle parts of games.

"I have my bike," she said.

"It's safe?"

"Locked, anyway. I suppose."

"Leave it, then. We haven't far."

Estrin shot her motorcycle a mournful look. "Where to?" she asked, in tow.

"My hotel."

"You live in a hotel?"

"No."

"Then why—"

"It's safer." To Estrin's grunt of incomprehension, he simply replied, "Never mind." He put his arm around her shoulders, though at Estrin's height that was less like holding a person than resting on a banister.

"The swallow," he told her as if beginning a bedtime story, "takes off when it's young and flies all around the world. For up to four years it never lands, sailing over South America, Africa, Australia—thousands of miles, the circumference of the earth several times."

"Does it mate in the air?"

"No, after sowing wild oats in Tierra del Fuego, the swallow settles down to raise a family. Buys a station wagon and gets fat."

"Thanks," said Estrin.

While no longer rolled up by dark as it once was, central Belfast was deserted after the pubs closed; their heels rang down the walk.

"Another parable," said the American, whose voice, cowed by quiet, had gone soft. "A few years ago back in Philadelphia I decided I was sick of my ratty underwear—it was stained, the elastic shot. So I treated myself to, like, the best—in one store, silk, maroon, black lace; as my stack piled down the rack, other customers began to stare at me sidelong. I bought thirty pairs.

When I got home I spread them out and not only felt insane, I felt deprived. All I could think about was going out and buying more."

"You're obsessive."

"Not so simple. It's greed. The same thing happens when I'm not halfway through a meal and I start thinking about a second helping. Or a cassette's not nearly over and I decide to play it again. It's a hunger like C. S. Lewis's magic Turkish delight: the more you eat, the more you want, because you didn't taste what you had before. When I decide in the middle to play a song again, I stop hearing it the first time. I have a problem with wanting what I've already got.

"Anyway, that's what happens with me and maps," she explained. "I spread them on the floor like underwear. I no sooner get my butt to Belfast than I start frantic plans to fly to the Soviet Union."

"Still have the silk drawers?" He raised his eyebrows.

"Nope. After the shopping binge I stopped wearing underwear altogether."

She couldn't match his stride, and kept trying different rhythmic combinations, 3:2, 5:3, like solving an equation, and now tangibly hung back. "Listen," she fumbled. "I don't do this sort of thing much anymore."

He stopped and kissed her hair. "Now, what sort of thing might that be?"

"I guess that's my question."

"Always in such a rush. Don't we need something to discuss before we can discuss it?"

"Sorry. You make me nervous. I don't know why."

He liked her for the confession. He took her hand, swinging it a little, feeling . . . content. A mysterious sensation.

5

Cape Canaveral on York Street

Estrin was pleased he led her to Whitewells, old Belfast, one of the last monuments downtown to an era largely expunged in the last twenty years blast by blast. At the corner of Royal Avenue and York Street, its Edwardian opulence put the rest of the town center to shame. The "Belfast Is Buzzing" campaign proudly celebrated a commercial reincarnation not unlike having been born a prince and coming back a sow. The lines of shoe stores and garish plastic marquees may have made locals proud, but they made Estrin feel temporary, trivial; she might have preferred the atmosphere had the shops remained bombed out. Yet only a few chipped stones on the hotel suggested nearby explosions; more than its architecture, what impressed Estrin most as they walked in was that Whitewells was still here.

Not that they got far. Two steps in, they were met by a

security façade more imposing than at most airports. While the doorman respectfully recognized "Mr. O'Phelan," even Farrell laid his jacket on the X-ray belt, walked through the metal detector, and raised his arms to be searched. For the first time in this Province, Estrin's adorable round cheeks didn't roll her past the guards. They impounded her can of Mace, and a far more than perfunctory frisk recovered a Phillips screwdriver Estrin had rummaged for all week. They took that, too.

"Jesus," Estrin exclaimed when they were through. "I'd hate to see what they do to suitcases."

"Something between homogenization and genetic engineering. If Watson hadn't discovered DNA, Whitewells would have found it at the door. Best security in all of Europe." He clapped her delightedly on the shoulder and left for the key.

Estrin sank across the carpet. Security curtained away, only formidable Old World appointments presented themselves. Whitewells was a bulwark of a building, with that airless quiet of a bomb shelter or a bank vault. Even the decor was safe, with conservative furniture, all dark, woody, and green. While oceans crushed the rocks of this island, the fountain here purled coyly: surely water would only wash your face. In Whitewells every element was contained: the fire would never pop beyond its grate, and whatever the powers of earth in this place, they were marshaled entirely for your protection. Estrin was reminded of the feeling of the world when she was a small child, when everything seemed oversized, looming, more real than you. The tables were long and steady, the chairs sturdy and stable, with fat, affectionate arms. Upholstery skirted their formidable square chassés to the floor, like RUC Land Rovers. Wainscoting was so thick you could run into it; the ceilings were corniced, the paintings mostly frame. Grandfather clocks, above ordinary time, were stopped at twelve.

Grazing the lobby, Estrin's eyes struck Farrell by accident: a few deft strokes from a distance, more sketch than sculpture. And she'd never seen a man whose apparent age could shift so. Joking with the receptionist, he could have been her brother;

turning, her father. Both versions were striking, though Farrell had that quality rare in men of not seeming to know how attractive he was.

Joining him in the lift, she could tell they were watched by the way the staff deliberately looked elsewhere.

Later she would notice the lovely room, with no smeary seascapes or little broken coffee machines; for now Estrin could attend only to the bed, rising at her with its big white spread. Despite her nervousness, she felt simple. Hanging her coat, she didn't mind having nothing to say. She sat on the edge of the bed and took off her boots; allowing her hair to drape on either side of her face, she looked up and smiled.

Farrell slipped off his shoes and stretched on the bed to its foot. He did not reach for her, but closed his eyes and rubbed his face. Estrin massaged his temples. He rested his arms and didn't touch.

"You know, if you'd like to just sleep, that would be all right," Estrin offered.

Farrell kept his eyes closed as her fingers moved into his scalp. "Don't think the old man has it in him?"

"I think you're tired."

"Yes," he said, pulling her closer. "I am shattered." He was an angular man, but the kiss was acquiescent; he was shaking.

For all her avaricious crackling of maps, at last Estrin Lancaster paused in her gorging of whole foreign countries to remain in a single room, really a small room, in one odd city with one difficult character, but as a result something paradoxical happened and, instead of feeling hemmed in, Estrin found the world of Whitewells and this man on its bed the source of infinite, patient fascination. As the universe shrank ever further to two patches of face, Farrell's mouth opened into a cavernous place, large enough to walk around in, get lost in, take the underground. Her passage echoed down his throat. Farrell had swallowed the world, and all that ever was could be found there—the Taj Mahal, the Eiger, the Ganges, Cape Canaveral, the Smithsonian

Institution, and Estrin's favorite *U.S. Out of Nicaragua* coffee cup back on Springfield Road.

She actually forgot about the sex, since she was not waiting to get on with something else. Sometimes she forced herself to pull away from him so she could enjoy going back, each time to visit new tourist attractions—the Pyramids, St. Stephen's Green, the Roman Catacombs. They were luxurious kisses and, while soft, not that disturbing invertebrate *bleah*, where the tongue dissolves into a pool of gelatinous mouth-flesh, like lapping at soup with no bowl, kisses without rim. No, even as their tongues wrapped, Henry Moore, one form into the other, these were kisses with structure and purpose, like good sculpture always turning, one plane leading endlessly into another, until you are back where you started, with no sense of having been there before.

Farrell held her neck and pressed her deeper. The farther they tunneled down each other's throat, the more it seemed unfair to be kept so far apart. Even if the evening was one-off, he was a slime, this was a pickup, Estrin was ready to offer money or favors or flattery, anything at all if he would only keep her in his bed the whole night.

"No, don't." Estrin stopped his wrangling with her silk. "I can't stand being undressed. And you'd never have a chance with these leather pants, they would take you hours."

This next business was also simple, without the zip by button hassle Estrin had grown so weary of, but with the neater, practiced efficiency with which people can take off their own clothes. She did not want to think about clothes.

Without them he was just as long, but even more narrow. So meager and unmuscled, his body looked easy to draw, though you would need a ruler. As a result, though hard to read at dinner, here he printed legible right angles, undivisive, direct. His skin, surprisingly tender for a man his age, pimpled with a dot-matrix of chenille. His legs dangled off the mattress, the wan, desperate sticks with knobbled knees that crowd Save the Children posters.

Even his penis, though long, was unusually slim, and less bullying than most, a limb more of grace than aggression, smooth and abstract like the rest: Giacometti.

Be that as it may, Estrin looked in his eyes as she hadn't for a few minutes and remembered his name; remembered other people saying it, the way they said it—with an inching away. She recognized his face as the same from yesterday: stony, blasé, *You're all witless gobshites*. As he slid into her easy as you please, like popping in an open back door, she recalled that only a few minutes before she'd have knelt on the floor for one more kiss— from a stranger, whose powers of affection she knew little but whose powers of disdain had already shown themselves to be monumental. In fact, Estrin had risen in the ranks of menials all over the world because she was reliable, but once in a while even Estrin slipped, and flat on her back now, she had that feeling of having been trusted and suddenly remembering she did not lock up.

It felt better than she remembered, but she hadn't remembered because she didn't want to. Estrin twisted underneath. She avoided seeing his face now because she already cared what it was thinking, and this could be a nothing, a fuck, she didn't know him— *Get out!* She managed not to say this out loud, and kissed him as if stuffing a towel in her mouth. Farrell was whipping more quickly and screeing like seabirds, but Estrin only whimpered. She'd put her life together and made do. She had a job now and a house and coffee filters and always bought milk for the morning the night before. She belonged to a gym and her running time was good; the phone rang when she came home. The Guzzi was tuned and she loved spending her free days by herself blasting across the island—to Bushmills— Estrin was in fine form, often excited by this new city, even Provo poppycock, Ulster slang—*stocious, legless, half-tore*, as many words for drunk as the Eskimos had for snow— For once in a country that spoke English, with more mountains and comically crummy food— *bangers and chips, pizza and chips, chips and chips*— It had all been enough without this—

His fingers on her shoulders bit flesh. Below him, Estrin put up feeble resistance: *she would not come*. A traveler may be excited, but never satisfied. Besides, can't you understand that pleasure is grotesque? What can possibly happen next but that someone will take it away?

Farrell immediately reached over to shake down his overcoat and didn't explain. He located an inhaler, which he sucked on, sitting up. This was not romantic.

He slept on the far side of the bed in a ball. A small person with the rest of it, Estrin lay bereft on the wide white sheet. She tossed, always hot or cold, pulling up the blankets, throwing them off. She felt deserted, and irrationally offended that he could sleep.

Yet by morning she, too, was deep in, and it was Farrell who roused her into his arms with a remark about feeling neglected.

Farrell eyed her from the safety of his Unionist tabloid. He had barricaded himself at the breakfast table with ten different papers, even for Farrell generous. He never knew what to say to women mornings. He watched her smarm her mug over her forehead, against her temple, down her cheek. She had a warmth with objects, he'd noticed in 44, the way she tapered over her fork, smeared the flat of the knife, traced the flute of her plate—she seemed to savor the setting more than the food.

As he walked her back to Bedford Street, they discussed the Guilford Four. Approaching her bike, Farrell felt Estrin drag at his hand.

"Well, it's been fun," said Estrin defiantly.

"Yes" was all he said. He waited for her to remove the padlock, zip up, strap on her helmet, and actually turn the key. As she revved the motor, he slipped his hands in his pockets. She fed the engine more petrol than it needed; its revolutions grew louder and more shrill. He could feel her clutching through disappointment to disbelief to rage like gears, and he waited for the very last stage—ordinary pain—at which Estrin unexpectedly switched off the cycle and stared down at the tank. She looked up, her face not wobbly but impassive and open.

"This is it?"

"Not unless you prefer, my swallow. Myself, I'd like very much to see you again."

"Then why don't you take my fucking phone number?"

"Now, that's a thought. You Americans are so well organized."

The exchange done, she started the bike energetically; he squeezed her shoulder and leaned down to shout, "And it was more than fun!"

She tore out from under his hand, grazed his toe with her back wheel, and ripped past the BBC.

6

Roisin's Furniture Goes Funny

"Now, why go to that confounded funeral, Roisin, when I've the afternoon free?"

"You know very well why. Didn't you just go to Mc-Michael's? Even Seawright's, and that was appalling."

"What was appalling, love, was blowing up his car. The yob was a bigot, but last time I read up, that wasn't a capital crime."

"It should be," she muttered.

"Sure we'd all be six foot under in no time."

"Well, last time I read up, walking down the road on the border wasn't a capital crime, either."

"The soldier says himself, the gun went off by accident."

"Angus, catch yourself on! I suppose Cromwell's invasion was an accident, too."

"Cromwell's invasion was three hundred years ago, Christ!

This Brigadoon drives me to distraction, always blattering on about Oliver and James and Billy, as if they were all on their way here to tea. MacAnespie will be investigated—"

"That's rich. Just like the Birmingham Six?"

"The point is, you attend, at the end of the day it's one more Nationalist demonstration."

"And Seawright's was a Loyalist one."

"That funeral was part of my job. Your job is to stay home and find it all too painful to bear."

"Even a poet needs to make political statements."

"Bollocks, haven't you had it up to your bake with political statements?"

"It's more you have, and only with mine."

"I'll not get into the whole kit, since I said I'd an afternoon free and not the rest of my life. But I do wish you'd think things through a bit more, lass. You call yourself a Republican, but you've not a single decent word for the South. It's the DUP fellows steam off to Donegal on holiday and say it's brilliant. You, Rosebud, come back from Sligo raving. 'Their veins run with Fairy Liquid!' you says."

Roisin laughed. "I said that?"

He snaked a finger down her arm, and Roisin shivered. "Aye, you've a right decent sense of humor, when you let it out. Loose a few more crackers instead of all this howl about creepy trees and menstruation, maybe I'd show at one of those do's of yours."

"Angus, you wouldn't go to my readings if I tap-danced with Dame Edna." Roisin struggled halfhearted toward the clock. "I'll need to leave in twenty minutes."

"I vote we have our own wee service." He slipped his hand up under her blouse. "Why, this afternoon I personally volunteer to cross the sectarian divide."

Angus MacBride was a vigorous, aggressive lover who didn't fancy diddling about for hours trying to satisfy his woman but pleased himself. Roisin preferred this. She enjoyed being taken, even forced a little. Besides, a too solicitous lover made Roisin feel watched, and his attentions often backfired. She had difficulty coming anyway, and under pressure to perform, her excitement withered. She wondered how men, their pleasures so apparent, ever achieved an erection with a woman in the room. Chichi clitoral diligence had, like every fashion, hit Ireland ten years late, and arrived in Roisin's life with her last boyfriend, Garrett. Roisin would find herself boated on a horizonless sexual sea, what had begun as a careless afternoon excursion darkening gradually to nightmare as the light began to fade and the bed rocked on. Frankly, the two- or three-hour fuck is highly overrated. Garrett had dutifully rubbed away until her vagina was raw, her labia numb. Once they'd endured a few of these sessions, she hadn't the heart to admit to him that short of success after ten minutes the project was hopeless, so the marathons went on until Roisin began to dread going to bed. She tried cutting his efforts short by faking, but this only seemed to inspire Garrett to more, like a pinball player determined to rack a higher score. Further, he wouldn't allow himself to enter her until she was "done," by which time Garrett himself had wilted. So then Roisin would take the helm and dither, though she absolutely refused to put the thing in her mouth. Ironically, he seemed to have the same reaction she did to being conscientiously serviced, and if he did come, it was a nervous, exhausted spasm after more toil, and this from a man who had apologized at the beginning of their relationship that he had trouble with premature ejaculation.

When Garrett announced that he'd started seeing another woman, Roisin was sure he'd found a buxom, thick-armed Andytown wench who boiled potatoes whom he could throw down on the lino when he pleased, to blast away and zip up after five minutes, better than this overwrought, internationally famous poetess for whom he had far too much respect. Angus didn't have enough, but then she'd do without if respect took the form of obsequious deference in bed.

So Angus plundered on, joyful and oblivious, with the rhythmic grunting Roisin trusted. It would never occur to Angus to fake excitement in a hundred million years. If he didn't relish making love to her, he'd get up and do something else; for there is nothing so comforting as the obviously selfish person: he will take care of himself. Left to her own devices, then, Roisin relaxed and enjoyed some moderate success. This particular afternoon she preferred to lie back and watch, for finally, at the age of thirty-seven, Roisin had discerned that you didn't come as a responsibility, a victory, or even as a compliment, but because you felt like it.

The timing of the ring was so perfect, and so close to perfectly bad, that they both had to laugh. Still panting, sweat streaming, Angus reached for the receiver with " 'Loo?" in a could-be-anyone voice. While he didn't want to be recognized, he liked the territorial implications of answering her phone.

Angus looked at the receiver like something with a bad smell and discarded it. "Fancy. Rung off. New boyfriend?"

Long after Angus had gone, Roisin lay on her back with her eyes open, the duvet up to her chin. Only the ebb of light and the beat of her body marked the passing of time. Roisin rarely listened to music. She found quiet a marvel. And she found doing nothing a marvel. How spectacular that you could simply lie here and the day would sift by. Roisin considered this her secret. On either side of the house, women rustled up tea—boiling, toasting, dragging children to the table. Tellies blared, papers flapped, electronic games wheedled away, but here Roisin folded her hands over her chest and could detect only the faint on-and-off hum of the refrigerator, her legs laid out like the dead's. But she wasn't dead! That was the secret. Under the slanted ceiling of the top floor, cozied by the faded blue wallpaper flowers and the shadows easing over them, Roisin could roam the moors of her head, heather purpling, grass bent, as a young girl with a long dress in a breeze. She wondered at the bustle of women in this town who always had to be a-doing, boys who tore off in stolen cars through checkpoints, even romantics who yearned for the days a lad could light off to sea. She didn't see the scrabbling for adventure, when all you need do is pull a comforter to your breast. For there was always a ship waiting in Roisin's port, with sails like skirts; her own breath blew the wind.

Only when satisfied she could remain this way forever would Roisin get up. She dressed slowly and considered the match of colors as if someone would call, though she'd probably spend the evening padding the house, reading snatches of poetry, and washing the dishes just to feel the water on her hands. Roisin always dressed well, especially for herself. She chose purple and green, like the hillsides in her mind tonight, a soft sweater, low shoes. She tiptoed downstairs as if not wanting to wake herself up.

She'd not combed her hair or made up her face—which she would also do, meticulously, whether or not she stepped out—so when the mirror in the dining room ambushed her she jumped. Especially the last five years, Roisin was mindful of mirrors and did not let them sneak up on her. And after each passing birthday it took a fraction of a second longer to prepare for them. What was required was nothing less than a mirror of her own to fight back, a careful preconception of a face to fend off heresy. As the two versions grew increasingly disparate, it took more energy to generate the gentler portrait, and Roisin marked the positions of store windows and bar glass like the mapmaking of the blind: she needed to anticipate them without seeing them, for a careless glance could ache up the back of her head for hours, like a baton clubbing from the peelers.

Tonight, however, she braved the image, unprotected by eyeliner or inner vision: this was her face. In the droop of her cheeks she saw her mother. Otherwise, there was less of a slump than a shatter to it. Her tooth enamel, skin, and dry, separated hair all crackled like crazed celadon. Her eyes were green and men admired them, though tonight she noticed a twist in their center, a wringing—they wound you in at a curl. It seemed the face, she decided, of a woman who had once been very beautiful. More truthfully, it was the face of a woman who had always been almost beautiful: her looks required a leap of faith. The rub: one so many men had almost made. She was the kind of woman whom men date weekly, routinely, for years, whom they think they love and maybe even think they'll marry, until overnight they find the "real thing" at Robinson's and in two weeks' time are off to Australia with a cropped blonde.

Maybe that explained the twist, as if she were wincing from flattery unreceived. In her best dress she might earn "lovely," but never "gorgeous," and certainly not that rare adjective some women pull from even dull men that is so unusual and right that the remark achieves a beauty of its own, and rests beside her as a compliment in the best sense, a woman by a rose.

As for the shatter in the face, that was easy: it was time and an inconceivable parade of disappointments. That she had recognized their pattern seemed not to free her but to doom her to it. Roisin went about her romances like any bad researcher who writes his conclusion before his experiment, so that long telephone sessions concurring with Constance Trower that she sought out abuse, that she could only admire a man who didn't admire her, only inspired Roisin to ring off and march out to prove how very, very right they were.

Looking herself in the eye for once set a tone for the night of uncommon bareness. The feeling downstairs wasn't bleak exactly, but unadorned. Trinkets in the sitting room did not blur into a nest of comfort and civilization but remained discrete. China bird. Broken clock. Alabaster ashtray. A *What Doesn't Belong in This Picture?* where the answer was that nothing did. More, the room was rife with futility. The empty Carolans tin on the mantel had seemed too handsome to throw out, good for sewing perhaps, but Roisin had a cabinet for that; or knitting, but she didn't knit. Candy dishes proffered no chocolates, bowls no fruit. The alabaster ashtrays were too lustrous for cigarettes, so she smoked with saucers instead. Those napkins on the sideboard were far too dear to dab spaghetti sauce, so she would set her place with pyramids of peach linen and then run to the kitchen to wipe her mouth on a paper towel. Her antimacassars were so elegant that she sat forward in her chairs, to avoid soiling the lace that was there to protect the chair from her head in the first place. Nothing made any sense! Likewise, the furniture did not cohere—the sofa ignored its end tables; chairs sat back to back, not talking. The house hadn't changed except that some artifice or optimism was removed, some essential squint that made the rooms more pleasing and sane. It was a house without lies, and it was frightening.

As this quality only intensified, Roisin was unsurprised when a short while later she looked down at her kitchen table with the rude revelation: This is my life. For she not only touched up her face for a mirror but routinely prepared a version of her existence that did not include evenings like this one: a biscuit, crumbs of Cheshire, a leaf or two of lettuce; a book breaking its spine at a page of inexpressible boredom; stray lines on the back of a brown Telecom envelope, with a word crossed out, replaced, crossed again, and filled in with the first one. This was a poet's life. What did others see in it? Why did the word sing? So her lover had taken her that afternoon; a poet was granted a lover, maybe even one taboo. Tonight, however, she conceded the larger problem was not his religion but his marriage. Roisin was having an affair with a married man; she was thirty-seven and it was nearly too late for children; she had poetry, but while she'd never admit this to Angus, Work only meant so much to her. Weeks and biscuits crumbled on; the shatter deepened; the twist took another half turn. What did she have but the blue-flowered wallpaper and the quiet of her own sinking ship, the slackening flap of her sails? Roisin St. Clair, one more gifted but sloppily understood poet reading on Thursdays at Queen's about eerie weather and trembling leaves when the crowd was only itching to make it to the Common Room and toss a few before last call—

She realized the phone had rung several times already, and rushed gratefully to the intrusion—why, every once in a while the outside world came through.

"Miss St. Clair, I am a friend of Angus MacBride's."

"Of whose?"

"Please," said the voice, pained. "I'm sure Angus appreciates your discretion. But I mean a *close* friend. I need to discuss a matter of our mutual concern. Best in person. At your convenience, of course."

"Kelly's, then," Roisin faltered. "Tomorrow, half-four. How will I know you, then?"

"Your photo on the back of *Known Facts* is most striking. I could pick you out of the top stands at a hurley match. I'm sure to find you at a small bar."

A pause; a click. Roisin cocked her head. The voice had a caress in it. Despite the ominousness of the call, when she looked about the sitting room her objects were restored to meaning and memory, collusion, the useless at least pretty. The chairs were in earnest conversation. Back at the kitchen table, the Cheshire was dry as wine, brilliant white and tart. She poured sherry into cut crystal and picked up the book again, engrossed, jotting from time to time; and some of the lines on the Telecom envelope showed great promise.

It was this particular hand on her shoulder from behind that spurred Roisin to think how some strangers touched you and made you angry, others only made you feel warm. Turning, she was tempted to decide easily that the difference was whether or not they were attractive, but she had liked the hand before she found the gaunt, tailored gentleman who belonged to it. She later theorized there was a class of men who filched at you, sliming for what they could get—a pickpocket job, their touch was theft. Others did you a favor: their touch was gift.

"*The* Farrell O'Phelan?"

"I don't know, are you *the* Roisin St. Clair?"

"I take a sorrier article, I'm afraid."

"A back booth, then, for two sorry articles."

"I never believed you were real! More like the Lone Ranger or Robin Hood."

When he ordered coffee rather than a drink, she trusted him better, for no good reason. "As Robin Hood I have resigned. I asked you here over an issue partly political, but largely personal."

"Politics is always personal here."

"And how. So you understand: alliances are not simply to positions but to people. As such, our friend Angus MacBride is irreplaceable. For years he's managed to conceal from the Prods that he's intelligent. And he's one of those rare fellows who can pat you on the back and turn a phrase with the latest idiom, and only later in bed might you realize what he said was anathema to you, if then. That he's reasonable and open-minded about solutions to this situation is known only to his closest associates like you and me. To the rest he plays the part of a hardheaded holdout to perfection. I'm not telling you anything you don't know. And sure I don't need to tell you, either, that his drinking is out of control."

Roisin inhaled. Anyone's confidence hit up her sinuses like eucalyptus. "You fancy?"

"He is drinking not only after political functions but before. And are you aware that the glass he keeps beside him at press conferences is filled with vodka?"

"Angus has always been well oiled, Mr. O'Phelan."

"Have you ever added up how many quarts that engine takes?"

"I suppose about half a bottle a day."

"I will infer you are not talking Beaujolais. And Miss St. Clair, that's the liquor you *know* about. Even so, that's hardly well oiled, my dear, it's pickled. Now, a friend of mine in the SDLP is your man's physician. I've glimpsed the reports. I will spare you the details, but the outlook is grim."

She gasped and pressed for specifics, but he was not forthcoming.

"So you see, I'd be leery of intruding on your privacy without cause. Angus speaks highly of you, though rarely, as he ought. I've come to believe you exert considerable influence on the man. As his friend and supporter, I appeal to you."

"To do what?"

Farrell spread his hands. "Haven't a clue. Mind you, for several years drink was more my own speciality than politics.

73

Like most such experts, however, I'm a better source on how to get in than out."

"How did you"—she nodded to his coffee—"get out?"

"I'm not, entirely," he admitted. "Otherwise," he patted her hand, "a long story. I turned a corner. I hadn't a woman to help me. And little good she'd have done me if I had. I was a spiteful drunk."

"Are you still spiteful?"

"Perverse. Telling me I'd had enough was the fastest way to get me to kill the bottle. Angus is more adult. I sense in him more of a—desire to please." Retreating from the border of insult, he added, "And wisely he might please such a lovely lady." Farrell broke his gaze and withdrew his hands to his lap.

"I'll think about it. I can't promise anything."

"I can give you one piece of advice. Angus and I have a complex relationship. With your concern, he might behave himself. Had he an inkling I cautioned you, he'd booze himself to death inside the week."

"Why?"

"Trust me."

"Why should I?"

He laughed. "What is it you've heard about me?"

"That no one knows whose side you're on."

"Seems you've done a bit of line crossing yourself."

Roisin fumbled with her jumper.

"I'm sorry. I don't mean to pry. Still, it must be difficult for you," he ventured, "not being able to pour your heart out to girlfriends on the phone."

Her eyes shot up, but he only looked sympathetic. "Yes, it's claustrophobic."

"Then"—he looked off—"I can't remember the last time I 'poured my heart out' to a living soul. Sometimes I'm afraid there's nothing to pour. Like Talisker at the end of the day—you know, I used to drain a bit of water in and rinse it about just to get the last drops out?"

"Sad picture," said Roisin.

"Only thing more depressing than a drunk jarred is a drunk sober."

"I meant the one of your heart."

"I did want to mention"—he changed the subject—"I'm an admirer of your work. Especially *Bare Limbs on Basalt*. Though I imagine *Neighbors Who Watch the Shore* has received more critical acclaim."

"Yes. *Basalt* is out of print."

"Unforgivable! I know some editors at Blackstaff; we'll see what we can do."

"Och, you needn't. Please don't."

He laughed. "You mean, please do. I heard an Irish comedian claim the other day that it was a stiff shock to go to the Continent and discover that there when they asked if you wanted a cup of tea and you said no you didn't get one. But it's no trouble, and that volume deserves to be on the shelves. Does that collection include 'Stibnite Crystals with Druzy Quartz'?"

"No." She looked at him in amazement. "That was only published once, in *The Honest Ulsterman*, three years ago. It's unimaginable you remember."

"Hardly. I quote a few lines from 'Stibnite' in one of my speeches. Since I repeat myself appallingly, that means I must have recited them two dozen times."

"What lines?" She leaned forward. Her tea had gotten cold.

7

Constance Has Inner Beauty;
About Farrell We Are Not So Sure

Though accustomed to shenanigans, Constance had found her
assignment to dig up all of Roisin St. Clair's published poems
unaccountably disturbing.

Still, she found every damn one. If anything, Constance was
competent. In the UWC strike of '74 she knew where to get
you milk. She was a wizard with maps, a seamstress with itin-
eraries. She negotiated library stacks the way most women
ranged confidently through Co-op. She was unintimidated by
computers. She remembered post codes, account numbers, train
schedules, hotel rates. Traveling, she packed dresses that didn't
wrinkle, and never forgot her toothpaste. She knew the best and
cheapest shops for anything from light bulbs to woolens, and
unlike Farrell would never buy top of the line unless it repre-
sented fair value; yet she never shopped for pleasure and stocked

huge boxes of detergent and froze family packs of chicken to save trips. She could spell out any of the maze of acronyms in Northern Ireland and the complete title of governmental applications. She could get carpenters on the dole or file compensation claims with the NIO. As a result, she had imbued countless other women with that particular modern bravery, bureaucratic courage.

For Constance believed goodness was practical. So she would watch your bicycle while you ran in the smoke shop for a paper. She would give you clear directions to the bus station. She might not routinely shell out spare change to bad buskers—not to encourage a poor choice of careers—but she would recognize honest embarrassment in a checkout line and fill out your bill the pound three you came up short, all with a brusque officiousness that eased accepting her money. She arranged funerals while everyone else was weeping on dales, amid even her own tragedy making sure you had bread with your broth, a lift home. She remembered birthdays; if her gifts were dull, they were at least handy. And because she understood kindness as concrete, that Farrell had saved specific people by removing real wires from gelignite continued to impress her far more than all his talk and referendums now.

While Constance roistered through her workday with arguably masculine zeal, she was perfectly feminine; she simply wasn't pretty. Her homeliness did not spring from an overindulgence in crisps or an inability to rouse herself to the swimming pool, for no amount of slimming or breaststroke would sort out the slight squarishness of her head, the meaty Dietrich thighs unlikely to return to fashion in her lifetime, eyes a wee bit small, a wee bit close together—or was it far apart? The subtlety of good looks astounded Constance herself. There had been times in a public bath when she had stared at a handsome woman in a way that made the other uncomfortably assume Constance was—no, it wasn't that. She was riveted by beauty because it would have taken such a tiny realignment of her own features for Constance to be beautiful, too.

Though her appearance pained her certain evenings in the loo, it was not her obsession; so she didn't deny herself a pavlova or marshal two hours a day for the pool. Consequently she'd thickened a bit, and was showing every promise of a dumpy middle age. In her work this had proved an advantage, and Farrell seemed to treasure her ordinary looks as if she'd deliberately purchased a spy kit. The haggard pre–Jane Fonda generation of housewives in West Belfast was only skeptical of well-manicured single women of thirty-nine who'd rediscovered seamed nylons streeling up to their doors for information with skinny necks and tasteful pendants, refusing a biscuit with their tea. Constance always had at least two.

Further, she followed every City Council motion and had memorized a generation of sectarian debts. She could quote whole paragraphs of the Anglo-Irish Agreement verbatim, and knew the history of each civil rights and paramilitary group down to half the membership. She had swallowed the entire attic of the Linen Hall Library, and to Farrell O'Phelan she was indispensable.

Her ambition, to the word.

Constance considered Farrell the most perceptive man she had ever met. Unlike all their other colleagues, who would, opportunity given, take a snipe or two, from a little nail bomb of petty complaints to single high-caliber potshots (last week at the Peace People executive: *He's a cowboy. Fundamentally the man is irresponsible*), Constance wouldn't hear a word against him. She'd thought well of the man even in his gawky stage, before the hotel and the European suits. She'd first noticed him at a UUAL rally as a heckler, where she'd been protesting with NICRA on the sidelines. He'd been articulate and, though vicious, formally polite; it was the only time in Paisley's public life she'd seen him paralyzed for an instant.

She was an intelligent woman. The nature of their relationship, well, it was perfectly clear, perfectly. Yet she was sufficiently accustomed to being depressed to still get up in the morning even if she expected things to be basically as dismal when she went to bed that night.

Depressed? Who said that? She did not consider herself depressed.

That's how depressed she was.

No, it was all right, the days flapping with *Fortnights*, evenings with a fistful of toast as she stared out the window at the branches webbing over the panes like the veins in her eyes. She merely needed a polestar. Like the reference draftsmen use to give a landscape proper perspective, she needed a disappearing point. Farrell O'Phelan was a dot off her page.

Once more he had not asked her out exactly, but they were beyond that. Even Oscar's didn't bother with reservations anymore but routinely saved their table. And after a fourteen-hour workday she would let him pick up the tab tonight. With half an hour before his return, Constance luxuriated around the suite, a paler but softer place without him, still steeped in his presence but spared its pricklier forms. She loitered into his office and eyed the correspondence. Constance could be trusted implicitly around open bottles of expensive liquor, cold cash, but curvaceous addresses on envelopes flushed her with wild kleptomania. The artless girls in the Tissot prints arched their eyebrows, goody-goody.

She disciplined herself from the post, on a whim creaking instead into the closet to finger Farrell's bomb disposal suit. A reek wafted from the hanger as if she were releasing something that wasn't supposed to get out. The suit made her feel nostalgic; a little hurt; delivered. Constance had secured it for Farrell's Christmas present that last year. It had taken plenty of finagling to pinch the suit from the British Army, the kind of project Constance could sink her teeth into. Though used, it was in good condition. Farrell had never worn it. Och, he had his reasons. It was heavy, sixty pounds or so, and limited mobility. Furthermore, it smelled ghastly, permeated not only with the acrid, almond tinge of explosives but permanently imbued with nervous sweat. *Like breathing pure terror*, he says. And sure he was a fastidious man, a fresh shirt every day, starched. As a child, grotty hands made him cry. As an adult, nothing had upset him more than the Dirty Protest; why, he was positively relieved when prisoners moved on to hunger strikes. Maggots in spoiled food, shite spread on the walls because it dried faster that way, less noxious than in a pile . . . Even reading about it now, he would agitate around the office and go back to biting his hands.

But the stench of the suit had been an excuse. He preferred pinstripe. And if a bomb had ever blown he'd wanted to go with it.

Farrell was himself thinking of Constance as he whistled up the walkway. He was sometimes concerned on her account, and wondered at how often this compassion expressed itself as rebuke. The problem was, he liked her too much. She was good-humored and bright, earthy but not crude, and, for all her community adventuring, essentially shy. As his hours in her company racked up, they only improved. However, if they had too good a time, the next day he'd be brisk and find something wrong with her work and disappear.

When he found her in his office—where she had no business—Constance was perched on his desk tugging at her stockings. As she whisked the skirt back down, Farrell couldn't help but think, *What heavy thighs*. She seemed to see this in his face, and instead of boistering the incident away, she timmered to the other side of the room.

They didn't talk. Farrell dialed. Constance scuffled by the closet. Sometimes he could not bear that she knew him so well. He might have preserved more of a private life, but he ended up telling Constance most of it just so she would tend to its aggravating logistics. So the rare times he was up to something that left her out, the air knotted like the roots of trees.

Farrell turned his back. He lowered his voice into the *Little White Girl*. He rested the receiver and waited a punitive beat.

"I do not like to be listened to while I am making a personal call."

Constance realized with confusion she'd been eavesdropping. There should be no such thing in this office. *She knew everything.* "You might've said."

"I shouldn't have to."

Constance felt suddenly estranged. She didn't know quite who she was or where. Rather than the disorientation seem odd, she was astonished she didn't slip out of kilter more often. She was impressed with having negotiated so many ordinary moments of her life with such social grace in the past. She felt someone should commend her. "Sorry."

"Likewise. This evening I am engaged."

Constance remained still, as if for a long exposure. The shutter clicked; she had misunderstood *engaged*. Her very heart had stopped for the picture, and while the word returned to its routine usage, her pulse was sickening.

Farrell was surprised, expecting a scene. Her face was impassive. She looked nonplused. "Tomorrow," he offered as reward. He tucked his red handkerchief into his pocket and poofed it out again, smoothed on gloves of tight cream suede. He pecked her cheek on his way out with an exaggerated *Mwah!* that was insulting.

He forgot she was still in the room and turned out the light. The smell of the bomb disposal suit lingered behind him. Standing in the dark, Constance felt as she had at three years old when she was first aware of her arms when walking and was mystified by how to hold her hands.

"I'm aware that Americans compulsively ask what you *do*. I've restrained myself, but I can't stand it any longer—what *are* you?"

They were back at 44, only the second time, but this established that to whatever degree there would be an always, they would always eat at this place.

"This is Ireland. We should begin with what I was."

"Sixty-nine?"

"A drunk."

"Seventy?"

"Keep going."

"Drink is all you did?"

"It's a full-time job!"

"Until?"

"Well into my twenties. I lived at home. My father lambasted me, my mother sighed and left St. Patrick's medals dangling inside my overcoat. It was quite satisfying. Might have continued indefinitely but for the Troubles. I lived in Glengormley, a mixed neighborhood that has yet, even now, to see many tiffs. Horrifically, people get along. Watching news reports, you Americans must have assumed the whole Province was smoking. But swaths grazed on placid as sheep. We watched that footage just as you did. *And the peace pockets were the hellholes*. Och, sure I ended up in the odd fracas on the Falls, a good place to find drink after hours. But I didn't spend every Friday out rioting with the rest. I wasn't invited. I began to feel left out."

"You're included now?"

"Of course not. Exclusion is an emotion; you don't live it down. I was a sickly child. I couldn't play football. Later, when the boys around me were nipping off to smoke on Sundays, I was still an altar boy, fasting, writing religious sonnets, forswearing sugar in my tea."

"And you promised yourself every night you wouldn't wank under the covers. It didn't work."

Farrell's fork paused halfway to his mouth. "Please."

"You have a prim side."

"I prefer the word *discreet*."

She trailed a nail down the heartline of his palm and kissed the pulp of his fingertip, like sucking the oyster from a quail. "I don't often meet men I can embarrass."

"You can be one smutty item, I must say."

"See? When was the last time I heard *smutty*? Ireland. The last bastion of real sex. Real sex is disgusting. Real sex is repressed. Mash down on anything that hard and it just spurts out higher somewhere else. Because every night you plonked away despite yourself, right? And it was great. It's never been that great since. I'm telling you, all that Catholicism did you a world of good."

"I thought at one time of becoming a priest."

"Naturally! Walking around with a hard-on sixteen hours a day, what else was there to do but become a priest?"

Farrell wiped his chin, following Estrin's hands as she ran them over her arms and bare shoulders. He liked watching a woman touch her own body. "We're still on the starter," he pointed out. "I can't imagine how we'll make it to coffee without getting arrested."

"Still, you're no priest, with that American Express card."

He shrugged. "Whitewells."

"The hotel?"

"*My* hotel."

Estrin sat back. "How did you come into that?"

"I saved its life so many times, it thinks I'm its mother."

"Say what?"

"The man who owned Whitewells, Eachann Massey, was a Catholic. But even Republican sympathies and a son in the Officials couldn't protect the hotel. Once the Provos and Stickies started feuding, the son was a fair liability. Whitewells has always housed plenty of journalists and foreign politicos, and makes an attractively high-profile target."

"Oh," Estrin sighed, "I would hate to see that place blown up." Locals felt the same way, for Belfast's notoriety was often priced with simple disappointment: just, *Och, no. My parents honeymooned in that hotel; they still tell stories about the fruit. We couldn't afford to stay there ourselves, but some days it's worth a few extra p to take the weight off in those enormous chairs downstairs and have coffee with whipped cream and scones with wee jars of black currant conserve—* And then someday you're shopping downtown and the pressure changes in your ears; all the windows in Anderson McAuley rattle. You feel nervous, excited, and stretch with everyone else who knows nothing as the peelers cordon off Royal Avenue with white tape. But the excitement dies down and the klaxons leave off until it's next Saturday and there's nowhere for coffee but the top floor of C & A or dingy old Kelly's, where it's weak as water, and freaking hell, you'd just as well go home."

"I'd hate that, too," said Farrell. "Why I've taken measures downstairs."

"The security is new?"

"The place was wide open in the seventies. Threats, car bombs out front every month. But Eachann's IRA connections and Republican politics made it awkward to call the army. So he called me, several times—'81, his sons picked off, one by the Provos, one by the UFF, wife long gone, middle of the hunger strikes Eachann dies, of all things, from natural causes. He left the hotel to me. Claimed if it hadn't been for O'Phelan there'd be nothing but a carpark to leave."

"Why had he called you in for bomb scares?"

Farrell looked pained, for he liked to tell his stories systematically. Conversations with Estrin didn't work that way. "For five years I was an independent bomb disposal man."

"Independent? Why didn't you just work for the army?"

"If you're going to pretend to know me so instinctively, my dear, you're going to have to ask better questions."

"No, I can see you in the military. An officer. Shaving in the desert with two tablespoons of water, and no one understands where you keep finding a clean shirt. Brilliant but unorthodox campaign, blind dedication of the men . . ."

"T. E. Lawrence. They don't make them like that anymore."

"I guess I was observing: they do."

He smiled. "All the same, you're hardly describing any of those poor grubby bastards stationed in these hinterlands. And I'm Catholic; as an Ammunitions Technical Officer I'd likely be shot by my 'own people.' Mark the inverted commas, please."

"Who are your people?"

"I am affiliated with no one. Which has driven the entire Province to distraction."

"And more than a few women," Estrin hazarded.

"You have a terrible time staying on politics for more than fifteen seconds."

"Not really." She would not be ruffled. "I just don't see politics as separate. More *stuff*."

"How adroitly put," he said sourly. "At any rate, it took effort to keep the business from growing. Countless eejits wanted to join. I said no. I worked alone. I refused to become one more woolly do-gooder coalition. Mother of God, look at the Peace People: in no time, a snarl of hostile camps scuffling over their constitution, while every streetcorner busybody sniffed about Betty's mink coat. Envious, divided, a model of the conflict more than a solution to it. I aimed to avoid that.

"At first, I'd do anything to save a life, a knee, or property I happened to like—Whitewells. Anything to take the mickey out of a load of rubbish. I've snipped up Gerry Adams's sound system. I've bribed an army helicopter pilot to hover over an Ian Paisley rally close enough that no one could make out a word and women lost their hats. I ran my own dirty-tricks squad. It was all supremely down-to-earth, if sometimes adolescent."

"Why are you still alive?"

"Good question. You're getting the knack of this place."

"Yes," she said dryly. "So I don't need to be congratulated every time I seem to realize the IRA is not an Individual Retirement Account."

"Sorry?"

"You were saying: why you're not dead."

"I took care to be a thorn of equal length in everyone's side. If I dismantled a Provo gelly bomb in a hijacked oil tanker, I'd be sure to loose an angry ram on a Save Ulster from Sodomy rally on the weekend. A balancing act of impartial disruption. I convinced each faction that I was a sufficient liability to its adversaries to keep about."

"Were you ever interned?"

"Oh, aye. In the first instance, I was pleased. There was a time in West Belfast no one would trust you if you hadn't been in the Kesh at least seven days. The second and third instances I could have skipped. Face-offs in a white room and a single mattress chained to the floor. A chair if you were lucky. Sleep if you were lucky. Water if you were lucky. I wasn't lucky."

"Do you still get harassed?"

"A certain Lieutenant Pim from Thiepval arrived on the scene of a rather wicked job I had already finished; he was charmed. That poor pillock actually did try to get me to join the army. He wanted to work with me. He liked me. He wanted to be my friend."

"So?"

"I didn't oblige, but Pim did. He fixed my computer file. Whenever I'm stopped at checkpoints now, they go back to their Land Rover. They come back smiling, and nervous. They shake my hand. They tell me, Safe home. They hope the delay hasn't caused me any inconvenience."

"What does it say?"

"Haven't a baldy."

Estrin eyed him critically. "I bet you loved being interned."

"Answering the same question fifty times? Spread-eagled against a wall for six hours?" He considered. "Oh, aye. Those were some of the great moments of my life."

"As opposed to now?"

His face shadowed, its parallels listed. "I came to realize I was entirely motivated by self-glorification."

"You're not anymore?"

"I have made repeated efforts at becoming a butterfly. Sure I'm as much of a worm as ever."

"Does anyone do anything for anyone else ever?"

"I've seen it," he admitted. "Singed passersby combing into McGrady's for more survivors as the bar burned after the blast. But most heroism can be explained away as extended self-interest. To make allegiances is to preserve the race, the Catholics, your own family; however your lines are drawn. In which case I am biologically flawed. I do not ally. And I not only refuse to defend my people, but I'm out to destroy myself. I'm a failed mutation, a danger to the species which fortunately has not reproduced. I am a rocky, hostile island. Don't wreck your ship on my shore."

But the warning turned on itself. *I am so wonderful that I know what's wrong with me.* Estrin was reminded of medieval monks who would whip themselves, feel righteous for whipping themselves, whip themselves for feeling righteous, only to feel righteous all the more and whip themselves again—an endless spiral of shame lapped by self-congratulation. In Ireland to run yourself down was to prove what a fine fellow you really were. "Self-criticism," she observed, "is a form of preening."

"You then, my swallow? Are you the world's helpmate?"

"It's all I can manage to avoid being a flat-out shithead. And people bungle so much doing 'good,' I figure it's safest to do zip. I don't hit children; I don't litter; I also don't work for the Peace Corps in Zaire. I try to have no effect on my environment whatsoever."

"But doing nothing often has a great deal of effect. And I get restless. I have to do something even if at any distance I find myself comical."

"So what do you do now?"

"I'm not nearly so colorful a character, I'm afraid. I've gone from prankster to community handyman. At the moment I'm negotiating for the release of two boys held at Secretary of State's Pleasure. Rather than finagling whirlybirds to descend, I'm trying to get them up again; a woman in Armagh with a house near the heliport is losing her nerves. I've helped the area around my office organize against the rebuilding of an RUC station there, since the last thing that keeps you safe in this town is the proximity of the police. And we got blown up last time; it's someone else's turn.

"As for the disposal business, I have moved from defusing bombs to politicians. I set the North before myself like a chess problem: As long as the Brits are kicking doors in up the Falls at 6 a.m., firing after eleven-year-old joyriders, and tossing the odd innocent in the Crum without charge, the IRA will flourish; as long as the IRA flourishes, so will the UVF, UFF, and everything else beginning with U. As long as paramilitaries thrive, the troops stay; as long as the troops stay, paramilitaries thrive: a perpetual-motion machine that slows only from the physics of exhaustion."

"I have never been anywhere with such a plethora of neat formulations about itself."

"How to get the troops out without leaving behind a month of Bloody Sundays? Next to the North, chess is Snakes and Ladders."

"So this is the game you play now with Angus MacBride."

She thought he'd be pleased she'd recognized his friend at the distillery, for they'd not been introduced. Instead, he snapped, "In reference to my current work, you are not to mention anyone's name in public under any circumstances. Understood?"

Estrin rolled her eyes. "Melodrama."

"Drama," he corrected. "You Americans have the hardest time getting it through your heads this is not a TV show."

"Spare my countrymen for an evening and just insult me."

"I expect you to keep your mouth shut. Straight enough?"

"Quite. I'm suddenly remembering an appointment later tonight."

"If you can't take a little flak across a table, you should keep the date."

"Ah—Farrell," she sighed. Sometimes the best way to win is to quit; one hand clutched her napkin, a white flag. "Listen, this isn't my country and I do put my foot in it. I actually asked a Catholic at the entrance to Sandy Row whether he sympathized with the Provos. The walk was crowded and he looked at me sidelong and said, Some other time. I felt like a twit. I don't know the rules yet, and on a second dinner certainly don't know yours. I'm sorry I used anyone's name and I won't again, but please don't rub my nose in it or I really will go home. Because I try, but I slip and some days forget if Molyneaux is UUP or OUP, or especially why that matters. Some days I wake up, I can name the number of my house but not what continent it's on, the day of the week but not the year. I have too much to remember and more to forget—I need a little leeway."

"Tenderness," Farrell corrected, taking one hand from her forehead, the napkin from the left.

"How," she faltered, for Estrin routinely steadied herself by being inquisitive. "How did you learn to do it? Dismantle bombs?"

"By one of the oldest traditions in the world," said Farrell. "I apprenticed myself."

When Farrell paid his membership to Linen Hall, he hardly expected to check out *The Beginner's Guide to Bomb Disposal*, but he had to start somewhere and had always taken refuge in libraries. Surprisingly, he did dig up *The Anarchist's Cookbook*, full of detailed diagrams on how to construct a book trap, loose-floorboard trap, ballpoint-pen trap—mere doddles. Sure, for a price he could have scored an Explosive Ordnance Disposal manual from the Brits, but this was before Lieutenant Pim, and Farrell's army connections were understandably slim; before Whitewells, and his pocketbook was slimmer. So his discovery of *Device* proved a promising, if aggravating, find. Its author, Corporal Porter Edwards Bream, was a veteran of the North Africa campaign from the Second World War, where he'd defused land mines for the Allies. Brutish things, they didn't apply. But his last term of service was in Northern Ireland. Funny, though nearly brand new, in a few months the book had already achieved that paperweight quality most published works are destined for—the kind of volume used to prop up film projectors or balance the legs of tables. Farrell took it home, and in all the years since the library had never requested its return.

Porter Edwards Bream was of Anglo-Irish stock, one of those sonorous codgers, you could tell by the flyleaf, who never went by less than all three names. *Device* was an essay. Farrell bristled at Bream's pretensions to philosophy, but had to admit that for a vanity press the writing was sharp. "A device is a device," Porter Edwards began. "Remember: big presents come in small packages." It was an odd ragbag of tidbits, stories, practical advice about the importance of paper clips. "Always be on the lookout for surprise," he suggested, "but do not flatter yourself you will see it in time. If you did, it wouldn't be a surprise, now would it?" Porter Edwards saw bomb disposal as metaphor. In the end, he said, the trick was all internal. What would destroy you, as in any Greek tragedy, would be your own character. With booby-trapped bombs in the North, you would be hung by your own predictability—like the boys who were blown away by a pressure switch triggered by the ripping down of slanderous, anti-British posters on a gable wall. You had to overcome yourself, become larger, so you would cease to be manipulated by what you were like. And devices taught *humility* and *respect*. Farrell gagged. Whole chapters read like reruns of *Kung Fu*. "On Immortality and Arrogance" particularly got up his nose: "If you believe you're immortal you probably think you're special. You're not," Bream wrote flat. "You're a dummy. Everyone thinks that. It's only the rare fellows who grasp they can die who have a clue."

Though by all indications Porter Edwards Bream was a whopping pain in the arse, Farrell needed tutelage, and traced Corporal Bream to the small Yorkshire town of Beverly. At the first pub he hit, Porter's name worked a treat. "Watch yourself, now," Farrell was forewarned. "Bream's a touch of the second sight. Funny—creepy-funny. Might not like what he sees."

"Bollocks," said Farrell.

It took an hour to escape all the embellishments and cautions. Christ, the last thing anyone from Ulster hunted was another myth. And Farrell knew how to decode these fables by now: Porter Edwards Bream was an opinionated, abusive drunk. Locals indulged him from their own need, their pitiable internal poverty. Their awe was detestable. Their patience was detestable. They tolerated the corporal's endless boozy blithering just to have someone to talk about.

He found Bream in a palatial house tended by two doting women whose relation to the man was obscure. An enormous, cigar-fogged old gout, he was not surprised by Farrell's visit, or particularly curious. For a spindly Catholic to have sought him out all the way from Belfast seemed perfectly reasonable. He was dead senile, and through the afternoon kept falling asleep.

They despised each other straight off. "If there's anything I can't bear," Porter announced not two minutes into their acquaintance, "it's one more sod's decided he's self-destructive. Your sort's problem: you're not self-destructive enough! Little better at it and we'd be rid of you! Blast it, know how easy it is to die? If you can't manage to stick your head in an oven, what kind of nincompoop are you?" Porter slammed down a full liter gauntlet of single malt, and the duel began.

"If we're talking sorts," Farrell started in, "why don't we move on to yours: the fat, spoiled fraud. You fill out a bar. You rant through lulls in conversation, so the lot can lap their beer. Sure at the Rose and Crown didn't they wax eloquent on Porter Edwards Bream. Naturally that delights you. But without you they'd find some other puppet. They use you—you're to be wise, to be anecdotal, to be merciless. They make you wise, they feed you lines, they allow you to be merciless. Your audience demands it, all your orneriness and declarations and drink. A retired army corporal with *stories*. It's trite. You'll cough the same tales till you die, like phlegm. In the end, you're their creature. And you think differently. That's what's so paltry and sad."

"I don't think in those terms at all, who is whose creature. You're sick, man. You'll do a lot of damage thrashing about if you don't get hold of yourself. It's always the, quote, *self-destructive*, do they ever so much as bump their own elbows? Anything but! Oh, the *self-destructive*, they go for the rest of the world at the throat. Look at you! Trying so hard to hurt my feelings there's sweat in your hair."

If so, Farrell hadn't succeeded. Throwing insults at Porter Edwards Bream was like flinging Harp tins at a Saracen. Farrell could almost hear the clink, the harmless rattle down the street. He felt childish.

"I didn't come here for sophistry," Farrell dignified. "I suffered my share in your pretentious little volume, *Kahlil Gibran Joins the Army*. I need information, and about bombs, not about my soul."

Porter's smile spread like something spilled. "Liar. Besides, shaking out your grubby bathmat of a shadow is about all I can offer. The only thing an intelligent man wants to know about bombs is where they are, so he can arrange to be somewhere else. And the Confidential Telephone no longer rings on my desk, boyo."

The bottle trickled down steadily as an hourglass. Farrell could not remember a more exhausting session before or since. "If you're supposed to know so bloody much," Farrell slurred, "see so bloody much, what can you see in me, fella? Mystic guru bomb man? Oh, X-ray vision ATO?"

"I have seen through pressboard." Porter nodded; his eyes, for the all-seeing, had grown remarkably tiny. "I know what's inside a bomb by looking at it, though that took years. How they tick, people are easier. Come with instructions printed on the box."

"And what have you told me, huh, fella? Codswallop."

"Jesus God, you are desperate," Porter whispered.

"Holding out? Don't want to give away the big secret about O'Phelan? Know how many theories I inspire in Belfast? Think you're the first shaman to come along? Dozens. Women. Dozens. They're writing novels, some of them. Wanna write a book? About me? Better'n *Device*. Wick title. Wick book . . ."

"Go ahead, kick at me all you like. That's safe. I should keep you here, harmless. Neutralized."

"With all this revelation about my deep inner self, how could I ever leave?"

"All right . . ." Porter grumbled. "You want something? A

tidbit, a morsel, proof? Why so anxious for what you already know? That you are a bully. That you're bigger and stronger than you pretend. Asthmatic? Poser! And part of your power is getting people to feel sorry for you."

Abruptly, Farrell cried. The charges slipped into a tiny hole in his side. "It's not fair, is it?" he blubbered. "They do, they all feel sorry for me. Bugger, and every one of them's worse off by far—debt, dead fathers, husbands in gaol . . . They think that's all perfectly normal! Me, I've always had enough to eat. My mother probably bleeding loves me, even if I can't admit it. And, Port old boy, I can't explain it, but lately women fawn all over me. One more potted egocentric. You and I, we're the same, and you revolt me."

Farrell sniffled; Bream fell asleep.

It may have been an hour later that Porter roused himself from a snore. "My poor fanatic!" he sighed, air puttering from his fat lips. "Seared by the agony of the world."

Farrell looked hard. Was he joking? But Porter went back to sleep with a little smile. This was the joke: that even myths need myths, or especially, and after years of soldiering on as one himself, Porter had knighted a Greatheart in his own study, a hero for heroes—now, Farrell lad, where would you get yours? It was a way of no longer taking Farrell seriously, for in an instant he transformed Farrell to a like-minded larger-than-life to adore or deplore, rather than one tall stranger on his doorstep with whom he might permit a smaller, more complex relationship that in the end is so much more flattering. Farrell was surprised to find his new title a demotion. He had been cursed: a Character.

So that last bit, it was nothing but meanness. But as for being a bully, Farrell subscribed. He didn't change, mind you, but attended, how he enticed women with his own Troubles—now there was a capital *T*. The conceit was they wanted to cure him, but he discovered their sympathy was sicker than that: they thought his unhappiness was better than theirs. Incredibly, it was envy. The women saw themselves as merely neurotic, while Farrell O'Phelan was afflicted with the *agony of the world*—they could buy that? True, Farrell's desolation was his pride and joy; all polished up, Estrin, it is my *accomplishment*. But the value of the dolor relied on mirrors; it was a magic show. Alone in a room, he knew it for a shabby thing: a worn top hat, a few cards, a rabbit. Farrell's Troubles were just like theirs: his only access to the agony of the world was his own, one more private purgatory of billions, and this was the secret Porter wouldn't tell and Farrell intended to keep.

Like Estrin's monks, it was a circle: outsiders assumed Farrell was a saint; Farrell knew he was a shite; but, "The final irony," Bream noted casually a few weeks later as they dissected the mercury tilt switch, "is you're actually much nicer than you know."

"You never explained," Estrin pursued, "what got you into bombs in the first place."

"You like stories out of order. Why don't we begin with why I quit." He motioned for the check. "But first we will prop you on three fat pillows with a mug of hot chocolate. That is what you need, my swallow. For just taking your head off to the contrary, I learned from my work that I can be quite compassionate." He sounded perplexed.

8

Big Presents Come in Small Packages

Even before it fell to him altogether, Farrell had unofficially headquartered in Whitewells, coopting upper rooms for the private hair-tearing of women sure they'd been followed from Turf Lodge. From early on, he and the hotel were fated for each other. Amid so many alienated factions, Farrell and this institution were alienated from every faction. Where the one solace of having enemies is having allies, where the one comfort of having parts of town you cannot go to is parts you can, Farrell operated alone, equally unwelcome everywhere, only in this lobby at home. They were exiled lovers, on an island made of islands a flagless galleon, precariously afloat; in their grandiosity and hauteur, both anachronistic and often disliked, for they would not apologize for having a little class in a city that exalted tatty wool caps and outdoor toilets as badges of socialist nobility.

Technically Catholic, but declared by all sides open season, together they shipped an indiscriminate aversion in a place that recognized as valid any position but none.

For it was inexplicable how either Whitewells or O'Phelan had persisted. When the first rumors circulated of Farrell's one-man bomb disposal and dirty-tricks squad, locals laughed and acted surprised when they met him alive at the end of the week. Likewise, Whitewells, festooned up there on Royal Avenue, about the only truly splendid architectural enormity left in all of Belfast besides City Hall itself, had about as good a chance of surviving twenty years of bombings as a Methodist all kitted out in his orange sash pounding a Lambeg drum down the back streets of Ardoyne. With the Provos, the Stickies, the Irps, and a whole smattering of Loyalist paramilitaries from the UFF to the Shankill Butchers on the one side, and Farrell, six four maybe, but a Bergen-Belsen 155, and a ten-floor Baroque bull's-eye on the other, any shrewd bookie would give O'Phelan and his ridiculous hotel fifty to one. Yet despite the odds, Whitewells had still not been intimidated into the loose chippings and landfill of more acquiescent buildings; and Farrell continued to gangle into her lobby without a gun. Farrell and Whitewells recognized each other as being equally implausible.

Besides, the bar served Farrell after hours and didn't turf him out when he became—ah—expansive. Brandy and port came in snifters large enough for Farrell's attenuated fingers, where down the road they'd pour VSOP in a water glass, and when a drink looks like swill it could as well be. As for wine, they didn't stock the whites you could pour over ice cream. But it was whiskey Whitewells understood best, not just Black Bush but Crested Ten and Jameson's 1780; Islay malts, Bowmore, The Macallan, Laphroaig. When they made it hot, they warmed the glass and dissolved not too much sugar, pressed cloves neatly into the zest, and squeezed the lemon, and as for proportions, they seemed to understand that the charm of the drink did not rest in its hot water.

Then, the generous character of Whitewells was a credit to

Eachann Massey, a man whose problems were matched only by his patience in their wake, one of those exemplars who serve as veritable advertisements for suffering: surely if pain produced such grace it was underrated. His wife had walked into the wrong grocery back in '71 and inadvertently become one of the vegetables—no, you see, this is just the kind of joke Eachann had been easy with himself. Eachann's life might have been better off with a few more pounds of explosive under that counter, for she lived three more years propped in the kitchen by the radio, spud eyes, her hands moist and flaccid like overdone cabbage. Berghetta had been a lively, sarky woman, with a bit of a sally to her, a wide turn-of-the-century sway to her hips; it had been a fine marriage, and her death dragged out for months in anguish. Yet though the bomb was Provo, it made no impression on Eachann's politics. He'd told her not to shop the Shankill anymore, but the stores were cheaper and close by and no one told Berghetta where to go. Besides, she'd not liked what was happening, and Berghetta was one of those people convinced enough of her own world that she was sure if she proceeded as if things were as she wished the universe would conform. If she shopped the Shankill as if it were safe, it would be safe. In a way she was right—if the whole Province refused to acknowledge the lines of battle, they would not exist.

However, they did exist for Eachann, who chose a position before or beyond disgust; Farrell respected such people, admired their ability to take a stand, however flawed, take responsibility for the consequences of that position, even as he loathed the rhetoric and closed-mindedness certainty implied. The shrapnel in his wife's head had not fractured Eachann's politics, because they were not reactive. He'd maintained an opposition to the British Empire that was thoughtful and impervious, and he never feared anything would happen to challenge his perspective. As a result, he'd been relaxed and relaxing, for he did not have to constantly flog his ideas to other people in order to sell them to himself.

For what the copious flow of foreign Experts so regularly

failed to grasp here was the essential integrity of nearly every point of view. Each party had assembled a puzzle that fit together. The North as object was an ingenious curio which from one side appeared an ostrich; another, a postman; another, a washing machine. That's why arguments never went anywhere: each picture was true. (In fact, the terror of completely looking at anything from another person's perspective is that he is always right.) However, in the logical reasoning out of these positions, little girls' scalps plastered to the sides of houses, kneecaps shattered into their cartilage, a great Victorian market mangled and gave way to slapped-up, slick-bricked shops with no memory of high hats and fine, tiny-handled tea sets but only of polyester knits and Tupperware and destruction. From these reasonable positions sprang unreasonable children, who threw petrol bombs not because they were Republican but because they were bored. Though Farrell may have relinquished the satisfactions of surety, he did cling to one vision: that here the cost of conviction had risen too high, and he refused to have its price exacted from his island.

Hence the saving of the hotel over and over, for Farrell would not have Whitewells taken from his world. He imagined that the bomb that got away would crumble him worst if he remained behind. In his nightmares he never dissolved in a flash of white heat, but was left kicking through another rubble in the city center, as he'd once scuffed through Smithfield Market, finding caps of Crested Ten, shards of snifters, spoons, melted picture frames, smoking tufts of brocade, breathing the stink of materials you'd never think would burn. Maybe it was warped to feel so deeply for a building, but Farrell did understand the affection designed into the neutron bomb. Still, it would take him several of these rescues and a last night to feel the same protective passion for his own life.

Bream taught Farrell all he knew, which is not to say they grew fond of one another. Farrell battled for hardcore information about how to neutralize a trembling fuse through a barrage of philosophy. Though the hemorrhaged corporal made an unlikely mystic, every switch had its tract, like the Salvation Army, where you had to sit through "Rock of Ages" to earn your soup. Even the way Bream referred to bombs suggested religious awe, rarely pronouncing B-O-M-B, but euphemizing, *the thing, the device, what you're dealing with*, as the Orthodox avoid the real word for Jehovah. "Remember, no matter how many times you've seen the same box, the same size, the same switch, treat every device as a stranger."

"I treat my own mother as a stranger," Farrell quipped. "It shouldn't be so hard with a crate."

"On the contrary," said Bream. "It's bastards like you can get quite matey with crates."

They worked late, and Farrell was not allowed any whiskey until eight—when Porter would intone, *Ye-et I wi-ill be me-e-e-e-erry!* like the end of Ramadan. Porter himself wouldn't touch the stuff before the dot of noon.

"Who's to say," Farrell commented two weeks in, "I'm not in the IRA? In which case you're a right eejit."

"But you're not."

"No—"

"So I'm not."

End of story.

"Besides," Bream added the next week, picking up the way they did now, all conversations going on at once. "If you were a Provo, you might have had the courtesy to offer me a few quid."

Farrell shrugged. "You didn't ask."

"You're a taker."

This was true. He sozzled Bream's whiskey every night and never once replenished the cabinet. He sat down to meals and didn't offer to wash up, didn't question that the two women prepared them, and didn't even learn their names. Odd, fresh from such a guilty childhood. But Farrell had indexed the population according to how comfortable they were taking, and how much. The more you took, the more you got. Farrell accepted what was given him not because he'd been a spoiled little boy but because he was clever.

Porter was a regular anthology of grim fairy tales, but Farrell didn't always find these instructive—like the time Porter leaned over a clock and found the long hand actually touching the contact. The corporal ran. Nothing happened. Later he found that a blob of luminescent paint on the hand had insulated the metal from completing the circuit.

"So?" asked Farrell, annoyed. "You were lucky. Save the pointless anecdotes for the Rose and Crown."

"There is a point. Never reduce yourself to luck. I shouldn't have been bending over any clock."

"Then get a desk job," Farrell muttered.

"You have GOT to concede to operate remote!"

"*I am tired of operating remote!*" and though this was one more running argument, the cry came from so deep inside the Catholic that Porter retreated.

When Farrell left Beverly, Bream handed him a package of army pigsticks, all tied up like a pencil box for Farrell's first day of school. There was no smooching, no promises that Farrell would be in touch. Farrell did hear, not much later, that Porter had snuffed it. His off-license, the Rose and Crown, even the taxi company that slopped the corporal into the back seat evenings—all sent flowers. Farrell didn't. He felt no more grief over the old man's death than he would have over his own.

Besides, in Belfast Farrell had his hands full, with a lot to learn. Bream was right, the technology was always evolving; you had to keep pace with the state of the art. "Irish, don't study history for once!" Bream opined, warning that most of what he'd taught Farrell was outdated. "And every device captured alive is an informant." For neutralized bombs weren't simply triumphs but tiny universities you could take back home.

Farrell spent the evenings he was not out on call reconstructing the latest ingenuity, so when the circuit connected a light bulb went on. Good practice, lousy symbolism: explosion as bright idea. His homework grew more demanding by the day.

The Provos were getting crafty at packaging, scrambling their tokens of affection with irrelevant wiring, so that radiograms looked like the scribbling of disturbed children. Some of these boxes, too, were so rife with anti-handling devices that getting inside was a Houdini demonstration in reverse, all locked with chains and ropes and handcuffs with a clock ticking.

Still, those were the days, when disposal had a little variety. Lately all you heard was Semtex, Semtex, Semtex—Coca-Cola to British Telecom, every product line suffered monopoly over time. In the latter seventies, you found Frangex, Gelamex, Quarrex, and piquant blends of HME, from the sharp diesel of ammonium nitrate and fuel oil to the fragrant marzipan of nitrobenzene. (ANNI made you dizzy, and Farrell knew British operators who could no longer eat certain Christmas cakes, since the smell of almonds made them sick. Farrell, on the other hand, would walk in bakeries just to breathe. The smell was nostalgic.) Back then commercial was scarce and the opposition was resourceful. "I can walk into any kitchen and make a hole in the room," Porter had declared. "Soap suds, flour, seltzer; throat lozenges, sugar, cream of tartar, even dried bananas: add ten minutes of education and stir." Dead on, for Farrell dismantled bombs made of anything from fermented garbage to Styrofoam coffee cups, in casings from a tampon incinerator to a stuffed toy bear.

As a result Farrell's relationship to ordinary objects electrified. Piles of shoe boxes, a pocketbook by an empty chair, sacks of rice delivered to Chinese restaurants all shivered with menace; mailings from the Ulster Museum threatened more than harassment for checks. Not to mention cars. Farrell couldn't walk down the street without noting whether the Cortina there was riding low, or pass pubs without knocking on arriving barrels of Tennants, confirming by the *cong* that they were only full of beer. They weren't always, either. Farrell's whole world anthropomorphized. Call it paranoia, insanity, but for Farrell, whose environment had more the ugly tendency to go numb, in whose former life people had become objects rather than the other way around, the animation was delightful, like living in a cartoon where clocks danced, refrigerators talked, the cow jumped over the moon. So did Farrell, if he wasn't careful.

Those days, too, the business was surprisingly personal, if sometimes infantile—like the wine case left in Whitewells Magic Markered in three-inch-high letters, IRA on one side, TE-HEE, HE-HEE, HO-HO, HA-HA! on the other. He grew to recognize the style of particular bombmakers, each with their explosives of choice, a distinctive twist to their connections, pet booby traps. He gave them names, too: Rat, Mole, Toad, and Mr. Badger. Farrell had favorites. Irrationally, he preferred the better-made bombs. He scorned sloppy wiring. Inaccurate switches made of clothespins and rubber bands filled him with the same disdain he felt toward incompetence anywhere. Elegant devices filled him with admiration. He had to remind himself they were intended to spread old ladies on Fountain Street like sour cream, because prizing open a carton all neatly layered with Semtex and fresh herring, Farrell wanted to shake somebody's hand.

Farrell had run his private bomb disposal service for five years. However inconceivably, he was still alive and that made him cocky. They had been far more active years than he'd ever have predicted, for potty as locals considered his project at first Farrell found he filled a need. In the mid-seventies, Provisional bombings of other Catholics were not so rare. Weary of the dole, the odd Taig would join the army or RUC, double targets for being Crown forces and turncoats. "Known" informers could consider themselves fertilizer. For a time, Catholic bakers, lorry drivers, even binmen who served the army would sometimes notice fishing line over the gates to their walkways. (The Provos had a faddish side—for a while there, fishing-line trip switches were all the rage, and Farrell would constantly reach into his suit pockets to find stray lengths of nylon tangled with his change.) Furthermore, in the absence of police protection for large parts of West Belfast, the Provos had assumed law enforcement; their courts were quick, their sentences simple, since—well, you could hardly blame them—they couldn't maintain a private Long Kesh of their own. Robbery on behalf of the IRA was respectable, but the organization looked askance at lads who asked chip shops for donations to more obscure causes. As a result, Farrell had rescued more than one lowlife hood the world was surely better without, but O'Phelan's service was ever distinguished by its indiscrimination.

For Farrell's clients were by no means all Catholic. While at first none too eager to call in a papish bomb man, plenty of Prods were even less anxious to call in the army to complain those Provy wankers had hit their brothel, their unlicensed bookie joint, their cache of Kalashnikovs. Uncooperative victims of Loyalist protection rackets had often preferred Farrell to the RUC likely to press for names, and it was healthier not to turn in these civil servants on either side of the divide. Protestant businessmen sometimes planted bombs on their own premises to collect government compensation; Farrell had twice been asked to disassemble devices by next-door shopkeepers unwilling to inform, but equally unenthusiastic about getting in on the scheme. Besides, as far as the Prods were concerned, why not a Catholic bomb man? The thing goes off, one less Taig.

Just practically, it was sometimes simpler to drag that lanky bastard in, with an unclaimed package on a shoemaker's bench that could as well be cakes as Togel. The army would ship the whole block up the road and divert traffic and string that bloody white plastic cordon everywhere, all very well if the whole panto was still interesting, which it wasn't the third time in a week. O'Phelan was sure enough a wog, some even claimed not the full shilling, but he worked well and fast and alone and didn't fuck about, just sent you down the way, and by the time you'd scoffed a pack of fags he was done, like. The army would tinker for hours with their wretched robot, which never seemed to work, and send it into the shoemaker's from half a mile away, all for three sticky buns. O'Phelan? He looked in the bag. Took a bite. You bought him a drink, and that was that.

While the Provos were none too delighted to have their gratuities waylaid, they could only applaud Farrell's undermining of Orange racketeering and compensation fraud, and they took particular pleasure, being themselves keen for panache, in some of O'Phelan's more outlandish pranks, particularly the ones involving cattle—Paisley's ram, or the bull he rented for the Apprentice Boys parade. More than one pint was raised up Andytown Road after the Great Bonfire Sabotage of '79. No one ever figured out what exactly got sprayed or sprinkled or nested into the piles of planks and tires and shipping flats compiled over the months to celebrate William of Orange's tired old triumph over James at the Battle of the Boyne, but once those monsters went up, this unbelievable reek rose over the whole of the Shankill, to drift in a noxious cloud all the way to City Hall, with a smell so censorious it amounted to political commentary.

Besides, the Provies themselves had found Farrell handy on occasion, while not about to give the Brits the satisfaction, still happy to let O'Phelan risk scrapping with Loyalist car bombs rather than endanger their own personnel. And while the Provisionals were a professional crew whom, on a technical level, Farrell respected, you got the odd gombeen who'd made a bollocks of the science-fair project in his own basement and turned up in Whitewells very pale. Often enough they didn't want their cell leader to discover the cock-up, and there was that Seamus character a few years back whose gelignite had gone volatile under the floorboards of his own mother's sitting room—not only the gelignite was weeping. In these cases, no Provo was about to call in to the police: "Gee, we were about to blow two hundred pounds in a hijacked post van outside your barracks on Malone Road, but damned if John didn't bump the dowel and set the timer ticking. So could you possibly disarm the thing and keep it from decimating an entire block of Beechmont, including my house, or could you take it back with you so the little bundle of joy can explode in the bosom of the RUC, where it belongs?"

For what made Farrell O'Phelan's service possible was he didn't tout. In a city where everyone needed protecting from everyone else, there was a place for neutral resort. Surely any number of Farrell's customers would have turned to the army rather than no one had he remained curled around a bottle of Talisker five more years. But given a choice, it was often a gentler business to dismantle than to betray. And there was no question that a critical contingent of Farrell's customers would never have informed on their husbands, brothers, lovers if that meant taking the bus the next fifteen years to the Kesh. Sure that poor Sandy Row frazzle terrified by a Smith & Wesson in the house would never have offered any soldier as she had Farrell a hundred quid to burgle the gun from her own linen closet.

Because so many of his tip-offs came from women. Women who were tired of propping for hours in the emergency waiting room of the Royal Victoria, the cushions liver red, as if not to show stains, maybe a son this time, maybe only a cousin, the nurses lovely as can be but strained, running out of compassion, of comprehension, finished even with rage and just onto their jobs because it was the fourth gunshot wound that night. It was with the women that the "party" Estrin observed wore off first; the Royal Victoria is one shithouse party. So once more the lads would be a-scurry all important like, looking for an alligator clip, angry their black turtleneck was in the wash, and it wasn't hard to get the scoop if you were determined (they weren't supposed to tell you, but of course you were *married*, he was your *brother*). Nor was it hard to imagine later that night, back in the Royal, running out of cigarettes, forced to worry back and forth between the boy and that rattletrap car; the nurses always warned you not to leave it overnight or the joyriders would plow it through checkpoints and you could pick it up in the morning smoking in front of Divis Flats. Well, that was when they crept out as if for milk or some air or a jar and nipped to a phone box or down to Whitewells, to return utterly terrified, and later to suffer the consternation of their men cursing that fuckwit O'Phelan up one side and down the other, come three in the morning to sleep, maybe not well exactly but at least at all.

* * *

It was early 1982 and the hunger strikes were over. As in most pauses here, the Province was both relieved and deflated. While Protestants had pretty much ignored the strikes and were now glad to get back to Princess Di, with big color photos of horses and swish outfits on the front page of the *Telegraph*, Catholics were demoralized. Once more the mood of this city had seemed apocalyptic, promising to climax in—they didn't even know what; and once more the place had subsided. The Provisionals had won a whole new flush of converts, thanks to the careful, perfectly alienating maneuverings of the British government; Farrell suggested that Britain's every move in the strikes had been so brilliantly calculated to recruit for the IRA that you had to suspect Margaret Thatcher of being an undercover Irish terrorist herself, and when she died they were sure to plant her in Milltown Cemetery right next to Bobby Sands. However, the new ranks were at a loss—the final hunger strikers had been taken off and were back to potato bread and rashers; all the energy focused at ten funerals began to disperse.

Perhaps it was fear of an era having peaked that had made Farrell such a soft touch for one more job. The strikes had provided the freelancer with busy months, his favorite kind, grabbing taxis and snatching two hours' sleep at a time; having come into Whitewells the year before, he was more mobile than ever, jubilantly irresponsible with cash. However, even in this frenzy he had begun to feel insidiously irrelevant. Dismantling devices never changed why they were there and why another would spring up tomorrow live as ever down the road. Many of those days were so thick he didn't even have time for whiskey, and with a clearer head he had eyed the H-blocks, priests and Red Cross whisking in and out as Farrell raveled on the fringe.

For Farrell's disposal service uncomfortably recalled Uncle Malachi's vigorous attack on jellyfish in Donegal. At the time Farrell had admired his uncle's netting in the shallows as a tide of men-of-war forced vacationers from the shore. Uncle Malachi was the first independent disposal man in Farrell's memory, burying the stinging creatures by the dozen in gelatinous pits.

Farrell had shouldered in to dig and fill the six-foot graves of
sand. However, the holocaust was ineffectual: amid thousands
of men-of-war his uncle barely dented the population. At the
end of the week, even at the age of seven, Farrell had to admit
his uncle's self-important trooping of the beach with his net
dripping glutinous red strings was silly. The tide brought the
creatures in; only the tide could take them away.

So Farrell envied the more celestial bodies, princes of tides;
his peripheral mischief seemed childish, failing to satisfy his
growing appetite for the center. Farrell may have made a career
out of isolation, but less by choice than because he'd been an
asthmatic little boy, bound in coverlets while the neighbors
played rugby.

The boy who showed up at Whitewells that night, tousled
brown hair and sporty red cheeks, must have reminded Farrell
of the footballers outside his bedroom window as a child, and
of the others later, with anoraks and cigarettes and girls. He
couldn't have an anorak, it wasn't warm enough, so his mother
bundled him even at sixteen in an enormous wool coat that
reached below his knees—not unlike the coat he wore now, come
to think of it, though so much of what Farrell was at forty-three
he'd taken years to grow into. As for cigarettes, he tried one
once and it sent him shamefully to his inhaler. And girls? He'd
skipped straight to women.

The kid had scuttered across the lobby and clutched Farrell's
sleeve. "Farrell—I mean, Mr. O'Phelan," he stumbled, breathing fast. "Just the man I need, so you are. For fuck's sake, clear
the bloody hotel. There's a bomb—"

"Where?" Farrell steadied the boy's shoulders with both
hands. The jacket, he remembered, was oily.

"They put a bleeding gun to my head, mate! Nipped me
into a black taxi and some big tube skelps me with a gun, like."
The boy displayed a rather unremarkable wound on his temple.
"On Castle Street they stick me with a shopping bag—"

"Skip the yarn, boyo. Where's the bag now?"

But the kid stubbornly told the story. "Don't take it wrong,

107

sir, but when they cart me to Whitewells I'm relieved like. This is Mr. O'Phelan's hotel, I think. I'm to take the bag in and not come out with it, and Lord, Farrell, I'm shaking and I carried it to the roof, I hope that's all right. I figure it's safest like? Where you can take it on? 'Cause haven't I seen you slick as you please snip up a car bomb outside me brother's in Bally-murphy. I wouldn't call the frigging Brits if it were a live Pershing missile in this hotel. O'Phelan, that's what I say to anyone cares to know: you got something that ticks, you call Farrell O'Phe-lan—"

Right: over the top. How often had Farrell rehearsed the picture since, the shine in those eyes not fear but excitement, a tugging about the mouth where he might have found the twitch of pride, in the breath an intake of triumph. Farrell stooped solicitously to hand the kid a fizzy orange. An orange! The boy'd have half a bottle of Power's down him in the hour, and barely feel it, too. Wet bleeding-heart meddler, with nothing better to do than cock up his own people, in a *tie*— Well, see what would happen to that dandy pinstripe in ten minutes' time. Aye, that was the breath when Farrell remembered it later: as if the boy were taking in lungfuls of smoke, as if so close to Farrell he could smell meat cooking.

Farrell quizzed the proxy with the overenunciation of an uncle probing a three-year-old for what the nasty man had done to him in the park: Did he look in the bag? What did he see? *Exactly*. Did they tell him to do anything to the bag? Where did he put it, *exactly*? How heavy was it? Did he smell anything? Did it make any noise? The boy answered with the precision of someone who had looked in the bag a long time.

For, Farrell assured Estrin, there was such a thing as real humility and this was it. How often had he listened in pubs as men chatted up some frumpy clart. They told her she was beautiful and she believed them! Didn't the wretched girl have a mirror? Yet Farrell the savvy, the suspicious, was only another skirt, wasn't he, because the boy had chatted him up, isn't that right? And Farrell wouldn't see it because he wanted, like any girl, to feel pretty, when really he was about to get fucked.

Relating this, Farrell spoke of himself with contempt, but this time with no aftertaste of self-congratulation, no oh-what-a-worm-am-I. It was one thing to feel *I am so competitive, so manipulative, such a good liar; I am a raving self-serving loner*, which was all very nice actually, with a big isolated grandeur like Whitewells; quite a different business to feel *I am so credulous, I must seem like a prat.* Farrell would gratefully take the label of egomaniac over ordinary patsy. He would gladly be a drunk, but not a popinjay, trussed up and easily fooled by a fifteen-year-old boy ogling up at Farrell as if having just won an audience with Michael Jackson. Lord, vanity makes you a sitting duck.

The kid skidded out the door along with the evacuating top-floor guests, perhaps to keep his face from any of Farrell's surviving friends. Then, what friends? Farrell's careful dearth of affiliation lightened the consequences of his disposal.

Farrell smoothed into the lift. The gate sang shut. The right angles of the car seemed unusually perfect, each straight edge serene. The brass lattice shone a defiant white-gold; he admired the exquisite symmetry of its diamonds. The compartment resonated with such cold, mechanical accuracy that it was as if he weren't in a real lift at all, one of those poor approximations most human projects come to, but an earlier, purer stage of design—his feet rested on the draftsman's table. His own motions, too, achieved this quality—he reached for the button with that same precision he later observed in Estrin when she was half-jarred. The guests would be shuttled down the stairs, so the car sped uninterruptedly up; Farrell stood in the exact middle, so straight it was less like taking an elevator than growing rapidly tall enough to reach the top floor.

Before walking the last flight to the roof, he checked his kit, spreading the heavy leather case open on the floor; there was a loop for every cord, hook, and grip, snips, and one mangled paper clip he'd used for five years. Frankly, aside from pigsticks, it was a treasure trove of ordinary bits, like the desk drawers of a boy.

Up the stairs, his step sounded not loud exactly, but slowed from a single sound to a series of discreet grittings and slidings. His depression of the panic bar dissected, *tick-squeal-thunk*.

Farrell had often been asked, Isn't defusion exciting? or, Don't you get scared? He answered, "No," unable to explain that you didn't enjoy the luxury of emotion. Not only did the niceties of what you would order for dinner or whether you wanted a drink slough off, but so did your mother, your country, your age, the date, your sex; certainly your religion was one of the first frills to go, for bomb disposal was a regular short course in nonsectarianism. All that remained was yourself and the device, together so enormous that there was no space left for any feelings about either of you. He had heard of Brits losing their bowels, but only after the job was through. Because at the time you feel nothing. Farrell, who often enough when he felt anything felt rotten, revered this condition, though you were not catatonic—you felt nothing and everything, for he would recognize the exact temperature of that air as it hit his face when he opened the door for the rest of his life, and he could tell Estrin precisely what that roof looked like, down to which slates were loose, which were splattered with pigeon shite. He could tell her the shopping bag by the wall was from Brown Thomas; *Treasures of use and beauty/Pretty toys for children* gleamed in the light of his torch. Next to the bag was an ancient mattress with a pattern of mildew like the Shroud of Turin. While he did not have any feelings about these things, he did know they were there with a profundity which perhaps amounted to an emotion at that—a seeingness we have no name for.

. Into this blinkered concentration one thought did intrude itself; much as Farrell dismissed it as an indulgence, it would not go away. As he crunched closer and the bag mocked, *Things for the best-dressed man*, the thought insisted itself, petulant. *Fair enough*; he turned to it at last. *But quick now.*

Face it, the notion slapped at him. *No professional from NIHQ would ever get so close to that bag as to read the ad, save on a fuzzy video screen a block away. The army would use Wheelbarrow, and don't imagine you couldn't rustle up a robot if you tried. You could have sent it on the lift, hulking and chunking up those stairs—sure it wouldn't be as elegant, they're ungainly monsters, but could do this job as well. And don't claim you haven't time to think this through—your right foot is still falling heel to toe. You just don't want to hear, but you're going to: because for that matter you could have called the army yourself. No one would be implicated unless the glypes left prints on the putty, and that would be their own fault. So why are you here—from pride? What's going to happen to your pride if in the next sixty seconds that princely Dublin shopping bag turns into a frog? Answer me, do you want to die? Is that why you drink so much, to dissolve? And if so, why dismantle the bomb? Why not fling matches? Why bother with the bomb at all, why not dive over the edge there—it's ten stories. Why are you on this roof, boyo?*

Farrell was almost angry—his first feeling, which he could ill afford. He bore down on the bag: a simple exercise. The proxy had described a timer and a cigar box with wires—probably one of those 5 p copper dets the Republic had been shipping up by the binful lately. Sounded like commercial, though, which meant the modest size of the bag was no indicator of modest capacity; some of the smallest bombs were the most destructive. But at least commercial didn't have a mind of its own like HME—commercial went when you told it to. As for switches, he could rule out a tilt, necessarily set once the bag was at rest, which they'd never trust to a proxy; and the kid had described only leaving the bag and streaking downstairs. Likewise, with a clock it wasn't radio-controlled. He planned, then, to cut in if the wires were accessible, or to plant a disruptor if the mechanism was fully encased.

Farrell shone his torch into the bag. The box was as the boy had said, with the usual Boots clock, whose metal minute hand would hit the contact at twelve. He breathed easier; twenty minutes left. A disruptor was chancier than cutting the detonator free, and commercial wasn't likely to do anything resentful for being jostled. Gently Farrell rustled the bag open a bit wider, tipping it to get a better look at the sides of the box. The almond scent of Frangex wafted from underneath.

All his information intersected at once: the boy downstairs had talked too long for a fifteen-year-old convinced the building in which he was standing was about to take off for Mars, and the flattery had been too profuse: for the wire straggling from the box was unconnected. More; insulated to its very tip, it had never been connected. The minute hand had not yet moved, nor would it—the clock was not even wound. The proxy was a fake; the timer switch was a fake; but the bomb was not a fake, for in that tiny rustle, with sound so disassembled, there was one sound smallest of all that pierced the drone of traffic below, stiletto: a click. A distinctive click that Farrell had rehearsed up to his ear when laying out his practice toys five years before: the sound of a micro-tilt switch touching its plates. Inside that Brown Thomas bag was a birthday present for Farrell O'Phelan; why, they could as well have included a pink ribbon and a card.

He should have known he would be all right, for he was allowed the moment in which to think he would not be. The bomb that went off he wouldn't hear; for all his flirtation with explosion, in its most intimate embrace he would see nothing. *That was the turn*: to want to experience your own death was to want to avoid it. If you tripped your last switch, you never finished its pretty echoes on the plate; if you loved fire, inside a flame its curl and lick were only taken away; if you loved heat, you had to keep clear enough to feel the blaze. To love death was first to love, so that all his attraction to apocalypse was still attraction, live desire, and he'd been a fool, a raving nutter, to assume he actually wanted the Frangex to ignite on any evening—for love of death and dying were not only different; they were antithetical.

9

As You Are in Pieces,
So Shall Your Cities Fragment

"I don't understand. Why are you here?"

"I shouldn't be."

"Why didn't the bomb go off?"

"Irps. That's how you can tell an IRSP device, my dear: it doesn't work."

"What did you do when it didn't blow?"

He smiled. "I looked up."

Clear winter skies are rare in Ireland. This one, innocent, earnest, suggested the shoe box he'd constructed as a boy, with an eye hole on one end and pinpricks on the other—held up to the light, it had made a child-size firmament, and true to form, Farrell hadn't settled for random dots but had carefully poked out accurate constellations. Funny how you were never satisfied with anything until you made it yourself, when there was a real sky out there and all you had to do was lean from the window. Why draw mountains like saw's teeth when you could hike through the Mournes? Farrell wiped the last traces of vomit on his sleeve. He didn't care if this observation was succinct, for he was luxuriating in the lushness of his own mind; memory, on the edge of extinction a moment before; having been a boy— in this lifetime of unnecessary perceptions, they had always been his greatest joys, tiny searing moments of mental incision like the pinpricks overhead. It's true the sky was more lovely than usual, more blue, and the air, while cold, at least had temperature at all, and it was temperature itself he relished—but most of all it was thinking, *he loved thinking*, so when he thought, You prat! he was euphoric to have ideas about himself at all. Greedily he thought, *My mother feels guilty over my childhood and doesn't know how to apologize*; he thought, *And I will never let her*; he thought, *My sisters have been cruelly underestimated*; he thought, yes, right next to this, *You can give the Protestants everything they want in fact, but if at the same time they lose in theory they will keep fighting.* He seized at any illumination however small, rolling in his own head like somersaults in heather, like burying his face in a young girl's hair. Farrell watched the gradual shifting of stars with the much faster turns of the way he looked at them, the dizzying spin of explanations for why they were there, smoothing the contours of his own ideas, shivering across his intellect, running suppositions like scales, showing off for himself, reciting chess gambits and trying whole new daring attacks; setting up the puzzle of Irish politics, not quite sure how to move, treasuring the fact he was not sure, since so much of thinking, good thinking, is being stymied. It was voluptuous, autoerotic; he could feel the luscious bumps and quivers of his naked brain, sweet, moist, and veiny, full of unexpected leaps from left to right, until he came to the single insight as though emerging from a copse to a clearing, *I do not need the bomb. I am the bomb.*

Yet later he would return to the hotel, as he had this evening, once more weary of himself, impatient with Estrin's intrusions, with the ceaseless chatter in pubs and chip shops across this

island, but really because his own patter was just as circular, just
as stale, stultified by the same unmoving board the North set
before him, the lumps of his head gone dry. *But I did need the
bomb. I needed the bomb to know I didn't need it. I still need the bomb.*
He missed bombs but was sure he'd only lost the nerve for them,
and in this way had only taken a giant step backward.

"So that was the last disposal," he concluded. "And I didn't
even finish that. I went back to the lobby. Ordinarily I would
have dismantled the thing, pocketed the switch if it deserved
further study, neutralized the explosive. Instead, I called the
army. They used Wheelbarrow. Weren't about to take my word
for it the bomb was duff. Took forever, of course, and how I
recognized the pretentious officiousness of the bomb squad.
They could have it, I decided. I stayed across the way, at Kelly's
Bar. They had to carry me back to Whitewells. It takes real
application for me to get a hangover, but I'd applied."

"You stopped because you got careless, or because you got
scared?"

"I quit because I'd never been scared. I wasn't courageous,
but naïve. Everyone else in Belfast knew what a bomb was but
me, who opened them up like Christmas crackers. I didn't want
to die; I thought I was immortal. But not anymore.

"So the next day I changed everything. I stopped drinking
anything but wine, after eight. I gave up red meat, sweets,
cholesterol. I took regular exercise. For a while I even slept. I
instituted security at Whitewells that stopped just shy of the
rectal mirror search. And I retired utterly from bomb disposal.
I regard myself as a reformed suicide."

Estrin struggled up in bed, resisting fatigue she couldn't
justify; she'd only unloaded the kegs of Smithwick's that afternoon, run ten miles, had dinner. Farrell did this to people. How
little sleep had Farrell gotten, and for what exalted cause? Somehow his tale left her both entranced and disquieted. It was a
good story, wasn't it? And he wouldn't lie?

Her uneasiness was with hue: the story was colorized. He

couldn't leave it alone. He wasn't lying except in the way he lied all the time.

"Dostoevsky," said Estrin.

"Alyosha, Dmitri, or Ivan?"

"Moral nit-picking of Alyosha; dopey romanticism of Dmitri; intellectual impudence of Ivan. And you left out Smerdyakov: a bit of a bastard." (Farrell swelled like a tick.) "But I was thinking of his real life. When he was condemned to death and marched out to the square blindfolded. The firing squad cocked their rifles. *Then* the tsar commuted the sentence. Dostoevsky was obsessed with it, that moment."

Estrin's voice trailed off, passingly envious of his misadventure, wishing she could prop Farrell on her pillows and tell tales of Frangex; but she caught herself in time, realizing, though the stories didn't tell as well, there were plenty enough times careening a motorcycle down the coast road in the Philippines, between checkpoints on the Gaza Strip, when she'd banked a little low and felt the machine begin to slide, when she'd miscalculated an angle at 120 k and been forced into the oncoming lane, a breath from an Arab bus. He'd been talking, simply, of almost getting killed, and hadn't everyone felt that? Didn't we all walk the world immortal and get reminded? Get reminded one last time, too late? For Farrell had a tendency to absorb all the drama in the room, a sponge in a puddle. It was greedy, but it was also Estrin's fault for imagining there was a limited quantity of anguish in the world that he could steal.

For all his fractiousness, there was a side to Farrell that was irrepressibly kind. The pale, dilute blue pupils always glistened on the verge of tears; even at his most irate, they tinted with pity. True, the pity extended to himself, and he wouldn't like to hear that; but he must have suspected in moments of genuine self-scrutiny that it extended only to himself, and the way he looked back at Estrin now belied that. They were eyes that wanted most to protect you from themselves, and they would fail.

"So many countries, all on your own," he whispered, taking her to his lap. "Do you not get lonely now?"

"Get? Stay. But you, I wonder if you don't top me. You're about the loneliest person I've ever met."

Estrin searched the runny pools overhead, eyes that kept the same constant chemistry in bars or in bed: one part humor, two parts pain. He was hard to find in them. The amusement masked their surface, while the sadness blackened the centers to wallow in its own secret abyss, like a swimming hole whose location he refused to share. As you pursued him across the iris, he flecked from spear to spear, tripping creek stones, always a step ahead. To dive in that serous blue and aim for the deep part was reliably to hit rock. The amusement mocked you. The sadness denied you. *This is impossible*, they said. *I miss you*, they said. *Why can't you look into my eyes?* He would run from you, only to turn impatiently and blame you for not catching up.

Estrin retracted on her side. "Being by yourself beats bad company. Most company. It's underrated."

Farrell uncurled her. "It's easier."

He rose to slide out of his shoes and strip off the red tie. Farrell had his shirts commercially laundered, so when he raised his collar it stood stiffly starched to his chin. He paused and, on some whim for which Estrin would always be grateful, leaned down and kissed her, with that gravity so particular to the man. Why the picture of Farrell with the white collar raised would burn so lustrous in her memory she would never know, or why it was nice that he was in his socks. Maybe the raised collar gave him a touch of the priestly or pastoral, to remind Estrin of her father. Maybe a little synapse in her brain illuminated the moment like a flashbulb for no better reason than that his shirt was so startlingly clean. Maybe it was just a mental accident, like taking a picture of your thumb, but Estrin didn't think so. There was a purity to the image, even as he stood back up and wrangled briefly with the top button, in one of those quintessentially masculine gestures, like slipping a checkbook from an inside pocket. The light in the room was warm but bright; his cuff links gleamed; the shirt was radiant. He did not seem much older; Ireland and the United States did not seem far apart.

Surely she should have remembered making love to him with this same clarity, but in Estrin's experience it was hard to recall particular couplings. They seemed so distinctive at the time, but maybe they were pretty much the same after all; or possibly recollection blurred from interior shyness, censorship even, and her memories were pasted with bits of black tape, porn rags for sale in a decent neighborhood.

That said, tonight's episode would impress itself more than most. Before, like the Technicolors of his tales, Farrell had laid it on too thick. In fact, she found his most drastic moments his most pathetic. Both his thrashing at her hips and the extravagance of his bedtime stories were rooted in a sad little fear: that he could not feel. Farrell's compulsion to magnify implied the meager; and it was when he cried most loudly inside her that she was certain he felt numb.

However, this evening they measured out their pleasure in tiny, cautious doses. Private, Farrell pulled the spread to her neck. While only frenetic bounding had brought him to climax before, it was readily apparent he was in danger of coming too fast. Then he had whipped to such a rapid frenzy that he'd been gasping less from rapture than from exertion; now he moved more gradually as they progressed. The first time, too, he'd been half drunk and a little slack; this time, hours without a drink, he was fully hard and so a larger man than she'd realized—a pleasant surprise.

From the outside the couple must have looked boring: a lump under chenille, a rustle, a murmur. But no one was watching; that was the point. For in their weaker moments, Estrin performed for men, Farrell performed for himself. Relieved of audience, they did not try athletic positions but remained on their sides; it felt good that way, there was no reason to try something new. Farrell, rather than caterwaul, only sighed. Estrin kept two fingers on his shoulder, and these absorbed the majority of her expression—a light pressing, or a lifting until the whorls barely skimmed the summits of his gooseflesh.

For Farrell, too, the less they experimented, the more each sensation distinguished itself from every other, like that astounding variation among three white pebbles when you looked at them hard. Just as the grind of his shoes and the clunk of the panic bar had segmented as he approached the Brown Thomas bag, so the sough of Estrin's breath broke down, and he followed each inhalation's shutter from larynx to trachea to bronchia and back again. He breathed with her; as air branched to both their lungs, his head went light. Listening, he found she drew each breath a different pitch, with a characteristic flutter all its own. Sometimes she sucked in suddenly, then leaked back out, her mouth a patient puncture in a tube. Others she said, "Sh-sh," though neither had spoken, or whistled lightly through her tongue. On occasion she held a lungful so long that Farrell, too, stopped breathing to hear better, in irrational fear she would suffocate.

They didn't kiss, they'd not have been able to bear it. This was already far too much, until they slowed so completely an observer would have claimed they were sleeping. Farrell was caught in a single stroke, inchmeal; each fraction he pushed toward her, the pressure of those two fingers increased. He could not remember when it had been like this or whether it had ever been like this, though admittedly he wasn't remembering very hard—he didn't want the distraction. He would fuck this exquisite, tiny creature as long and as gently as he could and save memory for more disappointing nights—this memory.

Estrin's forehead rippled down over her eyebrows, and she turned her head a few degrees away. She could no longer withstand seeing his face straight on. She shifted her thighs so he no longer touched her so directly. Even as she organized Farrell's presence as more glancing, it grew only more unendurable, like days so bright that not only could you not look toward the sun, you couldn't stand its glare on the wall. Her tongue rose to form "No," but did not. Her back arched, but not very much. She touched her forehead to Farrell's arm. She didn't want to come yet, but it was hopeless. In return, quiet, low, doleful, a felt mallet pounded on her kettledrum. While Estrin thought she came again, she wasn't sure, for though she could now distinguish one hair from another on his shoulder, the pinkish brown around the edges of his nipples from the bluer brown of their tips, sighs of pure pleasure from their identical twins tinged with regret, she could no longer distinguish between Farrell's sensations and her own. Estrin saw water—wide pale-blue water, still. Farrell drew her closer and stayed inside, his erection dying as slowly as it had come.

Before he lapsed out, there was a second explosion, quite nearby. It resembled their own, for bombs detonate within the body. They blossom in the lower intestine and open to the ear, where the pressure changes as the air in your very brain tries to escape, like a sudden inspiration. Just as Bach had enlarged her in Chartres, deep C minor from down the street expanded Estrin's slight figure until she filled the room, inhaled Whitewells, and grew enormous with the city, round. All her pictures were dark and furred. The windows rattled. One pane splintered and pinged; a shard spat against the drapes and dropped to the carpet. The sound lay down slowly. A cold whistle trailed through the broken window, like breath on Estrin's tongue.

Farrell's renewed erection embarrassed him. Though too late to hide his revival from Estrin, he sucked from her anyway, to tuck away the evidence ineffectually between their hipbones. She didn't mention it. But it's physiological, he wanted to explain. Buses, you know. Buses do the same thing. *That was no bus*, he heard back. He was relieved to skip the conversation.

"Just down the road," he whispered, stroking her head as if she needed comforting. "Probably the courts. Didn't sound so massive. I'll get the window replaced in the morning. Bloody hell, if I'd known in '68, I'd have thrown every shilling into pane glass and flowers—orange, green, and white carnations, red, white, and blue. I'd be a rich man."

She didn't need comforting, or jokes. When the bomb went

off, she had only seemed alert. If she was disturbed, it was not by the explosion. Her eyes were open, vacantly wondrous. "Flowers?" she asked.

"Funerals."

Her head limp on her neck, it rolled away from him, her hand now dead on his shoulder, where two tiny bruises were just beginning to bloom.

Farrell was constantly having the experience of realizing he hadn't noticed people before. In fact, he rarely paid enough attention to most people to realize he was ignoring them. Waking that morning to find Estrin Lancaster rising from his bed for the loo, he found that though he'd spent two long nights with her, he had yet to notice her, really notice-notice.

Och, he'd listened to her, more or less, and filed away her vital statistics, though with much the same caginess of any politician who will remember the name of your baby for his next campaign. And sure he wanted her; just watching her grope from the sheets he was already rising to the occasion. So what did he mean, not notice?

Well, for example, he'd never even looked at her, look-looked. (Farrell kept two meanings for every word; with himself he identified the emphatic from the facile by using it twice. These amounted to two different languages, the second of which he never used, for if he were ever to speak in total sincerity—imagine—he would have to stutter, I-I am-am sorry-sorry, like awkward tribal languages whose plurals are formed by repetition. However, to speak this language would instantly devalue it, and then to himself, he supposed, he would have to say everything three times.) Now, Farrell had slept with a fair number of love-lies, each with her charms. What selected this one had something to do with light. The groggy winter gray sifting through the drapes did not fall evenly over her shoulders or paint a simple highlight down her spine; rather, each ray suppled in fluctuating shades, as if poppling the surface of water more than flesh—was he awake? No, really, that light was not normal, it was not lapping a smooth surface, and as she stood and stretched and walked around the bed, the grays churned and eddied over her back, swirled in her buttocks, and streamed in parallel shafts down her thighs: why, her entire backside silvered like a school of fish. He sat up a little and rubbed his eyes. Because this was not the ordinary sleek of a small young woman in decent trim. Either she was diseased, he was still sleeping, or that was muscle.

Which explained the other difference, the eerie spring of her skin. Estrin's shoulders were small round melons, underripe; they would not take the press of his thumb. Her thighs had the taut shine of aubergines, that same resonance, her forearms the wood and stalk of overgrown leeks—in all a body more vegetable than fruit, hard and green and indigestible, with a smack to her skin that inspired him to spank her.

On return she glared down at his erection as if it were butting into her business. "You know, for all this liberated lip service, most men are still oblivious to contraception."

"And most women still make broad, slanderous statements about half the population of the world. I'd think you were better traveled than that, my dear."

Seven a.m. on three hours' sleep and the *my dears* were already hackling. Traditionally they would wake fucking or fighting—or both.

"Don't you care if I get pregnant?"

"I expect you'll take care of yourself."

"Everyone expects that." She glowered. "And I always do."

"My relationship to sex is apocalyptic."

"Most people don't think of children as the end of the world."

"My, my. We are thirty-two."

"What's that supposed to mean?"

"Tick, tick, tick."

Estrin flung the blankets on Farrell's flagging enthusiasm and sat half off the bed. "Fuck you."

"Soft spot."

She reeled toward him. "Yes, but not the way you think."

"You want children?"

"No, I do not. Nor have I ever. And I'm sick to death of this secretly, secretly you do, wink-wink, nudge-nudge. Every year I get older it gets worse. Come on, admit it, all you really want is to be a mommy, right? And this gadding about on airplanes, you're looking for a man! Confess, that whole time in Jerusalem you were pining for a split-level outside Philly with 2.2, a cocker spaniel, and a remote-control garage." Estrin rose to gaze through the broken window, assuming a stance that would have entailed thrusting her hands in her pockets had she been wearing any clothes. "You have kids?"

"No," he said. "Though I had one child, shall we say, canceled."

"Catholic girl?"

"It wasn't easy."

"No, for her I imagine it wasn't."

Though unsure how he'd kindled her fury, he found this an interesting performance. "I meant for me."

"But you brought yourself to it. Didn't marry the buttercup, now, did you?"

"Not Germaine. I married another time, however. She wasn't pregnant. It was a mistake. I'm not likely to marry again. You should be forewarned."

The turret swiveled. "Right. Two nights of fucking and she'll be out this morning looking at rings." She advanced on the bed. "You don't want to marry again because you're so exceptional, isn't that right? Everyone else needs a hand to hold but Farrell O'Phelan?"

"I cannot lead an ordinary life. But I do find the odd hand to hold—even yours, my swallow."

"And the no kids, the abortee, you don't want, same reason? That you're better than the average bear?"

"With my work I cannot have children."

"You can, you've proved that once, maybe twice, for all the precautions you insisted on last night. Okay, but I could have predicted you didn't want a family ten minutes after we met.

My point is this: when I say I don't want to marry, do you believe me?"

"No."

"And when I say I don't want kids?"

"Not for a moment."

It dismantled her a little that he was so direct. "Right," she faltered. "*Spinsters* have missed the boat; *bachelors* have jumped ship. Farrell remains dashingly unattached; Estrin protesteth too much."

She ranged the room, picking up splinters of glass and tossing them in the bin, moving with unnerving ease for a naked woman. Farrell had never met a female who wasn't dissatisfied with some part of her body, which she would go to extraordinary lengths to hide. But barring a flag to her small breasts, Estrin's frame was impeccable—and that she seemed to know this was not altogether attractive. He missed the crossed arms, the clutched thighs, the panicked robing and dive for towels, the humanizing shelter of shame.

She unfolded the chamois from the shoeshine kit on the portmanteau, smoothing and refolding it like a baby blanket. "Why am I so proud of not wanting kids, though? God, what's wrong with us?"

She turned and studied Farrell and caught him looking at his watch. "I can see you, though. Sixty-five or seventy. With a much younger woman; suddenly fervid to have an heir. Going to doctors, taking her temperature. Then children wouldn't seem ordinary anymore, would they? So you'd wildly overdo it, and croak in bed." She laughed.

Farrell reached for her hand. "Kill me."

She bounced amicably back beside him, her mood swings quick and queer. "I could, you know."

"With just that broken window and hyperventilation. I have weak lungs." Even joking, he couldn't bring himself to say *asthma*.

"No, really. We should be so lucky in 1988 to get plain old

pregnant. But I am astounded you didn't ask this foreign flotsam about disease."

"I have assumed if you weren't forthcoming about your health in the first place, if I did inquire, you would lie. So why be unpleasant?"

She paused. "Why is it when you talk like that I get the creeps?"

"Haven't a clue. Just solving an equation."

"Would you"—she curled on his chest—"lie about that?"

"If I hadn't told you at the start? Of course. Brilliantly, and to the bitter end. Seventy pounds and bedpanned in rubber gloves, I'd still be gasping the diagnosis was a grotesque mistake. Never back down. Because as long as I stuck to my story, blood test or no, there's a very good chance you would believe me."

She turned over and mused. "Ten years ago, know how hard it was to get a guy to slip on a rubber? When it was *only* to protect the girl? Now it's to protect their pricks, the sons of bitches arrive in bed swathed from head to toe in cling film."

"Are you staging this whole scene to get me to wear a prophylactic?"

"God, no, that's like indulging yourself in a Tootsie Roll and forgetting to take off the wrapper. Me, what with Dieter shooting up again, I got tested last month." She slowed, deferent, unraveling a pill of chenille. "Which was hard," she admitted. "I'd waited three months, celibate, for the untoward to show itself. At the Royal, they were nice, but suspicious. An American. Whose last boyfriend was a heroin addict. That went over terrif. I was scared. And I went through the test all by myself, like everything else. Waiting two weeks for the results. Confiding to nobody. *That* is lonely. But I was clean. Boring, but diseases are afraid of me."

"Are you of me?"

"Better believe it."

"So you want me to wear—?"

"No, I doubt you've copped enough international ass to be dangerous. And as for Junior, I lift weights."

Only when they'd finished did he ask her to explain.

"I exercise like a lunatic and eat fish. I don't have enough fat to ovulate. I'm infertile, long as I lay off the cream buns."

"How convenient."

"And extreme. I thought you'd find it appealing."

Farrell phoned while she showered. He could have waited, less risky all around; he worried the water was audible through the receiver. But a naked weightlifting motorcyclist in his bath made the call much more fun.

As a result, at breakfast downstairs he was still feeling self-satisfied, so he wasn't prepared. The moment was infinitely small, but the bombs that go off in an emotional life are so often this tiny interior *poof* no outsider can hear, a dog whistle of an experience—sun on brick, a raised collar. He happened to turn back around on his way from the dining room to get his papers, to tell Estrin to order steamed milk. She was sitting. She did absolutely nothing. Except her face changed. It—sank to itself. It cohered. He would hate to have to explain this to anyone else, except that the subtle settling altered the way he saw her forever more. He had witnessed the miracle of self-return, and from now on he would treasure most in her that she existed when he left the room.

Soon it would become a sport: he would deliberately arrive late, to find her leaning on the seat of that crazy motorcycle chuckling at the Grand Opera House and a moment later not telling him the joke. It was a joke to herself, and he loved that. From now on he would leave for the bog and lurk around the corner to watch the muscles at her mouth, so tight from smiling to please him, collapse down, her hands rising to embrace her cheeks. That was the return: a meeting of parts, a family reunion. She reached for and held her own hand. That was what made her so portable, wasn't it? For all the starving and lifting and forcing herself up airplane ramps, there was a caretaking in her he envied. She cupped herself. Of course, this was not always so, but at least she knew moments when she was beloved to herself. *Beloved.* He was surprised to be able to perceive this, since it was entirely unfamiliar in his own life.

Maybe he occasionally paid attention after all. For suddenly Farrell saw not only the similarities she kept insisting on but differences she did not. Estrin may have known self-loathing, thick as treacle and that dark, but she was far less acquainted with a simpler and in fact far more disturbing self-dislike—the same inconsequential distaste you felt for strangers in dental surgeries with whom you avoided conversation. And she did not understand him, for she did not know the vacancy of a man who has let go of his own hand, or has never truly held it, because sometime long ago someone else had never reached down to it when it was tiny and damp and hadn't yet learned to gesture aggressively in pubs, slip out a credit card, snip detonator wires— or that was the way he explained it to himself, something about his mother. But he was beginning to realize that the mother he missed was *his mother*—a semantically difficult distinction—*his mother*, but not some namable woman with a reprimand of a face and overdone Brussels sprouts, for even Medbh O'Phelan's rare redemptive affections could not soak in. You could never hear what you were not somewhere in yourself already saying; Medbh O'Phelan was irrelevant. He had lost his mother inside. That was why Estrin shrank when he shrieked over her upstairs and his eyes filled with thick tears that would not quite drop and later absorbed back, unshared. She could not imagine years like fields, scrub grass, worse, carparks, gray tarmac, without hatred, just emotional nausea, long borderless days given structure only by the orderly demise of a liter, nights that never precisely ended but slumped upright in a chair. There had never been an arm around him; he'd struck no partnership; avoiding alliances, he had refused affiliation with himself.

Then this whole banjax was missing a pinion, wasn't that the score? There was bloody well only one of you, wasn't there? So how can you have a relationship with yourself of any description? You are your frigging self! There should be no such thing as self-love *or* self-loathing. Except this wasn't Farrell O'Phelan's private dementia, was it, since there are such words, coined long ago by other poor bisected bastards who died in twos. Or had they? Was death alluring partly because in being nothing there was only one nothing, you could not count nothings, you couldn't help but die whole? For in the worst of Talisker Farrell had looked in the mirror and seen halves of his face like shoes from different pairs; in fact, when he only saw two soles, the day was easy.

That was what Genesis was all about—you could find this in the journals of Farrell's early twenties at Queen's, recording for posterity he'd been a boring old sod then—expulsion from the garden was the exile of the self from the self. Good Christ, it was as if God had planted a bloody nail bomb in the human psyche, because this very thinking should not exist, those passages from twenty years ago should not exist, gangling Farrell O'Phelan sorting out the rabble between his ears while his city went up in flames. *Self-respect, subconscious, superego, parent and child*—whichever jargon you found more clever, they were all just names for bits when the while kit didn't add up. There was only one of you; it should speak with one voice, and it was insane that this orator should ever address itself; it already knew what it was saying.

Gritting down Royal Avenue with his papers, Farrell glanced at the headlines while surveying the damage: a car bomb, Provo maintenance work. They were obligated to *x* number of routine bombings, *y* number of assassinations, and at least one high-profile, all-out Incident a year, just to keep up appearances. He sometimes pictured the Army Council mapping out the year's campaign much like any advertising firm with a job to do, having another coffee, letting the conversation wander; bearing down again, the foolscap black with crossed-out ideas: ~~Anderson-McAuley~~ Primark; ~~Crown Court~~ three judges (in rapid succession?); drumming their fingers, trying to think of a new angle, combing the map for an RUC station they hadn't hit in a while, racking their brains for a catchy gimmick to sell the Struggle like any other product whose billboards had gone stale.

It was a common Belfast fillip, checking out your street and the photo on the front page and they being the same view. Farrell reviewed the blackened brick, two floors of windows out—it looked worse in the pictures. Here, not so impressive, tarted up in a day or two. Belfast worked fast with plate glass, from practice. Already the stationery had erected a sign over its demolished storefront, BUSINESS AS USUAL.

Now, didn't that put it in a nutshell. For even when he searched for the traditional twinge of Didn't-I-hear-that-blow-last-night, Aren't-I-where-it's-happening, he could only dredge up the sour savvy of *Aye, weren't we due*. It didn't even pique him that the journalists knew fuck-all, while Farrell had the contacts to worm out the real story down to who twisted the wires, where the det was from; he wouldn't bother. It was harder and harder to get goosed by these productions. Why, with his own local headlines in the *Herald Tribune*, the coverage had come to have the opposite effect. This was where everything was happening according to the rest of the world, and Farrell knew very well nothing was happening here, so where was the real news, or was there any? For Farrell often experienced the conflict as trumped up; when *Newsweek* bought it, the whole world seemed a cod.

Then, flimflam was just one phase, and there were so many others; later some detail, ironic, idiotic, would start him thinking. For while the Province had eerily stabilized, his mind had not, and ceaselessly turned and consumed this town, constructing models that explained it. As more glass and mangled car parts skittered at his feet, today's theory had to do with *bits*.

If your whole self was shattered, one piece chatting to other pieces, hiding from some pieces, wrestling with others, is it surprising the streets were in shambles, continents were drifting, the planet chunked part from part? You make the world in your own image. *As you are in pieces, so shall your cities fragment. As your bits are at war, so shall you fight each other*. Peace on earth would come only when people made one piece of themselves. And this was different from loving themselves or repressing their bad selves or facing up to their bad selves . . . Nope, the whole tinkling crumple was no-go. And so a *united* Ireland, *unionism* aspired to the same paradise, where you thought one clear thought without compulsively thinking the opposite at the same time, where your feelings about your father did not bifurcate like putting on someone else's glasses, with one picture vitriolic, the other groveling, gooey-eyed, little wonder you could never remember his face; where your decisions were not bicameral, whole bloody sessions of Parliament, but a slice like cutting cake, simple and over and unregretted, taking up no more time than a line space; where no one made cartoons with angels on one shoulder and devils on the other, no novelist invented Jekyll and Hyde. Both Nationalists and Loyalists were yearning for the same cohesion, why the solution to the Northern Irish problem was to line up the locals one by one, tilt their heads to the side, and pour Super Glue in each ear.

As far as Farrell could tell, however, the world was entirely peopled with heads in parts; he could hear them rattle as he walked by, those cauliflower clumps of the brain segmented every which way—lying from truthful, shallow from deep, waking from dream. As a result, though Farrell may have lived in a city whose inhabitants shot each other and magneted gelignite to cars, he remained struck less by their lunacy than by their integrity, for while Farrell mocked himself for being tortured, he did find living very hard and could not understand why more lives around him weren't utterly disassembled. He was impressed, for example, that on the whole the population managed to feed itself, sleep, and look both ways before crossing the street. He was mystified why you did not pass more people standing on the corner screaming. Others found the rate of alcoholism in the Province astounding; so did Farrell, but he didn't find it nearly high enough. He was in awe of rough sanity. While the international press questioned why so many murders, Farrell wondered, Why so few? And with their heads full of gravel, Farrell was most astounded by widespread self-affection, the way scads of people chose shirts they thought they looked best in mornings and ate breakfasts they liked, happily skipping articles in the *Irish Times* they did not find interesting. Farrell wasn't interested in a single article, and he read every one.

"So, was that your first bomb?"

"I've been here six months!"

"How do they make you feel?"

"Odd."

"Odd? That's all?"

"*Awed*," she repeated. "Full of awe. Grim . . . *Happy*," she announced. "Wildly happy, and that's the way most people feel here, too, perfectly, gleefully happy, and they never admit it. They wring their hands and moan, but inside they are eating it up. I've seen it on their faces as well as on mine. The smallest little child knows how delicious an explosion is, and I'm sick to death of old ladies not admitting they feel the same way."

Farrell had a strong sense of having had this conversation before. There was little to be observed of bombs he had not said or heard already. Though he'd raised the subject, he didn't want to talk about them now or ever again. He wanted to talk about bits. He wanted to ask Estrin whether she talked to herself, and especially, didn't that strike her as peculiar. But he suspected such an exchange in ready danger of going stupid. You had to watch the conversations you involved yourself in, because they implicated you—and Farrell despised thinking something precious to him and having it come out taradiddle. As a result, his most intimate convictions he never expressed. He'd been able to tell a woman he loved her, for example, only when he didn't mean it.

For Farrell didn't believe in language. Not like this one here. Look at her, scraping for those adjectives, when what was the difference between *awed* and *odd* in the end? Words had let him down enough times he had resorted to their more perverse pleasures, that shiny red apple you pluck when you say, "I went to the cinema," when really you went to the tobacconist. Sometimes Farrell would change trivial elements of a story just for the sensation.

"Next time," Estrin was saying, "we go to Clonard. Or to your place. Just not always here. It's artificial. Protected and tidy and tells me nothing about you."

"We never, but never go to my bungalow."

She looked stunned.

"Sometimes I forget where it is," he amended.

"I have to leave," she mumbled, her brow all piled up like an accident on the M1. "I'm supposed to meet Kieran this morning to fiddle with the books. Convince both the British and the Provos he's not making any money. Shouldn't be hard. He's not." Estrin screeched her chair out. Scouring her hands on the linen napkin, she could have been a mechanic degreasing with an oily rag. She pulled her leather jacket over her dress.

"Clonard!" he conceded after her, unconcerned by Estrin's huff. She was already hooked. The story of Farrell's Farewell always worked a treat on women.

He leaned back for a second cup of coffee. Now, that parting was typical. Not just "I have to leave," but "to meet whomever to whatever—" American. Farrell had *appointments*, full stop.

But Farrell was already turgid with the day's agenda. Midcup, he withdrew to look at himself, look-look. His mouth quirked; he heard an inward clucking. *How'd you land in this muck, me boyo?* He wondered did he feel bad? No, he checked, feeling his mind up and down as he might run his hands over his body after a fall. No, he didn't feel bad at all.

Farrell dabbed his mouth with his own napkin like a civilized man in a restaurant. Funnily enough, that boyo voice he heard—it wasn't his. It was Angus MacBride's.

10

The Vector and the Corkscrew

By the time he nipped in the back door he wasn't sure it was worth it. He'd had to exchange his Escort for a Council car, in case anyone recognized his plates. No, he did not want a driver. And all the while those thick-necked Sinner bodyguards leaning on bulletproof glass, smoking and tossing chips in his direction, as if to the pigeons, but barely missing MacBride's tweed slacks, their taunting remarks falling equally short of his ear. Hoods, no one would convince him different, and it remained one of the great scandals of Western society that this surly slag littering the carpark was actually allowed into the sanctum of City Hall like real human beings, and their cronies were elected to office and could even vote for their own murderous propositions at public expense. It brought the blood to his face that those pistol-packing wogs oiling out of the building now were actually paid by the people of the United Kingdom, and that money like as not could be traced directly to the blackened mangle of shopfronts on Royal Avenue last month. For pity's sake, Belfast putting Sinners on salary was like hiring someone to set fire to your own hair.

Then looping roundabouts for twenty minutes when the lass just lived up the road, shoving his floppy felt hat down his forehead, slipping on the dark glasses, and swathing the muffler over his chin until he looked like one of the Blues Brothers with a cold— There's them would find this a jolly game, but Angus was well weary of it, thank you very much.

He drew the scullery curtains before unwinding and plopped in a chair. When Roisin walked in, she jumped a few inches higher than usual.

"Have a seat, my pet." He patted his lap. "Though with a week such as I've had, all my vital juices are near drained off. Whatever you do, don't mention the word *Gibraltar*."

"You'd might have warned me. In a tick I'm away."

"Cancel."

"Can't. I've to meet—someone about my book. About reissuing *Bare Limbs on Basalt*."

"Sure we could ring up Blackstaff—"

"Och no," she said hurriedly. "I wish you would stop regarding my career as merely what I do to keep busy when you're not here."

"Women and their bloody careers! Aren't we straight from *Me* magazine. The point is, Roisin, I swapped the car and went through the whole fancy dress just to see you, love, and it's little enough to ask in return you reschedule a wee lunch. Who is it— Hilary?"

"No, someone new. And no. It's on."

A good politician, Angus knew real no's from the soft-centered and recognized this was, incredibly, a jawbreaker. "Fair enough," he grunted. "You'll not be long, then?"

She shrugged and drew on her coat.

"I'll wait, for I've work to do. Might be by the time you've returned I'll have eased back in the mood, like. There's nothing wilts a man like taking a back seat to blank verse." He reached for the phone and dialed violently, lurching to a frame of mind for busy signals and press releases from the one he'd prepared for playing with the tiny hairs in the small of Roisin's back. "MacBride here. That bandy boss of yours about?"

Roisin stood at the door, watching.

"It's not he figures the phone's tapped again, is it? Because you tell him for me that not a soul considers him that important! . . . Och, everyone's off to lunch, and not so much as a filled roll for a poor starving MP. How about you and me rustling us up a bit of champ, Con? But sure we'd fall in love, and then where'd we be? . . . You've a sarky mouth on you, woman. All the better to keep himself in line. No, I'll ring back. Cheerio." Angus beamed to Roisin; even missed contact with that snollygoster brightened his eyes. He slapped his mistress on the thigh; suddenly working for an hour or two appealed. "Awfully tarted up for an editor, love. I'm getting suspicious." He laughed and shoved his hat rakishly down on his head to fetch his papers from the car.

After her tepid kiss goodbye, Angus ranged the pantry in disgust: Weight Watchers cream of asparagus soup, thimble-sized jars of tuna, barely nibbled wheaten that would have made a bonny boom to knock down Divis Flats. And the icebox was worse; why, you could make a regular poem out of the refrigerators of single women (and why didn't Roisin write about *that?*): a wee drawerful of well-intentioned vegetables (I Really Should Start Eating Better), but the broccoli was sicklied o'er with the pale cast of resolution; you could have sold her carrots to low-budget reconciliation camps for making bracelets in crafts; the parsnips bowed, all weak and hairy like old men's legs. There were traces, too, of I Really Deserve a Reward: a package of Marks and Spark's chocolate meringues, one half eaten and both soggy—women! *Why couldn't she eat the whole bloody thing?* A container of coleslaw with one tablespoon in the bottom, God forbid she should throw it out. And then a silly array of costly gourmet jars in the door—pesto, mango pickle, ginger chutney—with nothing to complement, like dandies without dates.

The array made him doleful, not, for Angus MacBride, a common emotion. He wondered, this also rare, if he did Roisin a disservice; a delicate, fading flower maybe, but with the air of a schoolgirl still. In fact, he loved to pass St. Mary's letting out afternoons, with the girls' pert green skirts and shlumpy jumpers, the scrumpled ties; he always put Roisin among them, carelessly swinging her bookbag, looking down at the footpath with that funny combination of self-consciousness and utter unawareness of how pretty she was. She still had a girlish laugh, clean as a tin whistle, in a mournful Celtic key. (Never do to let it out, but he had a taste for fiddle-dee-dee. O'Phelan, of course, reviled it. Well, bugger O'Phelan. Hadn't a sentimental bone in his body—or had he? Sometimes Angus suspected that behind closed doors Farrell was a slobbering, maudlin old fart.) And maybe the lass was a reasonable poet; he'd have to take Blackstaff's word for it, since he couldn't abide the malarky himself. Yet here he was, keeping her to himself for the odd afternoon.

The queasiness didn't last long. Fact was, she was damned lucky. Angus MacBride wasn't meal-a-crushie, now. And they had their times. More and more he believed you snatched your afternoon here and there, you'd more than most. What was a life but a few days, one after the other? And if she didn't like it, she could quit, like. Angus was not by nature a guilty person. It gave him enormous power over those that were. Someone should tip off the Catholics: taking the blame never absolved anyone, or solved a woe. And it was funny if you simply refused to feel obligated to people how little you actually had to do.

He snuffled through the pantry a bit further before resigning himself there wasn't a morsel to be had. Why call it a scullery at all? Why not turn the room into a snooker parlor? So he went for his Bush, only to suffer a rude shock: disappeared. Angus banged cupboards. Was she taking a nip herself? Welcome to it if she replaced it. But here he was, stranded in this wretched

Catholic ghetto, utterly unable to walk into a pub within two miles, and to light into an off-license he'd have to bundle so up to the eyes they'd be sure he'd arrived to knock the place off.

Angus trooped the house, sourly looking for a place to work, the cheerful picture of nestling into a corner with a golden short at his elbow now giving way to a stark splay of papers on laminate with crumbs. The whole place enraged him today. It was too clean, for one thing, though had it not been he'd have complained at the grot. He couldn't bear the way everything *matched*. The walls and furniture and drapery in the parlor were all the same dim floral print. Further, each corner dithered with trinkets. Why, it was like living in an Oxfam outlet. And nowhere, for a poet even, was there a serious workspace, with paneling, books, good light, a map on the wall. Disgruntled, he settled back to the kitchen table, drumming his fingernails. They were bright pink.

You know, it wasn't cleanliness or clutter. There was something deeper wrong here, some critical lack of gusto. Sure the sorry appetite had something to do with her mother and Catholicism and Ireland, the whole desperate lot that would douse the fire in any woman, and did. Why, he wanted to take Roisin's hand, lead her to Stewarts and say, Here. This is the way you go shopping. You take a big cart, not one of those miserable baskets, and you hurtle down the aisles until the wheels rattle. You skip all those bitty tins and go straight to fresh meats. You have them special-cut you two-inch-thick fillets. You grab a hunk of Ulster Cheddar, a dozen eggs, two liters of *whole* milk, thank you, a pint of double cream. Lob in a slab of real Northern butter, and spare us that low-cholesterol E-Z-spread-golden-sunshine best shelved in hardware as lawn-mower lubricant. Vegetables? Haul out ten pounds of spuds, and do not mess about with lettuce, because it takes too much time to wash and too much time to eat, and in the end what have you got? Toss over a few chunky soups and a loaf of plain. What with large-size hankies and a pack of fags at checkout, there you are. You have shopped. Now, when you go home you will have food, where before you did not. For it was quite clear that when Roisin came back from Stewarts nothing had changed.

Grab hold, woman! Get your pinky out of the air! Muss up that sitting room; go buy some massive cord pillows, a leather recliner, and a sheepdog. Roller over the twee wallpaper, chuck that electric fire with the red light rotating behind plastic coals—who do you think you're fooling? Light a real bloody fire, stretch yourself out on the rug with a mugful of hot whiskey, and take off your clothes. Christ, what was wrong with people? What were they afraid of, and what in God's name were they waiting for? Day after day, the timorous huddled in well-manicured dungeons like these, terrified of living their own lives. Now, who bloody well was going to live them for you, and who was going to strike you dead if you lived them yourself? Sure you've had enough bad moments, unreported bank errors, spite on the phone, to figure out that Jesus is not waiting outside your door with a .22? Your countrymen, ladies, are blasting each other through chain link like mince, and what happens to them? They slink off to the Republic and toast the tricolor over a jar! Meanwhile, you're afraid to unzip your dress! Because why did Roisin always have to twitter about needing to visit or hoover or jot when he came by, whinging why couldn't they go out, maybe somewhere they weren't known—*China*, Angus suggested—before she "broke down" and went to bed? Just: take it! Angus wished that for once he'd slip in that back door and Roisin would grab him by the balls.

For Angus could tell you he wanted a steak or a woman or the Nobel Peace Prize, but at the end of the day Angus simply *wanted*. Consequently, he cheated with a clear conscience. He considered himself a dying breed, for how many men were left out there capable of bona fide lust? His infidelity amounted to a moral position. The mustering of that much sheer appetite deserved reward.

Because MacBride had less fled his fundamentalist upbringing than rounded it off a bit. He did believe in God, but Angus's God was a decent sort who sometimes looked the other way.

He wanted you to have a good time. And He knew the difference between a little carousing and real-life rank shite. Amid so much reeking degeneracy He couldn't be fussed about your wee departures; in fact, He surely found MacBride's good-natured boxspring squealing a welcome relief. MacBride's God was a bit of a lad. MacBride's God played rugby.

Angus would acknowledge that his religion was lazy. He went to church because he had to; C of I, but Angus wasn't particular. He merely aspired to a rough sense of there being an order out there that would take care of itself. Rather than call him to a higher perspective, Angus's religion dug him happily into the garden of earthly delights. Someone else was looking after the big picture, freeing Angus to call the woman with the tight red skirt into the hallway on some pretext and press her up against the wall.

Because at some of these Unionist do's the presence of several attractive women in the room at once brought tears to his eyes. It was a smorgasbord of a feeling, and as the definition of attractive spread with the demise of a bottle, the sensation grew only more uplifting; desire rose in his throat. For one of MacBride's gifts was seeing what made a woman beautiful— every woman—finding the floozy underneath the wee Presbyterian bow. Why, he'd even felt pulled toward Constance Trower, one plain Jane, and so efficient so she was, so very, very Good at Her Work, so upright and sensible. But he could see that one hand at her breast and she'd collapse like a house of cards.

Wasn't that the wonderful thing about women. Sex only made men sturdier and more willful. MacBride was convinced, for example, that his numerous extracurricular activities, within the bounds of strategic discretion, had only improved his political career. But women? Touch the right place in them and they folded up. He loved that one lost sound they made, a mewl of helpless surprise, and boyos, this isn't when they come; you just have to touch there and they go limp and spill, until the bed is a regular rice paddy. Christ, Angus fucks Roisin and bounces to the carpet for his DBA taping in twenty minutes and Roisin lies there as if she's been shot.

Angus gladly pictured himself a predator, all claw and yawn and stretch. He liked being a man, and thought he made a mighty good one; women had told him as much. So how could this paragon of masculinity be left in a scullery feeling so churlish, so girlishly petulant?

Fine. Maybe he wasn't spiritual enough. Maybe he shouldn't let it ruin his afternoon that his whiskey had disappeared and there was nothing to eat and his woman had dandered off lunching instead of bundling into his arms upstairs. And maybe there was something to this I'll-have-a-piece-of-toast, oh-no-I-shouldn't, want-won't. Maybe a hungry, thirsty, randy afternoon had freed him into the deeper folds of tempest-torn introspection; maybe the way was now cleared to face down the stark eloquence of a crust of bread and a white square of paper—the prime advocate of which, of course, wasn't Roisin St. Clair at all.

Such an ancient opposition; Angus had to smile. The great galumphing hunter versus the clever but obsessively self-scrutinizing prey, a creature so complete that he will not only elude your chase but lay your traps for you; better, his own. Farrell O'Phelan. You are so much your own worst enemy that I have sometimes resented you most for making me feel superfluous. We could put you alone in a room and come back the next day and you'd have neatly skinned yourself and hung yourself to dry with the guts in a pail in the corner, the blood squeegeed down the drain, the floor swabbed, the rag rinsed and wrung and hooked on the door.

The polarity went long and perfectly back. Sure, in school Farrell and Angus had both been highfliers, three-A-grade material, but MacBride's intelligence was so much more direct. He'd never had any problem seizing an argument and mercilessly supporting it. O'Phelan wormed around it, and though he'd follow through on the kill, in private he flirted with the other side—in fact, you could be sure that no matter what the lad claimed, he was secretly more attracted to saying the opposite. O'Phelan's sentences wove down the page like macramé, all to worry some niggling distinction that made zero difference in anyone's life, while MacBride's essays were short and punchy, with tight, muscular phrasing and relentlessly practical points of view. As a result, the kid now made a reasonable lecturer, since he could squirrel about a subject while the audience made cootie detectors from their programs, but he'd be a nightmare as a frontline politician; Angus was a genius. You wouldn't think it would take talent, now would you, to be able to say something in particular and then shut up?

But the harpoon of Angus MacBride versus the coil of Farrell O'Phelan—the dichotomy had extended to everything. Food, for example: O'Phelan didn't like to eat as a kid. Or he did— and he didn't—he did. Something queer. Whereas Angus: did. Full stop. Hungry-eat. Or girls: Farrell would skulk around corners and fixate on some brunette in sixth form who passed by every afternoon at 3:45. And funnily enough, he didn't pick out the poor, shy, misunderstood sort, the awkward artistic variety who might recognize a kindred outcast. Rather, he went for confident, garrulous, pretty girls with lots of friends. Angus had found this hilarious, since that was the very definition of the girls O'Phelan couldn't get. Why would such a plum choose a tongue-tied asthmatic? Even so, what did O'Phelan do? Zilch. Oh, he probably wrote about the poppet, though not to her. Why, he wouldn't even discuss his fancies, and when Angus ribbed him like any reasonable schoolboy, Farrell shot him the most acidic eyes. A violently private boy who never, in Mac-Bride's memory, got a single one of those gregarious lovelies to so much as hold his hand.

Angus, now—he'd tried to teach Farrell at the time. You like? You take. Any idea the number of women who will say yes just because you asked? MacBride got an itch for a girlie one day, he was on her doorstep the next. She said no (oh, rarely), sod her. By the end of the week he'd be off cuffoffling with someone else. Sure, some were sweeter or smarter or more—

adventurous; but they weren't that different, especially when you actually talked to them instead of ogling from the other side of the street. But O'Phelan would iconify the lass—it was so pathetically Catholic.

One thing they had in common was a preference for the other side of the fence. It was O'Phelan who'd admitted he liked Protestant girls' legs; their knees weren't all red and mashed from kneeling on wooden rails. More seriously, Farrell must have liked in them the same directness he found in MacBride—their simple Protestant laughter, with no hand over the teeth; the square posture of possessors; the sway of a ruling class that knew want-get rather than want-can't have. Anyone so tangled inside must have drooled at all that clarity—good grades, combed hair, clean nails. For the last thing O'Phelan would scan bus stops for would be more agony.

As for MacBride, he'd found Catholic girls more of a challenge, and once the Troubles set in, this predilection transformed into all-out derring-do.

Then, Farrell's failings with the ladies might have had less to do with sect than looks. He was tall, but that was the end of it—all limb. His sleeves left three inches of wrist to chap in the winter wind; his trousers never reached the top of his socks, so you could see how his legs had hardly any hair. Farrell's joints were loose and audibly creaked; his frame hung like a marionette, sticks on strings. The eyes weren't extruded exactly, but too wide-open. His hair was out of control. The cringe of shyness was almost feminine. Farrell's whole atmosphere was hysterical: he looked from side to side too often, moved abruptly and unpredictably, breathed too fast—asthma. His complexion periodically boiled. At any rate, if Angus had been a girl he'd have avoided O'Phelan. Even if Farrell wasn't exactly hideous, he did look strange.

Angus, on the other hand, was handsome. Beamingly, boyishly handsome, with a physical symmetry about him that suggested a stability of a larger sort. He had broad shoulders and a grizzly chest, short legs but otherwise perfect proportions, rich brown eyes that always looked *at* something rather than simpering off into oblivion. Angus imagined he would have made a fine World War I soldier, for he had a body made for uniforms, well cornered, erect, the kind PM's could successfully truss up in support of stupid, romantic causes, and somehow the very beauty and rhythm and material logic of the vision would inspire them to plant it squarely in range of a trench mortar. Angus was made for propaganda. Even now, a stone or two heavy and a few too many jolly nights on, he profiled well in papers and looked forceful on video.

So that was it? Ruddy, upright, popular Protestant, good at sports and trailed by the ladies, takes awkward yet bright Catholic introvert under wing, to teach him social skills and encourage his fledgling intellectual powers, to instill the confidence that has braced the Protestant from childhood? Right? And how admirable, even before '68, to cross the divide at all, much less to befriend such a sickly social millstone after one lucky lunatic interschool chess match! What magnanimity Angus must have displayed, and sure Farrell looks back on those years with tearful gratitude for the loyalty of a boy with no need to hamper his otherwise impeccable social stats!

An attractive version which, at the moment, thanks to Roisin, Angus did not have the chemical resources to indulge himself in.

O'Phelan *should* have been grateful, blast it! Och no, he flat out refused the first several of MacBride's invitations. Albert O'Schweitzer apparently had some elaborate schedule of duties and penances to perform. He was an altar boy, had a pathological relation to his schoolwork, and at any given time would be carrying on twenty chess games by mail with players all over the world. Further, he always kept a board in his bedroom, where he played against himself, and later MacBride sorted out that it was this game that absorbed the best of O'Phelan's attention. It was certainly the game that made MacBride—jealous.

So finally the saintly consumptive from Glengormley deigned to spend the afternoon with this suspiciously healthy footballer from Ballynafeigh, with his earthly ambitions and terrifying rapacity. The relationship started out as no ball of fire, either. They played chess, and Farrell acted bored. Between moves he would walk back to his own board and contemplate the *real* game. Angus smoldered. He was having a hard time getting hold of this acrobatic chess style, which never seemed to settle into recognizable gambits. And he was not used to any boy not falling over backward to ingratiate. So it must have been about the tenth afternoon, when Farrell was particularly ill behaved, sighing, standing up, looking down at the game from a condescending angle, picking up his pieces at their very tips and moving quickly as if fearful this lower level of play would contaminate him if he held it too long. Angus, however, had been watching, and after each afternoon had gone home and studied his blunders. He'd begun to discover that underneath some of these capricious moves of Farrell's lurked routine strategies. Either the sideshow aberrations were a deliberate diversion or Farrell himself didn't have the education to recognize the essentially mundane nature of his play; it was theater either way, which Angus now ignored to play the center ring. He traded off some pieces and cleaned up the board. He would never forget the look on Farrell's face—so repulsively pimply then—when he first glanced down at the game, his expression prepared with the usual yawning disdain, when he suddenly noticed he was losing. Not just starting to lose, but—in fact—Farrell sat down for once—in fact— He put his chin in his hands and sussed out his position. After five minutes he looked back up at Angus, there is no question, for the first time. Absolutely: the face that stared across that toppled king wore the look of someone who has just found a total stranger in his bedroom and who wonders how on earth this young man got here and how long he has been sitting there and why hasn't he introduced himself before. Farrell nodded, once, and smiled. Oh, it wasn't a happy smile; don't mistake Farrell for one of these sorts "just looking for a worthy opponent," don't imagine he was glad. Farrell hated being beaten, long his common denominator with Angus MacBride. Still, he held out his hand, and though the shake was weak, now Angus officially existed. It was no way to win Farrell's heart, mind you, but the best way to get his attention was to whoop his arse.

Somehow, in the gluttony that characterized MacBride from a small child, Angus felt Farrell had something he didn't and he was determined to get it. Like, when Farrell got excited, little apoplectic splotches rose to his cheeks and his hands went spastic. Angus just got louder, where Farrell would often lose his voice. What in all that did Angus *want*? Because whatever it was, he had still not gotten it; Farrell was holding out.

Angus had gone after it with a vengeance. MacBride continued to trounce Farrell at chess, getting only more solid, more methodic, better planned. To the Catholic's credit, Farrell threw no tantrums, cut the glancing down at the board and walking away, sat still and intense but polite and lost. And then he would get Angus tea and biscuits, and they would talk about Kant.

Oh, Farrell didn't lose every single game, but pretty much, when he won, it was obvious MacBride had been careless. All the same, through those years, while MacBride swallowed everything from *Modern Chess Openings* to the sorry little diagrams in the *Belfast Telegraph*, his opponent's game, without any study, also began to change. It never lost its daring, but it did shed its decoration. Every gambit MacBride played, Farrell digested for the next session. It took more and more reading to keep ahead. They never discussed it, but Farrell was breathing down his neck.

Only many years later did this subject come up, and Farrell was drunk. At that time, of course, Farrell was always drunk. Calculatedly, the accusation was in front of Angus's wife, Karen: "You never admitted why you stopped playing me at chess."

"I went to Cambridge! And on trips back I couldn't afford the time. I was organizing the YYY—"

"Crap!" Farrell had slammed the table, and slurped forward with a disgusting leer. "You *knew*, boyo. A few more months and you'd never have had another game off me in your life. You"—he jabbed—"you were afraid of me. You've always been afraid of me. And someday you'll know why."

"Fair enough." MacBride strode officiously to the cupboard, for he himself had been—imagine that—working instead of drinking from ten in the morning and was dead sober. He dropped the dusty chessboard in front of his friend. "Set them up. Or have you forgotten where they go?"

Angus drank black coffee, though he needn't have; it was pitiful, mate in twenty-two.

Farrell lurched back in his chair and poured whiskey in his glass as if it were diet apple ade. "You should see your gob sometime, when you win. It's sickening. Like a grinning fat-boy teacher just handed a lollipop. I can see sticky smears all over your puffy, self-satisfied cheeks."

"And you're the picture of chivalrous defeat?"

"You're greedy, fella. You're just one more complacent, overfed Prod, always looking over his shoulder lest the Taigs take his beefy, wheaty, sheepy land away. And you look over your shoulder, fella, and you see *me*. Farrell O'Phelan's been at your elbow since you were sixteen."

It pleased MacBride to remember this, since Farrell had to be mighty potted to get sectarian. Yet even after this bigoted tirade, when Angus had turned for a little support from his own wife, she'd gestured to the board. "What did you prove with that performance? He's poleaxed."

True enough; when Angus looked back, O'Phelan had passed out against the wall.

Then, Karen's reaction was typical. Wouldn't it make sense that the woman would be the one to throw up her hands and lay down the law: I've had it, that sloppy bar stool you brought home has to go? He's costing us ten quid a day just in whiskey, and he's abusive, what do you see in him, I don't give a toss if he's back to his ma's, tomorrow he's out on his ear? Och no! It was Angus who'd have had it up to his bake and Karen who wheedled to let his friend stay one more week. After all, when

Farrell left she was deprived of her favorite sport, which was sure analyzing the waster to death. Angus had never known a woman to talk at more length about a man; why, she couldn't have generated that much flannel about her own husband if you paid her by the word—all about Farrell's smothering mother with her double-bind signals and the essentially romantic, possessive dynamic of that relationship; Farrell's fears of desertion and the tyranny of his academic success, his cycles of "depression and grandiosity" Karen nicked from Alice Miller; how with his drinking Farrell was making a bid to be loved for himself instead of for his achievements, they were being tested, so it was more important than ever to dote on the bastard . . . Incredible, she never ran out! Why, he couldn't have reduced an opponent to less than O'Phelan during that time, most nights flat out on the floor with his fly open, a trail of saliva down his chin, red wine spilled over his shirtfront, and here his own wife would wipe the kid's face and change his shirt and hold half of him when they dragged him upstairs to bed. In fact, Farrell was light enough that Karen had occasionally carried him up by herself.

11

The MacBride Principles

When Roisin returned, the kitchen table was askew with newspaper clippings; the pad in front of MacBride was heavily crossed out.

Roisin read over his shoulder. "Not another one of those!"

"Those what?"

"Atrocity denouncements," she groaned. "I know you don't overly absorb yourself in my work, but you really should read this one. It's new." She delivered him a sheaf from her purse:

MULTIPLE CHOICE

We would like to express our horror at the sheer savagery and ruthless calculation of this gruesome act. This appalling atrocity absolutely beggars the imagination.

1. The spirit that motivated today's brutal massacre can only be decried as (a) satanic, (b) obscene, (c) brazenly hypocritical.

2. Such hell-inspired monsters will stoop to the lowest depths of (a) barbarity, (b) callousness and inhumanity, (c) vicious cowardice, having descended to (a) the worst kind of sacrilege, (b) a specially refined brand of depravity, (c) desecration beyond human sensibility.

3. These (a) diseased minds, (b) debased creatures, (c) malicious animals and their campaign of terror are a blot on (a) mankind, (b) the face of this country, (c) the name of Ireland.

4. We are repelled by this (a) fiendish Sabbath of bloodlust, (b) viperous bloodletting, (c) dark carnage of blood, consumed by a wave of revulsion beyond the limits of (a) disgust, (b) indignation, (c) contempt.

5. It is difficult to conceive of a more (a) cruel and coldheartedly sadistic act, (b) blackhearted slaughter so defying the bounds of civilized decency that the people who did it have no human thoughtfulness or kindness or sensitivity at all.

6. We are so (a) extremely, (b) completely, (c) wildly, (d) unspeakably, (e) unutterably outraged that (a) it's hard to find words to describe, (b) mere words cannot describe, (c) no condemnation is adequate to describe our (a) repugnance, (b) antipathy, (c) lack of enthusiasm.

"What's this supposed to mean?" MacBride bristled.

"It's all from the papers after Enniskillen. Did you know Tom King used the words *appalling* five and *outrage* six times in a single denouncement? And surely you recognize some of your own lines. I thought you could recycle them. No one would know the difference."

"I don't issue *poems*, Rosebud, just humble party statements. And since when do you write about the Troubles, anyway?"

"I'm not allowed?"

"Back to the old purple heather and blooming gorse. More up your street."

She folded it back. "Well, *some* people think it's grand."

"It's a dose, Rose. I don't get it."

"It simply means you might react honestly for once. The whole Six Counties would fall off its chair."

"You're on," said MacBride, fetching a drooping carrot from Roisin's icebox and speaking into the stem. "I'm delighted to announce to our Channel One audience that mourners in West Belfast have just ripped limb from limb two off-duty British soldiers. This is a great boost to the UUU, since we can finally move on from our unconvincing defense of shooting three unarmed Republicans in the back. More, the incident provides a prompt antidote to Michael Stone's lunatic attack on these same mourners two days earlier, for we have a kindergartner's attention span and will attend only to the last bad thing that happened to *our* side. Further, we are thrilled to confirm for our sectarian viewers that Catholics in Northern Ireland are the bloodthirsty barbarians we always suspected. We would like to express our special thanks to the neighborhood for performing so vividly in front of international TV cameras, though we would like to protest that British helicopter pilots were given exclusive rights to film the actual execution—think how much more toothpaste they will sell than the BBC. And on a more personal note, I would clarify that I did not know either of these young men personally and have no real emotional response to their deaths, that they merely represent a political windfall I intend to exploit.

"Until next time, when I'm sure to cash in on the grief of strangers with just the same ruthless opportunism as ever, this is Angus MacBride. Sure you'll see plenty of me soon enough at my next election, when I will broadcast a slew of half-truths about my essentially limp religious convictions and my sham of a marriage, neglecting to mention that I'm bumping the daylights out of a dishy Fenian poet whose father was a notorious Republican arms trader.

"Better?"

Roisin smiled distantly. "Angus, you're a horror."

"You see my point, love. What am I supposed to say? *Brilliant?*"

"It's no joke."

"Och, it was. You just didn't laugh."

"But all those denouncements—they're mouthing. They seem to be so sympathetic and humanitarian, when they really just stir up a taste for more blood. Or they do nothing. Maybe that's worse. Sometimes I hear you on *Ulster Newstime* decrying this or that bombing, and you could as well be reading the phone book. I do my ironing. I slice a piece of cheese."

"You've yet to suggest the statement I should make."

"Maybe none! Silence is better than fraud."

"Silence is not an option."

"It is, too. Maybe politically risky. But at least it would be emotionally true."

"Who sodding cares what's emotionally true? Women! There are other things in the world important besides feelings."

"Like what?"

"Principles."

Roisin shook her head sadly. "Maybe ambition. I don't believe you hold any principle particularly dear."

"What's got into you? What kind of ogre do you think I am?"

"I suppose I wonder."

"Damn it to hell, woman! I don't want to talk about this anyway. You came in here, I was in fine form. Now look."

"You didn't get much work done."

"I was thinking. That is my work." Angus dragged the phone over by the cord and dialed sulkily. He stood up and paced the scullery and stared into the next room. He kicked the baseboard. He snorted. He sighed and sat back down and leaned his head over the back of the chair, looking at the ceiling, tapping the receiver. He shrieked the chair out and again stalked the lino, a caged bear; then he laughed and laughed and slammed the receiver down, his skin now red and moist and his breath deep, as if he'd just walked off a squash court. He splashed his face at the sink.

Roisin rolled the carrot microphone pensively around the table.

"That dunderhead . . ." Angus toweled down. "Light goes on in that bastard's brain, he thinks the rest is technicalities. Which MacBride, of course, is to tinker up."

"What are you talking about?"

"This frigging conference. Don't you breathe a word of it now."

"Angus," said Roisin. "I've got used to keeping secrets."

So had Angus, but with that wanker on his mind all afternoon he felt in the middle of a conversation he needed to finish, and not with Karen. He'd talked so much about O'Phelan to his wife that, no, they weren't talked out exactly, but they'd arrived at their positions; though MacBride would be hard-pressed to describe hers. Whenever your man came up, Karen went dry. The distinctive wry smile on her needled him, the way she'd look down with her mouth cocked and keep peeling spuds or seeming to read.

"O'Phelan and me's staging this conference, see—"

"What for?"

"To solve everything, of course." He chuckled. "Now, were it a public conference, every party in the Province would be beating down doors to be the first to withdraw."

"Passive-aggressive abstensionism," Roisin filled in: an old discussion.

"Oh, aye. All we ever need do here is hold the Troubles official, like, and you'd have your IRA folding their arms and not deigning to participate. If they ever gave a war and nobody came, Ulster's the place. So the conference is secret, see, and like any exclusive do, everyone and his brother wants to crash the gate. We've even suggested there's something a wee bit illegal about it. And dead off the record. No press, no recordings, no cameras.

"Anyway, it's all to mobilize consensus on the power-sharing

referendum. Hash out the particulars. Not till the end of the
year, but the idea's to run it right up to the election if necessary.
Lock them all in a room. Pour enough gargle down their throats,
they'll come round."

"They hardly need more muddled thinking."

Angus looked up sharply. *"Where is my whiskey?"*

The carrot now converted from mike to rosary, which Roisin
clutched to give her strength. "I poured it out."

Even under his short beard she could see his jaw muscles
bulging. "Your drain was clogged?"

"You're drinking too much, Angus," she rushed through. "It
worries me. Listen to you, thinking the answer to our problems
here is for the Irish to drink more? And your health—"

"When I collapse stone dead on top of you upstairs, you're
to worry about my health, because only then will it be your
business, understand?"

This was not going as she'd planned. In Roisin's version
Angus ended up in tears in her lap, and then they sat down to
a sober, thoughtful cup of tea. MacBride made vows.

Roisin's fantasies were incompetent.

"Now, you're to buy a new bottle and I'll shelve it past your
reach, since you're obviously given to fits. Discussion closed."

Roisin felt a wisp of disappointment and stirred uncomfortably. It seems there had been an alternative vision. Not that she
was one of those who claimed women secretly crave a bit of
rough trade. But she did not mind the picture of nursing her
face in her hands, weeping bravely, and all to protect him from
killing himself. She wasn't fussed by bruises later as long as no
permanent damage was done. And she adored his remorse. She
relished telling the story afterward, though it jarred her to whom
she would wish to tell it first.

For while she might not enjoy being beaten, she had just
been beaten anyway, hadn't she? Angus had adjured her and
closed the argument, and she had a sick feeling she might very
well replace that bottle. But this beating was worse. Physical
brutality was a relief. In its readily apparent ugliness a victim

could find a mean little victory of her own. But when he oppressed her with his condescension, his willfulness, his big voice and sheer masculinity, she could not return with see-what-you've-done-to-me-you-animal. No, this was just defeat, because she was weak and too quiet, not as pushy or clever, and a girl.

"Point is, this bloody conference." Angus manhandled the conversation back to his work. "I'm to get Unionists to sit down with Sinn Féin. And after the lynching in Andytown! O'Phelan thinks I can waggle a finger and the Prods will come running."

"Impossible."

He laughed. "Not at all. You just don't send them the guest list!"

"Won't Unionists walk out when they see who's coming to dinner?"

"No, by the end of the year no one's going to want to be left behind. We're sorting this out, love, making history! And once power is devolved, we've got more than a wink and a nod says Tom's out and they put in a local. Your friend and mine looks to be a shoo-in."

She started. "Farrell?"

"Lord, no! Your humble servant Angus MacBride. So: vigorous campaigning, a fair lot of backroom fiddle, argy-bargy over Bush and conference engineers consensus; referendum passes; government devolves. New Secretary of State arranges IRA cease-fire."

"I think I missed something there."

"The cease-fire? We have plans A and B. A is nicey-nicey. Sheer bribery. Offer Sinn Féin a piece of Stormont. They've just enough greed and pretensions to being statesmen they might take the bait."

Roisin shook her head. "Sinn Féin is not the IRA and wouldn't have the power to call a cease-fire even if they wanted to. Britain would never include them in a power-sharing government unless they denounced violence sincerely. And if Sinn Féin abandons violence, they're one more tiny no-account Socialist Party, they might as well throw themselves into the Irish Sea. Besides, you're going to get Ian Paisley to share power with Gerry Adams? On what planet?"

Angus nodded with a funny satisfaction. By God, that lass had been listening of late. She never used to talk like this before. "Dead on. Hence: Plan B. Slam the lot in the blocks. Make internment look like a slumber party. Eliminate the grot. Been done before, could do it again. We know who they are. They call it a war; all right, then, fight one back. And win. Make them cry uncle." He smiled. "Uncle Angus."

"How would you manage that with power-sharing?"

"I said share. Not give it away."

Roisin found she was shaking. "I'm a Republican. Would you lock me in Long Kesh?"

"For writing wee poems about Enniskillen? Hardly. But should you start up the family business again, I'd drive you to Maze myself."

"Your cronies don't know the difference. They'd take one look at my address and go straight to the strip search. My God," she mumbled to herself, "I'm the lover of a Nazi."

"Typical melodramatic Republican overstatement."

"You're talking about a police state, aren't you? When you violate the rules of democratic process, you undermine its whole foundation. You're on a slippery slope to the Reichstag."

"Bloody hell, Northern Ireland *isn't* a democracy, this is supposed to be your line! Army on the streets, Diplock courts— Britain runs this place like an only so benevolent summer camp. Be good wee campers, or have your privileges revoked at any time. What you're always saying, and with which I, very privately, agree. I've told Tom myself, toe the line and keep your nose clean and look pretty for the *Boston Globe* OR be a shite. Britain waffles back and forth. A kangaroo-court system, unwarranted searches, detention without charge; a little censorship here, the odd murder there, and then they let the blight get elected to public office and give speeches in City Hall! If you're going to be a shite, be a brilliant shite, right? Because what's so grand about democracies anyway, when they elect prats? And even democracies aren't democracies, you know that! Where's all your cynical socialist rhetoric when I need it, that capitalism-media manipulation guff you grew up with? Look at America now: sure they 'choose' their President, but do they choose whom they choose from? And do they 'choose' what they know about those characters? No! Do they have the remotest idea why they vote for whom they do? Not a freaking chance! But does it matter, long as the place doesn't go to hell? Frankly, democracy is awkward and reliably a sham. It doesn't work very well. Where dictatorship can be a highly efficient form of government. It's underrated."

It flickered through Roisin's head that maybe he was having her on. Sometimes Angus exercised out loud. He liked to see what he could get away with.

"I prefer a government that doesn't work very well. Inefficacy is protection. Efficient? Efficiently what? Does it matter that the trains are on time if they're on their way to Treblinka?"

"Spare me, Rosebud, there's few things I despair of more than dragging out concentration camps every time a discussion gets sticky. Leave the poor dead Jews in peace. Can we get back on track here? I'm a decent person, and so is O'Phelan, though he'd never admit it to your face. But I just think there's a place for results. I live in a world with this table, that carrot. Solid, see. Not a bunch of what-ifs and therefores. I see it all the time, the RUC getting so tangled up in its due process, mincing around West Belfast, well, we can't do this, we can't do that, and are the Provies following any such rules? No sir! Someone's fighting dirty, you fight dirty back. It's practical. I'm practical. Okay, Gibraltar. You flush out a murderer, he'd just as soon shoot you as blink, and you shoot him first. Simple. And you save people's lives. You can't wring your hands your whole life. You were right, calling me on that: principle's only so important to me. It's a slippery bugger anyway, 'cause you can turn any principle around to support what you please. So I stick with reality. I care about what happens. And put in my hands, I could make North-ern Ireland a bloody decent place to live."

Angus was breathing hard.

"When you sink to a terrorist's level, there's no difference between you and him anymore."

"Am I threatening to plant a bomb in your courthouse if I don't get what I want? Were the Allies the same as the Axis just because they fought back? There's plenty of difference. That's just the kind of ooh-worms aphorism comes from liberal castrati have lost the power to act in the world."

Roisin's eyelids matted. "I wish you'd let me differ with you without mocking me like that."

"Don't get personal, Rosebud! How are we ever to discuss anything if you take it personal?" He ruffled her head and pressed it to his coat. "I know you're just taking the other side, and sure you should, it's good steam. But you've your own sensible bits or I couldn't stand the sight of you. It's O'Phelan's on my mind, see. Any idea the times we've been through this palaver? He has to hair-tear and screw everything apart until you're left with fuck-all—like tinkering with your car until it's strewn along the road in wee pieces, and all the king's horses and all the king's men can't put your Peugeot together again. I couldn't count the times we've started into some simple, tangible problem like how to win this election or even which pub to crawl, and in five minutes we're paralyzed over how morality is pure defense of self-interest, and that would be important if anything was im-portant, but it's not because meaning is socially created, but then if you can see that, there is no meaning until the two of us are plopped in the middle of the footpath with our heads in our hands, like the three sillies can't fish the moon from the lake."

"There's something to be said for self-examination."

"You won't catch me saying it. It's bleeding dangerous. I think? You stick with your common sense, your gut. Goodness? It's good to pay a call on your old gran. O'Phelan will tell you now, you don't visit the biddy because it's good but because it makes you *feel* good, so it's bad. So he doesn't go. That's improvement? And turn it around enough times, you call on her all right, but to Raskolnikov the bird in the back of her head with a meat ax. That's your self-examination for you."

"Angus—do you *like* Farrell?"

MacBride laughed. "That's like asking do I like my mother. You love her or hate her, there's no in between."

"So, do you love him or hate him?" she pressed.

The question sat him down. "Haven't a clue," he admitted. "Between O'Phelan and me, it's something bigger. I don't think there's a name for it." He laughed. "But don't I sound like the lad himself, now? You've never met him, have you?"

"You've not introduced us," said Roisin.

"I should, I should . . ."

Angus had repeatedly promised to introduce Roisin to Farrell for over a year now, but had never, strangely, come across. In the meantime, O'Phelan had surfaced so constantly in Mac-Bride's conversation she felt long ago she knew the man. "Why do you want me to meet him?"

"The bastard would sure make a play for you. It would exhilarate me to watch you turn him down."

She curved the subject. "You know, I can't imagine Farrell supporting internment."

"Farrell O'Phelan would support the Spanish Inquisition if it suited his purposes. He may twist his hankie in his leisure time, but he's the second most ruthless man I've ever known. Where he got the reputation as St. Francis is beyond me."

"Second most."

Angus beamed.

"I know West Belfast and you don't," said Roisin. "You won't keep those people down. Put a husband in jail, three sons will take his place."

Angus nosed into the icebox again, as if his steak and eggs might meanwhile have been generated by the sheer force of his hunger. "O'Phelan agrees with you. He doesn't go for Plan B, not because it's immoral, but because it won't work. Claims we'll never do a truly reputable job of oppression here. Opts for Plan C. Drab, but possible. Move, anywhere—power-sharing, integration, doesn't matter, just close the book, so it doesn't seem like if you kick and scream enough you might well get your way. Internal solution, we say. Then do nothing. *Absolutely nothing*. Take precautions, but let them blow up this station and that soldier and ignore it. Don't try for a cease-fire, don't pay them that much attention. Don't react. They'll get bored. The IRA will never quite go away, that's too much to expect, but they could simmer back down to lunatic fringe. Besides, O'Phelan says we'd miss them."

"You certainly would. Raving about the Provisionals is about the only time I see you completely happy outside of bed."

"Then eventually, should it be economically advantageous," he carried on, "you may get your united Ireland. And between you and me, I hope it happens. Just for revenge. Mean-spirited, vicious Proddie revenge."

"You lost me."

"Rosalita, I could taste it! Sure there'd be dancing in West Belfast to 'The Fields of Athenrye.' But the whole of the Bogside and south Armagh would wake up the next morning with a throbbing headache, in a right blue funk. Still on the dole, still married to a fat girn, and someone still has to fetch out for milk and a loaf. Except no more freaking riots. No more sonorous funerals, just your ordinary dead people. And those poor Provos, all used to sneaking off to Libya like your da, or riding Semtex under car seats, hearts whomping though checkpoints across the border—what are they to do now, go for drives on the Antrim coast and pick bluebells? Och, Rose darling, I would rub my hands, I would laugh myself silly. Stick 'em with what they want, I say. Just for revenge."

"Then why not get it now? Give over."

"Simple. Fact is—and you must never let this out—I don't give a tuppenny damn, really, which way this place tips. Makes no practical difference. But I won't have bad behavior rewarded.

When a child throws a wobbler you don't hand it a sweet. Meanwhile, the United Kingdom is a farce and will shrink to plain old England in the end. Republicans will get this island at the end of the day, so why not let the Loyalists win in the short run."

"They've had it for three hundred years!"

"So what's fifty more? Besides, it comes down to this: *I will not lose.* If I were Catholic, I suppose I'd feel the same way. So it's all a matter of who's cagier. Ask O'Phelan, there are no issues here. Winning and losing, it's one of the only political scenarios on earth with any purity left."

Angus had been ranging the kitchen rummaging cupboards like a full patrol of Brits; next thing he'd be prying up the floor. Much as snarling over the Provisionals was his most cherished pastime, he did not seem quite focused on this last part. His eyes narrowed off, his hand pulled at his tie, until he wheeled abruptly to his briefcase and rustled out a magazine. "Here." He mashed his big forefinger on the face of a bleary photo. "Tell me. That's talent? You find that attractive?"

Roisin took the *Fortnight* with a long, shrewd look at Angus before turning to the picture: an intent, inclined head with crazed eyes.

Angus recognized Roisin's smile as the same one Karen used and snatched the magazine back. "Well? That's Romeo?"

"No," she said slowly, unable to dispose of the smile right away. "More Peter O'Toole."

"You're codding me."

"No, early O'Toole. Just a little. And yes, he is rather attractive."

Angus crumpled the *Fortnight* back in his briefcase. "Don't see it. Never have. Skinny creature. No shoulders. Looks reasonable in a suit, I suppose. In the buff? Ridiculous. Arms too long. A glype. Should have seen him at nineteen. Covered in spots. A wonder even now his face doesn't look like a strip mine." Angus kept fussing with the clasp and it wouldn't close. Roisin looked amused. "Well, I can't comprehend it!" he exploded. "Even in university, you put O'Phelan in the same room with a girl, he lit out for the Cave Hill and she booked for America! And later, sure, he had his nutty romances, not with the barkiest items, mind you, but dead stupid, always trying to take care of him and coming to me on the sly to get him off the brew—"

Roisin's little laugh was of an obscure complexion.

"—Och, you know those motherly Catholic sorts spend their whole lives banging themselves up on a cross, as if a soul will give them credit later, when I don't figure even God himself gives them a glance. All that happens, really, is a lad takes their money and cakes and pot roasts and snuggles between their big overgenerous breasts, and walks off, pockets jingling with the silver. Well, if you were a glutton for suffering, O'Phelan was your man. They'd fix him breakfast, he'd call them names, but I understood—some women are like that. And then there was that deranged marriage after knowing the kid two days or something, which isn't even long enough to get her pregnant and have a reasonable excuse. Now, she was a looker all right, but they both thought they were making a bloody film, they did, because in real life two days of courting doesn't wash, thank you very much, which I figure they discovered about day three.

"Fair enough, those were rough times here; just walking down the road was dicey, and you never knew when the Seville with the Christmas tree air freshener dangling from the mirror would be your last parked car on earth; it made women do loopy things, though this one was Norwegian or something . . . In those days, the Norwegians were everywhere. All this, all right, but the last five years! The boy's a regular fancy man! And all I see is Gumby. About as sexy as the Harland and Wolff cranes."

"There's more than looks to attractiveness, isn't there? And everything I've ever heard about Farrell O'Phelan, from you or anyone, makes him sound a terribly fascinating man."

"FASCINATING?" It was so much the perfect word to set him afire that Angus might have stopped to consider she had chosen it with incendiary care. "Is it fascinating not to know what you

want, to be morbidly afraid of sex? Is it fascinating to be unhappy? Sure doesn't that cover most of the world? And is it even
useful, in a place as polarized as this, to be against everyone,
when the one relief of having a war is being on somebody's side?
And is failure fascinating? Because what's Farrell ever done,
what's he amounted to? Fine, he's a hotelier, and by sheer luck,
mind you, so he can get his shirts made with wee initials on the
collar and order twenty-quid French wines. But your man
dropped out of university! Not a term before earning his degree!
And that's typical, of course, not deigning to take part, quite,
in ordinary people's education, when who knows, maybe he got
one bad mark! He's like that, you know. All or nothing. Well,
pretty reliable, isn't it, in a world you have to share with a few
other folks, that means the choice is going to be nothing?

"But I matriculated, with a first, and went to law school; I
worked hard and nights, and finagled my way up the political
ladder during bloody hard times in this country. That's pedestrian somehow, knowing what you want and working for it and
getting it? Because what's so dead fascinating about going from
pundit philosopher to curbside dipso? That's what Farrell was
up to while I was in the stacks: splayed out on the lawn of
Queen's, where he no longer attended class, screaming at
marches too stocious to stand up or even to get out of the rain.
Still, didn't I give the kid a hand anyway, digs here, tea there,
the only meals the boyo ever saw save the rashers from the
women he lived off? And how many of my tenners went down
that throat? While things were right tight those years, and every
note I gave him went to Talisker—Rose, I won't touch that
brand now, can't even stand the sound of it. Christ, is there
anything less fascinating than a drunk?

"But right, now the women flutter around him, Trinity and
Oxford ask him to speak, *Panorama* has him on TV. And why?
Because of that rinkydink bomb-disposal business, when by all
rights that should have landed him not on the BBC but in a
private room in the Maze. It was illegal! He withheld evidence

from the RUC and willfully destroyed it! How many terrorists are still on the loose thanks to Mister Helpful?

"But that's Farrell, renegade risk taker, and it must make every female's heart go pitter-pat. And, you know, I could handle Sinn Fein if I had to, long as I held my nose, but I leave them to Farrell, because he likes consorting with scuts—"

"Oh, Angus," Roisin sighed.

"I just mean O'Phelan's worse than the tourists! And then he's so *unstable*. That's the attraction, too, of those stories you've heard? Why, O'Phelan himself will slip into any conversation in the first five minutes what a horlicks he once made of his life, and never without hinting that he might do it again while you're watching. Almost a promise, like. When what's wrong with being reliable, what makes that so flat? Couldn't we all fall apart now?"

"No," decided Roisin. "It takes a certain integrity to fall apart."

"Rubbish! All that precariousness is self-indulgent! And so is expecting some lovely will always come along and warm your broth and hold your hand!"

Roisin had started to laugh. Hard. She was clutching her stomach. It was the laugh that always melted him, the descending tin whistle, the eternal schoolgirl.

"Really!" Angus persisted, but her laugh was contagious, and his own mouth tugged. "Couldn't I be a perfectly marvelous piss artist? Couldn't I loll around on the floor from ten in the morning as well as the best of them?"

"No, no, no—" Tears trailed her cheeks. "No, you couldn't. You don't have it in you, teddy bear. So I'm sorry I poured out your whiskey. You'd never make a drunk, Angus. I'll buy you another bottle. It was all a mistake."

Angus chortled and agreed, but somehow felt—insulted, all the same.

"Oh, sweetheart," she sighed, stroking his face. "I wonder if you ever talk so passionately about me."

12

Americans Have Good Teeth

Clive Barclay was a doctoral candidate in political science newly arrived from the University of Iowa. Damien discovered the student morosely propped in the Eglantine Inn over a shandy. Clive had been trying to sample local drinks, but the shandy, half beer, half lemonade, was understandably making him woozy. His interviews about Gibraltar lasted only as long as it took a pint of Guinness to settle, for The Egg was a newish, mahogany-stained pub with bright-blue upholstery, chockful of Queen's undergrads. No place, Damien whispered, to find what was really going on. To get inside, you really had to go to a Republican club.

Damien dragged the latest American amusement to the Green Door, which frankly was inside only in the sense of being out of the rain. The Green Door was the butt of all Belfast, home of the paramilitary unemployed. The club probably owed its original reputation to Sylvester, which he spelled *Sailbheaster* to support the Struggle, Malone. Sailbheaster dressed in black jeans, black turtleneck, black leather jacket with black leather gloves even in the warmest of seasons. His dark glasses gleamed over Doc Marten boots propped on a back table, a black beret cocked over one lens. Night after night he perched there, sipping his one pint—his mother wouldn't give him money for more— licking his lips and sucking beer through his teeth. Should the odd stranger light in, Sailbheaster would finger his balaclava and confide, just between the two of you, he was recruiting for the INLA.

Sailbheaster at one time caused the patrons of the Green Door considerable embarrassment, but over the years he had achieved the status of mascot. When customers passed him on the way in, they didn't knock him on the shoulder like a boyo but petted his jacket or rumpled his beret, and if anyone had something to celebrate, they bought the recruiter a drink, like throwing him a bone. When they tired of Clive, they would feed him to Sailbheaster.

"*Taoiseach dail padhraigh pearse!*" Damien cried on entering with Clive in tow.

"Your head's a marley," said Callaghan.

"*Luchann alaibh*, Michael," said Damien, kicking Callaghan and jerking his head toward Clive. "*Ta Americanle. Ar freisin drinkoine. Te understandua, eejiteanna?*"

"Ach, right! *Ard fheis! Ard Chomhairle! Bus Eirreann!*"

"*Chucky arla. Slantia ceili an phoblacht.*"

"*MacStoafain o'muillior sinn féin! Fianna fail fine gael charlie haughey RTE. Clannad gay burn aer lingus.* Yeats! GAA! Och! Um, och . . ."

At one time the Green Door's loos were labeled in Irish, but the signs had to be changed because the customers kept going in the wrong bog.

Quickly the crowd circled around Clive and his microcassette recorder, graciously conceding to speak in English for the sake of their guest.

Callaghan began a tale, turning the white scar on his temple toward Clive. "It's after midnight, right. Out for a stroll all by myself like, and I look about and fuck me pink! if I'm not in the dead center of Sandy Row. Murals of King Billy and memorials to John McMichael swirling round my head, glossy photos of Princess Di gooning through in every window, red, white, and blue scuffing up my trainers. So I flip right off my chump—"

"Ends up in Sandy Row by accident, do you follow?" Shearhoon nudged Clive. "And lived here all his life? Sure the American here could have steered you clear of the hole, Michael."

"And I find myself shouting," Callaghan proceeded, not to have his story undermined. "*Black Fenian bastards*—!"

"Doesn't make any sense, lad," Shearhoon intruded again. "*Black Fenian bastards?*"

"I was half mad with discrimination in this vicious sectarian police state."

"Half tore, more likely," Damien muttered.

Clive pressed his recorder forward. "Do you experience regular infringement on your civil rights?"

"Does the Pope shit in the woods?" asked Callaghan. "Are bears Catholic?"

Clive looked confused.

"So before I know what I'm about," Callaghan went on, "out hunkers a pack of fifteen-stone Proddies—"

"Och, sure you got them out of bed!"

"Duffed me up drastic. So naturally, after getting patched at the Royal, I report my misadventure to your local champions of justice, right? Fill out the peelers' bleeding forms. Nip round to the NIO in the morning. Sue for *lack of police protection*. Well routine."

Shearhoon's eyes narrowed. "That red Toyota out front—?"

Callaghan jingled the keys for all to see.

"Fucking hell!" moaned Damien. "How much?"

"Five thousand quid," said Michael modestly.

"You sly old shitpot, you!"

"I seem to recall," noted Shearhoon, "you whinging for a car before your *misadventure*, do you follow?"

"Now, what did you shout exactly?" Damien tugged at Callaghan's shirt. "What street?"

"I don't get it," Clive interrupted.

"Restitution," Shearhoon explained. "For sectarian violence. The Brits have a rating system, d'you know? Set quid per broken bone."

"Stitches," Callaghan announced, "pay top dosh."

"But that's . . ." Clive calculated, "eight thousand dollars!"

"Not bad for a night's work, eh?" Callaghan winked. Everyone in the club was very proud of him.

Estrin had hitherto kept her mouth shut to hide her accent, the way some women avoid smiling to disguise bad teeth. At last she couldn't resist. "I read the other day that, in the last eight years, out of all the suits against the U.K. for tripping over loose paving stones, 98 percent were from Northern Ireland. Twenty thousand claims. In one district, like, sixty homes made up for a hundred and fifty stumbles."

"Aye," commiserated Shearhoon. "The state of the footpaths in this town is desperate."

"The crown forces maintain roads only for troop transports," Callaghan pointed out. "They couldn't be arsed over footpaths."

"Up to thirteen claims in a single family," said Estrin. "So maybe it's not the sidewalks, Michael. Whole families of spastics. I've met a few."

"Och, up the road from me," Damien volunteered, "a lad prized up one of them stones to throw at the Brits. His ma steps out to fetch him in and falls in the hole, see? Breaks her arm. Sues. Two thousand quid."

"Beautiful," whistled Callaghan.

Now Estrin had betrayed herself, Clive launched predictably into the whole where-are-you-from. On hearing Estrin lived on

Springfield Road, he sighed. "Queen's found me an apartment off Malone. It's very nice," he despaired. "But gosh. You must get searched by the army and everything."

"Only once," she consoled him. "They were surprisingly polite."

"Do the Provos give you a hard time? Hijack your car, take over your house?"

"No, it's not like that. I figure they know I'm there; it's a small place. But a little five-foot-two foreigner doesn't seem to worry them much. If you know anything about Provos, you assume they won't take me seriously because I'm a girl."

"Has stuff, you know, gone off?"

"Well, there's an RUC station across the way that gets petrol-bombed a lot—" She cut herself off, because she couldn't bear people who bragged about bombs. "But otherwise it's quiet. You go shopping, you put up with the Brits, it's—just poor. Mostly it's very poor. Excuse me." She ducked behind the bar to slice lemon for G&T's no one had ordered. She didn't want to be seen talking to Clive very long.

Luckily Duff took over, and Estrin rolled her eyes. Iowa! Back home they were aghast: *Belfast*. When on Malone Road you could as well live in Scarsdale—hardwoods, big brick houses, boisterous Presbyterians washing their cars. In one of those mysterious bodies that managed to be both scrawny and overweight at the same time, Clive leaned forward and dipped his head with bovine regularity. When patrons insulted him, he never looked hurt or angry but only the more interested. That Midwestern nasality twanged in her ear like a badly tuned guitar. No doubt he had Irish ancestors, and arrived with the usual prepared Republican sympathies, the whole tatty anti-imperialist Tinkertoy mock-up she got enough of at the Green Door and could not abide in Americans—

Estrin was not sure what did it, what turned. Duff's arm was still around Clive's shoulders, and the Iowan was buried gratefully in the huge staypuff armpit as in a beanbag chair. Shearhoon had been one of the first people she'd met in Belfast, during those long three months waiting for a black virus to show itself, avoiding men for once for their sakes, living in a bombed-out house with the ceiling caved in. How grateful she, too, had been for the snuggery of Shearhoon, the way he had hugged her just like that but never with the suggestion of a pickup, not only because he was a middle-aged fat man and she was pretty, but because he couldn't be bothered; why, undressing must have taken Duff an hour or more. How much he preferred to order her a "hot black Bush" and wink, to take her touring West Belfast in his sputtery hatchback, which the joyriders had so far ignored because it was too ridiculous to be seen in—fluffy furred seat-covers with tiger stripes. It smelled of dog and Duff didn't have one.

For it was Duff put her on to the Green Door, Duff helped her wrangle with the Housing Executive for 133, reminding Estrin that she had successfully negotiated foreign countries all over the world not only from self-reliance but because someone had always been nice to her at the start. And here she was avoiding Clive Barclay like a bowel-bypass bag.

Didn't Estrin know better than anyone how hard it was to travel as an American? Inside it, the United States may stretch from the New York island to the country highlands, but a quick ocean away the country shrinks to a coffin, in which the rest of the world will bury you. Oh, they know so much about you—your race problems, your swimming pools. Sure, when the crack is slack, you can always pick on the Yanks—their trumpeting laugh, their hot-apple-pie flab. How often had her foreign companions looked straight at Estrin's dark solid cottons and complained about Americans' loud polyester clothes? For soft as your speech, local as your larder, you will never defy the facts: you have a belting voice and you feast on croissantwiches. You have money but no class, good distribution but no culture. You have no sense of history. You shower incessantly; you are obsessed with flush toilets; you have good teeth. You are right-wing. You may have gone to Yale, but your schools have no standards, so while you surely have strong, unfounded convictions about Afghanistan, you picture the country somewhere off the coast of East Africa. You are boastful. You will confide the most intimate details of your personal life to strangers. Your loyalty is easily won, but just as easily lost. You have a Cadillac smile, and when you invite the natives to your home in America you don't mean it. You travel largely to collect objects and to confirm opinions already in trim by the time you leave Kennedy. Experience is one more object, of no value unless you save it on film and can therefore show off Armalite-riddled Republican murals to your friends in Coralville. You are fascinated with violence but fundamentally unacquainted with the real thing; you imagine blood comes in bottles like ketchup, and when a shoot-out is over everyone wipes up and orders carry-out fajitas. You think the world is one big Epcot Center got up for your entertainment. Since you do not know real pain, they can mock you with impunity. You do bleed ketchup. This is the box. It's smaller than a coffin, really—closer to the size of a TV.

While Estrin scavenged the world for extravagant Scots, crybaby Englishmen, slovenly Germans, fair-minded white South Africans, and Jewish mothers who won't feed you a damn thing, there was a generosity she was willing last of all to tender her own ken. With a father who gave a third of his moderate salary to the ACLU and Amnesty International and still felt guilty for indulging himself with a pint of expensive ice cream, Estrin had packed off with her inheritance of liberal shame, an apologist for her nation, racing to deprecate her people before strangers like a Wild West quick draw. After ten years of beating by joining, Estrin had become the worst of the lot. Estrin Lancaster was anti-American.

"Here." She put a double J.D.-on-the-rocks down in front of Clive. "Compliments of Philadelphia." She smiled, Cadillac-wide.

As her own easy derision of Clive Barclay haunted her the whole next week, she grew obsessed with the idea that everyone was making fun of her behind her back. Estrin's mere presence in

Belfast read as voyeurism to most, and maybe it was. When she mentioned attending the funeral of the Gibraltar victims attacked by Michael Stone, she noticed how locals glanced at each other and smiled. *And weren't you tickled pink there was trouble. Didn't the* pock-pock *of those grenades shiver your pretty neck? Bastard's trying to kill us and to you it's a merit badge, a story on the phone. You cow. Why did you even go if you think Republicanism is so empty? Looking to get shot at? Grow up. The rest of us are ducking while you're taking snapshots.* And Belfast after Jerusalem, the Philippines, Berlin—hadn't Farrell called her a "conflict groupie," and wasn't that as justified as lambasting Clive for his swish Iowa haven on Malone Road? Wasn't her own choice of Clonard, smack on the Peace Line, far more comic? Estrin felt tacky. When she worked out in the Queen's gym, she felt less the disciplined athlete than one more skinny single in her thirties, sweating off cellulite, afraid of getting old. The Moto Guzzi seemed ostentatiously tough, the rev of her throttle a show of bravado from the small. Her own vowels skirled in her ears; she virtually stopped talking. For she could hear how often her jokes were flat, her politics simplistic, her tales tattered from repetition and transparently self-serving. Even ordering farls in O'Hara's, Estrin read in the baker's eyes, *Another American, titillated*, and Estrin skeltered out, fumbling with the door, pushing when she should have pulled. She skulked after work to her house on Springfield Road, crunching around the carcasses of burned overturned lorries, thinking, Wouldn't Daddy approve—slumming with the underprivileged. Then, admit it, you really could wire home for money in a jam. This is playacting, *Strapped Like Me*; is there anything more bourgeois? All that travel seemed suddenly rootless and grasping. Meanwhile, the bulge of pints and the bars of the Multigym warped her reflection; the Guzzi's tailpipe pitted her face with bits of missing chrome; the round pushover cheeks bloated upside down in spoons.

By the end of the week she was so withered by her own condescension that Damien asked if she'd lost weight. At work she mumbled and was often asked to repeat the tab. She did not banter. It was Duff Shearhoon's pillow of a palm that raised her chin. "Why so tucked in, little one?"

She sighed. "I feel preposterous."

"Brilliant!" Shearhoon beamed around the club. "You'll fit right in."

Give me a break is an American expression. Her impatience with prepackaged socialism aside, many of these men had been kicked and jeered at as *scrotes* by the British Army, searched and detained just for being Catholic, refused the right to take a leak or get a drink of water for hours, and while a lot of the abuse was minor, it added up, and it was often the little things that got you; surely at one time or another they had all gone home red in the face from their spread-eagle in Castlereagh, vowing to get the bastards back. It was a big leap from there to the IRA and Estrin wouldn't make it in her most understanding of days, but she could see the jump was short on Whiterock Road. For everyone in the bar that night broke Estrin's heart. Somehow Estrin had spent two hours or something talking to Clive all about his parents' farm, one of the last small concerns left in the state. She'd had him describe the outbuildings and his mother's cotton print housedresses and the tongue sandwiches in his school lunches when he was eight—

It was all inconceivable now that she had somehow roped herself into introducing the guy to the Linen Hall Library this morning, another chilly parting with Farrell behind her and all her generosity and goodheartedness out the window. She saw Clive standing on the steps, a dowdy American grad student losing his hair young, looking all smiles and surely expecting Estrin to still be this friendly Philadelphian flat out riveted by what he'd fed his cows. She glowered. *Clive was boring.*

Clive began admiring how lovely she looked in a dress; she cut him off with "Well, get the flattery in now, you won't see this often," and swept up the stoop. Clive trailed after her, bewildered.

The library calmed the girl somewhat. Like Whitewells, its

wide banisters, thick tables, and embracing dark-green chairs suggested resort, as if there were some place on earth that was safe. Walls of hardcovers implied comfortingly that there really was something to say. Of course, it would take only one strategic brown paper package left at the desk to put a hole in that one—stray pages, music sheets, overdue notices fluttering over Central Arcade. But today Estrin let the library lie to her: there was such a thing as wisdom and order. If you had a problem you could look it up and have it all explained to you; chaos was misunderstanding. If the world seemed askew outside these enormous, mahogany-framed windows, you had done inadequate research.

When Estrin said *Politics* the librarian bloomed and said, "You mean the Troubles collection!" in the same voice she would have directed the girl to *Curious George Goes to School*. Soon a gangling young man with punked red hair and hoop earrings swung down the aisle singing The Pogues. "Right." He clapped his hands and took them to the attic, where book piles and looseleafs burgeoned between stacks. "So what's this thesis about, then?" he asked Clive.

"The Troubles," said Clive.

The librarian, Robin O'Baoigheallain, listened patiently on the edge of his desk. When nothing more was forthcoming, he prodded, "Right, go on."

Clive's eyes panicked the close-packed room. "You know—Protestants and Catholics . . . just the last twenty years, of course. The . . . Troubles."

Robin roared. He slapped his thighs. He dabbed the corners of his eyes. The Americans waited for the curator to recover. "Kid," he wheezed, "our first-formers do better than that. This whole floor is the Troubles. You'd as well write a paper on the Planet, A.D."

"B.C.," said Estrin. "Neanderthal man."

"American?" he noted.

"We're everywhere. And yes, I'm being condescending. I get tired of finding this petty feud so interesting. Of being so careful and understanding and conceding the complexities.

Sometimes this place makes me sick. Your collection"—she nodded—"makes me sick."

"Aye," said Robin. "Me as well. But it's brilliant still, what
we've got here. I can show you about. It's fuckin' brilliant."

It was brilliant: cases full of Ulster Volunteer Force mufflers,
UDA sweatbands, *Ulster Say's No* coffee mugs, *No Pope Here*
buttons, Orange Order tea towels; full-color Republican resistance calendars, hunger-strike postcards, Sinn Féin daily diaries,
tiny gold Armalites for the lapel—though, Robin noted, a few
of their own punters had complained that maybe Sinn Féin might
take the Armalites off their Christmas cards. Both sides had
contributed an array of cassettes, from *We Hate the IRA* to *Irish
Republican Jail Songs*, with three-color printed labels and professional recordings of "The Extradition Song," "The Sniper's
Promise," "Proud to Be a Prod." The funeral of Larry Marley,
attacked by the RUC in 1987, was now out in video.

Robin explained that every week somewhere in the world a
book was published on the Troubles, and the attic was running
out of space, the skirmish raw material for the voracious industry
of intellection: *Nation, Class, and Creed in Northern Ireland; Vogt:
Konfessionskrieg in Nordirland?; Guerre Civile en Irlande; La Rumeur
irlandaise* . . . Surely Linen Hall stashed the final triumph of
imperialism, where academics from Oxford and Harvard would
do their stint in the hinterlands, to poke and take notes as if the
whole Province had become an obliging laboratory, its factions
performing diseases. For the parties obliged—eager for attention, both Sinn Féin and the UDA promptly delivered issues of
Combat, Welcome to Fascist Ulster pamphlets, and *Ard fheis* agendas
by the box every month, anxious to be recorded, sonorous in
their responsibility to History, here a somewhat cheapened Muse
who mythologized tragedies overnight: if IRA volunteers were
murdered in November, their ballad would be out on cassette
to meet the Christmas rush. In an economy where DeLorean's
cars rusted in ignominy north of town and Harland and Wolff's
once great shipyard came so near folding for lack of work that
Protestants and Catholics were actually marching off to Margaret

Thatcher *together*, History was Ulster's last viable export, churned out and cartoned off, volunteers packed into caskets like so much soap. Weary of foreign hyenas picking over his stacks for scintillating tidbits to beef up yet another manuscript, it was little wonder that when Clive chimed, "I thought of maintaining this isn't a religious but a *tribal* war . . . and that the Protestants suffer the same *siege mentality* of the Afrikaaner . . ." Robin only winced.

Novelists, of course, had gotten in on the feed for years, until Northern Ireland could take credit for a whole rather cheerless genre, "Troubles fiction," shelved down one wall: *Tears of the Shamrock, Burning Your Own, Suffer! Little Children, The Armalite Maiden; The Begrudgers, The Pact, The Contract, The Committee, The Extremists; Blood Sister, Bigotry and Blood, Ties of Blood, Fields of Blood* . . . In front of these on the floor, paging limply through *Dreams of Revenge*, was a small mousy woman with thin, uncombed hair and dirty jeans. Robin whispered that she was a writer from New York City. She had evidently grown so terrified of suggesting Chichester Street became Wellington Place without being sure to mention that for a block it was Donegall Square North, or not writing a conversation that would fill the full forty-minute bus ride to the airport—inaccuracies in fiction that locals mocked over a pint—that she was now completely blocked, and spent her whole day in the library combing *Victims* or *The Provo Link* for mistakes to avoid. She cried a lot, said Robin, steering them away. Sometimes late in the day he'd feed her sips from his hip flask, like administering spoonfuls of cough syrup to a congested child, and one afternoon he'd gone so far as to suggest to her that once upon a time, long, long ago, there were novelists who made things up.

Estrin flipped through *The Irish Information Partnership: Agenda*. The *Agenda* was not a single publication but a yearly subscription. Hardbound, oversized, with good-quality paper. It cost six hundred pounds a year. Inside, every injury and murder was neatly categorized by religion and agent. Estrin stopped at "Fatal Casualties by Type of Incident," with columns labeled

Riot, Specific Explosion, Anti-Personnel Explosion, Gunbattle/
Crossfire, Sniper Activity, Ambush, Assassination at Place of
Work, Assassination at Home of Victim, Assassination at Place
of Leisure . . . It was cross-indexed. It had bar graphs. And it
would prove whatever theory your little heart desired.

"Clive," said Estrin, "why not study the studies?"

"Come again?"

"I mean it. I've never seen a smudge on a map so examined
to death in my life. You realize that even the deadweight at the
Green Door have been on TV three or four times? I've got
neighbors, housewives and unemployed plumbers, who have
announced they will no longer give interviews. Study that."

Clive looked skeptical. "I don't get it."

"Clive, why are we here? Last week there was a German
film crew up my street. They paid off a group of kids on either
side of the Peace Line to start a riot. The crew helped collect
bottles. A friend of Malcolm's ended up in the hospital because
he was turning to mug for the cameras and a brick smacked him
upside of the head."

Robin liked the idea. It was cynical.

Estrin weaseled out of lunch with Clive and remained to talk
with Robin, in whom the Troubles inspired only malicious disinterest—the black carnival had worn thin. Rapidly he deserted
politics to enthuse over the new Hot House Flowers and the
Traveling Wilburys. He collected 1930s sheet music. He showed
Estrin the prized curlew skull he had recently found on Bally-
castle beach. Amazing, he led a perfectly festive existence without the help of one car bomb or SLR. Estrin hadn't found anyone
like him since she'd arrived: Robin was the gem of his own
collection. He reminded her of her best friend in Philadelphia,
of her best friend in Israel, of her best friend in Berlin. It was
a rare business now in Estrin's life that anyone got to be simply
himself.

For Estrin knew she was getting older when everyone she met
reminded her of someone else. Strangers promptly factored into

primes—with the smile of some German's brother, the strident voice of a rival from ten years ago. For Estrin this was loss of innocence: people were no longer fresh. Memory tainted even stray passengers in black taxis—spectacles on the bumper seat clouded with a fellow counselor's lenses in Berlin. At bus stops a man would blur not into the person standing next to him but into the person who had been standing in exactly this relation to her five years before. Every new profile reiterated the past like elms down long French boulevards. Earlier conversations interfered with the current one, distant radio stations broadcasting on the same call number—metaphor as illness. When Estrin reached for analogy, there were too many choices.

Not only people but places bloated with recall. As Estrin churned the Mournes on her Guzzi, Kilimanjaro poked unbidden between the breasts of Hare's Gap. Even a distinctive landscape would remind her of terrain just like this—Irish heath recalled Scottish heath recalled that rugged purple country between Barcelona and Madrid . . .

Memory as contamination. While this cornucopic tumble of mountains gave her life an opulence, it wasn't clean. Anyone who liked to leave so much had a taste for a wiped slate. Yet lately, no matter where Estrin flew to, no city was new. Consequently, Estrin's geography was now a matter of mood. When she felt wondrous, light, strange, she was in the Middle East; wound up, festering, Belfast; quiet, the Philippines; bereft, Berlin. States were of mind. The most illusive of these was Home—again, a feeling rather than a place, and a sensation she felt least often in Philadelphia. *Home* was a name for moments that had struck and fled her all over the world, hit and run.

Plenty of people might be pleased to have collected such a formidable stack of conversational trumps—*Why, I'm reminded of the time I was stuck in the Egged station in Eilat sleeping on my backpack and I met this gorgeous Palestinian . . . Tasty, but still can't compare with the paella in Spain . . .* But Estrin had met such people and hardly admired them.

As whole countries had fallen to emotion, it was hard to resist

the solipsistic notion that characters she located everywhere—
Man with Hopeless Crush Who Is Sometimes Useful But Who
Will Eventually Become a Problem, Close Male Confidant Who
Never Makes a Move But with Whom There Is a Palpable Sexual
Tension, Attractive and Intelligent Female Friend Who Is Also
Jealous and Will Eventually Become a Problem, Object of Un-
believably Fucked-up But Intriguing Romance Who Provides
Final Inspiration for Leaving Town—were simply parts of herself
or her family, and she continually reenacted her core drama on
the stage of different continents. She'd have to kick herself to
note: no, Malcolm existed, Robin existed, Farrell existed, even
Clive. They were not her actors or her relatives but separate
people with their own dramas, their own families. Robin might
remind her of Yossi in Tel Aviv, but he did not remind himself
of Yossi, and it wasn't his fault if Estrin's vision was corrupt.

Sometimes Estrin envied amnesiacs. In fact, she wondered
if eventually she would become one, because didn't you finally
run out of space? By now the number of people she'd met over
her lifetime would populate Rhode Island. Any time now she
would convert overnight from transient extrovert to agoraphobic
shut-in, having groceries delivered, terrified of answering the
door lest she see a new face and it squeeze its way into her
tightly packed head and replace an old friend.

Maybe the idea of a limit was fanciful, but that she might
lose a taste for strangers was not. Estrin was in awe of the elderly,
how they managed the overcrowding. Alzheimer's must be a
relief: cleaning the closets, taking out the trash. At the very
least, surely there came a time when what you had lived so
radically outweighed what you had left to add that memory
tipped you into the past, logically and mechanically, like a scale.
For Estrin was disturbed not merely by the clutter of recollection
but by its eidetic power. She could easily see herself wheel-
chaired in a hallway transfixed by the TODAY IS THURSDAY sign,
denied so much as a personal bottle of aspirin but overdosing
on her own life.

Estrin may have known too many people, but more to the

point, she had already known too many men. Facing the grisly statistics, Estrin was disconcerted. She thought of herself as passionate rather than promiscuous. Yet take, say, one weekend fling or one-night stand, the utter preclusion of which intolerably deadened the world; one consuming death-grip, all-out Relationship—obligatory; and, as a relief from the latter, or possibly just to buoy an otherwise ascetic desert of a time that quickly threatened to become what your life was like, one Incredibly Nice Man, with whom sex is warm and personal and enjoyable and dinners are humorous and interesting, who sometimes shows up with flowers for no reason and is always prompt, who adores you and in no way deserves what he will get, which is to be destroyed by his own flowers, his own punctuality, his— we will not even call it blandness, but mildness anyway—softness, gentleness that you do not really want, and be headed off at the pass by the next death-grip clutching up the driveway who never brings flowers and cancels at the last minute and with whom dinners are often quite bitter. Now, if we conservatively average one such variety pack per year for a normal American reproductive lifetime, we are well beyond counting fingers and toes if you're single at thirty-two. For all that intrusive memory, she'd forgotten some of them, their fondness for corn muffins at breakfast, their preoccupations with whales, their names. Why didn't someone warn you it was only giving in to chocolate or sitting or wild boredom that saved you over the years from seeming a total whore?

As a result, too, Estrin was left less with specific characters than with archetypes, the oversized roles of Father, Big Brother, Nemesis, which, suits tried on by too many different builds of men, had been stretched and misshapen until they no longer fit anyone in particular—even most real Nemeses disappointed.

Except one.

Constance dreams she is on a bus. The girl in the next seat is chatty. They stop at a station, where the girl buys her Kit Kats and cigarettes, though Constance doesn't smoke. The girl rattles off detailed chapters of her personal life, encouraging Constance to eat and have a fag. The stranger isn't exactly pretty, heavily made up, dressed 1969, with beads and one of those loose-weave sweater vests once so inexplicably popular. She seems thin in more than figure; Constance doesn't always pay attention. When the girl announces she's getting married, Constance only bobs out the window at the Irish countryside, full of fog and wrecked, rusting cars. "To Farrell O'Phelan."

Constance feels the candy bitter in her stomach; the Kit Kat promises to persist for hours as chocolate can. She turns to the girl and stares. Her seatmate is still gabbling, with no evident idea Constance knows Farrell; Constance is hardly going to say. She would have liked to wake up then, but the dream goes on and on—maybe that's what made it a nightmare, the way the trip seemed to continue for as long as it actually would have taken to ride to Armagh, the girl nattering away, until by the time Constance did wake up she'd hardly started from the dream in alarm but had overslept. The bedroom was steeped in the smell of disinfectant and tobacco; her windows tinged brown. When she lurched out of bed she could barely manage weak tea. Bus rides always made Constance sick.

These scenes splayed beyond her sleep. Farrell's abrupt announcement that he was getting married so insisted itself into the blandest of afternoons that Constance could only interpret the pictures as presentiment. His resolve to remain single only made the prospect of a change of heart the more grotesque. She thought of having to be congratulatory, interested, what did the girl do—, how long ago did they—, will he still— But in these holograms her inquiry never went very far; she could ask only two or three questions, and crazy ones, *What color is her hair?* Then it was right back to the start, over and over: *Constance*— She would know what was coming next just from the way he said her name, as he had never quite said it before, with an overkind warning in it, a trying to gentle what cannot be softened in any way, so that by the time the rest of the sentence was out, her grip would already have tightened around her gin-and-tonic, skin squeaking on condensed glass: *I'm getting married—*

With the main course, a sweet, and coffee yet to go—

Constance, I'd like a divorce.

So. That was why she always pictured the event at a small two-person table. Ten years before, she and her husband, Martin, had gone to Dr. Wong's Welcome Chinese to order Peking Duck. They had never eaten Peking Duck. Martin introduced his proposition right after the Tsing Tao arrived, in much the tone of voice he might have suggested they go somewhere else besides the cottage in Ardara on holiday this year. Constance said nothing. The soup came. Globes of oil floated aimlessly across the dumplings, boats of scallion. She thought, *Spoon.* She looked down at the spoon. So far nothing had changed. She looked at her hand and tried to feel it, being its fingers. *I said, Pick up the spoon.* But they were not her fingers. She looked at her husband, Martin. He was not her husband.

"The soup is not good? You like something else?"

The waitress was distraught. Martin explained, nicely. No, they weren't feeling well. She didn't seem to understand his Tyrone accent. They were off form, he said again. Please cancel the duck. They would pay for the soup. Or even the duck if it was too late, but please bring the bill.

Constance only sat. She felt relaxed. Her fingers and mouth didn't work, but the rest of her seemed to, and they walked out.

The silence and profound inability to lift silverware had lasted for three days. The divorce had lasted forever. Constance had still never eaten Peking Duck.

13

Checked Luggage, or The Long Fuck

Constance had two fears, and this was the second.

The phone is ringing. Though terrifying, that is pretty much the nightmare, and a recurrent one. Except she doesn't want to answer. What is on the other end is unformed. If she picks up the receiver the news will become true. So long as she refrains, the event to which the call refers has not occurred. Gradually the ringing grows louder and more intolerable. She knows that the caller will never hang up. Holding out becomes a torture, but she will not pick up as a sacrifice, for every second she keeps from the phone is one more second the thing has not yet happened. When she claps her hands over her ears, the bell trembles through the cracks in her fingers. The whole room begins to vibrate; teacups chatter toward table edges. She knows if she leaves the house the phone will still be ringing when she returns, and that the sound will follow her down the road. In one variation, she does leave, and when she turns on her car radio, every station plays a ringing telephone. While the dream never goes this far, she realizes that eventually, from weakness, exhaustion, or resignation, she will pick up that receiver.

For whenever Farrell walked through a door ordinary as you please, she felt the same relief as seeing her suitcase conveyed through the rubber flaps at Aldergrove. Though the shuttle had never lost her luggage, there was always that experience, however brief—the belt a-churn with misshapen leather strangers—of that life in which it was swallowed up. Whenever she let Farrell out of her sight, it was with the faith and fatalism of air travel, for anyone who has ever checked baggage knows well that, once you have relinquished its handle and watched the grip wheeled away into the enormous, anonymous, thoughtless world, even on its return your relationship with the object is altered—forever tinged with gratitude, reprieve, the blessing of that rare confluence of mystical forces by which Things Work As They Ought: luck.

So each time the planet coughed him back up, rolled him through the flaps of his office on the Lisburn Road, she was glad to *see* him. The pleasure was literal—that, with all his annoying fastidiousness and secrecy and unpredictable lashing out, he was still walking and talking, and the rest was trivial; Farrell O'Phelan was alive. Why, some nights she worked herself into such a sweat that she couldn't wait for that rush of cool air as he opened the office door, and she would ring him at 4 a.m., hanging up as soon as the irate voice grumbled lusciously in her ear.

The appointment was in Newry, one of the few towns in the Province that beat Belfast hands down for sheer ugliness. In the same way that praise didn't faze him but criticism could cut him to the quick, beautiful landscape never lifted his spirits, but blemishes like Newry could ruin his day. Happily it was dark, and Farrell would miss the stairways of pebble-dashed row houses the color of dirty bathwater, scribbled with UP THE PRO-

VOS or INLA—even the graffiti there were drab. At the mouth of
the Bann and the foot of Slieve Gullion, Newry was an achievement, triumphing over its comely location with such profound
dowdiness. Then, this was the town that complained Catholics
were never let houses on the sunny side of the street. Amazing,
his people believed the Prods could even take away the sun.

Farrell leaned back in the taxi and returned to the metaphor
he'd been working on all day. Who had given him the idea?
Some woman, recently. Whoever, he'd been relieved to discover
that he wasn't a single flagging asthmatic in a world otherwise
peopled by tireless sexual enthusiasts. And for once he'd found
a political model that could keep him entertained all the way to
Newry, and probably back.

The Troubles were a long fuck. Not the languorous kind,
but those protracted disasters the woman had admitted to, when
you could have or should have come after ten minutes, had your
splendid or inconsequential catharsis, and dressed; to grab a bite
of lunch, read, draft a lecture—but you hadn't—you'd held back
out of greed or drifted from the peak like straying the towpath,
and there you were, still banging away when you could be at
the newsstand or, hell, halfway across the Atlantic Ocean in the
time it's taken you to wear another layer of skin off your prick.
Now, to pursue the analogy, how did one of those interminable
afternoons finish?

ONE: Finally, forcing it, you did come, in a little loveless
squirt, an excuse for an orgasm, its only pleasure that the fiasco
was over and you could at last light out to Wellington Park for
soup or make it to Simpsons before they ran out of the *Irish
Times*. While no more than a puddle on the sheet, the squirt was
still vital, since, sheepish though the two of you might feel inside
at what a bollocks you'd made of the afternoon, it still satisfied
pride: zip up, you'd done your job and it was over.

Yet this solution, a pale, symbolic conclusion, was difficult
to organize. Certainly this whole last six months, with Enniskillen, Seawright, McMichael, Stalker, the Birmingham Six decision, Gibraltar, Milltown, the Andytown and Avenue Bar

massacres, there was a sense that things were coming to a head. But how many times had it seemed like that here? Wasn't it just like when the sweat was flying and you were flaunting every which way about the mattress and you couldn't believe you weren't climaxing, but you weren't? When somehow the more flamboyant you got, the more likely you never would? Once exploding eleven civilians at a memorial service or riddling an open bar with automatics only constitutes one more thrust, how could you tell coming from a passing shudder? The more that happened here, the more every "atrocity" listed to ordinary wanking away. Even the word *atrocity* (now, now he remembered who the woman was) had fallen to the sound of *box* or *weather*, like the word *come* itself, which camouflaged so demurely in the scrub of *go* and *stay*.

TWO: You looked each other in the eye and confessed; with the right woman, you laughed, though that was rare. Bag it, pack it in, hang it up, we're tired and this is not happening, no way. We're dead bored. We're sore. Let's get dressed. It's still light out, and we could walk by the Lagan. Farrell would never forget a particular woman about ten years ago who had feverishly lavished herself on top of him for half an hour. They'd both seemed content, in the middle levels of excitement; the endless shifting of position as the clock ticked on had not yet set in. And just exactly as the first fear filtered through his head that he was not climbing but had reached a plateau, she stopped, cold. "I don't want to do this anymore," she'd said, and he was so uninsulted he replied, "Neither do I." She slipped off, though he was still perfectly hard, and sat cross-legged on the floor with the paper, cheerfully checking cinema listings. She would not be trapped by form, the rules of pride. She would not fuck just because she had started. A deeper, private pride prevented her from humping on when she had tired. In short, she knew how to quit. A whole province of such people could turn off the Troubles like a switch.

Then, how likely was that? How many women had resigned so gracefully, and had Farrell himself bailed out of anything, ever? Didn't he particularly remember that afternoon? Sure he'd met single remarkable cheek-turners here, quitters of the best sort, Gordon Wilsons, even if *I forgive the men who murdered my daughter* had, as Farrell predicted, become a cliché. But one and a half million people were suddenly to become so self-possessed, nonreactive, smart, *perfect?* And then the Kingdom would descend, he supposed. Right. If the Bible taught you one thing, it was not to hold out for the Second Coming if you couldn't even manage the first one.

THREE: You petered off. There are limits. Over the hours a man would gradually grow spongy. In one more experiment with nooky over or under or to another side, the implement would slip and refuse to go back in—not out of conviction, but only: I cannot, I cannot go on. Even if I think I should, I'm raw and slackened; I'm not unwilling, but I *cannot.* A simple organic failure. Was that the answer: to let the fuck squeegee on until unavoidable sogginess set in, the bog steeped in its own juices and sank, unable to rise to one more occasion, so finally on hearing of another rooftop snipe-shoot, another agricultural show blown to hell outside the exhibit on supercows, no one has any response whatsoever? Not because they will not—but because they cannot? Weren't there plenty of fatigued Hard Men in West Belfast whose erections had died?

But what if it was possible to hand the lay of the land on to the next man: Here, you, fuck her fresh, my balls are blue? On to young boys for whom all pleasure is new, with priapic hard-ons like plastic bullets? To sixteen-year-olds filling cider bottles with petrol, smashing toilets of abandoned houses with slabs of chassis from burned Ulsterbuses smoking in front of Divis Flats? These are the fuckers you expect to get tired?

FOUR: You took a little turn; she touched just the right place down at the root of you, and even after all this creaky seesaw geriatrics you really start to fuck, for true—how could you not have been doing this before? The position of course no longer matters, but only the abandon. You are all-out, driving home, until you come from the whole lower half of your body, you come from the magazine, a mortar load of a come, a bazooka come, and you blast her to bits, to hell—

Aye? Line up the rocket launchers? Isn't that what everyone wants, anyway? We'll all die at the end of the day, right, and who wants to cut out with cancer of the colon? Why not die shooting your wad all over the whole bloody island? Why not close your eyes and throw yourself into one blind, gushy, sloshy last screw? For even the odd facile visitor had suggested the simple solution of civil war.

Now, nearing Newry, in the drafty black taxi Farrell was sweating. His pictures might have solved nothing, but they were the right pictures. Farrell's people were fucking each other. That's what was wrong with so much of the day-old-bread political analysis dusting up in Linen Hall: it wasn't slick and viscous enough. Those Cambridge prats were too well schooled to loosen their ties, trace the insides of their thighs with the tips of their pencils, and scratch, *Right, Northern Ireland is a bad fuck. They're still getting off on it, but they can't come.* And it took more and more stimulation for either partner to feel anything at all.

After prolonged, pointed flappings of the peephole, the door opened to confirm the worst Farrell had heard about these people: good Lord, they had sunk as low as Callaghan. The two men said nothing. Farrell nodded in a more dignified greeting than the man deserved. Callaghan returned with the squeezed smile of a baby messing its nappies.

So the RIPs had resorted to mucking out the Green Door. Wasn't that the rub: you didn't need a license to found a paramilitary organization, did you? For the recently formed Rest in Pieces broke all the rules. They blew up far too many pensioners splurging home with jam tarts. And the Rips had not been briefed about pet death. In their most famous incident, they had bombed a children's birthday party in Carryduff, maiming two miniature ponies. Farrell had actually admired the job, for the bomb was the cake, wired to connect when the steel knife sliced two sheets of foil layered into the icing—great stuff, popped balloons, screeching kiddies, horsie-spattered wrapping paper, earning the RIPs headlines tall and black as the magician's top hat.

To the Provos this was a massive PR hemorrhage, for in the last ten years the Provisionals had pursued a deliberate strategy of targeting Brits and peelers as opposed to real human beings. Civilians were "mistakes," occasionally blown to hell because, gosh, they just wouldn't get out of the way.

But Rips claimed their difference with the Provisionals was ideological. They cheerfully admitted, for example, to being sectarian. This was a war against the Brits *and* the Prods. And if the whole concept of an Armed Struggle was to "make Northern Ireland ungovernable," then you just had to wreak havoc, full stop. The more gruesome the deed, the better the copy. They had a point—Rips got marvelous press, of which, they charged, the Provos were jealous.

Bollocks, the Provos told Farrell. A Rip wouldn't know an idea if it sat on his face. They hit on old ladies because, Jesus, Mary, and Joseph, the army had guns! Just as Loyalists had given up hunger striking for the Five Demands because they got hungry, the Rips didn't go after security forces because someone might get hurt.

Now they did anyway. The RIPs ratio of own goals to successful operations resembled that of divorces to successful marriages in the United States. And while these wayward hobby kits in Newry basements had the advantage of thinning Rip ranks in a pleasant natural selection—every people should be so designed that below a certain IQ they spontaneously combust—the Provos were annoyed that freelance incompetence was reflecting on established Republicans. They had worked hard to earn their reputation for discipline and technical sophistication, and prized more than any single trophy in the conflict the word sifted back from NIHQ that the ATOs had "tremendous respect" for the IRA. They were not about to return to the days of joke butt because of a small clueless fringe that didn't know the difference between Cordtex and jump rope.

So Farrell had been asked to negotiate; though he had enough on his hands with the conference and the referendum only eight months away, this headache was right up his street. Because the Provos were rapidly reaching the end of their fuse, threatening to march in and wipe the RIPs off the face of their earth, as they'd nearly done with the Officials in the early seventies. Before taking drastic measures, however, they had empowered Farrell, grudgingly, to offer the Rips membership in the PIRA, though everyone knew perfectly well the Rips would never be asked to do more than make trips to Busy Bee for carry-out coffee. Farrell felt uncomfortably as he followed Callaghan that this wasn't much of a chip to bargain with. Rips were sulky, unruly children. They had either been rejected out of hand from the IRA—which was now about as hard to get into as the Malone Golf Club; things were hard all over—or had been laid off when the organization more than halved its people in converting to a cell structure for tighter security in '77. Paramilitary redundancies, the Rips were an embittered lot, and on some level their strikes on pensioners were aimed less at Prods than at Big Daddy Provo, who wasn't going to tell them what to do.

So while quietly recoiling at the sight of Callaghan's backside—the tight beige shirt rode up his spare tire, trousers slumped down the crease of his bum—Farrell recited to himself all the advantages of the Rips coming under Provisional wing: better munitions, access to explosive experts, extensive network of safe houses, reliable escape routes to the South; established reputation, sound funding; smarter than you are, better crack, and from the look of that sorry Whyte and Mackay on the table there, pricier whiskey by far; why the Army Council never serves less than Jameson's—

Farrell smiled: after so much effort at dismantling the things, to be selling one organization to another because the larger one made better bombs.

There was something about the setup from the start that Farrell didn't like. There were five people in the room, and somehow that was one too many; and they were all men. With no female at hand he felt he had no one to appeal to.

Further, the house itself was an unending aesthetic assault. The curtains were nailed up, the pink carpet balded, the furniture bunched with sheets. There were jars. Everywhere, with bits, shells, short pencils written down to the eraser, a plastic swizzle stick with a whistle on the end, rocks that probably looked pretty wet on the beach but, dry, looked like driveway gravel. A single Judy Collins album, warped, Judy looking woeful; two paperbacks: *Serpico* and *Wildflowers of Antrim*. Not even bad taste, just no taste at all. The room did not cohere; like Ulster, it did not know what it was.

Further, it was a place without care: a petrified bouquet in black water. A calendar from 1982; a Yellow Pages from 1979; an unplugged digital clock stuck at 20:58, significantly. One dirty fork. And Farrell knew that fork. It had been there long enough to have become The Dirty Fork by the Brown Chair, and no one would ever move it or clean it because now it belonged there.

Farrell was hard-pressed to finger why the house disturbed him so, except that it seemed too perfectly his image of what would happen to his mother if his father died; or, if he was not to hide behind the woman's skirts for once, of his own life if he ever climbed fully inside a bottle of Talisker. He could see himself living here, and it was the queer tug of the place more than its tattiness that repulsed him.

More practically, it bothered Farrell that the owners of the house were not present. There was a dress on the sofa, photos of pimply children on the mantel—a woman did live here, if a bit depressed. How had the Rips gotten the house? And what had they done with its tenants?

However, he needn't have worried about the hostess. And he needn't even have worried about the impending Provy extermination of the Rips. It was time for Farrell O'Phelan's world to shrink perfectly to the size of Farrell O'Phelan. Because Michael Callaghan had a gun.

"Pull up a chair," invited Callaghan.

Farrell descended to the straight-back slowly. Callaghan rested the barrel against Farrell's temple, nesting it in the thick shock of gilt gray hair, of which Callaghan, with his own weedy remnants, must have been jealous.

It was one of those moments Farrell had heard others rerun, claiming how they never felt more alive, they never knew more clearly they didn't want to die . . . But tonight in no way repeated the Brown Thomas bag clicking pristinely on the roof. Farrell was far more overcome by a sensation of *un*reality: the gun looked a toy. It had such a deceptively simple feeling; the solid cold metal felt nice. He was reminded of the way Estrin always nestled her snifter by her eye, the way candlelight glinted through the cognac and threw amber patches on her cheek.

It was a salvatory vision, benevolent, golden, and he wrested himself from it, tempted by rounding himself into her globe, hiding under the dark curls, and sinking into a bath of Courvoisier up to his chin. He had to remind himself that the object at his head was lethal, for in Belfast you got inured to these things; Farrell had frequently ordered himself on the street to notice soldiers casually swinging their SLRs: *Remember what they're for? Those aren't hurley sticks, boyo.* And this was no cool glass of expensive brandy in his hair.

His body knew what a gun was. Already pressed wool creases clung in damp wrinkles to his thighs. Farrell had to stop himself from loosening his collar. His heart pulsed in his teeth; the jars with shells and pencils bulged forward with every beat. Whistles on swizzle sticks began to trill. Faded prints gorged with the unhealthy color of overripe fruit. Spotting the crusty fork, Farrell felt sick.

He wondered later at the deluge, the earthquake, the nausea tonight, when he had approached so many ominous packages in the face of which these symptoms had been mild. But somehow no matter how sinister a box or milk churn or oil tanker could appear, however he might anthropomorphize its intentions to get him, these objects had never crossed into the animate, quite.

He'd always felt he had the better of them; so far he'd been right. No bag, deadly as its contents, can conceivably equal another man flicking off the safety catch.

"What is your name?" asked Callaghan.

"You know my name," Farrell whispered.

"What is your name?" The barrel nudged.

Farrell felt his face flush. He didn't answer.

Callaghan went down on one knee. It was hard to say if he was smiling, but his eyes were bright. "I didn't catch that."

This time the voice sounded different, and Farrell realized that Callaghan would shoot.

Now it was clear why the gun had seemed "unreal." He'd seen this scene before. Farrell lived in an era when two dimensions had overtaken three. Real life was subordinated to wide screen, the very inventor of "real life"—for before the talkies, what other kind of life was there? The phrase itself suggested a lack of confidence, as if the audience suspected time between tickets amounted to a long advert. And here he was for once in this truly filmworthy tableau, and it didn't measure up.

CALLAGHAN (*increasingly threatening*)

I didn't catch that.

CAMERA SLOWLY MOVES IN on O'PHELAN's face, his eyes moist with a hint of breakdown; O'PHELAN's P.O.V.: pan of tawdry hijacked two-up-two-down; CLOSE-UP on woman's dress on the sofa. He glimpses his reflection in the photographs and is immediately steadied by it. CAMERA PULLS BACK; beside O'PHELAN, CALLAGHAN seems shabby and small. Suddenly we feel that the man with the weapon is not the one with the power at all.

O'PHELAN (*steely, urbane*)

Unable to even write the line, Farrell was overcome with incoherent, helpless fury. What a load of shite he'd been fed. The camera retreats six more feet; cables trail in the foreground, a pretty girlfriend paints her nails off set. Right. And if the line doesn't come off quite cool enough, they can shoot the scene again. *What a sell.* Because nothing Farrell had ever seen in a theater had prepared him for the banality of a Thursday night, filthy carpet, old calendars, and some greasy pillock who had Farrell suddenly and truly at his mercy and on whom Farrell would never necessarily turn the tables before the credits rolled. *What is your name?* Not an inch of celluloid had ever taught him what to say back. Because no one was actually going to shoot Clint Eastwood in the head.

Farrell looked at his lap. "Farrell O'Phelan."

Now it didn't matter to be seen loosening his collar. Callaghan was at last clearly smiling. "*What* is your name?"

"Farrell O'Phelan."

"I can't hear you."

"Farrell O'Phelan."

"I seem to have forgotten your name, now."

The rest of the room had begun to laugh. Farrell lost count of the number of times they asked him. The others took turns. Once or twice he didn't respond, but any resistance was pointless after answering at all; and though somewhere around the twentieth time he raised his voice in exasperation, on into the thirties he grew patient, dully prepared to repeat himself all night. While the interviewers varied their question a bit to avoid this, Farrell, in ceaselessly repeating the same syllables, began to trip over the words. This amused his audience no end.

It was the ultimate desecration, when your own name no longer sounds familiar, when there no longer seems any reason the *Far* comes before the *rell*, or the *lan* after the *Phe*—and where to fit the *O*'? Anywhere, anywhere at all, and why not add other letters, which he did, generously, *D*'s and *S*'s galore, until the answer to *What is your name?* was truly *I don't know.*

Little by little both people and objects popped from the room. The only thing in the universe which never disappeared, not for an instant, was the gun. In the end he clung to it, as a focus, until on into the thirtieth, fortieth *Farrell O'Phelan* he found a funny love for the weapon, as his sole purchase on why this was happening, why his own name had been parted syllable from syllable: Farrell was still alive, but his name had been shot.

At last tiring of the game, Callaghan licked his lips and glanced at his companions. "Yeah," he drawled, "that's what we thought."

The Rips rolled in hilarity. They were soused.

"And why are you paying us a call?" asked Callaghan politely. "Mr. O'Fanlon?"

"To invite you to form a Provisional cell," Farrell mumbled.

"Well, aren't we chuffed."

"We're chuffed," said another.

"Bleedin chuffed," said Callaghan. "But tell me, Farjet—and I can call you Farjet, can't I?"

"I suppose you can call me anything you like."

Callaghan smiled. "Right you are, Farthing. But why'd the Provies call you in, O'Phallus?"

"It was agreed both sides mistrusted me to an equal degree. It seems there was a miscalculation."

"Getting to be a regular poli sci butterfly, aren't we, O'Fairy? 'Cause we heard about your conference, like. But how's it happen the Rips weren't invited? We're hurt, mate—freakin psychiatric from neglect."

"Only the major parties—"

"Now watch yourself, Fartlett. You wouldn't want us to get insulted, like."

Farrell just sighed.

"Frank, call your man a taxi. He's a busy, important gentleman. Has places to be. As for you, O'Failing, tell your Provisional friends they can stuff their wee songs and codes of conduct and endless bloody boring pamphlets about Bobby Sands right up the arse. And if I was you, I'd get that suit cleaned. Such a class pair of trousers, a shame to muss them up like that. You smell something, Frank?"

"I smell shite, Mikey."

"I do too, Frank."

Farrell turned white.

"What'd you say your name was?" The barrel nuzzled his temple affectionately. "Farwell?"

The taxi took its time.

When Farrell tottered back downstairs, Callaghan had to hold his arm to help him walk. His knees trembled. Even beside the taxi and more or less safe, Farrell did not turn and fire a *Make my day*. In fact, for the whole night he had not cut a single smart remark.

A Rip leaned out the window overhead and screamed into the night, "How do they call you now?"

Squeezing the trigger of the door handle, the gaunt man in his wilted pinstripe answered unexpectedly back. "O'Phelan!" he shouted at the top of his lungs. "Farrell O'Phelan!" For the first time in two hours that sounded like someone he had heard of before.

In the taxi, he crawled into the corner and pressed his knees together, slipping his hands beneath his jacket to hold his own chest. Feebly he groped for insights. It struck him, for example, that the interrogation technique the Rips used was copied straight from Long Kesh. Further, he wondered with the amount of instant power it conferred why every sod with twenty quid didn't carry a gun. More to the point, why didn't he? And Farrell caught himself on: frankly, if Callaghan had asked his name saying pretty please, holding out a sweet, or palming a tenner, he would have refused to speak; before a pointed pistol he had answered. So for all his decrying of violence to well-behaved Trinity audiences, Farrell had neglected to mention one little problem: *It works*.

All these thoughts straggled with the wet coils of his hair. He did not have the energy to find any of this interesting. The most persuasive insight he took from Newry that night was that insights counted for bugger-all.

He had the driver stop in Hillsborough at a public house and went straight for the loo. He had not soiled himself since he was seven years old, but found the shame identical. He was surprised to find the damage minor; then, the feel of your own excrement to your bum enlarged itself as a lump in your mouth to your tongue. He used an entire roll of paper to swab himself clean. He left his Y-fronts in the bin.

At the bar Farrell ordered his first whiskey in six years. "Cheers," he toasted the publican. "To the mayor of Carmel."

"All right already!" The pounding grew more insistent. Estrin checked the clock. Jesus, she didn't think the Brits barged in *this* early. And the first search, okay, she'd been excited. But Little Miss Adaptable had learned the local irritation with her usual precocity. Douche-bags better not touch the rocking chair; the varnish was still wet. "Cram it, I'm coming!" Estrin bundled down to the door with as much hostility as it was possible to muster out of a dead sleep. That was a fair bit.

"Bend a hairpin in this house, I'm on the steps of the American Consulate by sunrise!" She flung open the door in mid-thud, and the man behind it shadow-boxed forward. "Farrell!"

He bungled into the hall, knocking into a table. "Are you plastered or what?"

Farrell only made soft sounds, snuffling, lowing, breath. He scuffed into her sitting room, but would not sit down. As he kicked at the carpet, his hands spread and swiped at books, a wineglass, as if to fling them, but his fingers swept shy.

Did it ever take work to get the story.

"Now let me get this straight," said Estrin. "They asked you your name—and you told them."

"More"—Farrell stared at the ceiling—"than once."

"Seems to me you were lucky. If that were the UVF you'd hardly have the leisure to repeat yourself. Just past the apostrophe your brains would have been a Rorschach on wallpaper."

"I might have preferred that."

"Well, what do you think you should have said?"

"*Fuck. You.* That's what. *Fuck. You.*"

"And what would that have proved?"

"You don't understand." Farrell was weeping. "They could have made me do anything. And they knew it."

"That's right." Estrin took his head in her hands. "And you did real good. Because if they asked you to recite Georgie Porgie with a clock on your head or read *Ulysses* while standing on one leg and swinging a dead chicken and you did, you'd have done good, too. Sometimes dignity is a luxury you can't afford. You survived. In the end that's proud: not letting someone tempt you into throwing your life away. This country is full of people dying for bullshit. That's not pride. It's low self-esteem."

"You cannot—allow anyone—to humiliate you."

"You can't allow anyone to *kill* you! If they brought you back here in a trunk because you wouldn't tell them your name, *I'd* be humiliated! I'd be embarrassed and I'd be furious! At you, asshole! Would you stop wishing someone would shoot you? Are you really just disappointed that you let another chance go by? Because I"—she kissed him—"I am not disappointed."

She'd been concerned he'd not fit on her mattress at six-foot-four, but curled on his side Farrell conformed nicely, tucking his head down, pressing his hands together, and slipping them between his thighs. Such a thin man, he collapsed into convenient luggage, a lover for travelers, like a folding comb or retracting clothesline from a bus station vending machine. In the dim streetlight through the window, the gray hair shone as it had long ago, gold. Most of the men Estrin had slept with sprawled over the bed, territorial, or took her to their chests, protective. Yet this one-man bomb squad, this fast-lane politico, this pinstripe T.E. slept like a child.

She stroked his head. "Over the top," she whispered, when sure he was asleep. He wasn't, and they both smiled.

14

Negaphobia,
and Why Farrell Doesn't Do Windows

Farrell woke convinced he was still in Newry. He had stopped answering their questions not from defiance but from weariness. He wasn't brave; he just didn't care. Apathy is another form of cowardice. They were going to shoot him, and Farrell could only roll over and sigh.

But the room was too clean. Where was he? The walls were white; the cornice and window frame British racing green; muslin curtains. Narrow, the only other furniture a white dresser and white cane chair, the bedroom suggested a ship's cabin, or maybe a little cottage by the sea, the kind you could track sand in and no one would carp. He liked the idea he could walk out the door to comb for driftwood, though where did he get that picture? Farrell didn't take holidays.

Up on his elbows, he looked over to find Ophelia beside

him, drowning in her fecund greens. One of his office prints. He was being followed.

He smelled coffee and toast. Downstairs he found Estrin on a ladder in the kitchen, hair bound up, draped in a big splattered button-down in which she looked unreasonably attractive. He watched her caulk a seam of Sheetrock. "You're handy with that," he observed.

"Physical competence," she declared with a voice that argued she'd been up for hours, "is the beginning of every other kind. I mean, look at that." She pointed to a table slapped over with streaky green paint of a shade that managed to be both garish and dour. "You wouldn't want to have a jar with the man who chose that color. You wouldn't want to get in the car of a man who couldn't tape edges straight or who let big drips dry down the legs of his furniture. Get a character to paint a table and I could tell you if you should lend him money or trust his version of what happened yesterday. In short, I wouldn't give two bits for anyone who couldn't spackle a flush nail hole."

"And I wouldn't give a tuppenny damn for anyone who couldn't find a good spackler to do it for him."

"You can afford to say that. You have money."

"I have means. If I hadn't come into Whitewells, I'd have dug up something else. Means are all. You overvalue the minion."

"Naturally. I am one. Coffee?"

Farrell wandered with his cup to the sitting room. The paint was fresh, the carpet new. Here, too, projects—stripped chairs, electric sanders, wallpaper rolls. Traces, too, of travel—Buchladen Ostertor matches, Israeli earplugs, flamingo feathers. Snapshots of dark men by empty liquor bottles. This was more ulteriority than he was prepared for this morning. The woman was incoherent: a weight-lifting motorcyclist from Philadelphia; a cook from the Philippines; a drug counselor from Berlin; a night-shift overseer for an Israeli plastic boots factory; a barmaid in Belfast . . . She was a dilettante. This morning he settled for one word.

He drifted to her books, expecting *Cal, Juno and the Paycock, The Uncivil Wars*. Instead, he found *All Quiet on the Western Front, Good-bye to All That, The Great War and Modern Memory, The Road to the Somme*.

"I suppose it makes perfect sense," he shouted, "that you'd come all the way to Belfast to read about World War I."

"It does, actually." She strolled in, paring plaster from her nails. "Grotesque, unnecessary, protracted—like a joke no one knew how to end, so it just kept going, shaggy dog. Big parallels. For years I avoided the First World War because it disturbed me. Now I like being disturbed. I'm beyond World War II. It's too easy. Auschwitz, Baden-Baden—*Yes, there's evil*: that comforted me a long time. Now I suspect the clarity. World War II lulls generations of Allies into believing that when the time comes the path of righteousness will be marked with the neon arrows of a Holiday Inn sign. In Germany, you get the feeling it will be just as badly marked as the way to Dachau and Bergen-Belsen memorials are now—tiny little signs, in neat, embarrassed printing, smaller and more obscure than directions to *Toiletten*. I've had it with goodies and baddies. I'm more fascinated by bungling and murk." She nodded at the window. "Trees without forest."

"What trees?" He smiled.

"The thing I really love about the trenches"— Estrin paused for a lungful of turpentine, varnish, and wet paint, white smells, tingling with evaporation and disguise; the whole house exuded this odor of opportunity, an American smell, as if you really could start over—"is the way soldiers would run into each other, like, having just shared a Dixie of tea a few hours before? They'd embrace! They'd clap their buddies on the back and cry. They'd congratulate each other, just for being alive. Because I can't figure why I don't meet everyone I know like that, every day. Presumably they could all walk out their front doors in the next ten minutes and get run over by trucks. Because the whole planet is a trench, isn't it? With trucks."

Farrell didn't want her to say anything funny or interesting or intelligent. Estrin was a diversion. You didn't store heavy cargo on the side or your hull would list, so Estrin had to be kept light. He found himself glancing at her from the corners of his eyes, so that for moments she would comfortably disappear. He didn't move much or abruptly, lest the house capsize.

"Russian?" A grammar splayed on the couch.

"*Da, eta moya kniga.* Soviet Union's the next adventure. Takes advance prep. Those six cases are the living bitch."

The fog of his waking was not burning off. Farrell felt lost, his fingers held from his trousers, extended, balancing. "I don't understand. You're going away?"

"Farrell—I'm always going away."

"When?"

"Oh, I don't know. End of the year, early in the next. I don't want to zip off to Leningrad until I get a grip on the genitive plural."

"But that's—eight months from now. Why paint your kitchen?"

"I do this everywhere, don't you get it? My flat in Jerusalem was exquisite by the time I left. Oriental carpets, Armenian pottery."

"Seems a waste of effort."

"No, I enjoy it. Besides, I sell at a profit and finance my next plane ticket. And most people assume I'm one of the last great anti-materialists. Hardly. The first week I arrive in a new country I've bought a potato peeler, a corkscrew. Week two, a dish drainer, a spatula. I suppose if I ever stayed long enough I'd end up with a microwave and wiener cooker just like everyone else. Actually, I love things. If I didn't, leaving whole furnished flats behind wouldn't have that satisfying sting."

"What about people?"

"I make fast friends. I fall in love. I flee."

He felt it again, the wave of exhaustion this small woman cost him. Again the itchy temptation to cheat, to merely find her amusing. "But if leaving gets too easy," he groped, "are you not skivving now? No career, no children? At the end of the day, is the challenge not to stay?"

She smiled, victorious. "Do I miss my guess, or are you usually on the other side of this discussion?"

Farrell felt tricked. "Quite."

"Besides . . ." she ruminated. "I'm terrified of dish drainers."

She didn't need to explain. Himself, Farrell didn't own one, that's how scared he was. He ate out for every meal; he never fried an egg or even made fresh coffee. Despite the security risk, he'd a girl come in to clean. If his sheets were tatty, Farrell uttered a furtive, peripheral grunt; Constance would shop. The bedding arrived on his desk in an unmarked bag. As for laundry (*The horror. The horror*—), Farrell bundled it into Whitewells every week, and though he'd admit this was more bother than buying his own machine, Farrell would go to a great deal of trouble to seem to be saving it. He had once lit out on an electronics spree, in an orgy of labor-saving devices, but later could not reduce himself to picking them up from the shop. They remained, he supposed, in the back of CVC in boxes. Since, the picture had comforted him: how absentminded he was, how above this world. More truthfully, he had not forgotten them at all. It was simply worth more to him to nurse this vision of neglect than to face the computer he would have to learn to use, the stack-system CD that would force him to have tastes in music and very possibly threaten him with the specter of enjoying himself. As he could hardly send Constance out for suits, he bought all his clothes at the same shop in London once a year, staging a carnival of credit cards and clerks. In the extravagance of buying out the whole department in extra-longs, he transformed this soilingly ordinary outing into an expedition salesmen would report to their children that night—into an event worthy of Farrell O'Phelan, drama from the squalor of shirts.

Domestic allergy helped explain why he loved not only Whitewells but all hotels—their impersonality, their cleanliness, their attention to his needs. Whitewells was a mother who never made Farrell eat his sprouts.

Besides, jealously as he guarded its location, he didn't feel comfortable in his own home. Maybe he'd made a mistake getting it redecorated. The idea had been once more to get proles to contend with the sordid home life—God forbid he should be discovered in a Donaldson & Lyttle's shopping for throw rugs. The result, however, was more estrangement he could ill afford. Already the place had seemed sprawling and a little austere, where he felt bereft and most tempted, unwatched, to nip out for whiskey. But now, with exotic trinkets suggesting trips he'd not taken, enormous bowls he could not fill, seascapes chosen to offend no one and therefore to truly appeal to no one either, Farrell had been redecorated out of his house. He could not find the light switches; he could not work the blinds; he had never figured out if the thing in the bedroom was a liquor cabinet or a hamper. Farrell persuaded himself he'd successfully transformed his bungalow into one more hotel suite, but the place had more the atmosphere of a house he used to live in and had shifted out.

Fastidious or not, Farrell found his digs most cozy when books and papers nested in every corner, jumpers crumpled in every chair. Even tea stains on the counter, rings on wood—at least these were Farrell's rings, Farrell's stains. For inheriting Whitewells, money, had this one deadly effect: at one time his own fear of dish drainers expressed itself with dirty crockery, tottery table legs, bomb-shattered windows he wouldn't bother to ring the NIO to replace for free, but still expression of a kind. With Whitewells, though, he could afford to hire Constance to buy his sheets, the hotel to do his laundry. Farrell mused he might be better off rinsing socks himself—for once to be on intimate terms with something.

Estrin, however, suffered a domestic terror of a lower order, for when he suggested breakfast downtown she preferred to eat in. And fair play to her—the eggs were loose, the oranges Israeli;

he could have sliced his coffee with a knife and fork. "You should try short order," he commended.

"I have."

"Is there any work you've not done?"

"Sure. Anything important. And anything for a long time." She hugged her coffee and eyed him from behind her wayward hair. "Are you feeling better?"

"I feel nothing. Is that better?"

She gathered shirttails to her lap. "I've never seen you like that."

"I've never been like that." Or so he assumed, though he could no longer remember last night, exactly. It had been cartoned up; he couldn't get at it. He was left with information. It was already a story he could tell. "I do feel," he amended, "disappointed."

"With yourself."

"Oh, aye. But with the event as well. It was tinny. Someone threatened to kill me and the experience still felt—"

"Fake," she finished for him.

Farrell was surprised. Tentatively, he confided about Clint Eastwood.

"I have an older brother," Estrin began, not changing the subject. "Dropped out of school at fourteen, ran away from home, hitchhiked. Mime and Stoppard, mescaline, Jefferson Airplane. I've always admired him, though don't imagine it works in the other direction. Billy started his own construction business, self-taught. I must have been ten when he first asked me, 'So when are you going to experience real life?' This became his litany. Ever since, I've been trying to be real. Sometimes I wonder if I travel just to impress my older brother."

"Do you think you could go back now and he'd say anything different?"

"Of course not. Especially, the more places I go he hasn't been, the more I'll be a piddler. I'm the velveteen rabbit who will always have a bit too much fur. The Philippines wouldn't count because I cooked, which was girl's work, the hotel was upper class, so I obviously couldn't consort with *real* Filipinos, and didn't I get a lot of sun? It was all very well to counsel drug addicts in Berlin, but that was no substitute for being one. I've begun to understand that *real* to Billy Lancaster means being Billy Lancaster, a disaster I wouldn't wish on anyone but himself."

"How's he sorted out now?"

"Moved to Allentown. Business fluctuates wildly. In the black it's steak and cognac, in the red cornflakes and cognac. Sometimes I think he uses Rémy instead of milk." She paused. "I lie. Lately he's skipping the cereal altogether."

"Your brother has a problem?"

"My brother is a festival of problems. If that's reality, Billy's real as sin. In the middle of a divorce, which gives him the convenient excuse to pickle himself just exactly as much as he would if he were still married . . . I'm sorry, this depresses me."

"Maybe not enough."

"No, I hate seeing him fall apart. It's hard to find people to admire. I like tall men, don't I? I like looking up." She reached for a crust on Farrell's plate, having eating nothing herself; it saddened him to see her eat scraps. Her diet suggested poor nourishment of larger proportions. "I'll probably try to debunk you," she added. "Don't let me succeed."

"I don't want your admiration."

"Oh, I forgot. You're a worm." She leaned over and kissed him, a critical caution clearly wasted.

"Anyway, I've decided this complex isn't exclusive to me. Like, I come from an ill country, but not sick the way foreigners think. Sure it's the land of *graniti* makers and soda streamers, but give us a little spiritual credit—I've never met a single American who claimed if he could only upgrade to a multisystem VCR he'd be happy. Stuff becomes part of the problem: the more bother it saves us, the less we've got to do; the better our recording equipment, the more abundantly clear that the music stinks. Because this fear I grew up with, it's infected the whole population like botulism, and a little goes a long way: we're not sure we exist. It makes us dangerous, because we could end up making trouble, like pinching ourselves to check we're still here. I dislike scapegoating TV, but it is true that my country watches too much. That sensation of looking at a screen, it's easy to keep feeling that way when you look out the window. I think that's why we overeat and obsess over sex: we're dying to get something inside. The real reason Americans buy so much is it's one of the only national habits that's participatory: it requires you to make decisions, if only between the blue one and the red one. In any larger sphere, we don't perceive ourselves agents. That's why we don't vote, not because we're cynical: we can't conceive of having any effect. In the meantime, what you were saying: we hire a handful from Hollywood to live for us, and they're only faking. So nothing actually occurs. Little wonder we elect an actor for President, we don't think we have a real President. You know how envious my friends are of my life the last ten years? And not because they're interested in Zaire. They think I'm *real* now."

"Are you?"

"Not a chance. I call this negaphobia, and it only gets worse. It's an affliction of middles—the middle class, the middle child. Between the wars. This feeling as if you're encased in plastic. The world bounces off, you're lifeproof. Triumphs and tragedies happen only to people in books. Serious arguments start when you leave the room; at dinner parties, you catch snippets of a lively discussion about population control in Kenya while you're stuck chatting about spider mites. Feuds, floods, and famines on every front page and no one invites you. Mommy didn't sit you on electric burners as a child, Daddy never made incestuous advances. Empires rise and fall while you make sure not to run out of toilet paper. All of North America could go up in flames, and that would be the morning you slept late. It's a sensation of being left out or artificial. Your experience is invalidated as being legitimate because it's your experience. Why did I go to Milltown Cemetery for the Gibraltar funerals? Of course I hoped for violence. I got it, and it didn't matter. All right, Michael

Stone missed me with his automatic, but never in the thick of
the poof-poof did I believe he could shoot me. Everyone ran
but Estrin. I swear, something in me's been waiting years now
to get raped, held up at knife point, taken hostage in the Middle
East, though I know full well none of that would be real if it
happened to me. Like Milltown, I walk dangerous neighborhoods—East Jerusalem, Mathare Valley, Smoky Mountain; I
camp on the West Bank. It's frustrating, Farrell—nobody ever
fucks with me. So when I get a letter from my mother imploring
me to stay clear of Beirut, it's not out of line."

"Instead: Belfast."

"Right, but of course when I get here it's obvious I missed
the party—Burntollet, Bloody Sunday, the barricades; the snipe
shoots, the hunger strikes. You can imagine I'm tired of listening
to locals coo about how this is nothing compared to '72. Car
bombs and murders every night. Okay, maybe it was hairy at
the time, but behind the tsk-tsking I can hear their possessive
satisfaction: *Boy, did you miss out on the heavy shit.* And it works!
I feel deflated. Like when Marcos fled the Philippines I had to
rustle lunch at the Coral Reef, 150 seafood terrines to prepare
for a conference of Moonies the next day. I was peeling shrimp
while everyone else was trying on Imelda's shoes."

"I think you've arrived here at an interesting time," said
Farrell.

"You're right," Estrin agreed. "Because negaphobia is what's
interesting. And you wouldn't think so, but Northern Ireland is
rife with it."

"Am I?"

"The worst."

"And your brother?"

She laughed, her head ajar. "Come to think of it, Billy is
terrified that any moment he will vanish."

Turning old tables seemed to cheer her. She showed him
the house. The shell was 150 years old; Estrin aimed to restore
the interior to its original style. In the foyer, tile stacked on
rubbled marble, by bags of grotting; heavy scrolled doors

propped in the halls, half-planed, with leaded glass. Insane, for upstairs beside the ship's cabin the ceiling was caved in, the shredded walls rotting with damp; windows were boarded. Only the back-yard loo worked; in the upper one, the big footed tub was filled with tins of paint. Farrell fought a rising panic that he could not bathe.

"I shower at the gym," she explained. "And the circumstances I've lived in? Just a working telephone brings tears to my eyes."

Out the back door scrabbled the Peace Line, which fenced Catholic from Protestant West Belfast. It was never clear which side it was protecting, unless both from the worst of themselves. Sure something there was that did love a wall in this town, for rather than campaign for its destruction, both Estrin's neighborhood and the Prods on the other side had recently applied to the City Council to please heighten the fence three more feet. The one cause that reliably brought the two sects together was keeping apart.

"There's a strange post-Holocaust feel to the back some days," she rambled, squinting into the gray. "*Peace Line* may be ironic, but at times it does seem peaceful, like today. As if everything is over."

She took him out front to show off her new grille gate; Farrell immediately thought what a perfect detonator trip it would make, with a latch convenient for fishing line.

"Funny, I'm losing a sense of conventional ugliness," she went on. "Like the Jews found Arab sectors squalid, not me—crumbling Jerusalem stone, rugs hung out windows to air, markets full of yellow fava beans and parallelograms of baklava . . . dusty feet. Soft. Biblical. More the new hotels in Tel Aviv that got to me. And here. Even rows of bombed-out houses—they can be soft, too. Smoked on the edges like charcoal sketches. Clonard exists in black and white; only the mountains have color. Then, starkness has its beauty, so does disrepair. Some of the most lyrical houses I've seen have been in the middle of forests—

abandoned and overgrown, vines through bedsteads, nests of blue jays in the sink."

It was not a beautiful area for Farrell; once more he felt an urge to wash. Across the street, the wide lot was vacant, covered in nothing so lively as weeds—strips of tire, tufts of charred upholstery. Down the road, the usual flagging array of drinking clubs and bingo parlors. He conceded that most locals were cheerful, and in his experience they didn't mind the ghettos, on either side of the line; few tried to shift out. But, Lord, it would take a foreigner to find it pretty.

He looked back at Estrin's house. A larger building than the part she occupied, both side sections of the red brick structure were condemned, their once bay windows sealed with breeze blocks. Between these dead wings, Estrin's central rooms flaunted their vitality, with lace curtains in the windows, a newly furbished *133* all shined up in brass, a glowing red door, an ivy planter. With this moment of cleanliness and care beneath shocks of rumpled beams, its blank gray upper windows staring out at the vacant lot, the house suggested a blind old man whose mind remained young. However perversely, someone was still home.

"Now I remember," said Farrell. "June '81. Four trim corpses into the hunger strikes. There was a blue van parked by the barracks there. The army dragged it down the way and the eejits did a controlled explosion."

"So I heard. But I understand it was bigger than they expected."

"It was a thousand pounds! You do not shoot into a thousand pounds! And they should have bloody well known better. That van would have been riding as close to the ground as a fat grandma without her stiff drawers. What did they think it was carrying, the Royal Welsh Fusiliers annual picnic?"

"You were just pissed off they didn't call you."

"Aggrieved. It was a plum of a bomb."

"I talked to the family that lived here. They were sitting downstairs when they saw the engine of the van plow through the front window, sail past their noses, through the kitchen, and out the back door. Like a cartoon."

"They weren't evacuated?"

"The army knocked, told them to go. But it was morning. They were tired."

Aye, that was West Belfast by '81. There's a bomb across the street, Sean. Another rasher. Dear, there's a van engine flying through the sitting room. Would you fancy another cup of tea?

"Anyway, 133 pretty much imploded from the blast. The Housing Executive was going to condemn the property; I convinced them to sell it to me, and for zip. I said I'd fix it up and leave. They seemed keen on the arrangement."

"Just don't put in good windows."

"I've been warned."

Farrell's need to wash was now overwhelming. He went for his coat.

"I'm reluctant to let you go," said Estrin. "After last night. You think you're all right. You're not."

"Have I ever been? My dear, I've been through dozens of these dramas. I'm still waiting for the traumas. My emotional life works on a delay long enough that I may be dead before the results come in. Unlike your Americans, I've had plenty of experiences; they simply don't affect me."

"My point earlier, I guess," said Estrin. "That no matter how many bombs either of us survives, we may never be able to equal the eventfulness certain miraculous people feel when they walk to the end of their drive to get the mail. A new bird at the feeder. The irises peaking. A postcard from Belgium and a magazine."

But it was like that for Farrell, this moment. The sound of her voice more than her point—the lovely throwaway casualness of it; her face against Black Mountain, the sleeves of the big shirt trailing past her hands like a small girl's exploring her father's closet. Funny, Farrell had an inkling then that the truly earthshaking news eluded his pile of morning papers, and he felt jealous not, as usual, of the turmoil of Sikhs in Pakistani riots, the brave protesters in South Africa, but of those old men with bird feeders, delighted toddlers with buttered crumpets, anyone who had pierced the world like a needle while he was stalking Brown Thomas bags; he felt left out just as he had in the early seventies in Belfast, except now he was excluded not from conspiracy and arms deals but from listening to girls by gates.

Farrell resisted this vision, its quiet, its repose. Was his frenzy mere distraction, a busyness not unlike imitating his father as a child, when he would play at being an electrician, self-importantly pack blunted screwdrivers and bent resistors, pretending to have calls to pay? Because Farrell did not have the courage to face whatever all those bombs and lectures and back-room palaver distracted him from. He felt he was frantically working with his back to something, too frightened to turn around and see if it was a cathedral or a sheer drop.

In response, Farrell turned up the dials. He reduced his sleep from four hours to three; his meals from two to one; his pleasures, to Estrin.

He would sneak the American, treat himself to her. She became clandestine, forbidden. He appeared at all times of night. He would phone, drunken and spent, at four, his voice dying off the ends of his sentences like a shout from a falling body.

He rang her once in a particularly indulgent humor. "Swallow," he whispered.

"Yes?" She'd been asleep; her voice was childlike.

"I love you." It was easy.

"What's that?"

"I love you."

"I'm sorry, Farrell, but I can't understand, what did you say?"

"I love you!" he repeated in exasperation.

After a muddled silence she stuttered forlornly, "Your accent, and—the connection, I—still didn't—"

"Forget it!" He clumped the receiver down with the annoyance of a drama coach whose recalcitrant student has refused to learn her lines.

15

Ireland, and Other Hospitals

The conference, the conference. It did not have a name, suggesting it was of many. There was only one, and the ground waters of the Province rippled with it. Everyone who was not supposed to know about it knew—as they were supposed to. Finally something would give, the deadlock of this tiny country with no government would break. And the world had been watching for twenty years, Nobels and Pulitzers poised for the occasion. In the endless onion of local politics, insiders outside insiders outside insiders, the conference was at the center, the destination of every secret, a hard core of inclusion beyond which you could not peel. At long last Farrell did not have his finger on the pulse; he was the pulse. MPs felt his wrist when they shook his hand.

In the very middle, where Farrell and Angus were pressed

up against each other, the last two layers of the bulb, there was one spine of information even Angus did not have—wan and willowy, easily bent. Farrell nursed the toothpick between his teeth.

Given half a chance the parties would participate by refusing to. In the North the most common use of hard-won power was to defy its employ. The triumph of Gerry Adams's election to Parliament was that he would not take his seat; Unionist response to the bombing of Enniskillen was for months to boycott their own council meetings. The strategy struck no one as peculiar. 1981, of course, was the peak of Irish self-destruction: after the Blanket Protest, when prisoners shattered their own windows to chatter, naked bundles in cells bare of the furniture they'd smashed, the Dirty Protest, when blanketmen smeared their cells with their own excrement in an orgy of maggots and stench that years later broke Farrell into a cold sweat, knowing the difference then, that he had never, would never believe in anything that much, ten Republicans, consumed by their own indignation, starved themselves to death. In fact, that oft-repeated ambition of the IRA to "make Northern Ireland ungovernable" meant in more down-to-earth terms no less than *If you won't let us have this country we're going to blow it up piece by piece*, expressing the juvenile illogic with which a child will break a toy he has to share. Farrell marveled there was a man walking the land whose spited face still had a nose.

Likewise, the Border Poll for which the conference was designed to marshal consensus threatened at all points to turn into a tiny Alliance Party bake sale. Nationalists had largely boycotted the poll in '73, and threatened to do so once more; the SDLP was none too keen on an internal solution of any sort, and claimed power sharing had already been tried and failed with Sunningdale. Unionists would refuse, without Angus MacBride's constant cajoling, to proceed with "the way forward" as long as the Anglo-Irish Agreement remained in place, and the referendum seemed to offer a tempting context in which to hammer this weary point home. And should either side neglect the poll in force, Britain would ignore it. Back to the drawing board.

Meanwhile, Farrell still never turned down a speech engagement, for he couldn't pass up an opportunity to blind one more complacent audience with epiphanies of apocalypse. He could always depress them with visions of murder and division irremediably drizzling on, Irish bad weather. But how much more he relished answering questions about what would happen in the advent of a unilateral British troop withdrawal: rampaging Protestant armies decked out like adverts for *Soldier of Fortune*; Irish Americans pouring in funds so the Provos finally get their sting missiles and matching uniforms; the South trooping up ineffectually to protect the Catholic minority. Eager to get in on the fray, Scottish and Welsh nationalists rebel; after a hysteria of secession, England is left with the Falkland Islands for holidays. In short, the collapse of the British "Empire." Farrell liked to proceed from here to the destabilization of the whole Western alliance, but they often ran out of time.

And maybe Farrell couldn't say no because he couldn't overcome the flattery when even the feeblest library asked him over. Why, hundreds of people would sit in a room with their hands in their laps and listen to what he thought. He liked honoraria, even the twenty-dollar check and shamrock tie clasp. He liked to be *flown*, that luxurious passive tense, just as he liked to be *driven* in taxis. He liked first class. He liked it in the States, where they routinely introduced him as *Dr.* O'Phelan. Deplorable not to correct their mistake, but damn it, Farrell had lived on the margins for twenty years and he was due.

And he was worthy; he would try, harder than anyone had ever tried anything, he would fly anywhere, his exertions more diversified than ever: adding another linking agent to remove him from Callaghan, Farrell continued to negotiate between the Provos and the Rips; he was still raising funds for the conference in America; he crisscrossed the North and the Republic alike to win every stray councilor's support for his Border Poll; and he still hadn't lost his more personal touch, arranging sentence reduction for a repentant Loyalist now eager to make TV spots for Confidential Telephone. The time between washing his teeth and reaching for his jangling alarm was now shorter than it took most families to have tea. Yet he never overslept, for the clock was supremely effective—it frightened him. The same cheap Boots make used to time so many of the devices he'd dismantled, its digits big and childish, with the deceiving, conniving face that had lied to him in the Brown Thomas bag, not even wound. Well, it woke him up.

While Farrell did snatch the odd sausage roll and wrangle an occasional appointment from a pub to a restaurant, he had to face the fact he was more or less living on white wine. Truly the rule about not drinking until 8 p.m. began to blur when you were finishing your third bottle at eight in the morning. But drink was work, intrinsic to Irish negotiation.

With poor nourishment, wine, the scurry down airport moving sidewalks tripping over bags and children, the storm down the aisles of Boeings to be the first off the plane, it was lack of sleep that slayed him. Now that four hours constituted an indulgence only after neglecting to go to bed altogether, he would wake to find air traffic routes scored under his eyes, trails of exhaust wisping across his forehead, cirrus clouds drifting through his skin. Confronting the mirror shaving became a grim ordeal, acid tributaries eating across his cheeks, his face an aerial photograph of defoliated Vietnam. Farrell's eyes went gluey; the stagnant pools of his pupils eroded a murky shore. Though he would miss more sleep rather than not bathe, by the end of the day his hair had curled with sweat and thickened with salt, because a day was too long, it was a *whole* day. Worst of all, that boundary itself gave way, for he slept so little that one day bled borderlessly into the next, and he surprised himself, such an extraordinary intellect dependent for a sense of order on the distinction between Thursday night and Friday morning.

While he'd once been charmed by his own cognition, now thinking was a tyranny, frantic, uncontrolled. Why, he even bought a Walkman, but even the *St. Matthew Passion* could not overwhelm the merciless chorus in his head: *Call on Devlin at the Maze. The Kesh? The prison "outside Maze." Never know what to call the bloody place. Matter? Does. Myth. War of Symbols. So the Rips want autonomy. Won't get it. Unreasonable bastards, will want a bloody dental plan next. Speech at U. Mass Wednesday. "The final victims of effective propaganda are those who put it out." Tighten. "Propagandists victimize themselves." Not quite. Title? Entrapment, a title with entrapment. You told the Swallow tea tomorrow, you'll be in Boston. Cancel, be sure to sound knackered. How could I sound any other way? And ring Derry. Ring Ohio. Ring, ring, ring* . . . Phrases, assertions, plane schedules batted birdlike in his rafters, airy, fluttering, a panic of wings.

Farrell started breaking things, knocking over his wine. Holding his after-shave one morning at the sink, he simply: let go. The glass smashed into every corner and the smell rose for days, reminding him that he could no longer go on automatic for these most rudimentary of chores. If he picked up a bottle he needed to concentrate: Squeeze your fingers.

The whole frame of his vision would jolt an inch aside; sometimes the vista winked out altogether. He kept his eyes open extra wide, remembering with the same deliberate effort of holding bottles, Eyes open! He refused to blink until the balls dried, in fear of the lids latching lash to lash, as he might avoid letting doors close behind him to which he had no key.

Beside him bar stools danced; furniture remained stationary only when he stared it straight down. He was frequently convinced that when he turned around he returned to find a chair in a subtly different position. Everywhere in the crevices of cabinets at the Maze reception, in the upholstery piping of the NIO waiting room, he saw silverfish; ants scurried the surface of airline trays, picnic blanket. Pigeons and kittens skittering under parked cars he always mistook for rats. Strangers distorted on banisters and the bevels of Guinness mirrors into people whose bombs he'd dismantled or whose rallies he'd sabotaged.

Soon he would become dangerously narcoleptic. Already a

moment would jump cut to beats later and he would find his companion several words on, his own chin an inch closer to his tie. Bad splicing, he called it, but the simpler word was sleep. He was falling asleep, in taxis, between points in his own lectures, dozing through a question from the audience and then answering the one before.

For Farrell had fought to dispose of bombs with every bit the military vigor with which they'd been planted, and now, deprived of that campaign by one shaky epiphany, he had launched into his political phase like the Somme. Yet he had to confess that there were nights he stayed up to the requisite hour merely staring at those soft women in the Tate prints, that there were days he whipped from Derry-Dublin-Derry because of deliberate sloppy planning, to make an enemy of his own schedule, to lance with cabbies, traffic, the very geography of his island as the North's own Don Quixote. Farrell was one more veteran who could not adapt to peacetime, like any UVF or IRA volunteer a career soldier, and saddled with the problem of ordinariness that descended even on battle if you fought every day. He no longer believed in fighting, but he did not understand what you did otherwise with your bloody time.

Furthermore, he suspected he stayed so busy to avoid his own simpering, predictable company. A rude admission: he didn't like being alone. He would ride all the way to his office to make phone calls instead of ringing from home, simply to hear Constance humming over the computer nearby.

It was on his way to Boston in May that Farrell noticed from paper banners through Central Arcade the approach of Mother's Day—and even this attention was unlike him. For there is a trick to avoiding obligation he had sorted out early. Maybe on Mother's Day flowers are in order, a card, a call. Those are the rules. But you can escape through a wee loophole: *I am like this*. All you need do is establish early that you are Not the Sort of Person Who Calls on Mother's Day, and lo, you are not. Expectation can be trained to zero. If you are Not the Sort of Person

Who: goes home at Christmas, returns phone messages, responds to letters, or "keeps in touch," there is no discussion and, surprisingly, no anger. There may be rules, but it is not so difficult to make it clear that these are for other people. And your mother and lover and sisters will all, oddly, admire you, speak of you wistfully around the Christmas tree, a little envious because they didn't feel like coming this year either. "What do you suppose Farrell's up to now?" they might sigh, surrounded by wrapping paper and noisy children and expensive indications of how poorly they know each other after all. In any country you can achieve the stature of a separate nation with its own laws and system of justice, and you will have diplomatic immunity in your own family. What you *are*—and you must play on everyone's sense of the incontrovertible, on fact—is your excuse: *I am like this*. So your sisters will eye you lighting once more into a taxi with the single briefcase for Boston, for you are Not the Sort of Person Who Checks Luggage, while they are stuck pawing furry slippers in Marks and Sparks for Ma. You are the tall one who, in a fit of adolescent brilliance, cast himself as the exception; it is not your fault that exceptions require majorities to whom the rules apply. So when you let the weekend pass by, long after your sisters' flowers have wilted on her table your mother will still love you, or whatever it is she does, and maybe even more than your sisters, because from you she can miss what from them she simply takes, and you will imagine (you have worked this out so beautifully that you actually believe this) that should you freakishly remember Mother's Day this year she would only be disappointed.

On into the summer the light lengthened as if to accommodate his hours, the sky staying up with him until three, rising at six. So surely what happened in New York in August was a gift, for on this quick two-day fund-raising trip for his conference an air traffic controllers' strike delayed his plane back to London for a week. Raving or palm-greasing, Farrell was not getting out of this city without a rowboat, and he didn't swim. A frustration, but the perfect opportunity to catch up on sleep.

He would not. He stayed up anyway, for no apparent reason. Drinking, reading, talking, it didn't matter as long as it lasted till three. Then he would reach for his trusty Boots clock and set the alarm for six. At sunrise he would pace his hotel room, "thinking."

For once he'd done his presentation for the III and drafted a speech for Women Together he was now doubtless going to miss, Farrell had nothing to do. Nothing. It was awful. He spent nearly a thousand dollars on international phone calls, but less for pressing business than maundering to Estrin, Constance, what'sherface, not even to talk but to stay awake. He watched himself stay awake. He would admit this was insane. But whenever he leaned back on the pillow in his stocking feet of an afternoon, he would bolt upright in five minutes, heart racing; he would put on his shoes.

Farrell wondered should he take a butcher's at New York, but he had no intention of gawking over the edge of the World Trade towers like an eejit. He had work to do, work— Not here.

Frankly, New York made him nervous. Its population was five times larger than all of Northern Ireland's. No one here knew his name, his exploits, the family he ignored. For that matter, they didn't know the Provos, Stickies, Irps, or Rips. They couldn't list the Five Demands. Bobby Sands could be a line of clothing, Stormont a resort hotel. They didn't know the Anglo-Irish Agreement from pork pie. They didn't understand his accent or his expressions, *bollocks, dosed off, gobshite*. This was an experience not unlike those narcoleptic absences, the blinking out of the world, only this time New York remained in view; it was Belfast that disappeared.

He did enjoy telling men in bars where he was from—bloody well wasn't Teaneck, New Jersey, now, was it? Their brows shot up. But all they knew was bombs. Not the school-bus incident versus the Falls Swimming Center versus Crossgar, just bombs. They asked him was it dangerous, and Farrell said rather, fudging; privately he admitted to finding New York a damned sight dicier than back home. While he usually felt tall, bulky black men swelling in torn sweats made him feel mostly thin. The cars might not explode, but were taped with cardboard, NO RADIO and EMPTY TRUNK. Panhandlers tugged on every block: *Buy me an apricot, I just need bus fare back to Macon, My baby has AIDS* . . . "Crack" was no longer good conversation.

He refused to debunk his own city, which enjoyed a New Yorker's respect. When they asked if it was blasted to bits, he didn't say, "Hardly," but, "In parts." Yet should he start in on British incompetence, they drifted to the baseball screen overhead.

"Does Sunningdale mean bugger-all to you?" he ventured once at McSorley's.

"Sunny Dale . . ." his companion ruminated. "He in the Bears?"

Och, it wasn't they refused to listen. Sure, he discovered plenty of rice pudding receptive well-meaningness, blank propped-up smily faces full of niceness to strangers, an unfastened Interest in Fascinating Places, but you could tell they hadn't a clue. Later, spending more and more money on his hotel phone, he talked to Estrin about her travels for the first time without derision. An American in Berlin, couldn't she as well have been a polar bear?

"Porta-problem," she supplied.

"Sorry?"

"I yak through dinner saying the same thing all over the world. I'd love to find a city where I felt confused. I envy you."

While at home he flapped for news about places like New York, here he scanned the *Times* for the North. In the Travel Section on Sunday, Farrell devoured an article on B & Bs in the Republic he would never glance at in his Dublin *Tribune*. He bought an *Irish Echo*, foaming when he found it full of easy expatriate Republicanism, a facile support for the IRA that would never cost anyone here Semtex under their Volvos. In his indignation, Farrell felt more normal than he had all week.

Finally, one morning in the hotel coffee shop, he found an article on an inside page of the *Times*, and it was so small! Six people had died, and it was only two columns wide! He crumpled the wretched paper. *Who* died? In Lisburn, but near Thiepval? Downtown? The "IRA" took credit, but which faction? They bombed a "Fun Run."

"Rips!" he exclaimed out loud.

A woman beside him checked her blouse. "Where?"

Uncontrollably, he strolled into O'Anybody bars with green awnings, full of third-generation immigrants whose idea of being Irish was to buy lurid emerald soft-serve on St. Patrick's Day. While delighted to hear Farrell's accent, they couldn't tell Glengormley's from Cork's; the punters slapped him on the back and started to sing "When Irish Eyes Are Smiling," but Farrell didn't know the words. They thought Charlie Haughey was on *Hill Street Blues*. With their own speech thickened as if by a mouthful of ballpark hot dog, aslur with *yeahs*, *okays*, and *I guesses*, these local O'Reillys and O'Flanagans were about as Irish as Yasir Arafat.

A few glasses down, Farrell lit into song himself. He'd been in the boys' choir as a child and never lost a serene tenor. He treated the lot to the latest Ulster diddy, "Song Don't Spike":

Agent O
Said don't let 'em go
And keep traffic out of the way.
F. said to me: Take out all three,
and make sure Miss J. can't see.
So I shot 'im, I shot 'im,
I shot 'im and shot 'im,
Sixteen times from behind.
I know I shouldn't oughta but the people of Gibraltar
Were uppermost on my mind.

Bombmaker Savage,
We caused 'im some damage,
To make sure he'd not bomb again.

Off went the siren, so I started a-firin,
He spiraled with his arms beside 'im.
I shot 'im, I shot 'im,
I shot 'im, I shot 'im,
I trod upon his chest;
And while he lay static, with my Browning automatic,
Used minimum force arrest.

Then we were seen
With our guns down our jeans,
Our berets and axes in bags.
I won't give a Provo a chance to abuse me,
I didn't shout a warning, but I did say "Excuse me."
Then I shot 'im, I shot 'im,
I shot 'im and shot 'im,
Till the passersby were sick.
I'm sorry, Mr. Mordue, but I really can't afford to
Let some poofta spoil my trick.

Six months later,
We're filling the papers
in Gibraltar to tell our tale.
Paddy McGrory won't swallow our story,
Nor will Felix or the bleeding jury,
So we shot 'em, we shot 'em,
We shot 'em and shot 'im,
So the world would always see:
You can't jail an SAS man when he's Maggie's assassin
On a shoot to kill policy.

So we shot 'em, we shot 'em,
We shot 'em, we shot 'em,
Cause we're soldiers A to D (yessiree!)
We shot 'em, we shot 'em,
We shot 'em, we shot 'em,
We're soldiers A to D—eeeeeee—!

Now, Farrell may have gotten carried away with those last *We shot 'em*'s, but face it, the piece was a gem, a coup, a prize, and it was fresh, *de rigueur* from the homeland, and Farrell O'Phelan didn't waste his time memorizing any old mumble from West Belfast except, give us a break here, it was hilarious. But no. Farrell might have gotten more laughs with Peter, Paul, and Mary. Later, he prodded these gombeens on current events, and though the shooting was the biggest story for Northern Ireland in at least the last three years, in New York *Gibraltar* seemed associated purely with some insurance company.

For now, however, he was not through testing, and sang on determinedly to the tune of "If You're Happy and You Know It, Clap Your Hands":

Would you like a chicken supper, Bobby Sands?
Would you like a chicken supper, Bobby Sands?
Would you like a chicken supper,
You skinny Fenian fucker,
Would you like a chicken supper, Bobby Sands?

No one seemed to find his selections inconsistent. Farrell quit. The North was a tiny, exclusive hell: only one and a half million people on earth would get your jokes. If you ever really belonged in the Province it would never let you go; conversely, if like Farrell you felt furiously you didn't belong there, it had roped you as well. Loathing for his island trapped him perfectly as love. And that explained why Farrell wandered one of the greatest cities in the world in limbo, for here it was meaningless to hate Ireland—why not hate Portugal, the color blue, Monday mornings, his coat.

Passing Keshcarrigan, he spent a hundred dollars on the very books he could get in Belfast, Blackstaff and Poolbeg. They even had an old copy of *Bare Limbs on Basalt*, which he bought on an odd whim. In Zabar's, he searched the shelves of brandied plums and satay for oatcakes and soda bread. At the White

Horse—there was also a White Horse at the docks—he ordered Guinness, and he didn't even like Guinness.

"Haven't a baldy."

Farrell's ears picked up.

"Och, don't get your knickers in a twist."

The barkeep. Farrell made a beeline. Carrickfergus. Turned out the boy was only over this year, and though he may have been a Prod half Farrell's age, and back in Antrim would have precious little to say to any Taig renegade, here they knocked each other's shoulders and the kid slid him a free pint. On hearing "O'Phelan," his stance and eyes changed; Farrell shifted in return, standing more at his old angle, his voice cutting with conviction and disgust. The lad had the lowdown on Lisburn, and the two of them bantered on until three.

Back at the Algonquin, Farrell stacked his books by the bed. Strange to have bought that anthology. He experimented with keeping the volume on top, and burying it between *Violence and the Sacred* and *Writings from Portlaoise*. Still, from anywhere in the room he could sense its presence, like an unpaid bill on a desk. Over the TV blaring back-to-back reruns of *Mary Tyler Moore*, the book accused him from the stack with a quiet that pierced both Rhoda's nightmarish blind date and the day Mary ran the newsroom.

The sting of mum reproof reminded Farrell of his mother. She'd never thrown tantrums, but clammed up. Silverware rattled in the scullery. His sisters had muffled into pillows, trying not to laugh. Farrell had never been inclined to. With the air too thick to breathe, he would wheeze in his room, stifling himself over his glass inhaler since bidding for attention with asthma seemed too obvious a ploy. This went on for hours, and finally he would weep and implore her to stop slamming cupboards and pressing her lips white, to kiss his cheek, to forgive him, though he would rarely know what he had done or whether he was the one who did it. Farrell was born into total responsibility for everything and total incapacity to make anything right.

As an adult, Farrell had thrown great drunken rages: *See,*

Mother? This is how it's done. What I would have given to hear you scream. How I would have eaten off oilcloth to see you smash all our crockery of an evening. As a child, Farrell yearned to be beaten. In her cruelty, his mother never raised a hand.

At last the silent suffering on the bedside table became too familiar to bear. He groaned and gave in, reading a few pages. He tried to decide if she was good. While he found plenty of weak lines, O.T.T., there were others, harder to dismiss; these he resisted. He was being unfair. He wanted her to be a bad poet, and wondered why. He tried to be open-minded. Yet beginning with optimism or disdain, he could not decide. Apparently he had to find her brilliant or abysmal. Those were his categories, there were no in betweens. Though he'd always cherished it, maybe his extremity was callow. Maybe she was neither a genius nor a charlatan. Maybe there was such a thing as middle-level talent. Maybe that's all there was: absolutes are abstractions. Maybe his inability to see shades amounted to a lack of subtlety, or worse. Maybe he was an idiot. And maybe the chiaroscuro of his own portrait was equally misguided. Maybe Farrell, too, was middling like the rest of them; the severity of his own character—the travel and insomnia, the forty-eight pairs of identical socks, the same swordfish steak in the same restaurant for two years straight—pretension or a lie . . .

Farrell quickly rang room service for wine. It hardly helped, rather made the point again: the fumé blanc as well was neither good nor bad.

On the subject of mediocrity, wasn't it impossible to avoid his father? Farrell disliked thinking of his father. His mother may have seemed petty and sharp to her neighbors, but Farrell knew her to be an awesome woman and could study her endlessly late nights in hotels. However, he refused to flatter his father as having afflicted him whatsoever: blame was credit. But didn't he resemble the geezer in the end, with that rancid contempt for Taigs and Prods alike, his paltry boycott of one? The way Farrell had lowered at the marches in '69, mocking legless from the sidelines, as if the whole of the PD was frantic for his lead-ership and he was holding out? Or even earlier, the way he used to hide in the linen closet for hours, bruised and brooding, until he gradually admitted no one noticed he was gone? Farrell always refusing to participate, when who wanted him to, who cared? With the useless defiance of his whole life, wasn't Farrell O'Phelan the original abstentionist; why, had he ever held a legitimate job? And where did he scoff the whole sniffy hard-done-by if not straight from his da?

Grievance was his birthright. Ruairi O'Phelan was deprived, though would have been just as deprived in Switzerland or Japan, born as binman or prince, for deprivation is a point of view. Ruairi was one of the lucky ones, with real complaints: in '68, he suddenly couldn't wire Protestant houses, and the Catholic jobs were sorrier and didn't pay; he never had a chance at a city contract. He could hardly run for office, and that he didn't want to never stopped him from whining at being shut out. Because the one thing Ruairi O'Phelan loved over anything he wanted was not being able to get it.

For the most rancorous of his gripes was not having quite enough of them. Some months were tight, but he didn't have the solace of unemployment. He had a job, he merely despised it. And he would despise any job, revile the most perfect family. Older, Farrell learned not to take the hatred personally: his father would loathe any old son. For don't imagine Ruairi nursed the least illusion he might achieve through his children. The evening Farrell announced he'd won a place at grammar school was the worst of his childhood. No, there was expressly no consolation. In what you could only admire as resourcefulness, Ruairi had wrung joy from his suffering, but you could not have that and joy from joy. Business breaks and unbigoted Presbyterians embittered his heart. But watching news clips of Burntollet, he jumped from his chair, eyes shining, his fist pounding into his hand, for all the world like another B-special with a truncheon. At last the black bastards had shown their claws! All that Republican jaw supplied a vocabulary for his larger feeling of being shafted: he was a Catholic but did not believe in life after death.

227

This was his only chance and it had gone badly. His politics expressed his larger disappointment at this one mingy life, where every passing stranger was a man he would not be, who would see what he would not see on turning the corner. In the end Farrell supposed he admired the old sod, for the envy was a form of imagination. Here this cabbage could be coulibiac; now could be two hundred years ago, before anyone repaired a toaster; I might have been born smarter and more handsome, in France.

"I was a bright spark," Ruairi would grumble. "I was one bright spark, a fair sight brighter than *you*." So every impeccable brown-nosing report Farrell brought home dripped with pools of sloshed Carlsberg by nightfall. On through the pints, his father would rip his son's chessboards, one reason Farrell switched to wood. And all that time Farrell wanted nothing more than to wire a kitchen in front of his father and have the refrigerator come on.

While thirty-page wine lists seduced his finer side, Farrell often grabbed a hot pretzel off street vendors in preference to the Four Seasons. In fact, much longer here would surely drive him to the monasticism of fifteen, to butterless toast and sugarless tea. In Belfast, good taste was an eccentricity, in New York an obsession. He was tempted to find the town frivolous. New Yorkers seemed to care mostly about film festivals; they would go on at length about novels, having read only the reviews; and they talked incessantly about food. While Nelson Mandela turned seventy in jail, Haiti fell to the military, and the U.S. Navy shot down 290 Iranian civilians by *mistake*, New Yorkers appeared far more fussed by the death of the casual screw. (Served them right—if they couldn't walk to the edge and look over, they didn't deserve to reproduce. Farrell had come of age in Ireland, where sex meant playing the odds—you needed nerve to take a woman in those days. Apologies to Estrin Lancaster, but birth control was ruinous. Fair enough, plague surpassed pregnancy, for as far as Farrell was concerned, HIV restored to sex its proper sense of peril.)

Walking back to the Algonquin late his last night, the strike over and his step light, he chose a dubious course and found himself square in Hell's Kitchen. He recognized this variety of quiet from curfew. Most of the streetlights were smashed. His loud gritty stride seemed to advertise new, expensive cordovans. In the shadows, groups of black boys slumped on hydrants, and it took Farrell blocks to realize the language they slurred to each other in was English.

Thinking, *Scintillating maybe, but enough is enough*, Farrell swung determinedly east on Forty-ninth Street, and nearly ran into something hanging on a drainpipe. What he mostly remembered were its eyes—Farrell apologized for the pronoun, but *his* was beyond overgenerous to incorrect. Terribly, they were every bit as intelligent as they were alien. *I knife you*, they said, *for a quarter. No symbols. No flaggy-wavy. No we call it Ulster you call it the Six Counties, let's fight. I don't care you call Hell's Kitchen Timbuktu. And you can go home and write all the sociological this, psychological that you like, point is, you go home at all, you're lucky. This whole city say I'm zip, but a flick of my wrist say I'm the most important man you meet your whole life. And the last—"* The teeth flashed, Cheshire on the pipe.

The only reason Farrell didn't run was for fear of inviting chase. *People were killing each other here and it didn't mean anything.* They would do you not because you were Catholic but because you were there. Around him a city churned with the nausea of insignificant violence. There was a war on in New York all right, but fought on all fours. It made Northern Ireland look like a fife-blowing, drum-rolling Napoleonic tea party. For once the dismissive term *troubles* seemed fair.

That night Farrell had no problem staying awake. Burning with raw, bare-bulbed anxiety, at last he suffered legitimate insomnia, no help from Boots. Because a walk through Hell's Kitchen made West Belfast seem cute.

On the plane back, Farrell drank red wine. Meaty, it warmed him. Every mile the pilot closed between Farrell and his wretched island warmed him more. He missed its ugly coziness, rank and sweet, like this cheap Beaujolais. Farrell's relationship with his city was that sick, incestuous intimacy of two people who have made each other suffer. It was the sour, helpless love you feel for a brother who has run amok.

Then, there was a perverse prestige to a bum brother, and New York had unsettled Farrell's contented partnership with the black sheep. He was briefly concerned whether Northern Ireland was important. Come on, Farrell had worked with *explosives*. He had brokered with the *IRA*. Belfast, too, murdered its citizens indiscriminately, thank you very much. They have drugs; well, we have bombs! Beat that! Carnage and destruction! Mindless meanness and corruption! Farrell laughed; people in D through H looked over. Truth was, he felt competitive with New Yorkers over whose people were the more barbarous.

Farrell basked under the lemon-yellow sign in Heathrow: BELFAST PASSENGERS ONLY. There was a hard gleam off the plastic, selecting him from all the other simpering destinations BA flew more decorative travelers. The very sound of the place had a gasp to it, an exultation. Hadn't he little use for the New Yorkers who'd toured his town and chirped up in bars, *Why, it's not nearly so bad as you're led to believe*, who described bakeries and record shops and normal cups of coffee. *For fuck's sake, we've been through hell and back*, he'd wanted to return. *Sure we deserve a bloody cup of coffee*. Stride lengthening, briefcase swinging, Farrell advanced on Gate 49 with the jaunty territorial pride with which he'd swaggered into his father's electronics shop as a child, pocketing bits of wire, climbing the desk chair, propping his feet up: *mine*.

On the shuttle Farrell congratulated himself. Through the impromptu holiday he'd tabulated shy of twenty hours' sleep in six nights. And he was satisfied to note that he was coughing, rather badly. With any luck, by the end of the flight he'd be running a vigorous fever.

16

The House in Castlecaulfield

Had Farrell been a product, Estrin would have returned him.

"I've never seen you turn down a glass of wine," she observed dolefully. He reached constantly for his inhaler, but it wasn't helping; the cough was worse than ever, his handkerchief heavy and yellow. His forehead trickled like the windowpanes outside, and it was pouring.

Reading him as a man who would balk at hospitals, she was alarmed when he didn't put up a fight. At a glance he looked seventy-five. With no raincoat, Estrin draped the old man in a tarp; clutching the streaked sheet to his middle and cowling his damp gray hair, Farrell looked biblical, but out of those new-fangled churches with banners and teak—a modern-day Jesus in plastic and slapdash slashes of paint. Only the face was Middle Ages—flat, white, and harrowing. The eyes were empty. When she moved him outside he went soft and obedient in her hands; it was gross.

When he whimpered where were they going and Estrin said the Royal, just around the corner, she could as well have said plague hospital. "City!" Farrell gasped, and though City was a longer ride, she wouldn't argue. She propped him on the bike and said hold on, but hadn't meant like *that*; Farrell squeezed her chest until they both couldn't breathe.

"O'Phelan!"

Nurses scurried. Estrin had prepared herself for the six-hour wait of U.S. emergency rooms, but they took care of everyone in short order and Farrell right away. Estrin stood trailing the tarp, feeling that hopeful uselessness particular to waiting rooms. She importuned to stick with him; surprisingly they said yes.

His temperature was 104. A nurse said she was sorry but they'd have to take a blood gas, and Estrin didn't understand why the woman apologized until the needle went in his wrist and for the first time in hours Farrell returned to his eyes. They shot black. He inhaled quickly and clogged. That was all. The nurse stood back with her syringe full, nodding at Farrell appreciatively. "Haven't I seen stagers bawl like babies. He's a hard one, your man."

Estrin was grateful for "your man," even if it was only an expression.

Farrell was careened into X-ray in an oxygen mask. Presently a doctor called Estrin in to view the film—both lobes were overcast. The lungs looked so small, translucent wings darkened by storm cloud. Oddly, she recognized him. Farrell was so thin that even under radiation he didn't look much different. And she'd know those close, sharp shoulders anywhere. There was something about his sheer narrowness that melted her, a boy hunched in the back of a classroom, hoping not to be called on.

"Overdoing it as usual?"

Farrell rasped, sucking a last sip through a straw.

"There's no doubt you should have kicked it, old boy." The doctor slapped Farrell's shoulder like the withers of a sturdy horse. "But sure we'll prop you up one more time. Pneumonia again."

When Farrell heard the word *pneumonia*, he nestled his wiry head of hair into the pillow with the finality of *So. It's bad enough*. He laid his hands on his chest and closed his yellow eyes. With the webbed corners of his mouth serenely upturned, why, Estrin swore that she had never seen him happier.

Pneumonia's called the "old man's friend," and for true, I do feel old, too. Everyone whinged about getting old, but Farrell thought dotage must be spot on. What a relief to have done what you had to do—or not. To have bleeding well not done it, and it didn't matter and to know that, flat out. It was that perfect, placid, bored wisdom he was aiming for.

As for friend, he'd never had one; maybe a disease would do. Now, that's intimacy, isn't it? Better than washing your own socks. You and your germs, locked in loving, dependent embrace.

MacBride? If a disease is a friend, maybe Angus fit the bill at that. They were both out to slaughter him.

Otherwise there had only been women. Even there, had a single woman affected him in his life? In regard to his emotions, Farrell was increasingly convinced he hadn't any. He thought of himself as an alien from outer space landed here by mistake—in Northern Ireland, of all the unlucky places—who was desperately trying to pass as a human being. He had studied the bereaved at Mass, noting what they did with their hands. He had pondered the expressions of happy couples in engagement photographs, with the clinical curiosity of a biologist examining cell reproduction under a microscope.

Remember the Swallow asking how you felt when you heard your own voice on "Good Morning, Ulster"? *I feel nothing*. You said it hard, a slap; she went quiet. *That's right, I can be brutal. I like being brutal. There's a feeling: I like being brutal.*

Because there's a way the meanness is against yourself. I felt that slap. When I shut the door in women's faces, I sense their cheeks burning on the other side. I like to make women suffer so that I feel their suffering as well—they are the host body. I like it when they fall in love with me because that's as close as I get to the experience. The creature from outer space feeds off human emotion, needs the proximity of lacerating, unrequited love to survive. Now there's a film for you: an alien stalking the heath who sucks hearts dry. Then, by now in Northern Ireland a creature who ate feelings would starve . . .

I am starving. I rarely remember my dreams, but many of the bits I recall are greedy: of cakes, tarts, pots of jam. And in real-life restaurants the cart wheels by. I don't eat desserts.

I can't eat and I can't feel and I can't breathe. Now what the hell can I do?

Drink.

Oh, God, don't laugh, it hurts. But let me tell you, I do love pain. I'd happily trade places with Nietzsche. They say he was in physical pain his whole life. And how much that explains. Well, that's what I require. Pneumonia won't do the trick; I need a condition. Something degenerative and incurable. Then I might cheer up, like. An excuse! Admit it, you shagging bastard, you want an excuse for spending all day, every day, in bed. Isn't that the secret of the alarm clock? You refused to sleep in New York because if you slept at all you would have hibernated through March.

Fucking hell, that blood gas was brilliant. No bits, what? No wee parts talking to each other? For once we had our united Ireland. You think I'm sick, but the pain, that's what's mighty about it: all of you hurts. A blood gas will cauterize your seams.

This breathing, or not, I have worked on this a long time: asthma is my life. I keep two sad sacks on either side of my chest. They are nearly sealed tight. Someday the tiny leaks at the top will pinch closed and I will float over oceans with two balloons of still, stale air. I have never been a man who could breathe. Air is not my element; I feel lost in it. I am a worm. I would burrow warm, muddy gardens, secret and safe in the roots of your peas.

You know how you die in crucifixion? You suffocate. You get tired, see, having to hold yourself up. When you let go, you collapse on your esophagus. And Christ tired fast. That's why he went first. He was already knackered, after holding himself up for years. Probably for the first time in his frigging life up there that he relaxed. And look at the consequences.

Do not imagine you can let up. It's only pneumonia. With anti-biotics, it will buy you maybe a week. Are you forgetting what it's like here, with women and hospitals? How fast the gaggles fasten onto another opportunity to take care of you? To arrive with pastries and worry and poetry? Sure they're already queued at the door! On your toes, man. Certain birds must be kept apart. Oh, bloody freaking hell, it's back to work, is it? Oh, aye. It's back to work.

Now, visiting hours at City are— Numbers bobbled, each the same as every other. And how long to get down the elevator, how long to get out of the parking lot? Or how about a different bird a day, like National Trust picture calendars?

Soon I will get in an airplane and fly to the Canary Islands. I will have lined up many appointments for which I will not show. I will not even tell Constance where I have gone. On the beach, I will speak to no one, and even with the ice cream vendor I will hold up one finger and hand him generous change. There will be no telephones. I will not read. I'll feed crab salad to sandpipers—

If that five-foot-two Schwarzenegger is a swallow, what's the other, a chickadee? A budgie? —A pigeon! Och, you are a vicious man. Why is it the only time I feel truly warmhearted toward you is when you're nasty.

Pigeons will coo in your rafters, grovel the slates of your roof. They will dive in their own cages; you may hook the door on their tails. You can band their legs with cryptics they don't understand. Easily ruffled, easily soothed; not beautiful, but then I am a fancier. Obedient birds, if not quite reputable, they may be summoned and sent.

But swallows sweep down when it amuses them—imperious, willful. And so small!

Besides, why waste an opportunity, the sweated bed, the listing head, the phlegm—the sympathy; admit it, you want them to see, all of them, look what you've done to me—somewhere in this is a terrible lie—I am so tired!

He had to—he needed—he could not remember. He was

left only with urgency of some sort. He did not want the urgency. *Please, please let me go.* He felt his body sink into the stiff hospital sheets. They exuded the same optimistic smell of Estrin's fresh plaster. Around him, his thoughts flapped like linen on a line: *More than merely consultative but less than fully executive* chimed with the incessant rhythm of a child's rhyme. *Poor canary, I'm contrary, a worm in your garden grows* . . . Swallow. His throat bubbled and closed. *Constitutional nationalism drawing on the threat of the unconstitutional* circled without a predicate, a chicken without its head. Farrell hoped desperately he was losing his mind, but with his luck someone would find it and bring it back, like the time he ducked behind a Donegal bluff to detonate some dicey gel-ignite, only to have a boy run up behind him shouting helpfully, "Mister! Mister! You forgot your bag!"

"What time is it?"

"Four."

"And visiting hours start?"

Estrin cocked her head. "Three."

Farrell's breathing increased. He fussed with his pillow. "I've had no other visitors, then?"

"Not today."

"What do you mean today, isn't it Wednesday?"

"Friday."

Farrell's smile was strained. "The rest of my life should be dispatched so painlessly."

"I don't think it was painless." Estrin had never seen him nervous. It made her more relaxed.

"So!" he chirped. "Anyone been in, then?"

"Sure. You're a popular guy."

"Caramel squares." He scowled at his bedside.

"I met a friend of yours," she volunteered languidly.

"Oh?"

"Woman."

"Mmm."

"I thought she was beautiful."

Farrell paused, and dived in, patting her hand. "I've been meaning to introduce you two, actually."

"Well, I hardly buy that."

"Why ever not?"

"You've never meant to introduce me to anyone in your life, not anyone. I'm modular. I plug in and out. Don't snow me about introductions just because they've already been made."

"I can see you hardly inherited your father's pastoral bedside manner."

"She broke my heart."

". . . Did you like her?"

"Quite. And she liked me. That's what was heartbreaking. She certainly didn't want to."

"She's a kind person."

"Horrifically. She made me want to give her chocolates, send her to Hawaii. Just to make up for what an unbelievable shit you've been."

"I don't think I've treated her so badly."

"Well," said Estrin, "that's what's so shitty, isn't it?"

"What all did you talk about, for Christ's sake?"

"You, of course."

"And what did you decide?"

"That you were a prick. That we adored you. That there was something wrong with us. That she and I should run off and get married. What women always say to each other. But of course, by saying anything but. You'd have enjoyed it, actually. Your kind of fun."

"You're getting an attitude, my dear."

"Yes," she hissed.

"She's a fine poet," Farrell defended.

"That surprises me. She doesn't seem like the type."

"But you said you liked her."

"Exactly. I don't like poets. The very idea of strangers caring fuck-all about your daffodils and your kitty cat and your predictably hopeless romances—you know I find it laughable."

"I wouldn't single out the poets. I find everything laughable."

"Oh, you do not. I am truly tired of your line about how you don't believe in anything. You're the first man I've met who rivals my own father's putrid conviction. All the while claiming you're caught in the jaws of the abyss. I don't think I should let you have it both ways."

Farrell smiled. "Dialectics."

"In America we call it bullshit. And now you're grinning because you're relieved. Back to the abstract. Anything but face your responsibility for Constance Trower."

Farrell looked vacant. "Constance?"

"She makes you uncomfortable. And she should. She's too good for you."

"Yes . . ." he said slowly. "I've told her so for years."

"You think I'm being harsh. But don't imagine I'm going to feel sorry for you and your beloved pneumonia. I'd have more respect for you if you took a reputable vacation like normal people. Majorca. Because you did this to yourself. You got what you wanted. Touché."

"I'd have preferred cancer," he admitted.

"Better luck next time. Because that's the ticket, isn't it? You go: to stop."

"Which I'm unlikely to deny. Such ironies are the tiny puff pastries of my life."

She was drifting back to his side, which they both seemed to rue. "You like it when I'm pissed at you."

"Yes."

"When I show *spunk*."

"My prickly pear."

"You're tired of women baking and sponging and rubbing your neck. Weepy, selfless pushovers who listen tirelessly to your stories of bombs and drink and self-laceration of which you yourself are sick to death. Gooey, gorgeous, ga-ga women enraptured by your contorted soul, eventually obsessed."

"Perhaps."

"Then, I know that."

"Yes."

"So I'm just trying to appeal to you. And I'm not any different, in the end."

He watched her go, the glaring red helmet swinging over her shoulder, before he answered, "No," a little sadly.

Pronto, he demanded the phone and, aided by a scrumptious hack, arranged migrations. Easy: after seven the Swallow would have to be at the Green Door. He triumphed back to his pillow, hands clasped.

For there was only one place Farrell loved better than hotels, and that was hospitals. He had long romanced alcoholism and insanity for the institutions into whose hands they might deliver him—where someone else took over not only meals but everything in between. When he was interned, gaol had invigorated him with its regularity and rigor. The physical abuse had proved bracing; the only torture he couldn't bear was the incessant blare of the TV.

So Farrell gave himself over to the ward's keeping, to the dither of nurses, the lap of mashed carrots and strained peas, the blithe drizzle of antibiotics from his IV. He breathed for them. He spit for them. He let them lay the sweet cold orb of the stethoscope all over his chest. For Estrin was right: Farrell would assume so much of the burden of the world that he would finally force it to relieve him, and completely. He would filch every responsibility within reach, with a view not to power but to total, childlike dependency. Not only did he not want to solve the bollocks of Northern Ireland; he did not want to butter his own bread. He would gladly adjust the tilt of his bed, a little up, a little down, for the rest of his life. He was content with a regimen of regular meals and the vista of Belfast perking on without him from his panoramic window on the thirteenth floor. A toddle down the hall past the booby floral decor more than satisfied his need to explore. He befriended the terminal, eased conversation with tense visitors at the next bed, and waved bye-

bye to little girls. He involved himself in petty intrigues, waiting for a roommate to head for surgery before really tinkering for peace for once and shorting out the TV. (He pulled the same stunt in Castlereagh one afternoon, but the level of electronic expertise among Republicans there had been understandably high; it was back on top volume within the hour. At City, the subterfuge bought him a full day of quiet.) Happily he harassed his nurses, crying, Pillows! Tea! *Telegraph!* For months he had given; now, with a vengeance, he would *demand*.

And he did not miss alcohol. Ah, the parental simplicity of *No, you may not*. No, he could not! Farrell may have become an obnoxious grownup, but he'd made an obsequious little boy.

When Estrin discovered him the next afternoon, Farrell was nested with the *Belfast Telegraph*, underlining and scribbling on a pad with kindergarten concentration. It was the first time she'd seen him read a paper with any pleasure—God, especially this paper, a monument to self-absorption, whose headline on the day John F. Kennedy was shot read, MAN FALLS INTO BELFAST LOUGH. It seems for once he was not clipping articles on Robert Russell's extradition to the Maze, but was marking stray phrases in Eddie McIlwaine's "Ulster Log."

Eddie controlled the one page of the *Telegraph* from which the Troubles were more or less banished. Eddie catalogued the Ulster of pre-'68, so as the SAS gunned down three IRA suspects in Tyrone, McIlwaine's headline read, COALISLAND CELEBRATES WITH DUCK RACE. Loyalist paramilitaries might riddle the Avenue Bar with AK-47's; "An Ulster Log" would bemoan the increasing scarcity of the corncrake. The rest of the paper wrangled with what really happened in Gibraltar; Eddie printed the scandalous revelation that when Roy Rogers and Dale Evans came to Belfast for St. Pat's Day in 1954, they were not really riding Trigger after all. Very well, a busload of soldiers in Ballygawley may be going up in flames, but McIlwaine would not have his readers forget the welcome return of the Chuckles Fun Band and a free class on Irish crochet.

"An Ulster Log," then, chronicled not the roiling insoluble hotbed that had fascinated the international press for twenty years but a frumpy backwater, Northern Ireland *sans* petrol bombs and barricades, where no UPI man would be caught dead; a frumpy, brackish place whose protests over the closure of the Ormeau Baths would never lure a boom mike. Home of the indigestible potato cake and the handwoven sweater that came down to your knees, Eddie's Ulster would never blacken your *Nine o'Clock News*. For Eddie's Ulster was innocent. And naturally, Eddie's Ulster was a bore.

Farrell had discovered Eddie McIlwaine today and was determined to pervert him. *Chuckles Fun Band?* You think you can get away, don't you? We're massacring each other and you can still write to us about birdies? No Troubles? Anathema! Farrell coughed with gusto as he flourished off his last line and handed the pad to Estrin.

EIGHTEEN YEARS AND UNDER NOT ELIGIBLE TO ENTER

> *A seven-day tour of Northern Ireland,*
> *with free entertainment in the evening thrown in:*
> *a kidnapped boy hidden in a monastery,*
> *a bit of a battering—stirring stuff.*
> *I get myself invited to the weekly mistakes,*
> *more forbidding.*
> *Scottish visitors pour into Larne for the experience,*
> *for there is to be a repeat of the*
> *slow, slow, quick, quick,*
> *slow action in the autumn—*
> *though you should make alternative plans,*
> *just in case.*
>
> *What intrigues me about the ticket isn't the price;*
> *it's the mature outlook:*

you could agonize for hours.
Their pet subjects:
"It isn't even a political thing";
"Really nothing in religious terms today."

Wearies of Americans may feign a pounding,
but in your heart you know how flimsy.
You feel nostalgic;
you're totally nonplused.
Remember Belfast when the city was opening up?
When group efforts paid off.
A blaze of publicity, a big picture to packed houses;
bus trips, Rotary lunches;
escape by stratagem, every kind of answer—
rare old times.
Some may not be as honest with themselves
as you are.

"Your decrying of poetry immediately made me want to write it," Farrell explained. "Besides, this method appeals to my sense of anarchy."

Every phrase had been compiled from the following innocuous sources: Eddie's "Tenner Tours of Yesteryear," about bargain bus trips of yore; "Lighting Up the Silver Screen," about grand bygone cinemas; a revival of the quickstep, slow waltz, and moonlight saunter; the Across clues in the crossword, and Farrell's own Scorpio horoscope. The title was culled from the advert for Bing-all! For Farrell, the project seemed to expose poetry and McIlwaine both. Poetry was found out as a load of arbitrary shite, a random coupling; and McIlwaine could not escape. Subconsciously the old boy was one more commentator after all; even on page 10, the troops had arrived.

Estrin had never seen Farrell so jovial, playful, affectionate. The austere, apostolic gown suited him better than buttondowns. Hands behind his head, feet dangling off the bed, with bare ankles and little brown slippers, he told anecdotes; the IV swung and squeaked on its hook. He touched her shoulder. He asked when was the last time she wrote home. This finicky maven of warm salads and soft-shell crabs cleaned his squares of gray cauliflower and stringy chicken and licked his fingers. He asked after Duff, Malcolm, Clive. He said something generous about MacBride. She'd not seen this man more relaxed after three bottles of wine. A prime time to pry.

"You know, you've never said much about your wife," Estrin ventured, propping her muddy boots on the bedding with pleasant presumption.

"When you were only married to the young lady for seventeen days, she's unlikely to come up in conversation."

"Seventeen days can be a long time."

The ward was quiet; the sky out the window a seamless gray; no other visitors were due for hours. "*Tarja*," he began, the *a* stretched, "was Finnish," which explained the reluctance of the name—Finnish lingers. "A hard, clear, passionate people. Like vodka. Like crystal. But with a warm wooden underside, like a coaster for your glass."

"Drink metaphors."

"Oh, aye. Those days were pre-reformation. And Tarja"— he touched Estrin's chin—"could drink even you, my swallow, under the table and down the stairs. A bottle of Absolut down her throat was no more than a quart of antifreeze in her car; she just ran smoother in the cold."

"Meaning your company?"

"Not at first. In the beginning it was—intense," Farrell shortened lamely, for one of the reasons he withheld such stories was he felt compelled to leave out the good part. He was constitutionally unable to exhort one woman to another—it made them edgy. Oh, they would listen endlessly to what was wrong with your ex-wife. But there was nothing wrong with Tarja; who wanted to hear that? Because if you left out the good part—that ice-blue stare with glacial splinters, that hair like hard winter sun—the story didn't make any sense. He *married* her! Still, he was going to hard-winter-sun Estrin? Come on.

"It was late '76. Tarja was volunteering for the Peace People in their heyday. She was filled with that fire for reconciliation I so revile, but which in her impressed me for my mystifying inability to defile it."

"Conviction."

"Revolting in most people, but in Tarja it had a purity you had to respect. And in the atmosphere of the time it was a bit easier to flog, even to me . . . We'd have long rows, and after I'd ridiculed her gormless optimism and her wet friends, she laughed. A bit like you, my dingy, slitty-eyed despair, she didn't buy it. She said I was *golden*." He seemed to find this funny.

"Golden?"

"Yes. That in her dreams I was ten years younger and blond and that I 'glowed.' That I wasn't the way I thought at all. That somewhere inside I was—jubilant." Farrell's laugh degenerated to phlegm. "But that was the way she talked, you see. Simple, eerily direct. I don't expect it was weak English, but the way she thought. When I hurt her, she cried. When she was tired, she slept. She'd stop in the middle of an afternoon and say, 'I don't feel like wearing green,' and change her shirt. She despised cruelty, admired self-sacrifice. Finland? She might have been from Mars."

"Why did you marry her?"

Because, you eejit, I was in love with her, but Farrell declined to answer this, not just for strategic reasons, but because it wasn't quite true. "We were living on an—extraordinary plane," he suggested. "I couldn't keep it up. I married her to crash it."

"Which worked."

"And how. Besides, I pulled one truly appalling stunt to bury us for good."

"This is another warning," Estrin groaned.

"Predictably, I was blootered from the moment I stubbed the ring on Tarja's finger. Ten days after, I'm propped in the Crown and I spot a woman across the room. Winsome. Funnily enough, Tarja was much more lovely. Then, I think I liked the mildness of the attraction. I could take it or not."

"You took it."

"We tore off in a taxi after barely a banter. Ended up in Ardara, on the coast of Donegal. Holed up in a B & B for a full week, doing laps from Pat's to Nancy's and back to bed. She was married, seven years, three kids. *And we told no one.*"

"You just disappeared?"

"For a Catholic to vanish in Belfast in 1976 was an unusually malicious prank."

"Ever go back to Tarja?"

"Had the taxi pull up to our tatty flat in the Holy Land. Strolled in the door and Tarja threw her arms around me and wept. Hadn't eaten or slept, half undressed. Had spent the whole week on the phone to the RUC, the Royal, City—would have been roaming the Cave Hill for body parts by the weekend. She finally got around to asking where I'd been. I said I'd been on a tear. I said I'd been fucking another woman. Then I said I was going for a drink. I remember, I felt nothing. When I came back later she'd cleared out. Except from her lawyer, I never heard from her again."

"Congratulations."

"It is possible to destroy a woman's love for you. With Tarja it took drastic artillery, but this was a direct hit."

"Are you proud of that story?"

Farrell paused. "I must make a frightful impression."

Estrin tufted at the half-dry paint on her shirt. "Sorry."

"That was the most wicked thing I've ever done."

Estrin looked back up again. "Then why"—she leaned forward—"do I like it?"

"Because you identify with the woman I ran off with," he supplied. "And not with my wife."

Farrell looked at Estrin in dismay: one more. Sometimes he was tempted to spy on families pramming by the Lagan, just to find out what they said, how on earth they spent their time. Because Farrell hadn't a notion what to do with a woman once he'd got her besides break up.

Considering where they were from, Farrell enjoyed watching Estrin pick at the Bramley tarts by his bed. "What do you think of reconciliation groups?" she asked.

"Not much. Even peace movements need murdered children."

"What about you? Whitewells, *Panorama*. You're thriving off dead kids with the worst of them."

"Oh, aye. But you should know me well enough by now: that brand of castigation only delights me. Which drove Tarja wild."

"So," she measured. "Supposing your conference flies, your power-sharing referendum passes, power devolves. After the expected, maybe even disappointingly flash-in-the-pan scuffle, the IRA simmers down to a few hardcore head cases, the Brits wheel off with a wave, and you're left with the RUC, in their regular annoying policeman way, pulling you over for speeding when you're already late for the theater. Mummy asks you for Sunday tea. What do you do?"

Farrell didn't hesitate. "Leave. There's Chile, South Africa, the Middle East. I despise my mother's Sunday tea."

"I think," Estrin announced, "this shambles will be sorted out by good sons who ask for seconds of potato puffs. Who switch off the news for *Eastenders*. You? You're a troublemaker. Your motivation is weak."

"I do, however, want to succeed. I can always find excitement in Burma." It was rumored that Burma no longer had any government at all. There was no rice in the markets, and the streets were quiet only because the country had run out of petrol. In the last buildings held by President Maung Maung, there were soldiers with fixed bayonets in every room, including the ladies' loo. When Farrell read accounts, he salivated. No danger of prams by the river in Rangoon!

"Farrell, if you can't handle New York, how are you going to feel in Burma?"

"You think you're the only one who can travel, my dear?"

"No, but—" Estrin stroked his damp hair. "Farrell, sweetheart, you're stuck here, you're hooked. You and your newspapers, you're as bad as any *Hausfrau* addicted to daytime TV. And if the series ever closes, you will be lost."

"And how is himself, just?" Constance was locking up in the carpark.

"Ebullient," said Estrin, once again having a hard time looking Constance in the eye. "Coughing, but improved. Sadly. So I'd skip the flowers and fruit. He'd much prefer a case of pancreatitis."

"And what's the crack? Has he the nurses knitting him mufflers?"

"The usual: solving the North's problems to put off solving our own."

"That order," Constance observed, "hasn't worked here for years. So you're interested in the Troubles, love?"

"What else is interesting here?"

"What's interesting anywhere?" Constance countered.

Estrin fidgeted with her helmet strap. They both seemed to want to talk to each other, and not. Constance would fuss with her keys, snap her handbag, shuffle one step toward the hospital, then edge back. There was a funny feeling that they weren't supposed to be doing this; that whether or not their conversation broke a rule of etiquette, it most certainly broke a rule of Farrell O'Phelan's.

"We talked about his wife."

"Poor Tarja. They say she was quite a looker."

"That's not always enough."

"It's a start." She smiled. "Sure it's always been a requirement. But don't you worry, love." Constance patted Estrin's arm. "Maybe the lad's met his match, so he has. You've more of a sharpishness about you—"

"Than all the others?"

"Than Irish women. We still sit back in pubs and let them

247

rabbit on like God's gift. You Americans interrupt from time to time. Now, good luck to you, love," she said hurriedly, cutting a glance to the far end of the carpark. "I've to bring his highness the post. Cheerio."

Estrin paused to watch the puffy ankles stride briskly to the lobby, her expression at the door set in a brave, spiteless warmth. Oh, glasses, a square jaw, an excess of moles and pug nose, but gentle eyebrows and full cheeks—in Estrin's book "a looker," for were their lives reversed, Estrin could not have faced Section B with so little bitterness in a hundred million years.

On to the Guzzi, Estrin passed a woman dabbing blush by her car; their eyes met in the compact. Estrin watched this specimen, too, glide into the hospital. Beguiling, if chilly. Mmm, nice clothes; why did Estrin always dress like crap? Not bothering to change from her painting shirt. And look at that, slim in a way Estrin, so short with muscled shoulders, never suggested— Estrin could seem small but never delicate, never so appealingly frail.

It was late afternoon, August; fog drifted in and out of sun. Estrin needed air and tore off down the Lisburn Road to the A1. Funny, only a mile or two out of Belfast and the countryside was travel poster. While often psychologically remote, there is nowhere in Northern Ireland you can't get to in a couple of hours; in thirty-five minutes, she'd crossed to Tyrone. Whimsically she lunged the Guzzi off the main road, to arrive in a tiny town called Castlecaulfield. On its outskirts she slowed before a house. Estrin killed the engine. The cottage was old, whitewashed, thatched, with creepers up one side, baskets of brambles by the door, dahlias; coal smoke coiled from the chimney, and surely on the other side of that window pies cooled, salt cod soaked under a cloth. With its flagstone walkway and dog at the gate, the cottage might have seemed trite, but its walls had too specific a character for that, lumpy bone from which soothsaying fingers could divine a particular life. In the late-afternoon sun, *golden*, as Tarja would recognize, the cottage exuded that radiant clarity of a wheelbarrow, a rooster.

What struck Estrin about the house in Castlecaulfield was that she did not live there. That she had never lived there. That she would never live there and would never try. Not that she couldn't, for there were plenty of like houses she could rent or buy, rising mornings at the twitter of corncrakes, to milk the goat, throw coal on the fire, and round up a fresh loaf of barm brack. Now, it was not 1800 and she'd certainly own a VCR, to curl up nights with *Lawrence of Arabia* one more time, but late afternoons with this light she would doubtless be reduced to poetry. A little boy cringed shyly in the doorway, and Estrin smiled.

She noted that even in this pastorale she was by herself, and tried to add the child; a husband. The pastiche curdled. Better not push it too far. The point was, the cottage was lovely, and pitched on one of the most pristine, luxuriant islands left in Europe, Estrin lived on Springfield Road. Further, she had refused Castlecaulfields all over the world. Surely she'd left the Philippines because the weather was too pleasant.

Because after two weeks in Castlecaulfield Estrin would lose her mind.

The dog had begun to bark with the hostility the woman in black leather deserved. She did not belong here, and tore off from all that quaintness and quiet back to the main road, comfortably agrunt with Pigs and Saracens, soldiers at their sites. You could tell the Catholic towns because the signposts were painted red and scratched with UVF. *Right, you call Castlecaulfield quiet, but it's halfway between Ballygawley and Loughgall.* Nicely balanced: eight obliterated British soldiers on one side, six assassinated Republicans on the other. Easily she could open her *Irish News* tomorrow and Castlecaulfield, like Ballygawley, Loughgall, Drumnakilly, Enniskillen, would be one more catchword for atrocity.

For as a break from pneumonia, Farrell's barbarous betrayal in Ardara, and Constance Trower's staunch, masochistic kindness in parking lots, Estrin had gunned off in search of a blown-up bus: an expedition of tacky voyeurism she rarely indulged herself in, but no one was watching. Unless news reports were running old footage, the remnants of the bus carrying thirty-six Brits returning from leave which the Provos had quite expertly exploded in Ballygawley had not yet been cleared away. Sure enough, making her way through several checkpoints—at one she did have to take off her helmet and let her hair tumble innocently over her shoulders, but not one soldier asked a single question, not even the UDR—soon the carcass grinned around the corner, cordoned by white tape, dotted with wreaths and cards from Protestant strangers. Estrin parked the Guzzi and shot the posted soldier a smile to buy her five minutes without being run off. The crumpled black frame was tilted up on the grass, like most wreckage emanating calm rather than tragedy, a peacefulness not unlike creeper fluttering on whitewash. Estrin wondered what she expected to find here, what she hoped to feel—anger, frustration, grief? A mere wisp of mystification curled from the mangle, like smoke from thatch. She did not understand blowing up those soldiers. And she did not understand the house in Castlecaulfield, either, flower gardens and finnan haddie and three-year-old boys. She did not understand anything, and she'd been all over the world.

Estrin met the soldier's eyes again and this smile was wan; he shrugged. She thought he was handsome. Like Estrin, he seemed less angry than disconcerted, a little bored; glad for a glimpse of a pretty girl.

"How'd you get stuck here?" Estrin called.

"The bus, you mean?" A Scot.

"Ireland."

"Pulled a few strings."

"Come again?"

"Takes a bit of work. Most of us ask to get sent over. Everywhere else, it's press-ups in cold streams; here it's the real thing. Now, best take yourself off, lassie. I'm not to chat."

With a last glance at the Real Thing, Estrin plowed back toward Belfast. The sunset was sooty, the horizon plumed with charcoal clouds; nearer to home, the air choked with the smell of burning rubber. Banking to Divis Street, she mocked herself, going sixty miles out to find a burned-up bus when there was one still smoldering just down the road from her house. Beside it at the exit from the M1, a gang of ten-year-olds with sticks and balaclavas had crowded a sedan; they pounded the vehicle and crunched in a windshield before the driver cracked open the window and seemed to answer the committee to its satisfaction; the boys let him go.

Right. The South had just extradited Robert Russell over the border today, and it was a perfect excuse for a party. Proceeding slowly up the Falls, then, she knew basically what to expect, for after twenty years celebrations of this nature were routine in West Belfast. Closing on the welcome wagon, she gunned the engine and downshifted; Estrin was in no mood for interviews. The kids waved their sticks and took advantage of their anonymity to shout, "Show us your snatch!" and thrust their fingers in the air. But Estrin recognized two boys from Clonard despite the masks, and called them by name; she'd given them both rides on the Guzzi in July. They gave her the high sign, and waved her on. Considering they were only ten, the extent of her relief seemed absurd.

Up the Falls, hijacked vehicles smoked on the curb every hundred feet, until Estrin reached the barricade, a double row of lorries, buses, and vans sealing off the road. Only black taxis were being allowed through by cutting over on the footpath; Estrin followed one of these.

The barricade was too magnificent to pass up; Estrin parked. One lorry had recently ignited, its tires liquifying onto the pavement. As one fuel tank and then another exploded, Estrin inhaled—it was beautiful. Petrol stung the air. In all, ten vehicles crumpled across the road in various stages of cremation, their smoke velvet, flames licking the last bits of upholstery and fiberglass clean. She had come upon the remains of a successful urban safari, cavities split open, cabs lolling off their trailers, trophy heads, the faces of young hunters lit with a lust for gasoline. What a shame the cramp of local housing prevented mounting whole trucks on the wall. Maybe they saved the horns.

The atmosphere was festive. Families with prams strolled down the center of the Falls for their evening walk, as in a pedestrian shopping mall, obligingly closed to traffic by local community groups. Malcolm Dunlea and his friends barbecued whole chickens on steering columns over the City Bus, now nicely burned down to coals; propped outside Mackin's, now doing a brisk trade in crisps and ice cream, Duff Shearhoon spread his shortleg on an *An Phoblacht*. Face bright red, he was down to a T-shirt and suspenders in the heat, West Belfast's Tweedledee. With the *fitz* of beer tabs and children chuckling, the atmosphere was Fourth of July.

"Lancaster!" cried Malcolm. "Where've you been, you've missed half the crack! Dark meat or breast?"

Estrin's drumstick left a smeary residue on her tongue. "You should publish this," she noted. "Chicken Retread. 'Hijack one large, untrussed postal lorry—' "

"Roast vehicle until crispy—"

"Season with RUC—"

They concocted a Republican cuisine, using all local ingredients: Bonnet-fried Onions on Blackened Capris; Scampi à Petrol; Pork Interflora; Beef Balaclava; Cortinas of Veal with Hatchbacked Potatoes, and a selection of sweets: Ford Flambé, Muffler Pudding, and Paint-Blister Pie.

Sailbheaster had stationed himself erectly by the barricade, and kept aloof from the picnic. His boots were shined for the occasion, the turtleneck depilled. When Malcolm offered him a wing, Sailbheaster stiffened with contempt, but when Malcolm's back was turned, the eyes inside the little round holes of the hood went soulful.

Clive Barclay was sulking on the bumper of a well-done Granada, snapping a few dispirited slides. He had just shot an entire roll chronicling the rise and fall of the Turf Lodge City Bus; in his eagerness, he'd opened the camera without rewinding and exposed the film. He'd begged the boys to hijack another lorry or two, as this lot here were well past their glory, but the hijackers were all anxious to get home in time to catch their barricade on the BBC. Malcolm offered to take the Iowan's picture in front of the crackling post van, and Clive begged Sailbheaster's balaclava for the shot; waving a plastic tricolor in one hand, a tailpipe in the other, he planned to send the photo home to Coralville to his mother.

It seems Clive had interviewed a few hijackers, but he couldn't get any of them to talk about Robert Russell; he got more than one "Robert who?" In the end Clive clung to the Green Door crowd, which now a little better than tolerated him, with that hair-tousling benevolence they tendered Sailbheaster. Then, the distinction any member maintained between his own form of the ridiculous and anyone else's was more or less arbitrary. Everyone at the Green Door was a mascot.

The crowd bristled happily on the arrival of a Land Rover, which had connived its way to the Falls through the gates of the Peace Line; the vehicle paused at the intersection. Yet in a perfect expression of Belfast's concept of the ordinary, with two piles of stolen property frizzling in the middle of a public road to their left, the constabulary turned right.

As she puttered home to run before work—and the club would be chockablock tonight—Estrin tried to imagine this ghetto with purely lower-case troubles: Eddie McIlwaine's West Belfast, the massive Republican murals—raised automatics over vanquished British soldiers—all pasted over with ads for Foster's; where likewise down the way on Sandy Row the flaming orange edifice of King William flakes lackadaisically off the brick. Where political graffiti (*SAS: You can't walk/or fly/or drive/so swim home; Impact here, impact there! RUC can't hide nowhere!; Stuff your census*—) fades behind *Frank + Molly; Rachel is a two-timing whore.* Where locals die of heart disease, whose funerals drone on without gloves or berets or Armalite salutes, just sniffling aunts with hankies. A town where if you hijack a public bus and burn it up you get arrested. Eddie more or less takes over the *Belfast Telegraph*, until "Roundabouts I Have Known" makes the front page. Unemployment, but no outrage; an odd hand in the till, but no racketeering. Sectarianism reduced to rumor and backbiting, the snarl of ordinary ignorance you find anywhere. And no soldiers. Estrin realized she would miss them, as the locals would miss them, remembering the IRA funeral the other day when the army stayed away and the whole event went slack; gangs had dandered off side streets well before the cortege hit Milltown. She liked waving to soldiers when they weren't used to that, and at Whitewells she liked being searched, with the suggestion she might be dangerous. She enjoyed watching Brits stalk Springfield Road like an episode of *The Dirty Dozen* in her own home. Sheepishly, she preferred news about one more UDA man splattered in front of his wife to reviews of the Balmoral Dahlia Show. She enjoyed bomb scares at Waterstones, the bloom in her head when they were real, the uncomprehending face of Windsor House with all the windows replaced with ply-wood, even if they did cost half a million pounds. Corrupt as the entertainment for which other people paid, the picture of this place simplified to a small island with bad weather and high cholesterol profoundly depressed her. She could not live in Cas-tlecaulfield, with brambles by the door, and the real story was that the people in Castlecaulfield couldn't live there, either. As she locked the Guzzi by 133 newly sprayed with UP THE PROVOS, Estrin reminded herself that without the Troubles she'd never have come here, and without them, like Farrell, she would leave. For worst of all, Eddie McIlwaine's Ulster would shelter no bomb disposal, no dirty tricks, no late-night palavering with Rips, in short, no Farrell O'Phelan, and she had to admit, with a flicker of fear, that this was the one absence which more and more she could not bear.

17

The Fall of the House in Castlecaulfield

"If you go straight back to your taxis and airplanes," she had threatened, "then I'll know for certain that all you really want is a comfortable disease."

It worked.

Farrell's first bona fide convalescence since he was a child was one of those brief times that a Normal Relationship—which Estrin had never seen but in which she persistently believed anyway, along with the Happy Childhood and the Warm Family Christmas—would herald as the beginning of a lifetime, to which they would later hark back at the age of seventy on a porch: *Remember, that's when we knew, over oxtail soup, saying nothing. You let me plump your pillow. I held your hand while we watched* The Quiet Man. *You told me stories of your mother threatening to put you*

*in an orphanage. I read you Paul Durcan. I garnished your haddock
with tomato roses. I learned to make real Irish soda bread that week.
You thought that was so hilarious, it made you cough.*

Oh, aye.

*Funny how everything with us started out as parody, didn't it? The
"Have a nice day, dear!" The smack goodbye.*

It took us a long time to admit we weren't so different.

*It took us a long time to admit that wasn't so awful, you mean
. . . Notice how my accent has changed? Yours and mine, they've met
in the middle.*

I have always admired the way you say gobshite.

But had she become more Irish because they lived here?
Where were they? Burma? The picture blurred.

For instead of marking a start or a discovery, the week pa-
tinaed with preemptive nostalgia: what they had, perfectly what
they would sacrifice. Because Farrell did not know what to do
with women, because Estrin could not live in Castlecaulfield,
they merely glanced in the window—at the rope rug by the fire,
bookmarked Dostoevsky, toddies on the hearth—before tearing
off again to ambushed buses and Chicken Retread. They would
never know, then, if the early-evening light shafted so fulgently
into the ship's cabin, streaking the green cornice, crosshatching
the wicker with the dying golds of Van Gogh, because it was
beautiful of itself or simply since it would not keep. This was
just September, and the sun rose later each morning, the chill
sharpened another degree each night, gales blew leaves with the
faintest yellow off their trees. Every tray Estrin chattered to his
lap was one less meal she would deliver him ever again, and
though this is always so when your time limit is closer to a week
than fifty years, the passing of such dinners gleams more keenly
on the edge of your cup. The very silver seemed to tarnish by
the day, and Estrin could swear that by the weekend single hairs
on her temples had turned gray. The convalescence took on the
poignancy of a terminal illness, with the illness rather than Farrell
facing a tragic demise.

It was the morning of the seventh day that Estrin padded in with coddled eggs, fruit farls, bananas with brown sugar, and sweet, milky tea, when at last she could distinguish his cheek from the bleached pillowcase; his breathing was quiet. Farrell's eyes trembled open, and shut with a flutter of dread. She wanted to assure him she could pretend, *What, Farrell, what improvement?* But when he opened his eyes again, he saw she saw and there was no chance. "I have an appointment" were his first words. He only downed the tea and gnawed a single bite of bread before putting the tray aside. "Tonight I fly to Ohio."

"Of course," she said.

They were silent while he dressed.

She woke damp, panting. In the dream she had stripped the pelt from the Persian, as easy as pulling the skin off a chicken breast because that's where all the fat is. The cat glistened bright red—for it was still alive, with malignant, shining eyes. A cat is a scrawny creature without its fur, she thought as it slumped against the wall. It was smearing her Laura Ashley wallpaper, so she picked it up. It scratched and bit her fingers. Spiteful thing. She twisted its slippery neck with both hands.

This was not the first dream about dead pets. Just last week, she'd been seated in her kitchen. Underneath the table her toe crackled at plastic. She peeked, to discover a black garbage bag, twist-tied. She went back to peeling cucumbers. Of course she knew perfectly well what it was; she'd only pretended to be surprised. It was the neighbor's bloodhound, in little pieces.

Roisin had a feeling there were more such dreams she didn't retain, probably worse. Some mornings she remembered nothing but woke off-form. For once, she wouldn't tidy the room before breakfast because it made her uncomfortable to look at the bed.

The Persian jumped up on the duvet and nagged for attention. Distractedly she stroked its long hair, until she looked down at her hands—skinny, but with long, sharp nails and flesh-pink polish, and somehow in this light cronishly wrinkled—chicken claws—God, she was getting old—and she pulled them from the pet, afraid of what they might do.

Like most events that had menaced her for a long time, this one had been easier than she'd expected. Constance was glad to get it over with, if only that now she could think about what it had really been like, rather than concoct wee horror shows that kept her up nights.

Reality produced several surprises. The girl was short. And American; she'd never figure Farrell for that. He did like foreigners, but of the more exotic sort. A bit loud, like most of her people, a bit ready with an opinion.

But most of all Constance was impressed with herself. Why, she could bear up; in fact, she loved it! How much more preferable this meetable short person with moments of awkwardness to the tall, arch paragons of her fears. (*So you answer Farrell's post, do you?* Brittle silver laugh . . .)

All right, loud, aye; maybe naïve; ludicrously young . . . edgy, high-strung . . . self-conscious, with gunge in her nails . . . Constance sighed. She could not even marshal much malevolence by herself. Sure the girl was lonely, in a foreign country on her own. And the way she talked about Farrell, Lord, the kid had it bad. You could tell by the way when Constance mentioned him she paid far, far too much attention; those dark eyes zeroed in, telephoto. And the quickening when she said his name, the way she would alternate between saying it a lot, for her pleasure, and then avoiding it and using pronouns, or changing the subject altogether out of respect or superstition. In fact, it made Constance nervous to observe anyone's feelings as so apparent. Maybe, then, secrets are impossible. Maybe the only thing that keeps everyone from reading us like open books is they don't bother, pure lack of interest our only protection. Well, in that case Constance figured she was safe enough.

There was something about the decision with which the girl's boot hit the footpath, the marcato of her sentences, the way she stood with a hand on her hip not the least bit like the wee thing she was, her brisk irritation when she shoved all that thick black hair from her face—maybe it was being American, or maybe it was the authority of younger women, born into that wider world where girls rode motorcycles; from wherever it sprang, Constance did not feel it. For all her officiousness, she could not walk down the street like that, all trussed in black leather. No doubt there was a length of stride, a directness of gaze, a tilt to the chin, a swing of a helmet at your side, and a subterranean smile tugging at your lower lip that you could only strike past wheeling internists, not because you were liberated, or American, but because you were beautiful.

That was it! That was what she couldn't stick! As if that weren't the one detail that was a dead cert, sight unseen! But the slide of those narrow hips from behind was unbearable. Why was her skin so smooth, when if there was a God in heaven she'd have a few spots! And what kind of shampoo did she use to get her hair so thick, sure they didn't flog it on this island! It wasn't fair! And well enough if she was a dolly bird, but whether or not she was brilliant, she was no dose—och, wasn't the torture not how-could-you-Farrell but that it made perfect sense, and wouldn't Constance fall in love with Estrin Lancaster herself?

She had. Constance was smitten. She had changed her blouse three times that morning and still wasn't satisfied with the blue knit. Why, she didn't fidget over what to wear for Farrell himself. But she was on her way to West Belfast and thought she might perchance run into his girlfriend.

"What do you do when a Loyalist throws a pin at you?"
"Run—sure he's a grenade in his mouth!"
"What do you do when a Loyalist throws a grenade at you?"
"Take the pin out and throw it back!"
"How do you save an RUC man when he's drowning?"
"Take your foot off his head!"
"What do you throw an RUC man when he's drowning?"

"His family!"

"What do you call four thousand Brits at the bottom of Lough Neagh?"

"A start!"

"What do you call two Brits going off a cliff in a mini?"

"A waste! You can fit four in a mini!"

"You know, they tell exactly the same jokes on the Shankill about the IRA."

The Green Door's merry recitation went quiet.

"The Proddies pinch them from us," said Callaghan. "And balls up the punch lines. Haven't I had to retrieve many a cracker filched down a black hole and half mangled to death."

The punters were watching; Farrell strode to the bar and stood right beside Callaghan.

"Been scarce of late, boyo," said Callaghan. "I do believe I've forgotten your name."

Too many customers found this funny.

"I expect if I held a gun to your head," said Farrell affably, "you'd remember."

"I'm not likely to recollect, then. I'd hardly put myself in a situation where that would be possible."

"Och, it's always possible," Farrell assured him, raising his forefinger to the man's temple and pressing his thumb. "Bang, bang."

"A fine way to suss out what a man's made of."

"Ninety-eight percent water," said Farrell. "Every one."

"I had it on good authority you don't carry a piece."

"I did at one time." Farrell's voice was soft, informative. "I didn't care for it. When I left it behind I lost my confidence. I didn't mind owning a gun, but I didn't like needing it. And the status was cheap. Why, any wet-nappied, half-bald, overweight pillock can point a pistol, right?"

"Drink up, now!" shouted Estrin.

"Sorry, mate," Malcolm told Farrell from behind the bar. "Last call is twenty minutes past."

"We'll see about that," said Farrell, his eyes following Estrin as she stacked pints. They rattled. She spilled a bottle of lager, upset an ashtray, and broke a glass, all in the space of five minutes. She avoided looking at Farrell so completely, she gave away he was all she could see. Bloody hell. It was depressing.

At last the club cleared down to Duff, who wheezed off his stool and winked at Estrin on his way out.

Sweeping while Estrin wiped tables, Malcolm whispered, "What's he hanging about for? Should I turf him out?"

"No, he's—with me," said Estrin uncertainly, feeling she should add *sort of*; she no longer understood what being "with" Farrell meant. All those farls and tea and movies and Castle-caulfield hand-holding and then not so much as a phone call for two weeks. It was getting harder to take, though when she saw his face she couldn't feel angry but only grateful.

"You don't fancy him, like? He's a bleeding old man!"

"I'm pretty ancient myself."

"For fuck's sake." He followed her to the kitchen. "Lancaster, you could pass for a fresh at Queen's. And in your head, girlie, you're fifteen."

"Going on ninety-five."

Out front, Malcolm collected his books to go home, and Farrell noticed the chess set on top. Studying the boy, Farrell might have recognized himself twenty-five years ago, dragging his own worn chessboard on top of Kierkegaard all over Belfast, but the book was computer science. And the kid was too handsome, too well proportioned. His hair fell in disarming curls and would never suggest electrocution. His legs were surely shapely enough on the football field, not snooker cues with toes. Malcolm was too likable, too well adjusted, and his clothes fit the fashion, those queer jeans that looked erased.

Farrell nodded at the box. "Chess?"

"Why not a game someday?" Malcolm proposed. "Maybe I could learn something."

Farrell smiled. "You being sarky?"

"Not about the question."

"Catch yourself on. How old are you?"

"Fischer won the U.S. Open at thirteen. Come on, old man. What are you afraid of?"

The obvious answer decided him. Farrell slapped the boy on the shoulder. "Fair enough, then, knight's odds."

"No, sir. Square game. Tomorrow?"

"After hours. But next time you'll have to pour me a drink."

Leaving, Malcolm turned and asked as an afterthought, "Are you good?"

"Am I good? Now, that's a question I don't ask myself lately."

The door closed, the bar went quiet. "I rather like this club with no one here," Farrell commented.

"It's my favorite moment in the day, when the last customer's out. I love workplaces when they're all mine. That's what you don't understand about minions. It's the minions have all the power, really. The ones who know where the extra champagne is hidden, stash the rare bits of roast beef for later, and between themselves crack the best jokes at your expense. Customers are minions. Customers are at the tail end, and they have to pay for every pat of butter. And boy, do you have a man by the nose when you control his drink." Estrin held the neck of Farrell's white wine just out of reach.

"Please. No games. I'm tired."

"You're always tired. No games? You just arranged one. And if you could wait for this bottle two weeks, what's five more minutes?"

"The Swallow is piqued?"

"I don't know if I've a right to be. I've never known what my rights are. You've been careful to arrange that."

"Your 'rights'? I imagine you can get angry whenever you like."

Estrin pulled the cork. "I mean, what are you? Are you my boyfriend?"

Farrell winced. "I'd hoped you and I were beyond these tawdry distinctions."

"You mean incapable of them. Farrell, are you seeing other women?"

Farrell took a sip. "I could say: That's none of your business."

"That's what you're saying, or not? Because if it isn't, don't say it."

"Have I ever put that question to you?"

"Pointedly not. It's annoying."

"Such a traveler. Don't you prefer to keep your freedom?"

She considered. "It's not called freedom when you've nothing to escape."

"I don't follow."

"I just wish once in a while you'd get jealous!"

"I am." He held her neck. "Hopelessly. Of every man who rattles through that cage. Of every hand you press with twenty p. Of the soldiers you wave to, the shopkeepers you banter with, even young Malcolm Dunlea. Satisfied?"

Her neck arched against his palm. "You've avoided my question. Because lately I need to know where I stand, Farrell—"

"Swallow." He pulled her neck back. "You are my only passion." He kissed her summarily, like sealing a letter with wax—he'd issued his statement. Estrin draped into a chair, marveling, *Imagine. Some women get yes or no.*

"Are you really going to play Malcolm?"

"Oh, aye."

"Think you'll beat him?"

"He's sixteen!"

"Just be careful. Malcolm is very sweet."

"I should let him win?"

"I guess not. Still, I don't play chess, but can you at least arrange the game so it's close?"

Farrell laughed. "My dear, you and I are quite different."

"Which one of us are you criticizing?"

"You. You're much too pliant, self-sacrificing. Kindness is the mark of a loser."

"That's such a dreadful thing to be?"

"Yes."

"Plastic," Farrell despaired, squinting at his queen.

"Still works."

"Barely. I'm one for trappings. Ivory, green felt pads. These pieces make the game seem so unimportant."

"Isn't it?"

He liked Malcolm. "Quite."

For all their triviality, Farrell aligned his pawns with quiet, remembered glee. It had been a long time. He rarely thought of chess anymore, yet one look at this board unshelved a whole way of thinking that he now employed in only the most shadowy of terms. The uncorked bottle of wine was poised by the board, the barrel of a starting gun.

Farrell held out both fists, and was pleased Malcolm chose white. Farrell preferred black, the disadvantage; it was bad enough to be playing a boy.

Farrell extended back in his chair; Malcolm leaned forward on his hands. The first few moves went fast and easily. Farrell sipped his wine with less urgency than he would usually down his first glass of evening. Maybe Malcolm would learn something at that. A nice kid, really; cheeky, but Farrell preferred that. And if Farrell didn't miss his guess, the picture of a certain supple American bum bending over a dustpan had kept the boy up nights more than once.

Farrell looked down at the board and shook his head. "You're sure you want to do that?"

"Aye."

"Look hard now. I know you've taken your hand off, but I'd let you take the move back this once."

"No, we play by the rules. The move stays."

"Fair enough." Farrell sighed, and began his dirty duty. Part of Malcolm's education, then. Hadn't MacBride taught him this lesson more times than he cared to count. And hadn't it been good for him at the end of the day. (*Liar*, Farrell heard unexpectedly back. *That defeat is improving, a platitude for failures to console themselves. Hardly; it eats you alive. And those games at sixteen are still eating you and they're only getting deeper, closer to the bone. That shite. That smug, to-the-manor-born, self-congratulatory Prod.* Fucking hell, at least twenty-some years ago Farrell did have feelings.)

From the other side of the bar, Estrin eyed the game, drying glasses. She supposed, predictably, Farrell was on top—he looked relaxed, he made jokes; Malcolm hunched with school-boy concentration. But they seemed to be having a good time. And no doubt this was as engaged as she'd ever see Farrell O'Phelan with children. In general, he spoke of them like a tribe of pygmies he'd read about once in *National Geographic*.

However, when she wiped down the bar, she noticed a crease or two on Farrell's brow. He had drawn more upright. He tucked his hands between his thighs. He'd gone quiet. The bottle of wine had disappeared, and he signaled impatiently for a second. His opponent stuck to Lucozade. Malcolm wasn't being creepy; he didn't put his feet up, light a fag, cool about the club, but remained dutiful, patient, direct, hands flat before him on the table, his expression less self-satisfied than slightly perplexed. Malcolm expected to lose; he'd confided as much before the game. After all, like every other boy in West Belfast, he'd grown up on tales of Farrell O'Phelan: not the sort of larger-than-life you beat at chess.

This time it was Malcolm who asked, "Sure you want to do that?"

Farrell snapped back, "Of course I'm bloody sure, or I'd have moved somewhere else, wouldn't I?"

Malcolm shrugged politely and took Farrell's knight. Bring-ing the next Pouilly Fuissé, Estrin looked down at the board. Not knowing the game, she couldn't decipher their positions, but there was something about the starkness of the grid stripped down to so few pieces that tightened her stomach. Farrell rel-ished showdowns, the cold absolutes of capitulation and con-quest; Estrin, they appalled. It had always bothered her, for example, that contests won 10–9 had exactly the same result as 10–0. It didn't seem fair.

Estrin was in the kitchen, but she heard the "Aha!" clearly from there. She ducked out to find Farrell's face flushed more brightly than since he'd had pneumonia. He was scooped gluttonously over the board with a look she'd sometimes seen on Duff Shearhoon poised over a pasty supper when he hadn't eaten for an entire three hours. When Farrell pounced on his castle, he dropped it back from above the square so the plastic pipped. Spittle webbed at the corners of his mouth and, pronouncing, "Mate in four!" he sprayed saliva over the board.

Malcolm slumped back for the first time in the game, and flicked his king on its side. "Aye." He allowed himself a bit of a glare, but otherwise made no remarks. Methodically he picked up the pieces and placed rather than pitched them into the box. Of the two of them, with the boy so controlled, it was amazing Malcolm was the sixteen-year-old.

"A kiss for the victor," Farrell demanded, but when he smacked her, Estrin flinched, his kiss landing awkwardly on her nose. She wiped it with the back of her hand, feeling like a cheap, irrelevant prize. She read the SMASH H-BLOCK and STOP STRIP SEARCHES posters she'd read a hundred times, rolled up her sleeves though she was chilly. While she'd been frustrated by Farrell's melodrama, his elusiveness, the transparency of his own self-torture, she had never disliked him before.

Malcolm jerked on his jacket. "Right. I'm away," he said tersely, though not without turning to Farrell to add, "And I was dead on, mate. I learned something."

"Malcolm, wait!" Estrin caught up with him at the gate. "I'm sure you had him nervous for a bit. Good job." She kissed him carefully on the lips.

But Malcolm was unappeased and looked at her far more sourly than he had at Farrell. "You could do better, Lancaster." He brushed her temple. "Watch yourself."

Instead, she returned to watch Farrell, more what Malcolm

meant. His flush subsiding, his hair still teased from his head: it was like watching a junkie come down. He would be solidly depressed within the hour.

So it was a brief and pathetic fix, but he was hooked, wasn't he? That was it: he liked to win more than to please. He would sacrifice compassion and grace, even allow himself to become ugly, for a single feather in his cap. And in that Farrell had found all his victories hollow, Estrin didn't understand him.

"Whitewells?" he proposed. "To celebrate?"

"Celebrate *what*?"

In the end she went to Whitewells out of pity.

"Had him nervous for a bit?" Malcolm fumed the next night in the kitchen. "He was dead! Two more nails in the casket and we'd have dropped him and his bloody plastic king in a hole!"

"What happened, then?"

"I just—" Malcolm threw the dishrag at the ceiling. "Bolloxed it. Wasn't thinking. One gormless move, and knew it soon as my fingers left the pawn. Aye, and he knew it, too, mind you. But this time, do we get *Are you sure, would you like to take that back?* Not on your life!"

"You said it wasn't important."

"Aye. But it's important if you fancy a dickhead. And I don't care for him. He's too serious for you, and he's too old. I think he's a cod up one side and down the other. Fatuous and cutthroat. Smarmy—"

"Malcolm!"

"Well, he doesn't—"

"What?"

"It's not my right to say. But mind what I told you. And if you've any trouble with the ghett—which you will have—come to me."

"And what would you do?"

"At least play the bugger again and beat him dead to rights. Leave him looking a right eejit. If I've the bastard's number, that's the best punishment. I'd say take you off him, but, Lancaster, I'm not convinced losing you would pain the man much as it ought."

"Is it true? I thought Malcolm might have been exaggerating. Did he have you hammered? Did you win only because he made a mistake?"

"Losing is always a mistake, isn't it? But aye. He had me crucified. I would have called the match, but I kept playing, on the off chance of just that sort of carelessness."

"So you took advantage. Of a moment of weakness."

"That's what games are about, my dear."

"I hate it when you call me *my dear*."

Farrell smiled. "I know."

"You're not ashamed of yourself?"

"For compulsively trouncing a boy? Of course I am."

"But you can't pass up any chance to win, no matter how inglorious."

"That's right."

"And you are proud of that."

"I take my opportunities as they're presented me. Some are more honorable than others. But I'll take them all the same. Pride has nothing to do with it."

"No, I mean it's like everything you think is wrong with you. You love it. You wouldn't be any other way. There's no fucking difference for you between self-criticism and showing off."

"There's such a thing as neither, *my dear*. There's such a thing as stating fact."

"Crap! You adore your isolation, your competitiveness, your stoicism, your obsession with control—the whole cut-off shtick. Get off it, you think you're bloody marvelous!" She was breathing hard.

"And so do you."

The last breath was sharp, and she turned from him. "Yes."

* * *

While Estrin may have known nothing of the Normal Relationship, she knew this wasn't it. She'd been going out with Farrell for nine months now, but lately felt as she did biking through strange cities, looking around and finding a familiar pile of pistachios at the corner shop and realizing she'd been here before; torquing off again, taking exactly the same perverse turn, and staring once more at the same nuts after going through half a tank of gas. It was simply an inability to get from A to B. With Farrell she could not name where they were not getting, though eventually nonevent becomes event—for each return to that same corner has a little less charm. One more dinner at 44, the same, but it should not be the same, so it was worse. As always, he would be obligated all weekend and not explain why. He would still only tell stories at least five years old, as if a statute of limitations had finally run out. She assumed in five years' time other women would finally get to hear about Farrell and the American over a Bushmills washback. He would still reach from the bed for the phone in that single motion from waking to the bedside table with which chain-smokers will reach for a cigarette. He would still drag the phone around the corner and shut the bathroom door on the cord, and he would never later refer to the call or to whom it had been placed.

And while splitting nights equally now between Clonard and Whitewells, they were not even. On Springfield Road Farrell could slip out an open letter while she made coffee. He could squeeze the foam-rubber earplugs from the boot factory, ping the Weitzen glasses nicked from her corner *kneipe*, rattle her pink pebbles from the Philippines, mock her rows of Shipham's salmon paste, each jar holding about a tablespoon, Estrin's idea of dinner on melba toast. But Whitewells told her nothing but why his credit card was platinum. The stationery was blank, the rings of glasses wiped away. The staff smiled too much, stopped talking while she went through security, and began again only when the lift gate latched tightly closed. Whitewells knew its master and kept his secrets, while Estrin's life splayed over 133.

The only reason Estrin kept her privacy intact was that Farrell was insufficiently curious to pry.

Yet in the same way that when you are lost or stuck you get increasingly annoyed, Farrell began to pick. When he drank he used to extol, romance; now he was more likely to get contentious. He condescended when she didn't recognize the names Peter Robinson or Ken Maginnis, and claimed if she'd lived in the Middle East she should certainly know Gemayel. A conversation over dinner became a regular current events quiz, and Northern Ireland was not enough. When was Pinochet's plebescite? What were Benazir's chances now Zia was dead? And why didn't Estrin know anything about the Dukakis platform, it was her country, wasn't it? And one argument in 44 lasted all the way to brandy, whether short bomb warnings did or did not serve the IRA's purposes; she suspected he really had no opinion at all, or even agreed with her, but preferred to fight.

Further, he needled her about her menial jobs, poked at her lack of ambition, struck poses of weary amusement at her weight training, a regimen she would never cancel, not even for Farrell. He made caustic reference to the Lancaster Fan Club at the Green Door, and one evening he asked her, carelessly between spoonfuls of soup, when she was going to leave.

"Leave?"

"You know, for the next war-torn politic where you will dabble on the fringe. The next torrid ten-month affair with foreign exotica. What's on the agenda now? Afghanistan?"

She actually punched him. The cream of leek spilled onto his lovely suit. "Fuck you! Don't you care? Do you want me to leave?"

Farrell mopped at his jacket and said quietly, "You have done nothing since we met but prepare me for your departure, Swallow. I am only taking you seriously. What is the longest you've stayed in any country in the last ten years?"

Estrin mumbled, "A year and a half. That was Berlin."

"And then the boyfriend—"

"I flew to Belfast the day I found the syringe."

"So on the outside you're here another four months."

"What would you do if I said I had a reservation to Leningrad next week?"

"Try to take you to 44 one last time, I suppose. Wish you well. Maybe buy you a little something."

"And kiss me on the forehead." Estrin would have plunged herself in the Lagan, but they were not on a bridge.

"What do you expect?"

Burn my ticket, hide my passport. You're a trickster, you've sabotaged Ian Paisley rallies, you could at least keep a small American in town. "Not enough," she said, and folded her napkin.

On their way back to Whitewells, their dynamic once again achieved the funereal nostalgia of Farrell's convalescence. Stringing down Donegall Square East, Estrin checked out the latest car-bomb damage by the taxi rank, as always searching for something piquant, a clue, as if a boy's mangled toy truck, a single bloody tennis shoe would bring some poignancy to bear on an otherwise mundane scene—for true in Belfast, you grew inured to this; the entertainment value of bomb sites lapses. Gnarled window frames, broken glass, blackened doorways, powdered brick: that was about it, and that was always about it, with varying numbers of locals in hospital. What she was looking for, then, was an explanation. Though with an authority on Northern politics at her side, she could hardly inquire after all this time, *What is this about again? A united what again? What?* The most helpful single commentary Farrell had offered her was "It's about nothing"—concise, but too succinct—and the puzzle remained inscrutable as ever.

A compelling puzzle all the same, and for once Estrin looked around and noticed she was here, in a remarkable if bizarre town, where the gutted Victorian Assurance Building was as routine passing scenery as the Wimpy's up the road; next week the Wimpy's would be hollowed out, and that would be routine, too. God, it was fucked up, but she loved Belfast. The infrared camera on City Hall followed their progress down the block, its one sore eye. The skein of shattered shopfronts, Land Rovers squealing down Wellington Place, the RUC chatting in their nicely ironed light-green short sleeves and handsome black flak jackets, and the tall man swinging by her side with soup on his coat all sharpened, bittersweet. For Estrin no longer walked a city of this world but a street of next year's memory, another home she would leave, one more recollection to infuse with sudden color and fade as she cruised down a boulevard in Leningrad.

While she could always pop back to Belfast, Estrin had a rule: *Never visit*. The image wormed in anyway, with a stranger lodged in 133; staying in Whitewells and having to pay; scheduling out a week or two of trying to "see everyone," but Malcolm would have left, like all the bright kids, for across the water; Clive would have flown back to Iowa; maybe she'd be lucky and Callaghan would finally be locked in the Crum. While for the first year or so she would have read every article she found on Northern Ireland, eventually one more barracks bombing would flap from her breakfast table half unread. So what would they talk about, as she shared a fag with Robin in the attic or bought Duff a pint? Farrell would be involved with another svelte, well-preserved woman in her thirties, whom he would take to 44 and lead up the lift in Whitewells. The three of them would hardly get together when Estrin dropped back into town, but she would feel her replacement's presence in the niceness of the date she and Farrell did have. Suddenly 44 would seem shabby, and the chef would overcook her fish. At dinner Farrell would act much more interested in her life than he ever seemed now, but from politeness, inquiring whether she found *glasnost* real or a show. Estrin would have the opinions lined up, and they would make it through to brandy, which she would need. He would pick up the check, despite her protests, and walking back along these same streets bend solicitously toward her to hear from fourteen inches overhead. Though not yet midnight, he would claim he had changed his habits and tried to get enough sleep now. It had been a long day, though it was lovely to see her again. With a kiss on the cheek he would hand her a key to a room on a

lower floor, and she would smile weakly. And very likely antic-
ipating the nightmare of such a civilized evening, she would visit
town in two years and stay instead at the Wellington Park and
not look Farrell up at all; or she would obey her own rules, flirt
with this one more city, and then let Belfast go. Forever. She
dropped Farrell's hand.

"I'm depressed," said Estrin.

"Have you made any plans?"

"Only vaguely . . . You know, the Program. But I told you
back in January: I'm almost thirty-three and I've been on the
road ten years and I'm tired."

"Do you ever think of staying here?"

"I'd need a reason to. I don't have one, do I?"

He said nothing.

"I don't actually have the money for a plane ticket. I'll have
trouble if I can't sell the house."

"I'd gladly buy your ticket if you're tight."

"Thanks. That's generous. I'll let you know."

They walked on, not touching. It was dead quiet.

". . . My Russian is coming slowly. I wouldn't go until after
Christmas, maybe not till spring . . ."

"Good," he said genuinely, and in a rare moment of public
affection he put his arm around her in front of Whitewells security
staff and kissed her hair.

Upstairs, Farrell broke records. His face turned the ominous
plum of summer thunderstorms. His breath rasped with the
rapidity of a marathon runner on his twenty-sixth mile who would
not quite make it. Over her, he gradually routed Estrin from
one side of the king-size mattress to the other, until she was half
off the edge, arched, with her hair brushing the carpet. She
reached down and gripped the iron frame to keep from falling
on the floor altogether. After all this frantic whipping in and out,
Estrin herself had stopped feeling anything, and as a result saw
the two of them with uncomfortable sobriety. She felt lost. She
was not sure she was the cause of his excitement at all. She was
not sure this was excitement. She felt left out, and she couldn't

help but wonder if Farrell did also. In which case, who was conducting this elaborate tryst without them. And she worried about his heart.

But they didn't stop. Whoever was doing this, they had been going at it for at least a full half hour. Estrin, while doing little of the work, was now slicker than in the weight room; between them, there was almost no friction, not from excretions so much as from sweat, and besides, for all his howling, he was not quite erect. Perspiration ran down Farrell's temples, dripped to the tip of his nose, and splashed in Estrin's eyes; the salt stung. Clutching the bed frame was like doing a prolonged set of tricep curls; at last her grip slipped and her neck flattened on the floor, chin smashed to her breastbone. Farrell gurgled, a milk steamer, his nozzle choking in her froth. He was out of control, or perhaps in the end he wasn't, and that was the problem.

For far overhead, Farrell floated. *I am Ireland, divided. I am no longer the bomb, I am the North. I cannot explode.*

"Sir?" The door pounded. "Are you all right in there? Sir? Is everything all right?"

Farrell stopped, wheezing. "Fuck."

"Sir, should we call a doctor?" piped from the hallway.

Estrin giggled.

"Sh-sh!"

They both lay still until the girl seemed to go away.

Farrell pulled Estrin off the floor and collapsed back on the pillow. "You own the entire hotel and they still won't leave you alone."

The bedding, long since a casualty of their Olympics, was strewn all over the carpet, so there was not so much as bedspread fringe to reach for when a key sounded at the door and a maid burst in, leading the man from the front desk. Estrin bolted upright; Farrell gasped.

"Sorry, sir," the girl stuttered, paralyzed by the expanse of naked flesh. "We thought—"

Farrell hurled a pillow at the maid. "*Sod off* or you're bleeding fired!"

The clerk dragged at the wide-eyed maid and slammed the door.

"Well, that was a climax all right."

Farrell flicked on the TV. "Sorry if that embarrassed you. New staff."

"The old ones are used to this? You do know how to make a girl feel special."

Farrell turned from the screen. "I don't like it when you're hard like that."

"Farrell," said Estrin dryly, collecting a sheet, "I can't cry *all* day."

He flipped channels impatiently. If he was searching for *Neighbours*, she could find him rude. But he was certainly scrounging for news, in the O'Phelan mythology sanctified, relating as it did to both Interest in the World and His Work. Left to his own devices with a TV, Farrell would catch *Newsroom* at 5:00, *Inside Ulster* at 5:40, the *Six o'Clock News* and *Inside Ulster Update*, switch to *Six Tonight*, which would piece him through to the hour-long in-depth *Channel Four News*, to pace the room till the *Nine o'Clock News*, take a break for the bog at 9:30, and swill a glass of wine before *News at Ten*, *Ulster Newstime*, *Newsnight* at 11:00, and would stay up just to watch the five-minute *Ulster Newstime* at 12:50, after which he would gaze blankly at "God Save the Queen," feeling cheated, poorly informed. Estrin had watched him: he would scrutinize the same footage repeatedly, even the weather. During breaks he'd flap papers, and on maximum overdrive he could get through the *Irish Times*, the *Newsletter*, and *The Guardian* at the same time he listened to BBC 1 and still tell you at the end of it word for word what Nicholas Witchell reported from Tunisia. While Estrin knew better than to complain or compete, she could not help but suspect that all these updates on the Middle East were a substitute for information considerably more at hand.

In the wasteland of nonevent between *Ulster Newstime* and *Newsnight*, Farrell paused at a documentary about American evangelists, now replaying the service where Jimmy Swaggart confessed to visiting a prostitute and begged his parishioners' forgiveness: *I am a sinner!* Tears streamed down the preacher's face much the way sweat had dripped down Farrell's with Estrin half off the bed.

"The question is," said Estrin, "does Swaggart actually feel penitent? Or not?"

"He well regrets being found out."

"No, all that blubbering. Is it real? Or is it a performance?"

"He has no idea," said Farrell readily.

"What do you mean?"

"Do you not find when you tell a class lie you believe it yourself?"

"A little, maybe. But I still know when I'm lying and when I'm telling the truth."

"Then you have only lied badly. And that statement shows a simplemindedness I wouldn't expect from you. Most people consider themselves truthful. When they lie, say, about what has happened, they are presented with a contradiction. Somehow the circle must be squared. It is unpleasant to change your concept of yourself from paragon to liar. It is easier to change what happened."

"That sounds like a kind of insanity."

"Who's not insane?" he asked tersely.

They watched women ascend the platform and weep along with Swaggart, blessing him with their hands.

"But what does he *feel*?" insisted Estrin.

"Nothing. Or exactly what you see. Don't you understand?" he asked impatiently. "Right, it's dicey to tinker with events, though not impossible—look at the Gibraltar Inquest; those witnesses haven't a clue what happened in that shooting anymore. But emotions aren't facts. They can be controlled, even concocted. Surely you've noticed that you can make yourself feel?"

Estrin stared at him, and let the sheet fall to her lap. "No."

"Well, then." Farrell turned gruffly back to Swaggart. "We are profoundly different people."

"Yes. I'm beginning to think so."

"—Now you want to know what's *real*." Farrell jabbed the broadcast as the throng gushed around its fallen evangelist. "*That* is real. Swaggart's congregation genuinely forgives him. It's a masterful piece of manipulation. What's interesting is that it works. Not whether he's sincere."

"Nope," said Estrin, sagging on the bedstead. "I don't care if it works. I care if he can slobber like that and really be thinking, *Heh-heh, I am pulling this out of the fire, aren't I brilliant?* I care if that's possible."

"Have we been living on the same planet? Of course it's possible. But Swaggart is more sophisticated than the way you describe it. He's not secretly snickering; your man is 'slobbering' inside and out. But he made himself slobber. Haven't you watched newsreels of Hitler, Mussolini, Churchill, for that matter? Or Paisley. Great manipulators first and foremost manipulate themselves. Once you can work your own jacks, the rest of the world is a regular switchboard."

"Once you can 'manipulate yourself' you've lost your grip, haven't you?" asked Estrin, sure he was no longer listening, for he'd found the news. "What does that mean? If you're just one more jack, who's left working the board? That's like getting down off the podium and sitting in the congregation. There's no one to give the sermon anymore. Besides, once you're that far gone, don't you begin to forget what all that manipulation is toward?"

She was right; he ignored her for another murder in the UDR. She shut up. After the news, Farrell pulled on his shirt.

"What are you doing?"

"I have an appointment."

"It's after eleven!"

"You're welcome to stay here. But don't wait up. I'm not likely to be back tonight. Order yourself a drink, have some coffee in the morning. On me."

Once more he stood before her in his shirt and socks, his collar raised, exactly the same vision that had sung so back in February, though now the image was reversed: he was fastening rather than loosening the top button, and whatever luminosity shuddered from the man, the hue was opposite—then gold, now violet; the points of his collar perked wickedly under his chin. It angered her he was so handsome.

"Not a chance," said Estrin, swinging out of bed and shaking through the spread for underwear.

"There's no call for you to be upset. You know my work demands odd hours. It was hard enough to carve time to see you at all."

"Who said I was upset?" She jerked on her crumpled dress.

"Can I call you a taxi?"

"I'll walk."

They adjusted their clothing in silence.

"You're glad I'll leave for Leningrad, aren't you?" said Estrin, tearing snarls into the teeth of her comb. "It makes all this groping possible."

"You're being bloody unfair."

Garrisoned in her leather jacket, Estrin waited as Farrell put on his shoes.

"Farrell O'Phelan." She stopped him when he reached for the doorknob. "Do you feel anything for me at all?"

"Estrin Lancaster," he sighed, sweeping the hair, sticky with static, behind her ear, the sound of her name in his voice odd; it seems Farrell referred to Estrin almost entirely now as a bird. "I love you."

It was an assertion he would need to make twice that evening.

She was right; it was the bits again (he had been listening): what did it mean to "manipulate yourself"? He wished she would resume the casual brutality of when they first met: *Oh, Farrell, that's bullshit*. And the shatter was worse than ever. He talked to himself, interrupted himself, contradicted himself, until sitting alone in the back of a taxi was a veritable session of the Belfast City Council.

Funnily enough, despite all that deceit palaver, he had lied to the Swallow rarely. Farrell preferred to put a napkin over the truth to mashing it into something else altogether. He thought of himself as duplicitous, when maybe he was merely discreet. He remembered, for example, the fudge about exercise their very first night. Sure, once upon a time during the big survivalist turnabout after the Brown Thomas bag he did try a fierce running regimen, from four to eight miles in three weeks, promptly checking into City Hospital. She was right, he had the temperament; just not the lungs. At a distance, however, he found athletics an astounding misappropriation of energy and regretted the lie. Besides, it was more Farrell's style to hide something he had done than claim something he hadn't.

However, there were two whoppers now, if running was one: for no, he had never felt jealous of anyone in the American's life. When he looked at photos of Germans and Arabs on her bookcase he felt bland. And the flap of buffoons at the Green Door merely amused him. Frankly, he was beginning to see all the familiar signs: the way her voice shook when she asked about other women—why, she'd obviously worked herself up to that for a week; the ease with which he'd derailed her; and even tonight, crisp sentences, a clip-clip-clip down the hall, but not so much as a where-are-you-going. This whole caper was getting so flipping easy, it was almost less fun. His most impressive achievement so far was some nights forcing down two dinners.

In the shadow of the Boots marquee, he confirmed he was rather sore. Now, the pneumonia had been beautiful, but there were forms of exhaustion with which women were less sympathetic. Fortuitous he hadn't come.

A job, another job. He realized he did not meet women and bombs much differently: keyed up, concentrated, a little empty. After all, they were both sensitive, volatile; but while you had to maintain respect for what they could do to you, they could both be disposed of.

The incoming memory was unsolicited and slowed the wide, professional stride toward one more device to dismantle; Farrell stopped tugging at his cuffs, smoothing his jacket. He was twenty-two years old. Germaine had been only a year older herself, but she had a precocious drowsiness—she blinked slowly. Every movement she made seemed effortful; he wondered why that was attractive. She'd lie back on the bed, her hands dripping from their wrists, as if even a look at the clock was too much trouble—then, why would she look at the clock? Germaine had all the time in the world. That first afternoon, she'd made him read the listings, though the last thing he wanted was to watch TV, and lay ignoring him, gnawing on bits of dulse, to which she proved addicted. She wasn't wearing much, an old shirt, and gradually her thigh slipped next to Farrell's as he sat at rigid attention on the next pillow, scowling intensely at the set. He'd been far more terrified of Germaine than any basementful of Ampho years later. Eventually Farrell would wing it with HME in the spirit of blind immortality, but with Germaine he was mortal, all right, and his legs embarrassed him, so calfless and thin; he was sure his asthma would start up and she would laugh. But even when his lungs did close at first, the familiar strangle shrieking over the telly, she seemed to think that was normal enough and told him, with sensual boredom, to turn off the program. Back then, he had been so grateful! His admissions, too, had none of the proud edge that Estrin detested, just, "I'm ugly," he said, remembering his Y-fronts had a hole and hoping there was no brown smudge in the back.

"No, no," said Germaine, unbuckling his belt more efficiently than he ever unfastened it himself.

"I'm too skinny," he said. "I have spots."

"You're lovely," said Germaine. "Here"—she stroked his concave chest—"your skin is smooth. And here," she said, her hand further down, "is smooth as well."

He had shaken the way he always should have around Semtex and never had the sense to, the way he could no longer tremble around women far more trim, experienced, and poised than Germaine Ormsby. He looked down at himself and saw only one big elbow. From the dulse, her kiss was salty, oceanic. "Shouldn't we—do something?" he fumbled.

"Of course," she laughed. "I had something in mind."

"No, I mean to—"

"Oh, that." She slid down. "Must you always have everything all chalked out?"

Wouldn't Mother be pleased to know how promptly Farrell had been punished, like a good Catholic? Didn't Germaine get pregnant that very first time.

But he never regretted it. Even in that awful London clinic he'd sat on the grotty couch pulling the memory tightly around him like an anorak, and though it no longer fit him so well as he strode from his hotel at forty-three, Farrell tried it on once more, the way every subtle shift of position had been like opening a door. He'd made sure not to doze off in case he missed something: the pad of her finger nested in the depression behind his earlobe; his thigh between hers, comfortable precisely for being so thin.

And now he would rather sleep. That was the grisly truth. Sex was exhausting, and had even officially joined His Work, though it had been work even before this last bit; one reason Farrell slaved so hard was that he experienced every part of his life as work, so he might as well get credit for the effort. Dinners were work, casual conversations on the street positively overtime, and now this last sanctum—what should serve as the very definition of not-work, if there was such a thing—had become as laborious as drafting a lecture for the Trinity department of poli sci. How fondly he remembered recovering from pneumonia at 133, if only that for once a woman let him climb into bed and just lie there.

So now he reached for the satisfaction he had learned to savor in place of Germaine, for if we are all in essence a particular age (Estrin was ten), Farrell at his inmost was not twenty-two or forty-three but thirteen, wrists dangling out of his unstylish navy coat, bare ankles glaring below the too-short trousers, class oddball, whom girls would only kiss on a dare, to run down a playground, laughing. While the trace of a polished nail down his ribs may have worn thin, his telephone still rang in these deeper caverns, the tears of pretty women trickling through the ancient cracks: however after the fact, Farrell O'Phelan was having his day. There was a name for this emotion, and of course it wasn't love at all, it was spite.

However, just tonight, balls aching, suit incriminatingly wrinkled, an envious eye turned to the drunks in doorways who at least got to sleep, Farrell Finger on the Pulse did not feel smug but curiously used.

18

Form over Weight

"You know, you *do* have a lisp!"

"Sorry?"

"*The barest lisp.* I never thought about it before." Estrin pointed at the magazine, cross-legged on the bed. "This poem. It sounds amazingly like you."

"You don't say?" Farrell took the *Fortnight* and read down the page:

TWO VOICES

You go to church, love,
but your speech swells with a salacious underbelly,
fingering, dirty; your man the heretic
dislikes naming parts of the body.
On the whole he sounds abnormally polite.
Your suggestions are guttural, up in my ear;

your man's, sibilant—
he has the barest lisp,
which no one seems to notice
but me. Your questions pitch in major,
his in minor key.
Your invitations reach, grip,
and pull me in, hands wrapping the back of my neck;
your man's drift off, smoke from a chimney,
the Mournes sinking to mist.
In the arches of your chest,
vowels echo in the big Protestant sanctuary
of a good living congregation.
Yet for all your man's haranguing,
the preaching of the unconverted,
emphasis with wine so spit flies,
his i's remain diffident, e's whispered secrets
between pews at Mass.
Your consonants dig in,
the heels of heavy boots;
his are light-footed
and leave no print.
You will explain the difference
as between confidence and uncertainty.
For me the difference is shape:
you aim straight out.
So much of your man dips back in again—
he talks while he inhales.
He curves forward and withdraws,
to pierce himself with s's,
corkscrew. Most of all you want to know
why I care—shape? I lie by an arrow.
I curl by a spiral prick.
I ask which is better designed
to uncork me.

Roisin St. Clair, 1988

"Don't see it." He tossed it on the spread.

"Right. You're the one who hears his voice on the radio and 'feels nothing.' I guess you feel nothing when you read about it, too."

"I don't think about myself as much as you do. I'm not interested."

"Who's Roisin St. Clair?"

"Haven't a clue," said Farrell. And that was the truth.

Estrin kept a regular regimen: alternate days she weight-trained; on the others, she ran ten miles. She was allowed one day off a week she did not always take.

There were variations. While in top form she could average a 6:35 mile, her time would inch up or down and served as an interesting barometer: slower, she could be sure of getting a cold, or she was depressed. Estrin was rarely certain when she was depressed and had to check her watch, just as some people will to confirm it's nighttime when others can simply notice it's dark.

Lately her time was slow.

Further, while the amount of weight she pressed would edge up through the season, with those inexplicable spurts and plateaus characteristic to the sport, her speed and form varied a fair bit: the rapidity with which she brisked from one station to another, the crispness of her pull, the grace with which the slabs of iron rose and fell on the Multigym. These daily differences gave each workout a color, her life an emotional profile—the bench press was her analyst's couch.

Over the years, the nature of the regimen had also varied. Some winters she'd swim, mix in wind surfing or sculling, but that there was a regimen of some kind, and a vigorous, even fanatic one, had not changed since her early teens. As a result, even when she'd first gotten her period it was irregular and rare, and since fifteen she'd taken a progesterone supplement to menstruate.

Like Farrell, she was not a team player. She would never

enter organized marathons, weight competitions, or swim meets. She would not even play doubles tennis. And while she preferred racket sports to the drearier lap and clang of more isolated disciplines, she could never rely on squash because she could never rely on another person.

It had been almost four years now since Estrin had been back to the States, and one of the ugly revelations of that last visit had been the athletic revolution overtaking her country, obsession with fitness now demoted from an element of personal to national character. Estrin ran in Philadelphia to find a splatter of purple joggers suddenly underfoot, like droppings. Worse yet, a gaggle of female weight lifters in pink tights had roosted in her local gym, so unsettling the atmosphere that she switched to swimming that season, before she hopped a plane for Israel and left the whole unpleasantness behind altogether.

For back when she was thirteen, Estrin had been looping the football field when the rest of the junior high was bingeing fish fingers. She began weight-training at twenty with her first motorbike, needing upper body strength to control the machine. She'd been the only woman in her university weight room, and the men were resentful. It took months to win them over, until, eyeing her diligence from a station away, they granted her a grudging respect—the boys even seemed a bit proud of her by the time she left. The point being, she had not picked up weights from admiring Cher plug Jack La Lanne. Then, Estrin figured this happened to eccentrics in the States all the time: suddenly the entire country is playing Go, wearing your Kenyan kikoi, collecting Fiesta ware; you and your innocent, solitary interest in kayaking is suddenly engulfed by 250 million people doing nothing else. You're on your yearly trip down the Colorado, but this summer there are collisions with slick, expensive shells, problems with campsites. So do you quit? Do you allow these nouveau kayakers to crowd you out of a hobby you've nurtured since you were ten? That was America: it would swallow you. Because how could an obscure thirty-two-year-old traveler point to an entire country and claim, "You don't understand! They're imitating me!"

So Estrin decided this was one more test. Tolerantly, she would allow her culture to borrow her fixations, confident that in the long run it would give them back. She would wait the country out, sharing, in her maturity, her weight rooms with the girls who read magazines. Sooner or later an article would tell them to do something else and she'd have the place to herself again.

For Estrin could not afford to give up athletics out of any transitory rebellion. She did not know quite why she worked her body so hard, but she did know sport was a linchpin of sorts, and if it was ever pulled, every discipline in her life would collapse.

Because Estrin might have quit men, countries, and her entire family, but never a ten-mile run. Once tied, the battered gray shoes took over. Sometimes the shoes ran ahead. Though inside she might feel tired, a separate energy burned from underneath her. It seems she was blessed or burdened with a body that would exhaust itself well after Estrin herself; the body would overtake and outlast her. Aging to herself by the day, it mocked her in the mirror with its sleekness and impatience. Sacked out with a whiskey late at night, she would puzzle at the withers twitching her lap. For while Estrin felt the immanent approach of some interior end point, the dumb animal was romping mindlessly on. She wondered what it would be like in the years to come, trapped in this horsy, quick, restless creature, dragged from corner to corner like a surly aunt on holiday, taken touring the town when she would rather stay by the fire and drink.

However, much as she might relate to her own body as a pet, it was a beloved pet, and continent to continent she depended upon its constancy, its recognizable Braille rippling under her fingertips, its bravery in bad weather, and whatever it was that took over the knotted shoes and would not relinquish until the gate closed back behind them over an hour later, she suspected this was the real Estrin Lancaster, what Farrell would claim you had no business having a relationship to because it was you. Estrin might have her bad days, or even bad whole countries, but as long as the animal did not falter, finished its course, and never skipped a station in the weight room, the stars did not realign, the earth might tremble but never shook her off the planet altogether. Estrin would accuse herself of petty vanity if it weren't something more reverential, even more religious than that, for an eclipse of her calves would surely plunge her into black, heathen despair.

"I suppose raising a barbell or two is one of the few things you've actually accomplished." Dial tone.

Estrin turned red, rammed a musty towel in her pack, remembered shampoo. This was the story now: baiting hostility sandwiched with florid romance, neither of which seemed true. Last week he'd given her a book on the Soviet Union. She was not sure which of them he was trying to punish.

Estrin had chosen two hours in the gym over an increasingly rare dinner with that man. He understood perfectly well why she couldn't skip weights, and that was what made him so angry: how dare any girl be as inflexible as he was.

Today there was something curiously unpersuasive about her preparations.

Likewise, when she marched through reception, dressed brusquely, and pocketed her locker key down the hall, Estrin felt papery. She had the nagging feeling of having forgotten something; though she'd dutifully remembered soap, socks, ID, she seemed to have forgotten why she was here.

Ordinarily the Queen's weight room felt homey, though it would hardly strike strangers so: neon glaring from two stories high. Rubber tiles flapped on corners, paint chipped from free weights. Handles were missing on the Multigym, and there were never enough cotter pins. Much equipment was jury-rigged, bars bent, benches propped with two-by-fours. The aluminum mirror made you look fat. Men threaded aimlessly between dilapidated stations with no urgency or routine. As weight rooms went, this one was not serious. But Estrin enjoyed the atmosphere here, haggard and outmoded, for since the Green Door, she was re-fining a taste for the second-rate.

The mumble was marked with staccato clicks and clangs, sentences with excessive punctuation; barbells pounded the floor as the overambitious couldn't quite make the press. Usually Estrin found this funny. Tonight it jangled her nerves.

Officiously, Estrin adjusted the sit-ups board to maximum tilt. She hooked her toes under the padded rod and rested her fingers ever so lightly on her temples, to begin fifty fast, tight tucks. With sit-ups, prefer speed to repetition, and never let up tension until the conclusion of the set.

But when Estrin rose to her knees, her bluff was called: her eyes widened; the curl slowed, her elbows trembled. *When had this ever been so difficult?* Ludicrous; she began every workout this way, three times a week, and she'd been at this tilt for a month now. Estrin coaxed herself with normalcy, *This is what you are, this is what you always do, without this you are someone else, this is important*, and while all she got back was *So? Why? Be someone else, then; I'm not sure this is important*, she did rouse herself through forty-nine.

Forty-nine. Estrin looked around her, surprised. Why was the room still upside down? Her toes lost their grip, and she slid toward the floor.

No major lapse. Forty-nine, fifty, big deal—but that was the point. How hard could it have been to do one more? And very well, it didn't make any muscular difference, except Estrin Lancaster was a stickler, and if she went for fifty she did fifty, not one shy.

So the next set, more onerous than the first, she did fifty—a nervous fifty, a hysterical fifty; and on the third determined to do fifty-one.

She did not. It was fifty and again the stop, so when she

clambered off by the aluminum, she glimpsed the bloated image of a complete stranger.

Estrin shambled to the Multigym with her head at a tilt. There was an explanation. Adjust a few screws in the head, old girl, a bit of tinkering and you're right as rain. But she slipped the pin in at 24 kilos, feeling a complete fake, and again the first shoulder press was rude. The weight rose with no enthusiasm and would even have mocked her if the nature of the Multigym had not been essentially stoic.

Beautifully, exquisitely stoic; Estrin had always admired the venerable contraption. She liked to picture it square and mute in this room after hours, austere in the darkness, comfortable in quiet, with no need to lift itself. Masses of metal, like rock, exude a great stillness despite how you might force them to move, and Estrin felt she was violating the eloquence of the iron today by provoking it to squeal absurdly up and down.

At the station next to her, a scrawny student was wrenching at the seated cable row with far more kilos than he could handle, not exercising his lats at all but his lower back. A sorry performance at which Estrin would ordinarily crack a private smile, but tonight she glowered. Turkeys did not understand the first principle of lifting: *Form over Weight*. In fact, Estrin had often tried to work this paternoster into a wisdom of wider applications. That it was better to do small things well than big things badly was too mundane, for the insight was grander than that: *Form over Weight*—maybe best left alone, majestic in its obscurity.

However, during the next two exercises she watched her own form crumble. Over the bench press, the bar wobbled. Her preacher's curls were stingy. And the evidence was clear. Ordinarily by now, her veins would have risen, her arms hanging short like a gorilla's; her wrists would have pumped with blood until her watchband cut circulation to her hand, her skin taut as the rubber of a water baby. But tonight her watch was perfectly comfortable. The veins, if anything, had crawled back to the bone. Her skin was white and dry.

It was not until the wide-grip pull-downs, though, that Estrin began to confess this was not simply an off day. *Help me*, she implored, and to whom? *Oh nuts, I am not halfway through.* She kneeled on the mat and crossed her ankles behind her, exhaling as she pulled the bar to the back of her neck, but while she had always rather relished the implicit supplication of the position, in the past she had knelt and bowed her head to grace, to power, to concentration, to excellence, to lifting more and more weight with all the more impeccable form, to the Great Protestant God of Dissatisfaction, tonight she was Catholic, confessional: *Forgive me, Father, for I have sacrificed, for nothing. Hours and hours I have entered this room to spend the precious energy of my life for nothing. To raise iron and not children or standards or even roof beams, metal which will fall back to the floor when I am gone. Father, I run for nothing. I run toward nothing. I have only understood flight, I have never run to anyone's arms. Father, sometimes I'm sick and still won't stop running, and I shit myself. Farrell did, too, but he was trying to stop people from murdering each other, and I shit myself for nothing. I have caught myself on, Father, as they say in Belfast. I lift weight without mass.*

The iron bullion clanged back to the stack from three feet up the cable. The entire room paused in its reverberation and turned to the American. She was still on her knees, rubbing her hands; the bar swayed crazily over her head. They watched as one of their regulars stumbled to her feet. Usually Estrin tossed her damp hair from her face and bounded from the room with a salute, joking about having earned her pint. Tonight she looked down. She scuffled. Wasn't the wee Yank, someone commented, a bit poorly?

The cap was off the Bush before the coat was off her back.

"When you pick up that glass, what are you reaching for?" Estrin had once asked Farrell. "Peace? Excitement? Death?"

"Effect," he considered. "Of what kind? Well, that hardly matters."

So in its expression of nonspecific desire, drinking was almost abstract. It struck her that the cult of alcohol was not all bad. Its belief in resort was still a faith of sorts. Estrin poured another short. Convinced there was no comfort, she wouldn't bother.

Distractedly, Estrin crumbled soda bread. The loaf was stale, and somehow this cinched finishing the whole hunk. Eating the bread made her feel bad. That was the idea.

Estrin moved on to the raspberry preserve, scooping it out by the fingerful, toward the bottom of the jar having some difficulty with her knuckles jamming around the neck; she licked them clean. The more reasonable approach to these foods would have been to spread the raspberry *on* the bread, but that would have been civilized indulgence and this was abuse.

Though in a small kitchen, Estrin pipped from counter to sink like a dried pea in a Lambeg drum. She killed the Horlicks malt powder, but scrounged little else—dry muesli; the plain flour took considerable swill. Trouble was, no fudge brownies lurked in her cabinets. In groceries, Estrin blinkered past butter icing to carrots. So she poked at treacle and hoisin sauce straight from the tins, the combination gratifyingly horrific. Until finally she remembered the Stilton cowering in the hydrator.

Unwrapped, the cheese wafted and drove Estrin back: an ambivalent food. There was something repulsive about Stilton—its rind of festering blue-green and weak pink, so redolent of decay; its smooth, rich meat so sickly sweet, but veined with corruption, edibly spoiled. Stilton is insoluble, opaque. She could never eat enough of the cheese because she didn't understand it. She sliced it surgically with a sharp knife into thin specimens, laboratory slides. Every slab disturbed her more than the last, which ensured she cut the next. There was something wrong with Stilton and there was something wrong with a taste for it and there was something wrong with Estrin, so Stilton was the ideal food. Bridging liking and not-liking, the flavor suggested revulsion was a form of appeal. She finished the cheese.

Estrin opened the refrigerator three more times. A piece of lemon pickle gave her acid indigestion. She was still hungry.

She would stay hungry, too. Standing at the sink spooning malted milk was like trying to fill one hole by filling another, so that every time she looked at the hole she wanted plugged, it was as empty as before. What's interesting is that knowing full well that the malted milk was landing in the wrong hole did not stop her from shoveling it in anyway, because when afflicted with this gnawing emptiness, you have to do something, even if it is wrong.

Confused, Estrin wandered to the living room. It was hopelessly early, only seven o'clock. The kitchen safari had taken, maybe, twenty minutes. While she could limp through a light dinner with Farrell from 8 p.m. to closing, it was possible to consume three or four thousand calories in a quarter of an hour. How much your whole life was, as Farrell would say, trappings.

Likewise sex, the nitty-gritty, took less than five minutes, as Estrin noted with a glance at her watch when she was through. You could keep most of your clothes on, unzip, get the job done, buckle your belt, and there you were. For women, there wasn't even anything to wipe up. But this time, not even bothering to recline on the sofa but remaining upright in an uncomfortable chair, Estrin admitted as she never had exactly that sex by yourself did not always feel good. In fact, masturbating tonight had much the same quality as the Stilton, the like–not like, the little badness. Under the unflattering overhead light, she pictured herself slouched in the untidy room with paint cans, jeans binding her thighs, her stomach bloated with whiskey and muesli and lemon pickle. Though she'd read often enough you can "satisfy yourself best," her fingers felt ignorant. The orgasm was boring and laborious.

While relieved it was over, with the nagging twinges of renewed tension Estrin suspected it was not. She only halfheartedly tugged at the jeans. Estrin often experienced lust as pain, only to be met with pain—grasping down again, she felt no pleasure. Scratching was more satisfying than masturbating tonight, defrosting the freezer would have been more fun. This time at least she came more quickly, but the orgasm was worse, heavy, hesitant, a shudder. It did not round up nicely but stuttered off, unpronounced. Promptly, the itch grew more insistent than before, so it was no use pulling up her jeans again; doggedly, Estrin went back to it, with annoyance, only wanting the twist between her legs to go away.

It was after the fourth time that Estrin realized she had a problem, for while to come this many times in an evening was not unusual for her, in company or by herself, to still feel this randy after was. Launching dutifully into number five, she found both that she didn't have any choice and that another go would only make the urgency worse. She pressed her crown to the chairback until it hurt. Her knuckles chafed on her zipper. Her socks flopped off her feet, comically, but ugly-comic. She slouched lower, and coming was stupider, slower, a squirm, a turn in her chair. Six. She counted orgasms like sets, first with perverse fascination, later with increasing terror, as six only went to seven, ever less full, ever more demanding when it was done. Her buttocks ridged from the seat; the taste of whiskey in her mouth turned rancid. Soda bread, Horlicks, and raspberry rose. Estrin crawled up and splashed some water on her face, but it dried quickly and left the skin tight. The chair was waiting.

Estrin came twenty-five times. By the end she wept, arced so far off the seat her knees hit the carpet. *Please, please don't make me, please no more, please—* Finally the gullet could swallow no more, for the last climax was one or two spasms, a little gag.

Estrin stood, shaking; her head was light, her clothes damp, her skin blotchy. Her right hand ached, and her genitals were swelling. Incredibly, deep inside the sore, abused flaps the tingle tugged again, petulant, unsatisfied. Estrin hung her arms, a haggard mother who would finally let the child cry. Worst of all, she checked her watch to find the entire erotic nightmare had consumed only an hour and a half. It had at least exhausted her, so breaking three records in one evening, she faltered up to bed at 8:45.

*   *   *

The next morning, Estrin tried to act normal, and nearly carried it off except for a few telltale flaws, the kind by which an astute dealer can detect a forgery. Reading the paper, she had to keep going back to the beginning of the article to remember what country it was about. In Safeway, while one jar of jam, a single package of biscuits were routine indulgences, Estrin looked down to find several foreign products in her care, even losing track of her cart in baked goods because she didn't recognize the lemon Swiss roll, iced fruit buns, and Madeira cake as groceries she had chosen. Oh, it wasn't like being someone else entirely; the basket was piled with the usual four pounds of carrots, two cabbages, and whiting fillets, but instead of one drab allotment of petits beurres, there appeared chocolate oatmeal mini-flips, Walker's thick-cut shortbread, and bourbon creams. The world had not turned on its ear, but there seemed to be a tiny hole in the universe through which these alien packages were streaming.

She returned to collect her laundry. She stood for several minutes waiting for Estrin to stuff it in a duffel and strap it to the bike. Estrin didn't. She shrugged and went downstairs to cut wainscoting for the dining room, hoping Estrin would show up to tend to the clothes before the cleanerette closed. Sawing the baseboard, she would ordinarily have drawn straight forty-five-degree guidelines, but today she only eyed them, resulting in cockeyed corners of a sort that signaled, according to Estrin herself, that you shouldn't lend her money or ride in her car.

At 4:00, in her most magnificent impersonation of the day, she bounded upstairs in a performance virtually indistinguishable from Estrin Lancaster getting ready to run.

Though the blue and the green shorts were both clean, she insisted on rooting through the entire pile of dirty laundry for the red ones. She paused with an irregular shiver between tying her left and right shoes.

The weather was nippy but dry; nothing to complain about. The first few strides, her molars clacked. Her feet went *plop*,

plop, plop, not *pet, pet, pet*. She concentrated on not reading the *An Phoblacht* mural one more time, and consequently read every word.

Over and over, five miles uphill, and why? Here she was, always switching countries, how was it that wherever she went she re-created what she had before, one more ten-mile course? Change itself became the same old change, newness got old; even the erratic became pattern. There is no such thing as perfect randomness, she remembered that from math. Randomness is an abstract ideal to which you can only imperfectly aspire, for in her determination to do nothing and live nowhere, she always fell shy; as an absolute, too, no rule asserted a more ruthless order than chaos.

Her shoes splatted; her fingers fisted; her side stitched. The only part of Estrin that was really running was her nose.

Suddenly, outside the cage of the Felons, the *plop, plop, plop* went quiet. She looked at the fence and the view did not shift. Fence. Estrin looked at her shoes. Suede slick, stripes torn, heels rounded, toes worn to sock, the pair would have constituted a remarkable monument to perseverance had they not been deathly still.

Estrin felt calm. She had not, in fact, decided to stop. She had stopped, which is different. She read a poster for *Diary of a Hunger Striker* at Conway Mill. Well, well, she thought, almost cheerfully. Soon the sky would fall, pigs fly, and the law of gravity be repealed. Orbits and the behavior of molecules in a gas were no longer reliable. Your pet would bite. Maybe that explained the self-appointed apocalyptics on street corners: they had risen to do what they had always done, until one day they had not: the end was near.

Estrin wandered back through Milltown cemetery, humming. Protestant vandals had recently attacked Republican headstones with a sledgehammer; crosses were toppled, a statue of Mary dethroned; the big black honor roll of the County Antrim Memorial was cracked. Impressive work, she thought, big rocks.

But the destruction did not make her angry or sad. It had happened. Estrin kept humming.

Back down the Falls, the letters I, R, and A did not form an army. All of West Belfast floated before her in pieces—soldiers stalking backward, children throwing stones, quotes from Wolfe Tone bobbed separately past like balloons. The afternoon felt festive, like schooldays ended early from a sudden snow, a presidential assassination. She had reached for a little knob in her own life and turned it off.

Because what made this woman's to-and-froing possible was that Estrin herself was immovable. She had not changed her hairstyle since she was ten. She would not have dinner with you because it was Thursday, and that meant the weight room. Philadelphia to Bangkok, she always brushed her teeth beginning with the right back molar. In theaters she sat in the very front or the very back, always on the aisle, the better to *get out*. If you had not been to the movies with her before, she would reliably subject you to her theories about where you placed yourself in a crowd: Estrin didn't understand people who sat in the middle. She wrote letters on narrow-ruled notepads, and it didn't matter if none of these details cohered neatly into Traits—the important thing was that she would never walk into a stationery anywhere on earth and pick up wide-rule paper over narrow without having suffered a brain seizure. A tiny, stubborn bump on a big planet, with no profession, no family so's you'd notice, no national allegiance, Estrin was only conceivable for being a homebody, staunch, cranky, conservative, and for two days in a row now she had been winking out like a badly screwed in light bulb.

So Estrin walked into her living room as if a new acquaintance had invited her in for tea. It was only 5:00, with extra time now to do her Russian exercises before work, but Estrin picked up the grammar with the polite disinterest of a guest paging while her hostess put the kettle on. She flipped it open to the last chapter she'd memorized. None of the words looked familiar. Though technically studious, in fact she'd been losing vocabulary by the day. Estrin would pick up a *karandash* on the weekend to find by Monday it was merely a pencil.

Estrin was poor at languages and had slyly sought countries where English sufficed. This time, for more foreignness, farther afield than ever, she would relinquish the very words in her mouth. If that terrified her, so be it—*harder, farther, longer*—the shadow of the lamp pull crossed the dialogue, a raised whip. Farrell's *A Day in the Life of the Soviet Union* glared from the table, a beautiful hardback of well-produced photographs at which she had barely glanced. But it was a nice present. Wasn't it?

The grammar dropped. Her hands felt alien to her thighs, her body a jalopy pieced from different cars. The half-trimmed baseboards, half-refinished furniture, and half-plastered ceiling no longer exuded the atmosphere of projects that would be finished. Photos of far, far too many men leered from the wall.

Where is my mother? And has my mother ever dissolved in the middle of her own house? Mother, do you ever lose your way from the kitchen to the foyer? Mother, I am unmoored, I have come too far! Like the afternoon when she was three years old: Estrin looked about her, having adventured past her stoop, chin raised to the wind, patent leather braving down the pavement, and suddenly did not recognize the neighborhood. At least at three she had cried, and a kind old man had called the police; they had driven her back up the street in a squad car asking, patiently, as she wept, "Is it this house? This one?" Finally, though the whole world had grown strange and even that last house looked foreign, as it would evermore, slightly crooked, ajar, her mother shouted from the porch and tumbled to the car. But when Estrin got lost at thirty-two there was no flag of an apron, and across the Atlantic her mother would die without a daughter. Estrin was not even disoriented down the block but in her own living room; there was no kindly old man, only a not-boyfriend who couldn't tell the difference between an emotion and a model airplane; the British Army crouching down her street with SLRs had replaced the friendly Philadelphia police, and she could not cry. She could not marshal nearly so focused a sensation as loneliness or fright.

Estrin discovered she was standing, for she no longer felt related enough to her furniture to sit in it. For once time had passed quickly; she would have to hustle to be on time for work. Necessity is a kind of solace; however haphazardly, Estrin fit herself together again and stood at the door in her leather jacket, with her keys, her helmet, though with that vaguely unwholesome air of the repaired. She glanced behind her before killing the light; like the manse in Philadelphia, 133 would never look the same again, an architectural changeling. Likewise, outside, the countryside looked arbitrary. Estrin had no idea what she was doing in Northern Ireland. Eventually this happened everywhere, and more than men or wanderlust explained why she had to leave.

Maybe you've seen it now: both had lost their mothers. Farrell because his had held out, refusing to give him anything until she got everything, until she got more than he had or was. Farrell had offered, too, had sat before her as if on the other end of a seesaw; feet dangling, he had never weighed enough for her. He could not remember a single time she was pleased—chess was trivial, though she would cluck when he lost; good grades were only to be expected; his Christmas presents were squandered money or too cheap. With choices of failure and lesser failure, disapproval and disapproval in the extreme, he had found an eerie freedom—how little difference if he curled with Talisker. Long ago he'd climbed down from her teeter-totter, leaving her, arms crossed, still waiting for his spindly soul to lift her off the ground.

Maybe that accounted for her nagging efforts to feed him when he went home—and how ironic, all that chopping and baking, when in any of the important ways she had starved him to death. Besides, he was uncomfortably reminded of Hansel being fattened up. For what? Or if the feeding was not ulterior, it was at least guilty—and should that parade of apple tarts be apology, he turned desserts down flat: he did not accept.

Estrin, however, had a fine mother. Ruth Lancaster had cut

the sections of her daughter's grapefruit. She had hugged the girl tight even as she felt the child stiffen like overwrought metal in her hands. Estrin left those arms behind because she could not afford the comfort. Her mother's generosity was too easy. It wasn't fair to be loved for nothing. There were people like Farrell out there working so hard to be held, and here Estrin had come into her embrace with all the injustice with which others inherit mansions, swimming pools, mink. Estrin traveled the world to prove she was worthy of what was given her without leaving the house.

And so, exactly, this was duplicated with their mothers inside. Estrin would never brave enough tortured countries, win enough strangers, press enough weight, cut a perfect enough corner at 85, keep a fine enough figure, or fire a sufficient quiver of exotic stories over wine. Farrell would never lose enough sleep, deliver enough useless lectures, leave enough women, dispose of enough gelignite. And so long as they could never win themselves, they would never win each other, for you cannot earn what is free.

19

Notice-Notice

"I've been approached to do a reading for Campbell. A lunch, to raise funds."

"You don't say."

"I thought I might do it." They liked to experiment on each other. "After all, you and I have never had the same politics."

"You've never had any politics."

"You sound like my mother."

"*You* sound like your mother. Genetic Republicanism. The ballot box—*in one hand*—gets passed on with the dark hair."

"Unlike Loyalists, I suppose, whose every generation arrives at its own considered, thoughtful position?"

"If you're trying to tell me you'd campaign against my referendum from burning national aspiration, your head's cut."

"Maybe you should be stopped. If the Border Poll falls on

its face, no harm done. If it succeeds, all hell could break loose."

"It's a tea party out there now?"

"*Yes.*"

"Sure there'll be some kicking and screaming, but whichever way you turn, you step on wee toes."

"Why do I have the feeling whenever you use infantile imagery you're referring to the Catholic community."

"Honestly, Rose, you are getting stroppy! Time was you were glad to get a glimpse of a weary old Prod's P.O.V."

Roisin studied the weary old Prod. Other women got to watch their men push children on swing sets, trim hedges on Saturday afternoons. Roisin was convinced she spent most of her time with Angus watching him dress. Today this annoyed her; so many of his suits were brown. They were all too small. While the round butterball hammocked over his belt used to charm her, the teddy-bear vulnerability, the ready-made pillow, this great soft welter of accumulated indulgence, now he simply looked fat. And he always wore nubby tweeds, cords, wide woolly cravats. Lately she'd come to prefer silk.

"Besides," he grumbled, snuffling around the carpet, boxer shorts in the air; oh, it was gross. "Sure we'll keep our noses clean, put together a bloody utopia. But if that doesn't work, kid, I swear to God I will make Adolf Hitler look like a Boy Scout. You thought I was codding. But I will not have your hoodlums run my Province."

"*Your* referendum. *Your* province. *My* hoodlums."

"Where is that sock!"

"You could not conceivably get Farrell O'Phelan behind widespread oppression of human rights."

At least that got his bum down. "And that would cock up the whole kit, I presume?"

"He's come to have a lot of influence. More than you think."

"Thanks to me! My legitimacy! My contacts!"

"He made a few of his own. The ATOs at Thiepval think he's brilliant. But I forgot. You're the one who saw his potential in grammar school. Who lifted him from the obscurity of the Fenian cesspool."

"And not entirely out. Why I trust him."

"Do you trust him?"

"To be a scoundrel. I understand scoundrels. You, my pet, are a romantic. There's more to the beast than kisses."

"You don't think Farrell's a romantic?"

"Can play one, aye. Could join the RSC. But Son of Corrymeela he is not. Selfish, grasping—"

"Catholic."

"Every Proddie sentiment is not sectarian, love. There is such a thing as personal antipathy."

"I mean he's on my side. He can't help it; he was born there. For Farrell to support internment, you're right, would be genetically impossible."

"No, love." He tapped her chest. "Means just the opposite. There's a special wee hatred that your people reserve for their own kind. Ever listen to Provos talk about the Officials? Better yet, Sinners about the SDLP? Makes their steaming at British soldiers sound downright affectionate. O'Phelan? He doesn't frighten me, because I'm too far away. I'm in the other camp, and we've struck an allegiance of sorts. But, Lord, would I hate to be right next door."

"Like who?"

"Och," he laughed. "Any girl."

"Angus . . ." Roisin was doing her nails, red. "Do you ever wonder why I should want you to win? Especially if you are appointed Secretary of State; what do I get out of it? You and the wife, up on the podium, grinning for the cameras, flapping Union Jacks. I can't even wave from the crowd, sure I can't. I catch it on the news."

"You're to light out for Piper Heidsieck and leave the door unlatched the next afternoon. Private parties, pet, are the best crack."

"Does it ever strike you that I could ruin you?"

"In a word? No."

"Meaning I couldn't or wouldn't?"

"Meaning what good would that do anyone?"

"Angus," Roisin abjured, "you said so yourself: since when do people only do good?"

Lately Farrell could not watch the news sitting down. He would perch on the edge of the bed and then pace, glaring at Channel 4 and rattling his soda water, anxious for eight o'clock. Ordinarily this time of evening, Farrell would shave and unwrap a fresh shirt, break the baby-blue paper band; swish the tie around his neck, chin high. Nestling into the shoulders of his jacket, he would assess the effect. Everyone assumed he was so thin because he ran himself ragged; in fact, he dieted to a scrupulous 155. He would send a pair of trousers back three times to get them tailored right. Farrell was vain. And a former eyesore primps with a special gratitude. Every night, now forty-four, Farrell checked his face for spots.

Tonight, however, through some miracle or mistake, he'd no dinner date, and he missed dressing up. Even the news was more interesting when he was ignoring someone because of it. These broadcasts were particularly thorny as well, because every other bloody interview was with Angus MacBride.

Farrell should have been delighted. Plugging the referendum, wasn't he? And hadn't Angus weaseled himself onto every story from the IRA postal assassination to the privatization of Shorts. But if he was pushing the Border Poll, why did he keep sneaking in his own stats? You'd think the lad was up for re-election himself, the incessant mentions of the European What-have-you, the New Ireland This, the Washington Democratic That, the Royal British Something-or-other Award, law school, Cambridge—

Cambridge. About an hour ago, that was the thorn, and it was still in his side, about the size of an ice pick. More truthfully, it had wedged there twenty-seven years ago; why, it was a miracle Farrell could walk.

Why did you not go to Cambridge? Not for the education, for
the sound of the word! And was that sound worth all the testing,
the expense? Unquestionably! And fine if you were turned down
or couldn't afford it, but you didn't even apply.

MacBride never let you forget it, either. You gave yourself
away there: how much have you played the loner just because
a bit of company might show you up? You didn't even write
away for an application. MacBride never hesitated, with that
putrefying, clear-eyed assurance of his, *of course* the only question
was Cambridge or Oxford. And after losing and losing to him,
at chess, at sports, at girls, you folded like a ten-high hand.
MacBride may think he's better, and though you are better,
you're not sure and so you're worse.

Hasn't it been the pattern of your whole life, to make a
bollocks of it so you have something to overcome? Wasn't that
what Talisker was all about, a ploy by which getting up at eight,
putting on clean BVDs, and ordering coffee instead of a short—
from your peers proceeding with any dowdy Monday morning—
was transformed into an achievement for which your mother
would kiss your cheek? But you can't ever play it straight. That's
why MacBride started hammering you at chess, isn't it, because
your gambits were too clever, too squiggly, too oblique? But he's
caught on to you, as he's been on to you ever since, as he surely
is now—and if so, what is he planning— How he frightens you.
How hard that is to admit.

Because it intimidates you how much people *like him*. You
can only cut a phrase with a knife. In company you are sharp
but wounding. Fair enough, plenty want you, like the women,
since like children they see something they can't have. And in
your distance, you blur; they see what they wish. Angus is up
close, no tricks, and still charming as hell. Angus imagines he's
an ordinary fellow, while you find him a marvel.

Playing yourself at chess, didn't that tell all? Ingenious! How
could you help but win? Isn't that why you originally pressed
for an independent solution for Ulster, economically goofy as it
proved, because you liked the idea of your own tiny country

where you seem important, and didn't MacBride have to grab you by the short and curlies with graphs and studies to give it up? An *independent solution*, that would be your favorite. Why, the only opponents you've ever taken on board were bombs: objects! That was the secret to Porter's self-destruction: when you only fight yourself, the contest is rigged.

Aye, your schoolmates assumed Angus went to university across the water because the Prod had more money. An inconvenience, MacBride's family was no better heeled than yours. No, the only reason you didn't apply to Cambridge was you were afraid you wouldn't get in. So this ate and ate at you, every summer Angus returning with his pip-pip, here-heres, until senior year you did something furtive, bizarre, and maybe even degrading.

You wrote Admissions. You claimed to have taken the years after grammar school in the civil service. You had passed your A, O, and S levels, and you would now like to apply. You filled out the forms and told no one. You were invited to sit the special qualifying exams for Cambridge and Oxford. You told your mother you had research for papers in English libraries, and boarded the ferry for Liverpool for the first time in your life. England was not so terrifying; you were mostly afraid of running into MacBride. They treated you nicely. They gave you a dormitory swanker than your room at home. You spoke to no one, though others—English!—were friendly. The food looked all right, but you couldn't eat. And after all this, the test was just a test. You've always loved tests, the way the path is laid out for you: B, not C. If only the rest of your life were an exam. In the Catholic Church, you pass whether or not you've earned it; you pass shamefully. In your own home, you have never passed, but the test is fixed. Here the questions were clean and straight, in fact, so easy you were dejected, sure you had done badly because you had obviously missed what made it so difficult. You packed your spare shirt unused, for the one you were wearing hadn't even gotten sweaty.

When the envelope came you trembled, but the surprise wasn't the news it bore but your own reaction: you were not relieved or exultant, but destroyed. The letter only proved what Angus had maintained from the start. Had he ever claimed you weren't good enough? No, Angus knew you could get into Cambridge, and that's why he mocked you. You tucked the envelope in your OED, in the drawer for the magnifying glass along with one crusty condom. The Durex was weeks too late, but this gracious letter was four years too late, and pathetic.

That was a week of test results. Germaine, you were so obliging. For on the arrival of that letter my sails went slack. How could I finish a paper for this Bally-Boondocks college when I could have stretched the lawn between those tawny spires? I know it's English, pretentious, a sell, but that was the most beautiful town I ever saw. You may have been my first girlfriend, but that April I fell in love with a life that I stole from myself. Meanwhile Cambridge was wasted on prats. Those students did not love libraries as I loved libraries—low light, whispers on musty air, maroon, manila, and marble, tiptoes on spiral stairs. But I did not love Queen's University. Surely a degree in philosophy from Queen's qualified me for nothing but despair.

So, never in England my whole life, I go twice in a spring. You were so overwhelmed I would go with you instead of sit my exams, but you did me the favor. How I clutched at your misfortune, how happily I jumped my sinking ship into that lifeboat of a ferry. What an Irish story we made, having to go get an abortion with my girlfriend and so destroy a fine career—in what, mind you? And do you think I didn't know that if we'd waited two weeks for the term to finish we'd still have had time to clean you up? You were my excuse, turtledove, and I have used women as my excuse ever since, for less and less honorable journeys. They have picked me up and saved me, fed me, dropped me when I arranged that, and most of all explained me; why, without women and Angus MacBride, I'd disappear.

That's right, MacBride, for that's what the competition was

all about: context. It would be lovely, for once, to win. But Farrell preferred inferiority to Angus MacBride over no relation to anyone.

The papers were deceptively quiet. There were rumors of the conference, of course, of "talks," but after a whole winter of Molyneaux's "talks about talks about talks," most readers skipped to acrostics. Fluctuating support for the referendum copped the front page with every quiver of a percentage point, but after sixteen years without a government, the better part of the Province denied the possibility of change with a kind of ferocity. Meanwhile, the Provos, having raised a ruckus of car bombs and assassinations in August and September, had cooled back out, well aware that when you kept up a "resurgence of violence" for any length of time it was no longer a resurgence but simply the status quo; you got trapped into spending all that Semtex and personnel just to maintain the impression that nothing was happening. It was more cost effective to lie low, so when you did blow up a bakery, customers actually looked up from their treacle cakes instead of blowing off the dust to count their change.

Farrell saw Estrin when he could. He did not know quite why, except she was texturally important to his life; she was a smooth place. He had a vague feeling of preferring evenings he saw the American to certain other evenings. And though he could tell any stranger that Estrin was planning to leave Belfast within the next few months, he had never once told himself.

As an exercise this evening, once again he paid attention. She wanted him to ask her to remain here. Then she would leave. He was amused by her tactics—she'd long ago dropped tugging his sleeve outright; why, she even resorted to Northern Ireland.

She was affecting a desperate good humor. She laughed too much, after nearly every sentence; her voice was high and a little nasal, her gestures manic. She was actually wearing a touch of makeup, unlike her. Maybe that was it—her face seemed fuller and flushed. She devoured their entire plate of bread.

"I accommodate myself too fast," she was saying—damn, Farrell had already missed the first part; this was going to take work. "I'm one of those people who would wash up on the shores of a desert island and have a hut, a set of fishing lines, and a regular afternoon swim by the third day. I can travel because I'll relinquish one reality for another without much of a fight. One reason I understand this place. Someday you should get me to explain my theory of overadaptation."

"Go."

"Just, Nazi Germany, Khmer Rouge, South Africa—the problem is overadaptability, Darwinism gone awry. Like finding yourself in a dream and not trying very hard to wake up. In wildly short order an entire society can make do. Like, oh, I see, last week you earned a loaf of bread by marketing cold cream, this week by throwing bodies in pits. Here, the North has adapted, beautifully: your business is blown up, you get restitution from the NIO, all in a day's work. They hack up stray Catholics, you strafe their bars—both executions of cultural norms. That's the way it works now; this is the dream."

Farrell translated: If Estrin left Ireland tomorrow, he could turn her off like the *Six o'Clock News*. *That* was overadaptation.

"It comes down to conventions of scale," she maundered. "Last fall a few blocks from me one kid shoved a younger kid on his stoop. Instead of shoving back or tattling to his mother, the younger shot the bully in the head. My neighbors' ideas of everyday fairness have been altered. In Belfast, murder is within the realm of ordinary revenge."

It occurred to Farrell that the main thing Estrin did was talk. He was hard-pressed, then, to explain the little excellence off her, a sheen—pewter. In Belfast terms, your woman was *sound*. Still, it pained him to see how hard she tried to please him, talking politics when Farrell would much rather discuss *Who Framed Roger Rabbit*. And despite her animation, when Estrin rose for the bog he watched her face go limp. Tired? So you're tired, Swallow, at thirty-two? How many projects have you seem crumble, how many convictions fall away? How many people have you been, how many earlier exhaustions have you plumbed and overcome? Don't you know this is only one in an endless series of evenings you're sure you can't survive?

He worried about her. Travel was going to get harder when her looks had faded and foreigners didn't fall over themselves letting her flats and offering her the management of pubs. Estrin should have children. Otherwise she was just going to get drier and tighter and take to drink, that was clear. There was something especially depressing about women drinkers—sloppy, without splendor. Drink drove them to corners. Farrell pictured Estrin at forty-five. She was not as strong as she imagined. Shuttling cups of coffee in some Scandinavian diner, or wherever she was when her motor ran out. Black wages, the same blouse five days a week, not that she cared. Still eating practically nothing, dry toast; thinner than ever, but drawn, veins varicose from serving smorbrod all day. The exercise long ago by the wayside. Gin bottles lining the windows the only decoration in the flat she let from a family that was concerned.

Farrell was amused he chose gin. He didn't like it. Estrin didn't, either.

When she walked back across the room, he started. She could have passed for sixteen; her hair was washed and for once not pulled back but curling softly over her cheek. She look inexpressibly lovely, and Farrell laughed at himself: the diner in Sweden with the gin bottles in the flat, that was Estrin's terror, and it was absurd. Yes, she should have children, but not to save her. You're an altruist: because the world would be better. Estrin's family would be sarcastic, with the scowling strong opinions of American kids; smarter than you sometimes wished, why, you couldn't have talked like that at their age—smart in that way only children can make you feel stupid. One would be obscenely private, the one their mother liked best. None would understand their mother, though they'd make a sport of trying, studying the snapshots of foreign men in attic shoe boxes, squeezing the foam-rubber earplugs from Galilee, now gone a bit hard. Estrin would be unpredictably terse and unpredictably affectionate, and would ruin at least one good son by being so gorgeous, even, yes, at forty-five. For Estrin would grow old beautifully, because she did everything beautifully—the excellence was grace. And eventually she would stay put, in a sprawling jumble sale of a house full of frayed New England quilts, unmatched dishes, Monopoly sets missing Chance cards, and motorcycle parts. Neighboring children would all wish Ms. Lancaster was *their* mother. In some capacity, she would rise to responsibility, as she did everywhere. Estrin was stronger than she knew. She was a supremely disciplined woman, and if drink was ever getting the better of her, she would give it up. He would run into her someday and be proud.

She ordered dessert. Not fruit salad, either, but white chocolate mousse torte. She fed him bites, but otherwise dispatched the entire slice. Finishing off that much whipped cream in a sitting was the single most wonderful thing he had ever seen her do.

In the ritual walk from 44 to Whitewells, her voice lost its pinch and filled with layer cake. "Irishness, Britishness—I don't understand it!" She swung his arm. "What you are, having to give it a name. Everything I am, I resist: American, female, thirty-two—it all makes me crazy! I mean, sure I like Ray Charles and strong coffee, but even personality is a crutch. So is culture. I constantly run into other travelers knitting national portraits like little booties. Now, maybe you have to assume some shape, but I see people as closer to gas or vapor than furniture. Besides, if there is such a thing as identity, then it just is and you don't have to worry it. You *are* a chair, a cabinet, and you know the nicest thing about furniture is that it doesn't sit around dithering whether it's a table or a lamppost when it's really a bookcase. —I wonder if you have the slightest idea what I'm talking about." She said all this so fast she was panting.

Farrell said, "No."

"I want to be bigger! Wherever I fly I want to be someplace else, though I still want to be where I am! Sometimes I'd like to evaporate." Estrin looked up; the sky was clear. "That's the way stars make me feel: as if I'm surrounded by everyone before me, shattered to pieces. A lot of people find starscapes depressing; they feel small. I feel huge, envious at worst, I just want to—"

"Die?"

"If that's what it's like? In a minute." She paused. "But first, I want to go to the Soviet Union."

Farrell laughed. "That's the only time you've referred to your next trip without sounding like Ivan Denisovich. Most nights you'd think they were going to scoop you up from the airport and ship you straight to the salt mines."

"I know," she sighed, and gripped his hand harder. "I've been a little ill." She didn't explain, and shivered.

Farrell hadn't gotten all that last carry-on but fit snippets into what he knew. Everything Estrin was she also was not. She had long insisted how much they had in common, and though he did not always see it, he did see this: they were both at war. *Bits*. Travelers gave themselves away by where they felt comfortable, and Estrin took to cities divided: Belfast, Manila, Berlin. Anything she claimed would also be a lie—Estrin had a flip side. She would not be ambitious, but she was; her very lack of ambition was not like other people's, not placid, but perverse, and fired with a black determination that made it an ambition of its own. Certainly her regular ascent in the ranks across the world was no accident but Estrin working hard and getting herself noticed and promoted because she did well. She wanted to be in control, ate carrots and ran ten miles a stretch, but later that same night could down half a bottle of whiskey to flee her own dictatorship, with considerable success. She was half adventurer and half middle-class Pennsylvanian; brave but still essentially safe, loving edges but never quite living on any of them. She wanted a man/she did not. She did not want children/she should.

She would not be a woman/she was one, and how; she wanted to leave/Christ, did she want to stay!

It had cost him to watch her. At Whitewells he imagined her leaving for Leningrad and his asthma started up; he could not make love to her. Neither could he sleep, so for hours he wrapped her to his chest as the gales rattled the window frames like Bloody Friday, the blankets tugged up to her chin, his nose in her hair. The feeling was of holding a feverish child, though he couldn't be sure; he'd never held one. He'd been one, piled so high with wool his fingers pruned in sweat, though his mother had never sorted out that a single coverlet would do if she only crawled inside and put an arm around his neck.

Odd that no one noticed. She had expected to wake that very first morning to splayed thighs puckered over the bed, to pimply, flaccid cheeks in the mirror. Instead, the withers twitched as always, and their regular ripple quivered: she no longer deserved them. She felt sorry for the hunkers, as for a trusting horse you know you are going to shoot. She would roll over and hide another hour. Sleep came easy; she got plenty of practice.

For Estrin had tendered her resignation to herself. Surprisingly, the days passed with no less effort. Weights, with transport and showers, had taken ten hours a week, running five; and chawing a full pound of carrots took far longer than snarfing down half a dozen Bramley tarts, which Estrin could kill in forty-five seconds per. Not-studying Russian, not-refinishing the dresser, not-ordering the plumbing for the upstairs bath never filled an afternoon. As a result, she wandered around a lot.

But it was not so bad and Estrin embarked on her vacation with curiosity. She'd no idea if she'd entered a season or the rest of her life. So far indulgence was anticlimactic. She didn't look much different; one more month, as always, she had missed her period and would need to take hormones, so she was not as far gone as all that. Without exercise she didn't feel evil or free but mostly a little tired.

Only when the U.S. presidential election was upon her did Estrin realize she'd not written for an absentee ballot. She pretended it didn't matter or that she wouldn't want to vote—bullshit. She felt guilty. Daddy would be disappointed. When the night came, she didn't stay up to watch the results, but tuned in the BBC for a few desultory minutes, noshing oatmeal flips, before snuffling to bed early. At this point she was more likely to lose sleep over Pinochet, Bhutto, than Dukakis. For the United States of America had become one more foreign country.

But the oatmeal flips were American enough; Estrin's revolution was bourgeois. She didn't have the flair to become a card-carrying alcoholic or a legitimate pork pie. She could run through a bottle of Bush every three days, but never in an afternoon. She'd crumble through half a package of biscuits, sleep till eleven but not the whole weekend. She did not confess her decline to Farrell from shame she couldn't fail with success. If there was one thing he surely excelled at more than bomb disposal, it was undoubtedly going to pieces. Farrell would do better than surround himself with wrappers, butter in the corners of his mouth, to shamble toward the TV with a fistful of potato farl. Literature is fraught with the big Brendan Behan tragedies that make such bang-up dramatic endings for future biographers, but where were the women who went down the tubes with any style? Estrin groped for role models—*Long Day's Journey*, Janis Joplin. Why, surely a respectable degenerate would at least get herself addicted to morphine instead of mince pies.

Roisin had read her share of Shelley, Shakespeare, and did not understand why in earlier centuries rapture was exalted, when in the twentieth pining by the telephone seemed sick, the stuff of self-help groups in which frumpy old maids explained how they learned to stop waiting for a man and enjoy being alone. (Liars.) The sonnet had given way to *Women Who Love Too Much*; passion was a problem, like Bingo, on which dilapidated biddies squandered their social-services check for the week, pitiably hoping for the big number. Roisin scanned local magazines (*You,* *She, It,* and other popular pronouns): "What Becomes of the Brokenhearted? (The News Is Good)"; "Why Women Should LEARN to be Angry," where to be in love was to have something to get over, like chewing your nails. They told her to face facts, that the good bits don't last; that a relationship is practical, your mate is your friend, and it is less important at the end of the day that you shake when he touches your arm than that you both like fish.

Roisin had been born in the wrong era. She swept through her house in long silk robes, her cheeks damp, her color fevered. She lived on pale sherry and clear broth. She put on Rachman-inoff. Several times she nearly burned the house down, noticing the kettle was on only because the windows steamed up. Every-where lines scribbled, on the *Irish News,* inside Byron paper-backs, over the labels of HP vinegar and soup packets, and no longer the neat, round, well-dotted script of earlier poems but dashed, furious races to the end of the napkin and back again. And the letters! Scrupulously posted to the hotel. Not to the office, mind you; she did not trust that woman, so protective, thought she owned him so she did, when what was she, his secretary, paid his bills and licked his stamps, but the way she stood before the door the one time Roisin called by, like a football goalie she was, determined no other woman would score. Funnily enough, no one got Roisin more fussed than that bat-tleax, who had acted sniffish, mind you, ever since she found out about the toe over the old divide—wormed it out, so she had, och, Rosalita! Massive mistake. Then, that day your man had acted a bit put out, said Roisin shouldn't come round there ever, though she'd a brilliant excuse, well rehearsed and to do with poetry. But she'd not done it again, no, no, she had obeyed him at every point, and so far that had worked out, except she could no longer hold her hand steady enough to apply her eye-liner, and in shops she couldn't remember what she'd come for and would walk halfway home and remember and back again and forget—little matter, for the breeze felt so warm and the long, thin arms of trees reached out to her and her feet looked so pretty in their trim red shoes.

Constance went through Farrell's desk. An old habit which she indulged in shameful spurts. Peculiar considering the risk; he would have her carpeted and usually she found nothing—pens, bills, *The Protestant Ethos*, telephone messages she'd taken herself. Yet even the nothing interested her, the truly dry nature of his life sometimes, when he seemed so full of secrets. But a year ago the search had panned out: a handwritten ten-page diatribe from a woman named Decla: how badly he'd treated her, what a stingy, closed man he was, how brutal and manipulative, how she would never, never have anything to do with him again—and would he like to discuss this on Wednesday? Constance had laughed and, listening for the outside door, read it three times.

Well before the pneumonia, Estrin had dreamt of him in hospitals. White formless gowns flapped at his delicate ankles. "My finest feature," he claimed, the hem tickling tiny blond hairs. He padded her dreams in bare feet, helpless and trailing catheters, skin like dried apples. She came to visit. As the dreams persisted, his portrayal became increasingly decrepit. Farrell was only so much older than Estrin, but his dream image bent; he required canes and walkers, an arm up the stairs.

In last night's episode, his hotel room kept catching fire. She put it out, it caught again; she put it out, and Farrell wouldn't help, but lay on the bed in his hospital gown, staring at the ceiling as his mattress smoldered. Finally she couldn't bear fighting for him any longer and, instead of burying the fire, fed it, sticking bits of furniture into the fledgling flames and blowing on the coals. As she left the room, it turned orange behind her, and Farrell still lay on the bed, immobile, with a stoicism so violent it constituted an emotion.

Fresh from immolating the patient that morning, Estrin was startled to catch the face of such a young, buoyant man leaving security that night, joking with the porter. As Farrell strode to the desk, Estrin could read the headlines tucked at his sleeve: FATHER DENIES GANG WAS PLOTTING TO KILL KING; PROVO SCUM BOMB FAMILY ESTATE. In the warm crook of that arm, the news withered.

Because somehow the whole idea of something happening had to change. Maybe the main events of any time are not the bombs bursting in air, but *who was alive then*. So aside from the bollocks they had made of their relationship, for the first time Estrin noticed that she and Farrell were present at once; that obtuse as she found him, had he been born in 1640, the partnership would have proved considerably more difficult. Though he'd just bitten off her head for not knowing who Yitzhak Shamir was when she simply hadn't understood his accent, dawning over the insult came: *He's still here*, or even, *He has ever been here*. And one of these days, should some UVF nutter gun him down on Royal Avenue, as so many women feared, Estrin would still think, *We intersected*, and feel the coincidence of that, the luck—for even in the context of massacre these coexistences of his will have been what had happened.

People are events. They may be the only events—at Farrell's elbow the papers wilted; the walls of Whitewells wafted, cheap Hollywood flats. Only Farrell seemed real. Only those watery blue eyes had color. Yet what Estrin saw was not tall; for that matter, its eyes weren't blue. What Estrin saw wasn't even smart, though it may have had a sense of humor. Estrin saw *Farrell*. She could stare straight through every lamp and end table save this one moment by the desk; only Farrell was opaque. And for once she didn't try to understand him but only see him, which is different.

For there is a *bit* in anyone that does not need to be understood, though it may be amused by your efforts. It cannot be broken down; it is prime. In Farrell, it did not buy forty-eight pairs of identical dark gray socks, for it either has nothing to do with "character" or is the only part of character that matters. In Estrin, it did not lift weights, or feel compelled to, for it does not feel compelled to do anything, and would therefore survive poor cornering at 95. It is the part of you that sits in a wheelchair, that your children pay to keep in homes after a stroke. It is the part of you that thrives while you sleep, that you can run over with a truck. Likely to be your frustration, it does not get drunk. Some compensation, neither does it get fat. It may die, but nothing short of that. It is the you that does not see itself because it is itself and only looks out, and certainly it is the part of you that this part of other people will love—but there is no point to feeling guilty, suspicious, unworthy, grateful, or even proud of this, because most of all it is the part of you that you did not create: you do not get credit for yourself.

20

Harder-Harder, More-More, Worse-Worse: Estrin Turns into a Lamppost

Ordinarily Duff made her feel abstemious, for he had accepted that useful sacrificial role as the person everyone else was drinking less than. Why, beside this fattest, most slovenly and enduringly unemployed of members, there wasn't a punter in the place whose life didn't seem well appointed by comparison. But now when Shearhoon dangled a chip in her direction, Estrin recoiled because she accepted. He frightened her now, the whinny from his stool gusting through to the kitchen, where she fled to avoid him. And he was beginning to notice, for he made even more jokes at his own expense and began—a sure sign you were not the full shilling at the Green Door—to buy more than his round. The twitch quickened, his smile wormied, his constant *D'you know? D'you follow?* now so dissected his yarns that she could no longer make sense of them. And the only change she could discern in Duff's life was that Estrin Lancaster wasn't nice to him anymore. This made her colder still. She did not want to be important. How could she take on the literally one million calories of Duff Shearhoon when she couldn't prevail over a single jacket crisp?

In all, she had to admit that the new saturnalia was making her miserable. She'd cast off all her regimens, but had nothing to substitute in their place. And Estrin made a lousy blighter. She was irritable, bereft; not a single gob of jam or drizzle of whiskey gave her pleasure. Sex had turned furtive; with Farrell, she turned out the light before getting undressed. Her clothes were filthy; she had run out of clean dishes; the Guzzi was sputtering, and she would not set the points. While she had lost all comprehension of what she was doing on this island, she had made no plans to leave, though her "boyfriend" was no doubt collecting brochures from Aeroflot.

Estrin had relished nipping off the beam, with visions, tantrums, something you could lock up and put away, all expenses paid to Purdysburn, but this subtler crumpling was not within the realm of the asylum but more likely an everyday collapse common to every two-up, two-down on Springfield Road. She was merely becoming confused, vague, boring, and overweight.

That's right, though she had avoided mirrors for six weeks now, she happened, by accident, to look down getting ready for bed one night and there was a foreign little *bloop*, small by some standards but those had never been Estrin's; stand straight and suck in as she might, it was not going anywhere but out. Estrin made herself look at it, the soft white curve of it, where before there had been an undulation of abdominal muscles. *What are you?* It was happening: Estrin the bookcase was turning into a lamppost.

As she plopped on the edge of the bed, the blob lolled against her thighs, themselves showing a dimple or two but holding out longer than the rest, the last to go. It struck her that simple suicide was really a more attractive option than slow death by biscuit.

It had been a feeble experiment with an obvious conclusion. God knows why she had to be strong, taut, and separate, or why she had to move from Belfast to Leningrad, what she would find in another man there, what was wrong with this house here, but there is a point at which you have made particular decisions in your life, and though they may have been wrong, if you don't make others you have to stick to the old ones because they are all you've got. And Estrin had not. She may have been tired of running late afternoons, but she had not come up with anything else to do then; she had not come up with another person to be than someone who runs; she could not at this late date become Duffy Shearhoon. Estrin turned back to her life in hollow resignation, having deserted it and no longer believing in it any more than she believed in Northern Ireland, but she had no one else to imitate and nowhere else to stay for the moment. She would march herself up the road and out of the country, if not with eagerness, at least with obedience, so she spent the rest of the night trying to sober up and laying out the Plan.

She would finish the house, down to lace curtains, candlesticks, and fresh milk in the fridge. She would dust the sills, clear the drains of turpentine, shine the mirror, maybe run herself a celebratory bath. When everything was pink, with dish drainer, potato peeler, and corkscrew, she would slip the key on a separate ring and hand it to someone who would always keep the couch under the window, a hired caretaker for her past. For she would never see 133 again. She would not even take a snapshot.

The sale of the house and the Guzzi should cover airfare. With the work she'd put into this bombed-out hulk, it should bring more than the song she bought it for. The Swallow would fly in spring. Leningrad would be no skive. She would probably receive a visa for no more than a month, and Estrin planned on slithering in for a year. She decided to arrive and disappear. Half the Soviet Union operated black; a room and a gritty job shouldn't be hard to scarf up. And Estrin had never been intimidated by laws. They were ideas that functioned mostly through fear. If you did not cooperate by being frightened, their imposing net melted at your fingertips like a spiderweb. For practically, how much effort would this *glasnost* government expend to dig up an obscure American traveler who'd overstayed her tour? All the same, it would be hard. *Fine, it will be hard.* Estrin felt callous. *It will still be cold in spring. Your Russian sucks, but you can order* kofye, *ask for a* komnata, *and buy a round of vodka; the rest is frill.*

As for the *bloop*: Estrin paced until 4 a.m. with coffee, and made one more small though rather awful decision.

That night Estrin dreamt about Philadelphia. The streets had all been renamed after people who had become famous after she left the country, and she had to ask directions to her own neighborhood. She wanted to mail a letter home to tell her parents she was back, but she no longer knew the price of first-class postage, nor did she know the rates of a pay phone. Testing herself, she found she also could not remember who was President of the United States or the capital of New Hampshire. She tried to buy a steak sandwich, but reached into her pocket to find only pound coins, so the vendor took the sandwich away. When she finally found her house, her mother spoke Russian and Estrin didn't understand a word.

Estrin had fasted nearly every year since she was eighteen, but in the Lancaster harder-harder, more-more, worse-worse school of achievement each fast had been for a bit longer, and this one would go to the top of the charts: *three weeks*. Conventionally she scheduled the ritual to break on her birthday, December 17, a poor enough time for a birthday, so often subsumed by the season, even worse for starvation—she inevitably wound through champagne and plum pudding with cups of weak tea.

In the five days preceding the fast, Estrin's appetite flagged with dread, whatever she ate merely reminding her of what she soon would not. She was beginning to forget what it was like to enjoy anything. Lately she walked the streets with her fingers gnarled into grappling hooks, her face wrung like a wet sheet.

When she opened her eyes to the mountain of her bedclothes on Day One, she could as well have been staring up at Kilimanjaro from the foot. *You have no idea what you're in for.* No, she admitted numbly, padding downstairs to boil water and eyeing the sad little crumbs of her last meal: soup and a wheaten farl, which, in a nervous anticipatory nausea, she hadn't managed to finish. Estrin threw the hard crust away and sloshed the cock-a-leekie down the drain, steeping herself strong, unsweetened Darjeeling; coffee she couldn't bear without milk. She was already ferociously hungry and the fast was only forty-five minutes through.

Restless, she launched out and combed the city for a selection of herbal tea bags; tannic brews corroded an empty stomach. At Waterstone's she bought: *Famine*, about the 1848 potato blight, and Beresford's *Ten Men Dead*, about the 1981 hunger strikes in Long Kesh. She returned to 133 and arranged her teas, pleased with her discovery of "nettle," its bramble of punishment, tea from a crown of thorns. How pleased Daddy would be that his defiant, agnostic daughter was still hounded by the ancient metaphors. *Father, take this cup from me*—she wondered how long she could find this funny.

Until about four in the afternoon. She had sanded her kitchen table through three grades of paper; the dust caught in her throat. Inability to sneeze contributed to a feeling of triviality. She felt partial. The colors of the room bled weak, fey yellows and beige; the weather was pasty, but could not rain. The phrase she had marshaled to rally this first day, *an act of sustained concentration*, already rang false. Hunger only fragmented her attention: she looked at that smooth table and didn't care. Estrin could not for the life of her understand why she could not have a piece of toast. The first day is the worst, she remembered. Because you feel silly.

At the Green Door Estrin announced she was "on the wagon" until her birthday, which aroused little comment. The club was used to these easy disavowals, just as easily broken.

Day Two, Estrin started *Famine*, in decorative discomfort—those families would never have allowed the potatoes to rot in Estrin's hydrator. Still, the story was absorbing, and she read better without bolting up for biscuits, without drink. That afternoon she went running. Her time was slow and she felt crummy, but that was to be expected. By the evening of Day Two, she was calm; at work, funny and energetic. She had not lost her touch. She could run, she could fast. Now all she had to figure out was why either capacity counted for sweet fuck-all.

By Day Four she was hitting her stride, well into *Famine*. With the table refinished and the spare bedroom repainted, she decided to try the weight room. She also decided fasting was easy, and that was a mistake.

The weight room was a disaster. Though she limped through every set, Estrin had trouble with her heart. It palpitated; for beats at a time it would stop. Her stomach churned, her bile rose. After, she showered for half an hour with her eyes closed.

The queasiness persisted, especially mornings. Estrin decided against weights; she would only run. In previous fasts, even the longest, the two-week one, she had played tennis and squash, cycled, swum; but this time even the running grew more burdensome than she remembered. Her time slowed further. By the end of the week she had to admit she was *jogging*. Her vision would darken curiously. The tea slurped in her stomach and leaked up her throat.

With *Famine* finished and every character defunct, Estrin moved on to the David Beresford. Even early in the account, she gripped the arms of her chair in frustration. Bobby Sands inflamed her. By page 120 she couldn't bear to sit down and agitated around her living room, raving. *United Ireland!* Lord, hadn't she heard enough of that chatter in this neighborhood. *Dying for a united Ireland*, what did that mean? It was like dying for Munchkinland, like dying "because." And for status? So you got POW status. So you proved this was a war. Big fucking deal, call it a war! Aren't there stupid wars? Aren't there bad wars? Shouldn't most wars never have been fought, and aren't there wars of which half the lot are on the wrong side? Weren't there plenty of Nazis who called themselves POWs, and what did that prove? Her reading crawled, as every few pages inspired another tirade. Because the problem wasn't that she didn't understand. The problem (Day Eight. Day Nine . . .) was understanding all too well.

For if the hunger strikes expressed a microcosm of the Troubles, wills at impasse, Estrin had reduced them further still, Sands and Mrs. Thatcher in one five-foot-two American girl. Estrin, too, was a prisoner of war.

"It is not those who inflict the most, but those who suffer the most who will conquer." Terrence McSwiney, 1920 hunger striker and dead person. Sands's pet homily, and the loopiest assertion Estrin had read in her life. Languishing late afternoons with the book falling from her hands, spent from railing at Bik McFarlane, it dark so early now but too fatigued to turn on a light, Estrin Lancaster understood that those who suffer the most: suffer the most. That suffering *per se* was without moral qualities—for discipline, the Five Demands, pain is only pain and it is probably best if there is less of it. Estrin was surprised in reading the Beresford how Catholic she'd become, despite Presbyterian force-feeding: her admiration of agony, her repudiation of the mince pie, so reminiscent of Farrell as a boy renouncing sugar in his tea. And the repudiation for Estrin had extended to her whole life, so that now she'd found a man more like her and more splendid than any man in any country, she was bound to forswear him more completely than any man before, not to write or ring but to fly to the most foreign part of the world she could find, a cold climate where she would deny his very language. How she had out-Catholicked this place, out-Farrelled O'Phelan. She would deny herself so completely after three weeks of tea and eleven years of travel that, sidereal, she would evaporate.

For Estrin inescapably identified with the hunger strikers the more she despised them. Rising to boil water with her hands trembling on the arms of the rocker, watching the walls ripple as if underwater, feeling her heart thunder from the mere exertion of standing up, Estrin envisioned with feverish clarity the straight-backed chairs of Long Kesh, the single keg of water, and the helpless tyranny of their own demented determination. Because that first bowl of porridge left cold had sealed their deaths. How well Estrin understood, just as weak before an equally deranged resolution, for it seemed—and she was beginning to vomit some of the tea, that had never happened before, not even in the two-week fast in the Philippines—that she was physically allergic to food; anywhere near the bread box her hand crippled. Comestibles repelled her. The peculiarity of fasting is that there is no temptation. And the terror of fasting is that it is possible.

But the days were so long! Every task loomed enormous. She tried to keep working on the furniture, but even the smell of shellac turned her stomach, and the reek of paint stripper drove her out back to retch tea. Brushing her teeth, smoothing the enticing mint on her tongue that she could not swallow, was the best moment of her day: because it was over.

The second-best moment was morning, groping with hot, slit eyes to the calendar and marking off the day before with a big crude X, the scrawl of a prisoner chalking off a sentence on the wall of his cell. On December 17, she'd sketched a birthday cake, with confetti, streamers. Mornings through the first week she had embellished the picture with a wedge of Stilton, champagne, but no longer, for into the second week food had lost its frivolous, sensory appeal. More and more she wanted to eat to digest. Paging through the sixty-some-day decomposition of ten hunger strikers, one at a time, as each lost first his muscle, his appetite, his sight, his voice, and finally his mind, though never, through to the very last hour, his ability to mutely refuse salvation, Estrin grew less eager to taste Madeira cake again than simply to survive.

From a penchant for starvation in the past, much of the experience was familiar: the headaches, the excessive heartbeat, the nursing-home care with which she rose from her chair; the funny metallic emission from her gums. Cold lips, sometimes a touch blue. Looking up at the clock and realizing she'd been sitting in the middle of the floor doing nothing for over an hour.

Recipe fantasies. The phases: this is a cinch/this is a nightmare. I feel perfectly normal/I feel perfectly grotesque. Long sleep, attempted hibernation. Swings from torpor to irrational elation, bounding irresponsibly upstairs to clap Robin on the back even as she declined, easily, his offer of a Cadbury Milk Tray.

The elation, however, was rare. Unusually rare. The sleep was fearfully narcotic. Surely this was worse than before. She felt back for memories of last time in the Philippines, cooking all day, never able to lick her fingers. Lying on the beach weekends like washed-up kelp. It had been bad; it was always bad. But surely not this bad. Of one thing she was confident: the nausea was new. Oh, she'd been woozy from time to time, but actually puking up tea, never. And she'd never shaken so much; all her muscles ached, and her breasts were chidingly tender.

Estrin told herself that fasting had never been a picnic and she'd simply forgotten what real discipline was like. Certainly the pleasures of fasting are few, though there is one: the will is a muscle, and beginning the second week Estrin's began to burn.

Will, of course, has the same reputation for righteousness among Protestants as suffering among Catholics, but will, too, is a neutral quantity, as easily put to the service of evil as good— there is nothing so all-fired wonderful about determination to do something lunatic, any more than there is about misguided suffering. Agonized folly, disciplined folly, is folly all the same. And so Estrin pumped the muscle with shy horror. She was feeding an animal that was not quite tame. It's a queer business to not quite control—your own control. Weakness can be protection. Because Estrin's will was violent. Estrin's will was dangerous. And had she been locked in the H-blocks in 1981, Estrin's will would have slaughtered her with unambivalent joy.

There was one other pleasure, rather sweeter than the rising specter of a private Third Reich on Springfield Road. When she woke slow and groggy mornings, her hands would slip softly from her thighs, finding the scoop of her hipbones hollowed enough to serve soup, the rib cage sharp enough to carve lamb. Gradually and conditionally, warmth returned to her fingertips, and she smoothed the tight rump of her hips, finally earning a few tentative strokes of her own affection.

However, as she shrank down half a pound a day, unearthing the knolls of muscle that had so inexplicably persisted through her decay, the morning of the eleventh day, with her eyes still closed, her hands padded their way up this new body to find her breasts had remained curiously full. It was time for her period, but this was ridiculous. Estrin had never been big there, and in her heyday had nearly reduced them to pectorals. She cupped them impatiently getting dressed. They were too—female. They were an affliction. She marched to the kitchen to boil water, glowering as the swells bobbled ahead, and rinsed the *U.S. Out of Nicaragua* cup stained with rosehips from the night before. But when the thin medicinal reek wafted from the nettle tea bag, she fled out back with the dry heaves. Pale and bracing herself on the brick, Estrin returned to the kitchen, having a hard time closing the door. It was brittle out there, with a rare frost. She'd have to head back out for coal; her breath fogged at the stove. Without food Estrin got cold easily and huddled over the steaming kettle, shivering. She forced herself to dip the tea bag, and stirred the tea for a long time. She had to force down liquids or she'd end up in the Royal for sure.

Briefly the picture salved her: Malcolm stopping by when she didn't turn up for work, finding her on the floor in a coma and calling an ambulance, lifting her on a stretcher and saving her from herself. Estrin had led such a nightmarishly healthy life, she envied Farrell. She would like his lungs. Because no one ever took care of her. She would like someone to take care of her.

On the other hand, in a hospital they would ask what happened and they would try to feed her and she would shake her head and press her lips like a stubborn child. After repeated refusals she'd admit to having eaten nothing for eleven days and that she "only had ten more to go." The nurses would be horrified. They wouldn't understand the spiritual quest, that this was a return to herself, an act of loyalty and honor, even love. But Estrin knew from Beresford that they could break you, stick tubes in you and perforate your purity, pollute your exquisite Germanic perfection with glucose until you were any old hungry person once more. No, she did not want to end up in the Royal, and so she finished the tea and boiled more water, a good girl cleaning her plate. A different sort this time, fennel—why, what an opulent variety of tiny cardboard boxes lined the stove.

Estrin built a coal fire and, wrapped in three blankets, propped with *Ten Men Dead*. She was beginning to deal with herself as an invalid who had to be carted to different rooms, propped with pillows, and given something to amuse it. She was most captivated by the second hunger striker, Francis Hughes. Bobby Sands was overserious and wrote woeful poetry. Hughes, however, was a soldier. He always dressed in fatigues. He was credited with murdering up to thirty members of the security forces, and if you were going to make a career of killing people, you might as well do it right. He'd been captured by the Brits at last after being trailed for fifteen hours shot in the hip. When they operated on the wound, he spurned general anesthesia for fear he would talk. He was motivated by loyalty to his friends and good old-fashioned revenge, having been badly beaten by the UDR as a boy, a justification Estrin preferred to the right-to-national-self-determination, freedom-from-the-tyranny-of-capitalist-imperialism rinky-dink they never got quite right at the Green Door. And Frank was physically competent, good with bombs, the inventor of the historically important clothespin booby trap. He was handsome and a drinker, had a foul mouth but a beautiful singing voice. Of all the hunger strikers it was Frank who persisted in exercising in his cell: Estrin was in love.

But Estrin knew her own Francis Hughes, who'd not de-signed bombs but dismantled them, whose politics were fierce with respectable disgust. By early afternoon, after fifty-nine days of fasting, Frank had passed from man to myth, claiming, "I don't mind dying as long as it's not vain or stupid." Estrin let the pages flap and announced out loud, "Sorry, Bootsie, but it was stupid," adding, "I know all about stupid," and lapsing into now recurrent fantasies of Farrell at 44.

1. She has agreed to meet him, reluctantly. She arrives in her best black dress, drawn and tiny-wristed, skin translucent, tubercular: Dostoevsky. Farrell orders wine. Estrin orders Ballygowan.

"You're thirsty?" he asks.

"Yes." There is no explanation. The conversation is lively. He tells her about the conference. Her attention is perfect, her comments succinct, her humor dry. Farrell orders cherrystones, salmon, mixed salad; Estrin asks for a second mineral water. Farrell is startled.

"I'm not hungry." She shrugs, and smiles only on the teeth side of her mouth.

"You're quite sure?"

"Yes." Her hands are clasped.

Farrell is unsettled and gulps his wine. He eats guiltily, slurping the clams; they drip. In the end he gets quite drunk. Estrin has remained composed. For once she sees him across the table stripped of the glow of Pouilly Fuissé. In her sobriety she is critical but forgiving. She notes the Béarnaise sauce on his collar, the fishy webs in the corners of his mouth. He gets a bit sententious. Estrin becomes only more understated. Perhaps there is even an argument. Estrin wins it, though he is too sozzled to be aware of losing. That is all right. Because there is a subtitle running: *I have not eaten for eleven days.* And tomorrow this same fantasy would run again, with twelve. A number dominated her day. Eleven was important because it was just past halfway. She had never understood eleven so completely. It is prime. If you subtract it from twenty-one you get ten. Ten more days . . . tomorrow nine . . .

The fantasy was the not-saying. That was the extra challenge this time: to tell no one. Dining with Farrell and refusing to ask for admiration. Later, only after, would she permit herself to tell. Only on her birthday would she permit herself to tell.

2. December 17. Farrell has dressed elegantly. They are seated in 133. She has made the meal herself. The candles are lit. Casual, patient, she lifts the fork to her mouth. Chews thoughtfully. Swallows. She knows the nothing of this moment: food tastes no better than it ever did.

"I am a bit hungry," she remarks.

"Good," says Farrell. "Your appetite's been poorly."

"I'll say." Her voice is wry. "I haven't eaten anything but herbal tea for three weeks." Another slow, cardboardy bite of fish.

Funny, in this picture every time he doesn't hear her. He lets the comment slide by. The fantasy goes wrong. He does not drop his fork and say, "What?" He talks about the conference. Estrin shakes her head and feels sick. She can no longer keep down solid food. She excuses herself to the john and pukes. She returns blanched and barely able to stand, but this, too, he fails to notice. Later, when he's drunk, he says she is beautiful. But Estrin is not beautiful, she is damp and jaundiced. She has not eaten her dinner. She needs to lie down. When Farrell makes love to her he is, as usual, flamboyant, half off the bed, but Estrin is passive and whimpering and he doesn't notice. Why even in her fantasies did he never notice anything? Why, starving and light-headed in her half-built bombed-out house, no longer able to turn a page and still planning on running ten miles, could she not at least solicit his compassion in her head? For he was only critical now. He picked fights; and the sex, she could be anyone. Over and over she ran both visions, and each time the second, the birthday, went wrong.

And there was something wrong with the first one as well. Yes, if she went out with Farrell before the seventeenth, she'd drink mineral water and keep her mouth shut, but because he'd not admire her after all. Estrin knew this because she did not admire herself. Her eyes throbbed in their sockets and she could cool them. The beloved leg muscles twinged in rebuke, the only reason she couldn't feed them that she was a fruitcake.

Once more Estrin Lancaster sacrificed for nothing. At least in Long Kesh the hunger strikers had the illusion of cause, and they did have each other. As usual, Estrin had nothing and no one. Just like weights, Estrin fasted only for vanity, for prettiness, because she lived in a time when lovely women were thin. For power, but petty, personal power, a base control over her own arm as it reached not for jam jars but for camomile. Estrin had refined the perfect suffering that did not respect itself. At last Estrin could whip herself and feel only cowardly and small. Maybe she had something to teach those medieval monks after all: to end the cycle of self-abuse and self-righteousness, lose your faith. Whip yourself for nothing. Feel the emptiness of your gesture. For Estrin starved herself and knew only shame.

It was pitch-dark now. Estrin went upstairs to change, but would not relinquish the blankets and slipped into running shorts under a wool tent. There was one other problem with Fantasies One and Two: there was no danger of facing Farrell over fish or Ballygowan so far. The conference had started, and for all eleven days he hadn't called. Not once. Estrin dropped the blankets to her feet and drew a deep cold breath. So that was why she had to leave Northern Ireland, and soon. Why she had to leave Farrell O'Phelan. It was not simply habit, compulsive departure. It was not Fear of Intimacy, magazine. She would leave because she did not have him to give up.

21

Chemical Irritation

The Antrim Arms was bedlam.

"Telephone for O'Phelan—O'Phelan—" rose above the din.

"He's not to be had. I'll handle it." Angus threaded the cord through the wilderness of spent drink. "Aye, your man's in his bloody chambers, any message like? . . . *Rosebud?* For fuck's sake, is that you?"

The dial tone was the more annoying for his having to lurch back over the bar with the receiver for nothing, and in MacBride's condition it was some trick to spare the glasses in his wake.

If it wasn't forty-five seconds before the phone rang again. "O'Phelan—!"

Angus snagged the call once more. "Listen, lassie, if you're checking up on me, you may as well ask for the thing itself—"

"Farrell?"

"Roisin?"

A meaty pause, you could carve it. "Farrell . . . ?"

"No, love." Sure he'd made a mistake. If he wasn't bloody well hearing voices now. Maybe that thorny flower was getting to him more than he figured. "The boy's embroiled. I'll take your name, just?"

"Is that Angus?"

A Yank at that. This conference was making him jumpy. "Aye."

"We met at the distillery. About a year ago. You probably don't remember."

"With the motorcycle!" He lit up, though (was it the connection?) the quavering voice on the other end he could hardly associate with that dark, determined powerhouse at the Pot Still Bar. "Who could forget those leather trousers? And haven't we never met for a jar?"

"Right." She sounded curiously out of breath. "But Farrell isn't, ah—"

"Should I interrupt him now, you'd hardly want to speak to the dragon you got through to. But you're still in Ulster? Or would you be calling it the Six Counties now?"

"I'm not calling it anything." She was whispering! "Printable."

"Still in the North, then."

The laugh was weak. "Barely."

"I'll tell the wanker you rang?"

"No, I—no. No, don't, actually. Never mind."

It seemed she was ringing off, so he started to agonize back over the bar when he heard her say something more; he returned and she was gone—more awkwardness, and she'd been so smooth at Bushmills. Women: they could never keep it up.

Not until midnight did he and O'Phelan find themselves in the same room. Angus was well on, but the spirey man's proximity was still a splinter in his toe. Over in the corner, O'Phelan was bent over your man from the SDLP (the Stoop Down Low

Party, as they were known in their own parts, and a wet lot),
the bright spark who'd accused Farrell that afternoon of having
led the Province "down the road of no return, and back again."
Everyone else in the hotel had loosened the odd collar, but there
was O'Phelan still looking nicely turned out, thank you very
much, with his wee glass of white wine. That was the final cod,
wasn't it? Hadn't the Antrim Arms shipped in two cases of Chardonnay for the bastard, and wouldn't they need more. The kid
was fooling himself; he drank every bit as much as anyone in
the room, just siphoned it down as wine and had to run to the
bog. Angus preferred whiskey as more efficient.

For a rare moment unentangled from snarls of conversation,
Angus paused to inhale the piquant smog of smoke-clogged air,
boozy breath, brash proclamations, and insincere laughter—no
doubt about it, MacBride was happier than a pig in shite. Angus
enjoyed corruption. He liked puzzles where all the pieces were
queered but somehow fit together. He liked legal tax evasion
and dodgy investment schemes and lying to his wife. In short,
Angus MacBride loved Northern Irish politics. And not since
Sunningdale had he felt more perfectly squirreled to the very
center, a screw without which the whole table fell apart. At
Sunningdale, too, he'd been ancillary, young. Youth was overrated. He might not goal a football as he used to, but now he
could clout the DUP in the teeth. And just with a bit of a phrase,
mind you, a bit of a phrase. A wee reference to the Ayatollah.
(Had to qualify your metaphors in this place, where, if an MP
vowed to murder you in the next election, he meant with the
Browning in his belt. Angus was the only real politician in this
hotel. With the rest toadies and slugs, the conference was a
regular camping trip on the banks of Lough Neagh.) Tired of
hearing about Sunningdale, anyway. Everyone afraid of a reprise,
when what? Those poor Orange geriatrics were going to stage
another general strike? Half the lot couldn't make it to Finaghy
on the Twelfth anymore without a lift up. Sure, they'd barricade
Great Victoria with wheelchairs. No lads, the hard-liners have

had it, they priced themselves out of a province long ago. It was Angus MacBride's back yard now. Why, he liked to think of Ulster as one big family farm.

This Border Poll was a snorter, but all the better to win his Nobel Prize. Looked dicey but possible. In the meantime, this conference was the best crack he'd had in years. And he liked the Antrim Arms. A bit tatty, but you could put your feet up, and no lass dashed out with a rag when you upset a bit of lager on the carpet. Whitewells was too starchy. Wave your arm to make a point and before you knew it you were two hundred quid in the hole from knocking over some godawful Chinese vase. And every time he walked in that place he got angry. The ease with which the hotel had fallen in that character's lap. And its pretension! Very Catholic, very *Irish*: always slagging on the British, but wanting nothing more than to be wee landed English lords every one, down to the ascots and snuff. This was a town where everyone imitated the sort they hated: the Protestant paramilitaries aped the IRA, the Provos the British Army. No wonder at the end of the day nobody knew who they were, except the same. That's what none of them could stick. Sure there were differences with the mainland, the South, but here there were no "two communities," their "separate traditions," like classes of '63 and '64. The Northern Irish fought this hard from being so hopelessly homogeneous they could drown.

"Your girlfriend rang."

Farrell turned, and it was a funny little moment where Angus, maybe for the first time, did not like that O'Phelan was the taller. He looked *down*. "Which one?"

"You never mentioned you hauled in the wee Yank. It's not like you when you've plucked a bird not to stick the feather in your cap."

"What do you know what's like me, fella?" Farrell may have kept his tie on, but your man was half tore. "You've never known who I was. You've never known what I was capable of—"

Lord, the spit would be flying in no time. "Your motorcyclist, now," Angus interrupted genially. "I've always found American

women most generous, most open-minded. A progressive people. You find that so?"

"Throw your mind at a wall, MacBride, and it would stick.
A woman's just a pair of knickers with a post box."

"Oh, aye," Angus agreed. "But you, my boy, care about
what's *inside*. You and your American discuss the issues of the
day. You solicit her opinion about your work. You go to openings at the Federesky Gallery and sip Beaujolais. Your fingers
intermingle, and you discuss over cappuccinos whether you're
ready—"

"We fuck," Farrell cut him off.

MacBride smiled. It wasn't often he found himself the more
sober of the two; he slid his Bush on top of the piano.

"She's pretty," Farrell added.

MacBride stepped back; the *p* was a spritzer. "Oh, indeed.
And you can imagine how impressed I am that you've managed
to attract such a lovely woman. Intimidated, even. I feel small.
I look to you with an extra awe, wanting your secret. I think,
Angus, best keep any lady you fancy far from O'Phelan's
charms."

Farrell leered. "How I've fouled myself for you, MacBride,
you'll never know. What I've crawled through to wipe your nose
makes the blanketmen look like dental hygienists."

"Spare me, O'Phelan, nothing makes me more nervous than
your bleeding favors."

"Och no, Angus, I owe you so much. For your dogged friend-
ship with such a pimply schoolboy. For your tutelage in chess.
Propping me up and brewing me a cup of coffee when I was
down the neck of a bottle and *such* an embarrassment to your
C of I upper Malone T-T's—"

"Aye, and I never would have guessed all that'd be held
against me, like."

"We Catholics are ungrateful. Ask Maggie. She sends in the
army to take care of us and we only snipe at them. And every
time she whirls in here, she coos about how many leisure centers
we've got. Why do you need the IRA when you can play squash?"

"You sound just like your da," Angus swiped, and effectively shut Farrell up. Dead on. Because Lord, had that geezer ever driven Angus wild. Blocked half the night and typical Taig, professional victim, a string of excuses long as your arm. Never once heard the bastard take the blame for so much as his own cut finger. Once, tentatively, Angus had corrected your man's usage of "hegemony," and hadn't the ghett lit into a song and dance about how his language had been "robbed," how he was forced to express himself in a "foreign tongue," as if he hadn't been raised speaking English every bit as much as any poor Orange fourth-former. A dried-up, wicked scarecrow, Ruairi O'Phelan, who would *jab, jab, jab* at MacBride's chest, nailing the family's token Prod, the one sixteen-year-old scapegoat the electrician could get his hands on. Sometimes MacBride caught Farrell's face in a certain light and the resemblance depressed him.

A message from the Swallow was at least a relief from the regular spattering from the Pigeon, ill disguised, coy. One was worried; the other browned-off. An interesting difference, their defaults. When the Pigeon didn't hear from him, she assumed he'd been shot. The Swallow assumed he'd been an asshole. While the concern of the first was flattering, the suspicion of the second had proved more technically correct.

He rang the one, delayed the other. He did not quite understand what he wished to put off.

Farrell gave the conference an afternoon free, and though what they surely needed a break from was less politics than drink, the nearest diversion in Bushmills was the distillery. Farrell accompanied the rowdies with some reluctance. He'd not been back since that meeting over a year ago, and wondered if maybe he'd like to keep the memory clean. *Sentimental.* Best to go and keep his ears open for the casual, hungover aside that so often told all. The SDLP was the nugget, and they were making him sweat.

The distillery was in a dead phase of its production. The

massive mash tun, last time filled with steaming grist and threshed with a ten-foot blade, was empty and still. Its room, toasty then, was cold. The guide hurried their group, for the conferees weren't interested in the process but only the results—and these were the men to sort out the North? For sure it was the bar at the Antrim Arms lured most of this crowd through seminars all day.

Farrell looked forward to a good whiff off the washbacks, but these, too, were empty. Farrell opened the lids on each vat to make sure, and in every barrel the inside was chill and dry, with a wisp of wort off the wood like an afternoon you can't quite remember. Farrell pulled his coat tight and shivered. He was sober, but he'd had no sleep two nights running; the washbacks jumped. He kept starting, checking corners—there, darting through the door, tripping down the stairs, bouncing across the walkway: a tousle of dark hair, the gleam of a red helmet. He turned at the clop of boots (a cooper), the twang of American sarcasm (a tourist). He had awaited the big-breasted pot stills, but that room was closed entirely and their group went straight to the bar. The tour had taken ten minutes, and the conferees, glasses in hand, could not have been happier. But Farrell only wanted to leave. He wondered what he could have conceivably found interesting in the distillery before.

He did not phone until four in the morning. Estrin had just gotten to sleep. She'd been thrashing for hours, tormented with feathery visions of dill sauce. She repeatedly checked her pulse, until the hyperawareness of her heartbeat seemed to imply how immanently it would stop.

He was incoherent. Something about booze, which she could infer, and lack of sleep, hard work . . . How often had she sympathized with this bullshit. But for once she would not caution, *Farrell, don't push yourself, you have limits, your lungs, get some rest*, but drawled laconically, "Well, it's your choice, isn't it?" which she followed with pitiless silence. He inquired vaguely into how she was, and she said, "Fine," immediately furious he did not know what she refused to tell. It was Day Fourteen.

Estrin woke again at 7:30 and groaned. Sleep had become arduous, like everything else. Her dreams could no longer carry a plot or maintain a location, but frittered in a delirium of empty glasses, cleared plates, banished lovers. She never dreamt of eating, she never dreamt of sex. Only of strangers and stadiums and big, unfurnished flats; parties to which she was not invited.

She spent the morning throwing up (now routine, and subsiding after the third cup of tea), picking up a paintbrush and putting it down again, and watching the flowers on the wallpaper grow hairy vines. That afternoon she finished *Ten Men Dead*. Probably the book depressed her, but just now it made her livid, since everything did.

It wasn't exactly flattering now, was it, that the son of a bitch called, since she'd traced him herself and spent plenty of time at it, too, not that he'd call and tell her where he was, mind you, so she had to stop by fucking Whitewells, where they always acted as if they'd never seen her before, never so much as a nod of recognition, stony, every damn one, and no, they hadn't a clue where Farrell was—liars—so she had to call Constance, who was embarrassed and wasn't supposed to tell but did anyway, because Estrin sounded so pathetic. And now it was time to go to the Green Fucking Door. She couldn't find her fucking right boot and then the fucking Guzzi took forever to start and the light at the Falls must be jammed because she'd been at this intersection a fucking half hour, until Estrin actually shouted, "Fucking change!" and people stared.

Estrin had a name for this, it was Chemical Irritation, rage that heightened her life with an almost hallucinogenic intensity, except instead of the colors getting brighter they merely grew more annoying. In fact, what colors, since it was dark practically all day and of course it was raining, of course— NORMAL people traveled to Bali and got suntans and Estrin had to fly to Bel-fucking-fast, dreary, dank, and obsessed with its turgid, ineffably boring little conflict— NORMAL women ate breakfast, and lunch, and supper, with dessert and brandy, and then watched movies on TV huddled up to some reasonable excuse for a man. But *no-oo*, Estrin had to make for repressed religious countries and then find the ugliest part of the ugliest city and live there and starve. Estrin had to find a "boyfriend" who rather than hold her hand through the trials of her own barmy fanaticism was up in Bushmills pickling the last few brain cells functioning on this island. As Estrin whipped past graffitti with the rain needling her face, every scrawl of the I-fucking-R-fucking-A ground a whole layer of enamel off her molars. And all down the road, if every local wasn't dressed like a dog's dinner—

Do not imagine that when Estrin got to work her mood improved.

When she arrived, Clive had finally gotten an interview with some Sinn Féin menial who was making quite a to-do about not wanting to be recorded. Seated at the bar, Clive seemed to acquiesce, and slipped his tiny S911 into his breast pocket. He must have thought himself quite the sly fox depressing the Record button, and might have gotten away with it had the cassette not gone haywire; for midway through the interview the tape began curling out from behind his lapel. The Republican marched off in a huff.

Ordinarily Estrin might have found this funny, but the joke cost an hour of Clive's disconsolate blithering about how other people got away with things and he always got caught. For the rest of the night, too, Clive was unraveling the tape all over the bar, fussing when Estrin tried to wipe down the counter lest the recording get wet, and later asking Estrin to untangle a particularly nuggy morass. She gave it a go, but it turned out that threading quarter-inch microcassette tape through itself was the perfectly wrong task for Estrin Lancaster this evening; after five minutes, her breathing sibilated. Clive almost noticed the crimped fingers and dangerous little growl in time, but just as he assured her he could do it himself, she crushed it. Splintering that plastic casing, wadding up the tape, and throwing the lot at Clive Barclay was the only thing that gave her satisfaction all night.

Because everyone was in top form. Sailbheaster was whistling a medley of "My Favorite Things," "My Little Armalite," and "Blowin' in the Wind." Callaghan was gooning at the bar in his best beige, lager dripping from his mustache, repeating everything Estrin said in a broad, twangy attempt at an American accent.

Malcolm kept at her heels all night. He had a surprise, he said. Take a few minutes and come see his surprise. But the club was a-scurry with the all-important business of getting soused one more night, and she put him off.

"Aye, the Six Counties has gone twee," Callaghan was bemoaning to Duff. "Walk down Royal Avenue, look sharp lest you get mown over by a riot of housewives storming Anderson McAuley for pâté molds."

"Time was we knew how to riot proper, d'you know?" Duff concurred. "Waved a tricolor instead of a linen napkin. But these days a boy buys a round, it's down his throat in an hour, when a ways back a lad would save for the kind you served to British soldiers. And they'd not come back for seconds, d'you follow?"

"Have you seen what they've done to the Washington Bar?" chimed Damien. "The yuppies have shined up every chink. Looks like a bleeding Wimpy's. And they've shoved the boyos to the back, for they don't fit the new decor."

"The Washington, bollocks, the Britannic!" Callaghan exclaimed.

"Aye," Duff sighed. "The Crown has soiled herself."

"You been in?" asked Damien.

"Tried once," Callaghan snorted. "And this fat specky cod in the doorway puts out his arm, like. Points to a sign about PROPER ATTIRE. Told him my tux was in the cleaner's, thank you very much. Fucking hell, I'd not drink there if you put me on salary."

"All part of the picture," said Damien. "Don't you know

Maggie sent a check from across the water to do up the Crown's top floor. And you can wager the Washington's part of the conspiracy, and all those shoe stores in the town: more rape of our culture. Get the ladies addicted to bun warmers and Earl Grey tea, sure they won't bang bin lids anymore."

"Aye, the whole place has gone soft, like," keened Callaghan. "And you know who's the worst of the lot—"

"The Provos!"

"Better freakin' believe it! The gombeens poove about in ties. I tell you, Sinn Féin is the worst thing ever happened to West Belfast. A ballot box in one hand and after-shave in the other—"

"Wasting time in City Council screaming *Point of order! Point of order!* instead of digging their balaclavas out of mothballs. I don't give a toss for a Republican who can't fire off anything but his mouth—"

Estrin choked on an incredulous guffaw.

"But sure it's time for a change, d'you follow? Twenty years and how far are we, just?"

"*Exactamente!*" said Callaghan, who holidayed in Spain. "So they plant a wee bomb here, a wee bomb there. Who gives a frig? Isn't the whole kit accustomed to a bit of a bang from time to time? Don't grannies knock the plaster from their hair and take another spoon of egg mayonnaise? No, to shake this place up now you've to do better than knock a few windows out of Windsor House. And the Brits-and-peelers strategy is off the mark. It's civilian casualties have an impact. Look at Enniskillen: the Provos bow and scrape how it was a mistake, but I say it was fuckin' brilliant! Got wider coverage than any operation in the last five years."

"Aye, but there's press and press, Mike lad, d'you follow—"

"*Impact* is all that matters. The Provos claim this is a war and then conduct it like a badminton match. If this is a war, I say let's have it, all out. There's no such thing as a civilian in Ireland. You choose your sides and your weapons, and I am bleeding sick of waiting for some eejit to wave a flag and shout, *Go!* I am dead bored with reading about one more shooting here, one car bomb there; why, even Enniskillen was small potatoes—"

"So do it!" Estrin had run out of bar to wipe. It was a tribute to the durable powers of the human body that after fourteen days without food her face could still turn such a vivid color of fuchsia.

Callaghan turned. "*Por favor?*"

"Go ahead! Fly to Libya and stuff a few Sam-7's in your carry-on! Honest to God, it would be a relief just to see this crowd do anything! All this flannel night after night, and I have to listen to it, for hours. *Bullshit*, that's what we call it in America, you are *bullshitters*. Because for all your talk about Milltown, Andytown, Gibraltar, with all this aspiration to a united-fucking-Ireland, you think I don't know what you really do? You sleep till noon, kick around hoovering crisps until the club opens, and then drink yourselves psychiatric! You can't hoodwink me, I pour the booze! Okay, it's your life, but I just wish, if that's the way you want to spend it, you'd face that, snoot down your row of pints, and *shut up!*"

"Now, Estrin, love," Duff stuttered. "Don't you think you're being a bit harsh, now—"

"Harsh!" Her voice skipped up an octave. "I have hardly begun! Sailbheaster sits back there night after night mugging in dark glasses for the INLA until his mummy comes to collect him. In my day we played cops and robbers, but I was eight! I feel as if I'm running a babysitting service! And all of you hit on poor Clive every time you're short of quid, and score a stout in exchange for some bogus interview. You've never told him a damned thing he couldn't find in the papers, or worse, because you get the details wrong. And you, Damien, with all your bitching about how you've had it with this place and you're going to travel, you'll get a Guzzi like mine and—well, go! Go, go, go! I mean, it's like listening to a 78 of *The Cherry Orchard* on 33!"

"Well, aren't we the lofty one, Little Miss Well-Traveled,"

said Callaghan. "And what mighty works have you executed, that you sit at the right hand of you-know-who?"

"Nothing," she said squarely. "I have done absolutely nothing. But do you hear me whining about what all I want to do but the British won't let me, I can't because I'm lower class or a woman or short, or whatever excuse an American gets to use—or do we get any? No, at least I admit that no, I do not want to accomplish anything, I only want to have a good time—"

"Some good time," muttered Damien.

"And no, I have zero political opinions, and that may be deplorable to you, but at least I don't sit around pounding the bar and sounding ferocious and still having no more effect on my country than a sick mouse on the dole."

"And your fancy man O'Phelan," said Callaghan, "you figure he shows us up, like? He's a bloody paragon?"

"At least he gets off his butt."

"And on top of a fair number of others, I've heard—"

"What's that supposed to—"

"Sure we've all got our dreams, d'you know?" Duff interrupted quickly. "And when they don't come through—"

"You mean when they don't arrive in the mail—"

"A man needs the odd sip of consolation, d'you follow?"

"Yes, I follow, because if you aren't the worst of the bunch." She wheeled on Shearhoon. "All your stories about the old days, when the most you've had to do with barricades has been to become one! As for your literary ambitions—"

"Now I did send *To Kill a Whirlybird* into Blackstaff, and it was simply too radical—"

"When?"

"Sorry?"

"When did you send it?"

"Why, that must have been—"

"Ten years ago!"

"Well, perhaps the disappointment, d'you follow—"

"The consolation, more like it. And when did you write it, this grand epic of Irish resistance?"

"Why, I believe it was—"

"*Twenty* years ago! And when, Duff Shearhoon, was the last time you actually read a book?"

"Sure the other day just—"

"Sure you cannot fucking *remember*! I've traveled all over the world, but Christ, I have never been anywhere more calcified with self-pity—"

"Est—"

"Resentful of anyone's success—"

"Est!" Malcolm guided her to the back kitchen with a hand on her arm. He closed the door behind them and sat her in a chair. Her head fell over the back, and Malcolm stroked her hair. "What," he asked softly, "is wrong?"

The ceiling buckled; for a moment the wriggle of tiles disappeared. Estrin closed her eyes and said nothing.

Malcolm stooped at her side. "You look desperate, you know that? You're pale and skinny and I never see you eat anything, and now you don't even drink. I pass you in Andytown flopping by the mile; it's cold, it's raining, and you're bloody killing yourself. What's up, Est?"

She was not forthcoming. He rose and rubbed his own neck. "The rest could use a browbeating, but I wish you'd let up on Shearhoon. It's Callaghan should be carpeted."

"I know," she sighed, and didn't recognize the sound from her mouth; her very voice was losing weight. "But Callaghan frightens me."

"Why, just?"

"The others rattle me because they're all talk. Callaghan rattles me because he's not."

"You overrate the chump. A dozer like the rest, and he fancies you, like. They all do."

"Malcolm, what are you doing?"

From his knapsack the boy had produced milk and several packets of tinfoil, and was rustling over pots. "I told you I'd a surprise. There's not a meal to coat your ribs like Malcolm Dunlea's Irish champ. You've never had the real thing, says you. Now the spuds is all cooked—"

"Malcolm, we really need to cover the bar. It's half an hour to last call."

"Don't you be fussed, I'll pull the pints." He glugged milk in the pan and sprinkled scallions on top. "Meantime, you can sit back here—"

"No, really, I've had my tea." Estrin was sorry there was no one to get the joke; *tea* in Ulster meant dinner, and didn't it.

"Aye, your three leaves of lettuce and a Brussels sprout. Now the trick with champ is not to boil the milk but still cook your spring onions—"

"Malcolm."

"And then you build a big moat, like, with the creamed spuds—"

"Malcolm, stop."

"Fill the lake with hot milk, and then float your really massive lump of butter in the middle—"

"Malcolm, *I can't!*"

"But, Est—I brought all the bits—the best champ in West Belfast—"

"For Christ sake, Malcolm." She stood up. "It's only mashed potatoes." Brisking to the bar, she left the door swinging. When she returned an hour later, the pan was rinsed, all the foil packets bagged away.

Day Fifteen. Estrin continued to have trouble with her eyesight. In *Ten Men Dead* it said that fasting, you begin to go blind because your body feeds off your brain tissue for protein. Estrin told herself this was too soon, that she simply wasn't sleeping; as she wasn't, for she tossed by the hour with relentless visions of Francis Hughes. He limped her bedroom in Doc Martens boots, dragging a jug of plain water, Ulster's Ghost of Christmas Past.

Estrin abandoned the North and checked out *The Life & Times of Michael K* from Linen Hall. She read it in one sitting, though lines of text vanished from time to time. A clammy hand had guided her selection. Michael K begins to live entirely on pumpkin, and as in every book she'd read for fifteen days, the main character starved.

Day Sixteen. Estrin calmed herself, there was no doubt now she would make it. Then, Day Twenty-one was the point at which the Long Kesh hunger strikers were routinely checked into hospital.

It was Friday, but her customers were cool, as they'd been the night before. Damien and Callaghan stopped talking when she approached; Sailbheaster kept his gloves on, his jacket zipped to his chin; Clive arrived with a paperback of *The Crack* and though not turning any pages did not look up. Malcolm didn't tell Estrin about hurley practice. Duff moved his regular stool conspicuously from the bar, and ordered only from Malcolm; the twitch in his eye fluttered like the wings of a hummingbird.

So on Day Seventeen she did not find their silence inexplicable. Estrin was in one of her improbable phases of exuberance and hoped to effect a reconciliation without apologizing outright. She tried a joke with Clive; his eyes went small. She brushed past Malcolm and began to assure him that next week was her birthday, and most certainly they would have that champ, with bangers and rashers and potato bread besides, and a big bottle of Bush to wash it down. . . . When Malcolm only rolled a plastic bullet, she cut it short. They sure held on to a grudge. At least Duff would warm at her touch like the big ball of cookie dough he was, but when she turned to his stool, for the first time since she'd worked this job, it was empty.

"Duff's not in the loo, is he?" she asked Malcolm. "I don't see his coat."

"You've not heard the news, then. I was wondering."

"I don't like the sound of this."

"He tried to plant a bomb in The Crown Bar."

"But Duff loves The Crown!"

"Aye. Made it more of a personal sacrifice, like. For the cause."

"What cause?"

"Yours, I'd venture. I figure he wanted to *do* something."

"Fucking hell." Estrin sat down, hard. "All I had in mind was a poem."

A cathedral of drink in the center of town, The Crown was a cross-sectarian bar. Unlike the haughty, disinherited façade of Stormont, the grand but inevitably British City Hall bannered front and back with BELFAST SAYS NO, St. Anne's or St. Patrick's each patronizing its separate part of town, The Crown was a landmark on common ground, a corner Switzerland in gold, manila, and pale greens. Close-ups of the bar's watery stained glass, hand-painted tiles, and curling plaster ceiling lavished National Trust postcards. Neither side, perhaps superstitiously, had laid a sheet of Semtex any nearer than the big brown eyesore of the Europa Hotel across the road (open season and no loss). You could sprinkle the RUC over the glens of Antrim like so much gentle rain, riddle the island's best smoked salmon with grapeshot in Marks and Spencer, or drill your own grandmother with an SLR, but you did *not* bomb The Crown Bar.

For The Crown was a real reconciliation camp, unifying the intemperate, where Duff Shearhoon and his hefty counterparts on Sandy Row alike could extend in long confessional booths, shutting the dark wood doors with their leonine gargoyles tightly on the conflict. When the Troubles are cleared away, The Crown will be what is left. The Crown was above the Troubles; it did not need the Troubles. The name may have sounded British, but the bar was Irish to its girders, a world view: *Sure what's your hurry now, you'll have another Bush, you will, there's plenty of time for all your carry-on tomorrow* . . . The Crown didn't fast. Unquestionably, The Crown was the capital of Eddie McIlwaine's Ulster, and it was only a regular pilgrimage to such a shrine that made the prospect of the house in Castlecaulfield remotely bearable.

Duff Shearhoon so worshipped The Crown that he only delivered himself to its forgiving arms once a week, like saving the good china for Sunday tea. He could be found on Great Victoria Street reliably every Friday at three, an adventure that cost him no small huffing and puffing—busing his bulk even small distances amounted, in sheer poundage, to organizing a school field trip. The Crown was a good afternoon bar, shielded with stained glass, impervious to times of day; it was never too early for a jar. And despite the fact that Duff had been impeccably unemployed for years, Fridays retained their atmosphere of hard-earned holiday; from his youth as a civil servant, Duff still ritually observed the salient feature of a working week: celebration that it was over.

The Crown's recent renovation had been loyal enough, but its accompanying unveiling of the Britannic Lounge on the second floor was pure betrayal. A dress code? and a bouncer? What was left of it curled Duff's hair.

So it was a queer business that Shearhoon had failed to take the bouncer into consideration, who later that night described to the RUC a great heifer of a man in a shabby olive anorak clutching a parcel tied up with a manic amount of string. Admission to the Britannic was discretionary. Though the doorman complained the gentleman wasn't wearing a tie—and with Duff's chin, neck, and shoulders all roughly the same circumference there was nowhere for a tie to go—one suspected from the distasteful portrait of puffy lips and wheezy shambling your man's real objection was to Duff himself. The customer had appeared in a state of "agitation and inebriation," and persisted, gasping, that he had an appointment, d'you follow? Then, the rebuff went easily enough, for Duff was less likely to storm past the bouncer than need help up the stairs.

For how many times had Estrin listened to Duff grunt off his stool, whistling through flared nostrils? So she could picture him clearly on Amelia Street, ambling from the Britannic in the same bald corduroy she waited five minutes each night for Duff to wrestle on, with the affectionate tussle of a master with his aged dog. Bewildered by his package like mail order he no longer remembered writing off for, never in his life more desperate for a pint, he had gazed into the beloved amber windows glinting with the saffron memories of so many Friday afternoons gone by. In fact, the bouncer described the Britannic's rejected patron as merely standing beside The Crown for several minutes in a paralytic stupor, waving the package about as if trying to give it away, and at length galumphing wildly to a street bin on the corner and depositing the bundle on a bed of Harp tins. The package disliked being abandoned, however, and complained.

Much as the reluctance cost him, it warmed Estrin that Duff could not, in the clutch, sally into the welcoming fold of his beloved pub with so ungrateful a present. Maybe he imagined he could damage only the Britannic Lounge, since for true it was a sad little bomb, rural, HME, good for a sprinkling of injuries, a counter, a bar mirror, and a floor of windowpanes, or, apparently, one human barricade.

Estrin glared up at Callaghan from her slump. "You know, this doesn't sound like Duff's idea to me."

"How do you figure?" asked Callaghan pleasantly.

"Nothing would alienate this whole town more perfectly than hitting The Crown Bar. *Impact*," leveled Estrin.

"Aye, the choice was bloody brilliant," he concurred. "But the job was wick. Maybe you were right, Yank. Shearhoon was never much of a hard man, like. Suppose you feel a bit poorly, so you do. After the rousing call to action."

"Do I feel depressed, yes. Responsible? I told him to get off his butt. I did not suggest fertilizer. I mean, where did he *get* it, Callaghan?"

Michael shrugged. "This is West Belfast."

"This is the Green Door! Haven for the clueless and un-connected! Christ, you are a shit."

The pasty man scratched the bulge between his shirt buttons and squeezed the same old smile. He did not feel bad, and he never would. It is generally only good people who feel bad; guilt, unfairly maligned by popular psychology, is the signpost of decency.

Estrin was sad and she would miss Duff, but she couldn't quite cry. It seems the whole club felt this way. Duff was a man whom everyone had liked, and liking, as Estrin had observed herself, is a trivial, disposable brand of affection, easily replaced. Then, he had never asked for more. An entertainer, he would never bore his audience with stories of promising, witty schoolboys drabbed by careers of collecting rates, of fifty-year-old sons who would still return home every night after ten merry pints and weep themselves to sleep over parents more than a decade dead, of lonely fat bachelors. No, Duff was an anecdote.

Estrin did feel sheepish, though less for her tirade than for having taken politics too lightly here—*chicken retread*, she had used it for one-liners and passing dinners with Farrell. Suddenly all her theories seemed irrelevant or, worse, indulgent, and tonight all she muttered was "Christ, this whole thing is fucking stupid." Hardly profound, but Estrin was growing suspicious of profundity, so much pith for its own sake, those sonorous observations that existed more to be admired than to sort anything out. How much had any of her own pronouncements here made any difference? She remembered the packed attic of Linen Hall, lined with perfectly astute books, and so? Estrin promised herself to make no more proclamations, about overadaptation, identity; while a vow she would break, it would at least last the night. She did for the first time understand why so many Northerners left. Because there was nothing to say; because that never stopped you from saying it; because one day you walked in and Duff's stool was empty and you felt humiliated, for yourself, for everyone. There is only so much embarrassment a citizen can withstand in a lifetime.

The members had difficulty keeping a properly subdued face on the evening. Like Estrin, no one bawled. Instead, they set to writing memorial notices for the *Irish News*—in one of the more barbaric traditions of the Province, composed in rhyming verse. The session rapidly grew animated, with cries of "Swoon! Croon! *Would be to us a boon!*" They might recall the cause of their mission and tamp down, only to get into a loud row two minutes later over whether it was acceptable to rhyme *Duff* and *chuffed*. The memorials, too, had a strange tendency to go off in the second stanza:

> *You left this earth before we'd told*
> *How much to us you're worth.*
> *We'd love to say your weight in gold,*
> *For countless nights of mirth.*
>
> *But we'll have to leave it weight in coal,*
> *Or maybe only turf—*
> *Cause all the Green Door's on the dole;*
> *We can't afford your girth.*

Finally they settled down in earnest to compose a ballad, entitled "The Pints of Shearhoon."

> *National self-determination*
> *Was dear to old Shearhoon,*
> *So some noble organization*
> *Set him dancing to its tune.*
>
> *Sworn enemy of the army,*
> *The brave bard from Andytown*
> *Found the Britannic Lounge too smarmy,*
> *But only loved The Crown.*
>
> *A victim of the Struggle,*
> *Our burly volunteer;*
> *His package he did juggle,*
> *But the bloody thing went queer.*
>
> *While we'll miss the big Republican,*
> *Who surely had it rough,*
> *There's one still healthy publican*
> *Relieved the job was duff.*

A bollocks, do you follow?
For once it weren't the Brits.
You may find it hard to swallow,
But no other story fits.

We'd yet buy Guinness for the bastard—
He didn't have to die,
If he hadn't of been plastered,
Or he'd only worn a tie.

22

The Saint of Glengormley

It was Day Eighteen. Estrin sat herself squarely before her dingy morning maté and for once counted up a different calendar. She'd finished her last progesterone supplement four days before the fast, and it hadn't worked. She had to face the fact that there was one other reason women did not menstruate than that their fat-muscle ratio was so very fierce.

Not that Estrin for a minute believed such an absurdity possible. The fast had obviously upset her chemical balance in every way. It was only from routine caution that she mobilized for the Royal Victoria. Besides, getting the test was something to do. Estrin could no longer manage to cut molding or refinish furniture; she could barely read; a slow walk around the corner would fill her afternoon.

In the courtyard, a forbidding bronze of Queen Victoria brandished a scepter in Estrin's way, inflating its chins in disapproval that any institution bearing the Queen's name would harbor that clinic on the third floor.

Inside, Estrin took an obscure pleasure in the place. The Royal was grim. The bright kindergarten daffodils of Farrell's ward had disturbed her more than these yellowed corridors, for the mindless murals of City lied: they belied the corruption of the body, the horror stories the tower block disguised. City's demeaning floral optimism painted over tragedy with decor like a great big get-well card for the terminally ill. Estrin preferred to stare ugly mortality in the face. The RVH suggested leeches, nuns, unanesthetized amputation. Its nurses wore buns, its doctors wore spectacles. A place where sickness was still unsightly, from which the healthy fled—why, the Royal Victoria was a real hospital.

The waiting room of the clinic was itself a form of contraception, since ten minutes of reading its posters and you would never have sex again: AIDS: PROTECT YOURSELF; RECOGNIZING HERPES; WOMEN: ARE YOU BEING PHYSICALLY OR MENTALLY ABUSED? CHLAMYDIA: WHAT YOU DON'T KNOW CAN HURT YOU . . . Patients stared straight ahead, hands protecting their laps, seated mute and immobile in every other chair.

Once Estrin delivered her urine sample, she was invited into an office. The woman was nice enough, and wouldn't charge Estrin, though she shouldn't have been covered by National Health. She asked about Estrin's period, and Estrin felt irresponsible admitting she'd missed two. *Just give me the fucking results.* She did not want to tell this stranger about her "partners" or what she would do if the test was positive when the chances were so ridiculously thin—

But when the results came back Estrin felt calm. She did not say, "You're kidding," or ask the nurse to repeat herself. Estrin realized she had known from the start what the answer would be. Through that orgy of mince pies, she had gained enough weight to ovulate. She found she was smiling. Amiably, she allowed them to make a counseling appointment she would not keep. Really, she felt *amused*.

Leaving the hospital, she stroked her chin. She waved goodbye to Queen Victoria.

For now that the unthinkable had occurred she was impressed. Estrin felt more part of the human race than she had for years. Functionally infertile since fifteen, she was tired of being the exception. And though she had no intention of Francis Hughesing herself beyond two more days, at this moment on Day Nineteen Estrin Lancaster was dying, and she admired that inside this shriveled, moribund host another animal thrived, like lichen on a felled tree, flowers blooming in radioactive Hiroshima—

My relationship to sex is apocalyptic/Most people don't think of children as the end of the world.

Only now, a block up the Falls, did she think of the father. Estrin's laugh was not very nice.

She surveyed the prams wheeling along the footpath, so many women younger than herself rustling out of shops with whole families, the eldest old enough to pour petrol bombs. For the first time she felt envious. Fine, the ladies looked plenty haggard—they lived on chips and never had a minute's peace to themselves. But Estrin had a bit too much peace to herself. And while she'd seen their worlds as tiny, confined to this island and often to a single neighborhood, Estrin's world was smaller still, a portable universe of one. These women, too, had left the Royal's third-floor clinic and returned to a husband, of all things, with what they regarded as good news. Estrin recalled all the sappy fifties movies of her childhood, where the woman cries and the man hugs her and gets her a chair and won't let her carry the groceries. Crap, a load of crap; why, Estrin could not remember one time watching a sit-com where a pregnant woman totters back from a clinic after eating nothing for almost three weeks, dreading calling the father, who is off drinking with a load of paramilitaries on the Antrim coast, the mother not proud but apologetic: Don't worry, *fuck you, I'll take care of it.*

Well, he was good for the abortion anyway, and it would be expensive, entailing a shuttle ticket to London as well as non-resident medical fees. Since in Northern Ireland you could blow eleven Prods in Enniskillen to kingdom come but you couldn't scrape a tadpole from between your legs—

And wouldn't the bastard kidnap this misfortune for his own anguish, wouldn't he coopt her suffering if he could? Well, she wouldn't allow it. All he would have to do is pay. She would carry her own groceries: herbal tea.

Bitter. Back home, the house a shambles, teacups every-where, tea, tea, tea, fucking tea . . . No reason this altered the fast. Estrin sat and tried to feel pregnant. With only a few more days, she wanted to know what it was like.

That night the club was humming with the next day's Border Poll. At the last minute the SDLP had endorsed the referendum—Estrin felt the shadow of O'Phelan cross the club. News of the conference had been hitting the press; even the Green Door had heard of it. MacBride had been winking and nodding up a storm on *Ulster Newstime*, and it annoyed Estrin to see how he took full credit for the negotiations when she had watched Farrell drag himself out of bed with four hours' sleep for a full year.

After hours, Estrin lured Malcolm into lingering. He assumed she needed to talk about Duff, but she didn't bring Shearhoon up at all, instead ambling off on a queer tack about how she had no interest in deluding herself about sacrificing for a whole coun-try, but she could stand to do something once in a while for even one other person besides herself: "I mean, I'm sick to death of lifting weights, but I wouldn't mind pushing some stranger's car up a hill. I'm bored with running, but I'd gladly help you move— I'd carry books up three flights of stairs. And I'm fucking tired of skipping dessert to stay thin, but I wouldn't mind going hungry for a kid—I read *Famine* the other day, with all these mothers starving so their children could eat and I salivated with envy."

"Est." Malcolm took her hand with that paternal softness of

his so remarkable in a young boy. "Stop waffling. What's biting your bum?"

"I'm pregnant." It was the first time she'd said it out loud. She enjoyed the sound of it.

Malcolm rather enjoyed it, too. "O'Phelan?"

"Aye," she said, and laughed, catching herself—it was the first time she'd ever said *aye*. Must be the kid. He was half Irish.

"What's he say, like?"

"Not much lately. He doesn't know."

"You clued me in before the father?"

She sighed. "Tells you something, doesn't it."

"Are you going to get married?"

"Oh, Malcolm. All these guns and you people still live in the House at Pooh Corner."

"You wouldn't have it on your own?"

"No, Malcolm. I won't have it, period."

"Est!" Malcolm drew away. "Bloody hell, that's a sin!"

"Yes," she considered. "It may be." Estrin was interested. She had no previous qualms about abortion. It seems her qualms were only about this one. "Anyway, I'll have to fly to England. If you could cover for me at the club . . ."

Malcolm didn't respond.

"Boy, I should write my brother." She stretched. "Dear Billy: You will be relieved to hear I have finally experienced Real Life. I will promptly slaughter it, but I thought you'd be proud of me, for a day or two."

They stayed late. He massaged her temples, his touch subtly painful, the wrong fingers.

She walked home; in the last days of the fast, she couldn't bear the roar of the motorcycle. Her steps were short, an old woman's. Home, with tea, she stared into the coals of her fire.

("Are you going to get married?")

Stop it. He would never. You would never. Estrin apologized to herself: *It's the child. These kids start trying to survive you early; they know they have to fight, even at the size of a pea. And I am tired of fighting. I know you think that's because I'm a girl. Very well, I am a girl. And fine, I won't marry or have children. All the same, there's a waiting in me and there's the tiredness and there's all this running, away more than toward, and I don't see what's going to get warmer or closer. There is no luxury in my life. There is no leaning or holding, no enclosure, no shore. I can see myself older and I'm scatty. The eccentric aunt who never eats a meal. Thin and scrappy and spilling stories no one cares to hear. Well traveled and full of voices—old voices—Farrell's in the morning—"This orange juice is gorgeous!"*

At 4 a.m. it struck her that, though Farrell had called her often enough at this hour, she had never dared ring him past twelve. This was the last wild night of the conference and he was surely legless, but for once his politics dwarfed—the Real Life filled her with quiet power. So she rang and rang the Antrim Arms and would not stop hassling the bartender and other strangers until they finally roused Farrell O'Phelan himself to the phone.

There is a Chekhov short story called "The Bet." A facile banker wagers two million rubles that his friend will never succeed in a self-imposed imprisonment for fifteen years. Accepting the challenge, the friend condemns himself to a single room. Years pass. The prisoner spends most of his time reading. Meanwhile, the banker suffers a failing of fortunes, and an idle wager turns ruinous. He appears at the end of the fifteen years in a sweat. His friend has been strictly adhering to the terms of their agreement. So on the last day the banker is astonished to discover an empty cell, and a letter. The document recounts a growing existential disenchantment. In his exile, having read so much philosophy, his friend has grown contemptuous. As an expression of this disdain, he has left his room precisely one day before he could justly collect his money.

Estrin had always liked this story. The letter had been preachy but the gesture pure. She was never quite sure what it meant until the early hours of Day Twenty, cradling her tea.

* * *

"Wake up, you willick, or you'll sleep through till the polls close!"

"*I don't vote.*" It was a principle. Farrell slammed down the phone. Christ, the thing never stopped ringing, and hadn't this place wrung enough from him for three weeks—one party always stomping out and having to be enticed softy-softy back to the table, night after night half the lot soggy with drink before tea, the other half, Sinners and Paisleyites (they had so much in common), scowling in the back of the room sipping pure orange . . . Three solid weeks of a headache smack between the eyes, his sinuses drying in cigarette smoke like flaps of hung haddock, his back creaky from soliciting aggressive short people . . . And it took them a bit, but the crowd had warmed to the performance, the DUP spraying Sinners with Roachguard to eliminate "insects," sonorous readings of the OED entry on *scum* pitched against an equally loud appeal for the support of Gaelic football in Irish—bad Irish; the Union Jacks and tricolors sneaked up in the dining room early mornings, the ritual rippings down, the obligatory punch-ups, and then last night, inconceivably, the maudlin singsong around the piano as, unable to agree on "Say Hello to the Provos," "God Save the Queen," or "The Pope's a Darkie," they finally converged on "Barbara Allen," with the Sinners, DUP, UUU, and SDLP in four-part harmony, dripping on each other's shoulders and bawling on the refrain. Now Farrell could rest in peace, because he had obviously seen everything.

But no, MacBride had to harass him, and here it was still pitch-dark—what—eight— Didn't he go to bed at eight? Ah, p.m. Farrell rolled over. Fine. He'd wondered what he would do today, and now he'd done it. And thank fuck, he had spared himself megaphones pouring MacBride's syrupy voice down the streets of Antrim. How fitting to spend election day instead sleeping off three liters of white wine.

The sheet wrapped around his legs; Farrell declined to struggle. This was the kind of bondage he could get into: being tied to a bedstead, full stop. Had he ever loved a woman as much as a real feather pillow? Quiet sifted the room like dust. Curtains drawn to the dark, phone jack pulled; Farrell considered seriously if this was the finest moment of his life. Even in the disposal days he had never worked harder than this last year. The conference itself had been a marathon; now it was over. Across the Province votes were cast, and how delightful, whichever way they went, to be able to affect them no more. And for the first time since he was delirious with pneumonia he could not think of a single thing he had to do.

A memory squirmed. He did not know if he'd dreamt this. Yet on the notepad there, a scrawl, E-8, like a chess notation. She did ring, after all. Tea, she said. Never more insistent. Had something to tell him. Jesus God, when these women "had something to say" he suddenly remembered an appointment— in Venezuela! And she couldn't put it off one bloody day, *had* to be tomorrow night. With the election party starting that afternoon, he could tell already he'd be late.

Farrell sat up. No, no, no, he did not want this moment to be over. For a hospital, my kingdom for a hospital. Alas, he felt down his chest and inhaled, and it seemed he was in perfect health.

Braced with a shower, in a freshly cleaned suit, Farrell decided to enjoy the evening, what was left of it. Downstairs in the dining room he found a handful of other conferees who, after a devoted session that had lasted through to morning, would not be bullied by their parties to spend election day on knock-ups, shillying pensioners to the polls. Though the kitchen would close for the night in an hour, the table was laid in one stage or another of breakfast. It was the respectful, wry repast of the hungover: jokes were carefully not too funny, mention of alcohol was no go. Gentlemanly speculation over coffee and brown bread: even with the SDLP's grudging endorsement, the poll's turnout would be dicey. Shared incredulity that the constitutional nationalists actually swung round on an internal solution. General concession that the Provos would put up a ruckus, that it was best the next few days to avoid central Belfast. Farrell was surprised to discover he liked some of these codgers. The North attracted a different breed of politician than elsewhere. They had character, even if it was bad. He was further surprised that the men liked him, too. As they retired to the lounge, they gave Farrell a tiny standing ovation—*pat-pat-pat*—not too loud.

Ballot boxes were locked up overnight; counting would start at 9 a.m., so there was no point in heading back to City Hall till morning. The remaining conferees drove home or went back to bed. Farrell, liberated once more from the twenty-four-hour day, which was clearly only for ordinary people, stayed up to flip magazines. How arbitrarily you chopped your life into little pieces of days, weeks, years, when it was really one long uninterrupted sigh. He roamed the empty rooms of the hotel. The Antrim Arms had not begun to recover; and the sight of so much shattered crockery, ties looped over chandeliers, and three-setting political diagrams penned on tablecloths made Farrell encouragingly wistful: he must have had a good time.

Early morning he packed and, with nothing else on, took a walk to the Giant's Causeway as the sun rose. Stepping the hexagonal stones with the North Channel slapping under the peach horizon, Farrell observed, *It's beautiful*, clinically. Magnificent scenery always seemed to exclude him. It confused him. Farrell didn't know what to do with it. Just like: women.

Ah me. It was not true there was nothing left on the agenda; better get cracking. Farrell hiked back to the hotel, where the manager had put together a hefty bill for damages. Sensing he was making one of his usual mistakes, Farrell wrote out a personal check. A bad habit from that childhood of zero credit/total blame: he paid for things.

It was a brilliant, clear morning. Testing his immunity to scenery, he had the taxi take the coast road. Meanwhile, the X's began to flutter one by one into the pigeonholes of City Hall. Sometime in mid-afternoon they should have a profile of the results and turnout, and that was when Farrell would pay the call on Angus MacBride he'd looked forward to all year, if not for the last twenty-five.

Day Twenty. Goldenrod sun, light which cast the Falls in the hue of an earlier century. It was hard to tell if the shimmer off the neighborhood was due to the weather, yesterday's election, or the army, out in force. There was always more energy here with the Saracens plowing up and down, patrols jogging side streets. Their jungle camouflage amused the American, for there were few trees in West Belfast—the bright blotchy green only made the boys stand out. In effect, the soldiers *were* the trees.

Estrin walked downtown. The waist of her jeans puckered under her belt. She had excellent posture. Shoulderbones poked her leather jacket. Browsing in Waterstone's, Estrin selected, with care, *The Chocolate Book*. In Kelly's, when she ordered coffee and they put milk in it, she had to send it back. When it returned black she couldn't hack it, but the cup kept her hand warm. Otherwise, she felt startlingly normal, less shaky than for the whole last week. She paged recipes at the bar, determined to find the one concoction with the most butter and chocolate, and finally lit on Truffle Cake, requiring no flour at all.

Estrin shopped through early afternoon. Farrell liked good prawns, and they were hard to find. So was high-quality bitter-sweet chocolate. But Estrin, having waited twenty days, was patient. She bought expensive Côte de Jura, with a color like the morning's startling sun; freesia and mums to match; cognac. She took ten minutes in the bakery selecting her exact loaf of bread. The slabs of salmon were the color of steak. In the end, she spent fifty pounds she could hardly spare: part of the fun.

Roisin cleaned. She decided what to wear. She went to the Botanic Gardens and strolled through the Palm House. The extra oxygen lightened her head; the moisture felt kind on her skin. Later she shopped for perfume and new shoes. She called by the caterer's once more, who was annoyed at so much checking up on a two-person meal. Roisin was impervious to paltry annoyance. For touches, she returned to town for french roast and champagne truffles. She asked the off-license for a fine white wine. They suggested the Côte de Jura. It was dear, so she believed them. And brandy, she said. Champagne! They looked at her like, *How drunk does he have to be?* I don't know, she wanted to explain. Very.

It was unlikely Angus would get away from his election party, but in the fantasy they both came. Though apparently a ghastly mistake, in a way she had arranged it. Painful maybe, but enough was enough. Face things. They would each make their bid for her, furious with the other. She would stop them from coming to blows. This isn't your decision to make, for once, she reproaches them. Men, you never seem to recognize when for once a woman has the power. I choose. And I have chosen. She turns. *I love you.* The confession would seem brave, but only just before, and then when it came, it would be easy. *I have loved you from the first. I think I have loved you when you were only a name to me. I love you in the way we say the weather is fair, or that is a chair: my love is not an opinion but a fact. I love you in the same way I am five foot nine, and I could no more feel otherwise than grow shorter. My love is real as any object, and in this way it is simple and even ordinary. It sits with us beside the wine, stationary and calm, in the way of things. Because my love is not a demand, an assertion, a complaint: it is a fact. And I will love you every day for the rest of my life with this same ordinariness, just as I do laundry and fix lunch— your laundry; your lunch.*

By the time Farrell arrived, City Hall was already packed and perking; the stewards were having difficulty keeping out interlopers without passes. Outside, groups clumped around the building according to affiliation, breaking out packs of Harp on park benches. The entrance was looped with cables, and cameras boomed into Farrell's face as he shouldered through the crowd. Not only the microphones of RTE and the BBC nosed forward, but ABC, NBC. He failed to answer questions posed in Finnish, German, and Italian accents. Inside, the crowds were already impatient with the coffee served in the rotunda; flasks glinted down side halls. MacBride was easy to locate by the ooze of supplicants, that big red beacon of a face beaming the length of the chamber like an overgrown Boy Scout's.

And little wonder. By noon the votes were largely tabulated in counties Antrim and Down; the big white billboards outside the counting rooms scrawled with the approval of the whole Province. *My votes*, thought Farrell, and would not, just today, chastise himself for being small. Just: *My votes*. Inside, Farrell went up to the pigeonholes and stuck his finger through the grid to touch the actual paper. He was waved off. *But those are my votes. Mine.*

Plenty of hungry hangers-on sucked up to Farrell as well. Yet the attentions felt unpleasant. They were impersonal—to position, inclusion, info. How much would any of these prats have had to say to him in the days of Talisker? He found himself searching the chamber for someone to confide this to. Just as in the distillery, a figure flirted in doorways, with the elusive flicker of someone who was just leaving, or who had decided, with a glance in the room, not to come in after all.

Grocery shopping had never been more voluptuous. For all of yesterday's diet had felt cruel. While planning to scrape it aside, Estrin was still conscious of starving someone besides herself. She would like very much to feed the child a farewell banquet.

For this rebellion was of a premier order. While the fast had become almost easy and she could see her way clear at this point to Day Fifty-nine, when Francis Hughes had kicked it, Estrin had invited Farrell not for Day Twenty-one, but for *Day Twenty*. Because Estrin thought she was full of shit. Estrin had decided fasting for three weeks was dorky. It took a form of super-discipline to overthrow herself, an exotic will not to meet a goal but to reject it. She had never taken on a more formidable enemy, the absolute enemy who knows the position of all your troops and even where you are thinking of moving them. Having outflanked an opponent with perfect intelligence (*You're just weak, you can't make it . . .*), Estrin clutched her plastic bags stretching at the handles, the spoils of war. Her exaltation was indescribable. She bought nuts, ice cream, fruit, all for the day *before* her birthday, a date she could never remember celebrating precisely, and so, after thirty-two years and 364 days, it was about time.

The results of the poll were officially disclosed at 3 p.m. The power-sharing initiative had passed by 70 percent, better than expected, even endorsed in some of the border territories of Armagh. Turnout was hardly brilliant, but they were not suffering large-scale boycotts. In a politic of absolutes, the referendum had been destined to get slapped with SUCCESS or FAILURE and they had squeaked by.

The bomb outside Boots seemed positively celebratory.

MacBride slipped in a few interviews while still lucid; by six his only serious dialogue was with bottles of champagne.

The festivities were in a large rented room of the Europa. Big, square, brown, neon over unstable press-wood tables, the Europa met Angus's requirements perfectly. On the one hand it had ghastly decor, exorbitant prices, and appalling security; on the other, it was not Whitewells.

"Don't I deserve at least a glass?"

Angus pip-pipped as he had in Cambridge, and made a show of pouring for his old friend, but one he staged for the lot; Farrell was getting routine bluster, generic congratulation. This amounted to being ignored. Farrell would take care of that.

He retreated to observe. Amazing. MacBride had managed to mop up credit for the whole shebang. *But it was my bloody referendum. My idea. I put it across in Westminster. I sold it down South. I won over the SDLP.* And wasn't the conference the same: filched. Look at the news. It was actually being called the MacBride Conference. By election day it had become the MacBride Referendum. A tiny Catholic experience of plantation. And with his typically unconstitutional, two-faced Fenian terrorism, Farrell had exacted his revenge.

Farrell kept running in his head the moment this evening when MacBride would look at him *really*, for once the two of them in a room talking straight. Farrell could not recall a single discussion with MacBride when they hadn't, secretly, been talking about something else. The quality of their relationship had grown only more ulterior, and it was wearying.

As the party pickled on and Farrell decided he had earned more than one *slainte* of champagne, he began putting the impending showdown off. Why, by the time he angled toward Angus again, he was clearly forcing himself, and the glass in his hand was shaking. When he fetched the journal from his overcoat, the cover stuck to his fingers, tacky with sweat. By the time he sidled up to the thief of his referendum, Farrell had faced his disappointment: that he was not enjoying this; that he simply wanted to get it over.

"You've a room upstairs?"

"Aye, but not to spirit the likes of you."

"You had better."

"There's trouble?"

"There has been considerable trouble, which you were spared. Take your glass. You'll need it."

Grumpily Angus relinquished his limelight and led Farrell up to his room. Angus sat on one of the single beds and slapped his thighs. "Well, now. Let's make this jiffy."

Farrell remained standing. "I've yet to formally congratulate you."

"You couldn't have brought me up here for that."

"No, I brought you up to congratulate me."

"Spot on, then. Thumbs up, well done. Can we go? I've my eye on one silky slip of a girl worked terrible hard for the SAYS YES campaign; she deserves a reward."

"I'm pleased you've such a panoply of lovelies to toast our success. You won't miss one."

"Come again?"

It was not quite the look Farrell was shooting for, so he fired on. "Besides, I only borrowed her. You can have her back if she'll go." Farrell's coolness was a bit overdone. He had played this scene in his head too many times, and now found himself imitating his own images; reality was not measuring up. He tried to remember some of the zingers he'd concocted in the back of taxis. Instead, he was reminded of the pebble dash in Newry, bungling Eastwood's lines.

"Stuff your fancy footwork, O'Phelan. You've something to say?"

Farrell handed him the *Fortnight*. "I know it's tedious. But sometimes you should read your own mistress's poetry."

Angus scanned the page, then glared up for explanation.

"Surely you recognize the voice. It's been whispering in the back of the ear since you were sixteen."

Angus tossed the magazine on the spread. "Why can't you be a man for once and say flat out you're bumping my girlfriend?"

"Have been bumping; I am through. The point is, I did it for you—"

"How can you—"

"Hear me out. She was on the verge of leaking your affair. Once the rumor hit the *Sunday World*, she'd have wrecked you. *And* SAYS YES. Not just because she's Catholic, but in case you need reminding, you are a married man."

"Your head's cut. Roisin's no tout."

"Roisin St. Clair is an attractive but aging woman, childless and unmarried. Face it, in another year or two you'd be through with her yourself. She knew that. But in the future, old boy, try to pick your mistresses with more care. Roisin seems quiet, but she's scrappy. A tout? She could always pass the tattle off to herself as loyalty to the Republican movement."

"Roisin doesn't give a toss about the Republican movement."

"Aye, but she did about you, MacBride."

"In which case, how could it be in her vaguest interest to spill? She's kept her bake tight for two years. Your story's not holding together, boyo."

Funny, Farrell thought the same thing. "By the time I got

to her she'd concocted some remarkable fancies. All to do with myths of the two communities and that. You're Protestant; you can divorce. She reasoned if she car-bombed your career, you'd have nothing to lose by leaving your wife."

"Piffle."

"Yes," said Farrell sadly. "You have to admire women sometimes for what they can believe. I've urged Roisin to move on from poetry; I'm convinced she has a much greater talent for science fiction."

"So O'Phelan came to the rescue?"

"I'll be candid, I'm not sure how much I was motivated by deep personal loyalty. But I would not see the opportunity to sort out this Province glitched because you get an itch in your trousers late afternoons."

MacBride was finally growing incredulous. "You actually expect me to be grateful!"

"You bloody well should be. It hasn't been easy, linchpinning a delicate political scaffolding with a man who fingers down every pair of knickers with expandable elastic. Really, Angus, this womanizing has got to stop. I pulled you out this time. But I'm not about to devote myself to seducing your lovers in order to dismantle bombshells in your personal life. My disposal days are over. And this has been particularly sordid fiddle I don't wish to repeat. So settle down, or even stick to Roisin. I imagine I've rendered her relatively harmless."

"How could she possibly go back to this ugly old bear once she's sampled the refined wares of Farrell O'Phelan?"

"Well, she seems to have stomached both of us for some time now."

"How long?" asked Angus warily.

Farrell had an intuition he shouldn't say, but it felt too delicious, a spade in black dirt, a blade through wormy ground. "This whole last year."

"You are one stinking wog—"

"I figured you wouldn't shake my hand. But I expect in the light of day, as Secretary of State, you will see my administrations as more charitable. She's rather pretty in low light and a nice dress, but not my first choice. And certainly devoted—a little too. Clinging, in fact. Still, no one deserves to be shattered, do they? If I were you, I'd call round to pick up the pieces."

"I suppose O'Phelan the Fascinating has broken her heart?"

"Yes," said Farrell simply, and with a glance at his watch reached to let himself out, lest he make it two.

"You've always had an exalted sense of your own importance, O'Phelan," Angus called at his back. "I've brought you along for the ride. Yourself, you've never more than piddled on the sidelines. Disposed of a bomb or two, put up with Frankie Millar in The Crown. But I could have pulled this off without you, kid. You've always missed the ticket here: this game's all about who your friends are. I'm about the only one you've got. Right, for once you joined the proper team. But without me you're outside the fence—one more unruly football fan."

The lift shut. Farrell felt dimly depressed. In all, he'd found MacBride's reaction rather pale.

Even after twenty days, two extra hours were interminable. Her preparations done well before eight, she'd had to cellophane the salmon and put the bread back in its bag. She'd left the shrimp unshelled for casual effect, to seem to go to little trouble, though by now she could have shelled them several times. Estrin decided not to get angry. She would not be manipulated into one more trivial domestic, livid that dinner has been ruined! while the man is out tending to the affairs of the world. So she got depressed instead. The old pictures churned her head: nausea and inattention. She was nervous about digesting her food. She was afraid if she explained about the fast he would only find her potty. And she felt guilty for being pregnant. How quickly she'd assure him she wouldn't have the child, to prove it wasn't a ploy.

When the knock came at last, her dread had steeped the kitchen as the smell of boiled cabbage infused so many Irish walls, and she was sure he would scent the reek of her terror. So ethereal this morning in nineteenth-century sunlight, having worked herself to such a pitch whipping cream, whisking chocolate, never licking the bowl, only to sit here three hours with her feet up, now that it was past ten she was half tempted to tell him to go home. The evening no longer felt appropriate; she didn't even feel hungry; she'd rather go to sleep.

Ordinarily her visions of an event and its nature on arrival clashed so radically that the fantasy could not survive fact: afterward she could not even remember the mock-up. Whatever she imagined, at least she could be sure it would be wrong. So Estrin was startled to open the door to find the dream kick into real life. Right off she was looking at a bad night. He was holding the door frame on either side in order to remain standing. His eyelids drooped. She felt convinced if he'd shown up at eight, this evening would have gone quite differently, but that was idle speculation now.

"Hiya." The kiss on her cheek felt impersonal. More than three weeks apart, they did not feel quite comfortable with each other. As resort, Estrin fetched a bottle of wine he did not need. She poured two glasses, and held hers up to the candle; Farrell bent behind the glow: *golden*. Of all the women Farrell had mentioned, Estrin liked Tarja best.

"So, the poll passed," said Estrin. "Congrats."

"Aye, thank bloody hell it's over." Farrell flopped on the couch, loosening his tie. "I will spare you the regimen I've kept these three weeks, though you can guess."

"Why not," said Estrin. "I've spared you mine." Estrin twisted her wine, but did not sip. She had promised herself at most one glass, over the night—test the waters. But from even this she hung back. No ceremony? He didn't know. The glass seemed beautiful but small, both luminous and insufficient, like a promise to be broken. "But you expected it to sail."

"On the contrary, this election has been on the brink of disaster from the beginning. It has taken constant supervision, like minding a baby with the croup."

"What would you know about babies with croup?"

"I was one."

"Still are."

"Now that was frosty. Are you miffed? I've done something?"

"No, Farrell, you've done nothing at all. For a month."

"Haven't I rung up?"

Estrin felt heavy and wilted, so overwhelmed by a three-week swoon of puked-up tea, the smudge on the footpath of Amelia Street so recently Duff Shearhoon, that plastic cup in the Royal with its tiny potent tablespoon, the ghastly loom of *A Day in the Life of the Soviet Union* so soon a day in her own, that she felt curiously at a loss for conversation. She threw coal on the fire. He was beginning to miss out on so much of her life there was nowhere to start, nothing to say; they weren't even close. She looked over at the drunk man on her sofa and tried to remember her affection for him, the way she would sometimes search for a word in Russian she must have learned: *lyubov*.

She raised her glass. "We should toast. Tomorrow's my birthday." Resigned to it meaning nothing to him, she took her small sip of Côte de Jura and so ended a three-week fast twenty-one hours and twenty minutes early, its few calories seeping through the weakest of victory smiles. It drizzled astringently down her throat, and did not taste so different from camomile tea. Wine could not save her, neither muscle tone nor the Soviet Union could save her, and that man slopped on her couch most certainly could not save her, but, oddly, whole-wheat bread would. She rose abruptly from her crouch before the coals. "I'm off to get dinner," she announced.

"Is it ready? I'm famished. Haven't eaten all day."

"You poor thing!" Estrin cried. "It won't take long."

In the small kitchen, he was impatient. His long legs were in the way; she had to keep stepping over them. Though she intended a simple meal, Estrin was proud of her cooking and couldn't resist embellishments; last-minute tasks added up. Dividing her attention between the stove and Farrell, she boiled the dill hollandaise and had to start again. Farrell glowered.

"We should have gone to 44. It's after eleven. Maybe you should skip it."

"Tonight," said Estrin through her teeth, "I am not skipping dinner."

"This scullery is stifling. Sure you could survive one night without food."

"No," she said, "I'm not sure I could."

"Have you just a can of soup, then?"

"Farrell, when a woman fixes you dinner, it's supposed to be a favor. Not a problem."

"Have you just a biscuit, then? My dear?"

She plunked the plate of prawns before him and returned to sautéing mushrooms. When she looked around, he was not only ignoring the Stilton cocktail sauce but was eating the shrimp with the shells on. His expression was stoic and grim: he was hungry. He would eat these shrimp. He would be a good guest. They were positively indigestible, but he would say nothing.

"I can't stand it!" she declared, turning off all the burners and pulling up a chair. "I'll shell them if you won't. Here." She was messy but swift, and cleaned a heap to keep him happy. So much for leisurely peeling over confidences and wine. She swept up the shells and wondered whether it was best to cry now or later. Later. No amount of surly abuse, disappointment, no, tonight not Farrell O'Phelan himself would keep Estrin from trying to keep something down her throat.

"So how are the plans for Leningrad coming?"

"I've thought of Armenia instead. Spitak, or Leninakusk. Earthquake relief." Estrin's ears picked up, as if someone else had spoken. She wondered what she would say next.

"Fashionable. Right up your street. Disaster and more sectarianism—Armenians versus Azerbaijanis. But Armenia will hardly be de rigueur by the time you get there. You've got to stop arriving places when they're passé."

"That's my thought, I guess. That in a few months no one will give a toss for Armenia, some other catastrophe will be in vogue. But those villages will still need rebuilding, on or off the six o'clock news. I'm a good carpenter. And maybe that's the test—being willing to do something boring and has-been."

"The test of what? Your extravagant altruism?"

"I've never claimed to be an altruist," Estrin bristled. "But I do try to avoid being a creep."

"I am an altruist," Farrell declared. "One of a brave few. Because I'm an altar boy and a cynic. I dispose of people's pesky bombs and wash their mingin' laundry and don't believe it makes the slightest difference. I am an altruist and I will be the first to tell you that altruists are prats. I am the saint of fu-tile goodness. And I have defiled myself for its sake. I have wallowed in shite for this Province, for a crowd who only deserve to go to hell."

"Haven't they?" Estrin interjected, flaking open the salmon under the broiler.

"Och no, all the indignant UDA Methodists and devout, rosary-grubbing Provisionals are in seventh heaven. And when they do each other in, they drift straight to God the Father, smelling like the Anderson McAuley perfume counter. They have *beliefs*, you see. They are willing to die for their beliefs, and they are so generous with their convictions they'll let you die for them, too. No, these gombeens are as happy in Ulster as bunnies in a briar patch. It's me lives in hell on earth. And sure I'll only burn when it's done. Because haven't I delivered my soul up to grot? I have damned myself for gobshites not worth the parings from my toes. That's what's wrong with the Christ story, in my opinion. This cod about how he rose and floated *up*. A real savior goes down. When you take on the sins of the world, you sin, for fuck's sake! You smear yourself in its excrement like a stinking blanketman in the Kesh! No, my Jesus goes straight to hell. We'll meet down there, roast bangers, and play bowls. Swap yarns! My Jesus has some stories to tell."

"Sounds like you do, too," she said warily, and lured Farrell out of the kitchen by uncorking another bottle of wine. She brought the plates to the living-room table, with candlelight. How curiously, again, the scene was just as she imagined: the salmon red in the middle, its sauce smooth and weedy, the fine beans and baby corn bright and crisp . . . Farrell ignored his plate.

But Estrin pondered hers. She no longer comprehended food, for fasting reveals the secret that you never need to eat, really— see, not a nibble and you're still strolling streets right as rain. All the signs of a population that eats turn strange: fast-food parlors and groceries alike seem vestiges of a queer if widespread religion whose sham you have uncovered. Loyal to her own vows, however, Estrin partook—gently, in a tiny, well-chewed communion. It did not exactly taste good, but she hadn't yet run to the loo. And she did not feel guilty. This was the first meal she'd eaten for the last two years and not felt guilty.

"Estrin, my swallow," Farrell sighed, retiring from his untouched dinner. "I've wondered how I might have turned out in another town. This one has eaten me from the center. I feel like one of those shiny apples that deceive you until you take a bite. All around the core mealy and brown. I'm sorry."

"Farrell," said Estrin. "What."

He closed his eyes and ran his fingers through his hair. Rubbing his bleary sockets, he spoke in a blur behind his palms. "For the past year Angus MacBride's career has been in serious danger. And this must never leave your house. But keeping the whole slop to myself has been like not taking out the rubbish. It begins to smell. Angus has been carrying on with a woman, a Catholic, which doesn't help. She was talking. She needed to be won from him, and silenced. I did the job." Farrell emerged from behind his hands. "I believe she's quite in love with me now. The referendum is passed. And I'm left looking quite the ogre, aren't I? I feel shabby. I could bathe for hours. I could raise my face to a showerhead and drown."

Estrin put down her fork. "You mean you've been having an affair. Another one."

"Have I ever."

"For a year. All the while with me."

"It hasn't been easy."

"You seem to have managed."

"You're so cold."

"What do you expect?"

"A bit of compassion. I am exhausted—"

"You're always exhausted."

"When have I ever before asked you for sympathy?"

"Pretty much every time I've seen you."

"You're disappointing me. So icy. For once I take you into my confidence—"

"Farrell!" Her voice hit a harmonic. "We've seen each other for a full year; you sleep in my bed; I'm in love with you; and now you tell me that this entire time you've been fucking some other woman and I'm supposed to be *sympathetic*? Who do you think I am, Mother Teresa? Or just a moron?"

"Someone you are not, obviously." He drew himself up. "You're being churlish. And I thought that you of all people might understand—"

"*I do understand.*" Her voice descended again, deeper than usual. "That's the trouble. You're not remorseful at all. In fact, I don't think I've ever heard you sound ashamed unless you were apologizing for being nice! You and your 'futile goodness,' I sometimes think you had to give up bomb disposal because you figured out that it was useful! Pull off being a dickhead and you're crowing! Some poor girl in this city is crying her eyes out, and I'm supposed to hold *your* hand? You should hear yourself, you raise the hair on the back of my neck: *I believe she's quite in love with me.* One more heart to throw in the box with the rest, like tin pins for good attendance at confirmation class."

Farrell went stony. "I don't wish to discuss this further."

Estrin cleared the dishes and scraped the food in the garbage. She returned to stab at the fire. "I don't mean you shouldn't have told me, but—"

"Your point of view has been duly noted. The issue is closed."

For a second time that night, unexercised, Estrin's anger went soft. A wave of weakness crossed her; she dropped a shade paler in her face. Her intestines began to squirm. She was cold, terribly cold, and, though unable to wrest enough calories from either her dinner or the coals, crowded before the grate as if it could offer comfort of a more enduring sort. The truth was, she wasn't his wife or even his "girlfriend" exactly, and in the obscurity of their relationship he could hide. Had she a claim to legitimacy of any reasonable kind, Estrin might throw things, but under these conditions even to have raised her voice was pushing her luck. How little she had of him. And wasn't she leaving this country soon enough besides. Why bother to protest. How cleverly he had always managed to keep her helpless. He really was a remarkable man.

For the betrayal was too subtle to name. There is a way of lying that is simply keeping your mouth shut: he had never said he was not messing about, never explained his obligations, but the enormity of the not-said all these months bloated her sitting room, the countless conversations in these same seats when he had swallowed this story with his Chardonnay and spoken instead about censorship of Sinn Feín. Too, there are betrayals to promises specifically not made—had he ever vowed to be faithful, or to tell her when he was not? No, but the issue fell away before the larger betrayal that he had not made these promises.

She talked to the fire about Duff; she felt so far away it was amazing he could hear her without a bullhorn. And how they managed to move from Shearhoon to German concentration camps Estrin would never quite piece together the next day.

It was two in the morning. She did remember at some point mentioning having been to Bergen-Belsen. Farrell responded that he would never visit such a camp because he "couldn't take it."

"I bet you couldn't," said Estrin, propped at a broken angle in her chair. In the last two hours she had come to think of Farrell as someone she had once known. Her single glass of wine was barely touched. She pictured herself in a pillbox outside an RUC station. The door is locked, the windows bulletproof. The only way to get through is to speak in a tiny microphone in the glass. The sound is bad. There are guns if she wants them. In the glow of a three-grille space heater, Estrin is smoking and reading a magazine. She is a middle-aged man with no family, and will soon drive home and watch television. "You couldn't take not being an inmate. Auschwitz survivors must destroy you with envy. Christ, you look like one, you'd fit right in. You could not sleep, eat badly, work too hard—a camp with all your favorite pastimes, better than arts and crafts. Couldn't drink, though. That might prove a problem."

"Is nothing sacred from the whittle of your sarcasm?"

"No," she announced. "Nothing." (Inside the pillbox, it turns out the man is a cripple. He was shot by terrorists and can't move from the waist down. That's why they stick him in the guardhouse. But in his immobility, he is free. He used to play sports, but has grown philosophical about not being able to play. At least he doesn't lose anymore, he jokes. And really he doesn't mind. He's happier than he was before. He doesn't think about women; he's given them up. He's impotent. He works crossword puzzles instead. His life is small, regimented, and dull. He knows this, so there will never come a time it hits him over the head. He has no friends; his parents are long dead. He is impervious.)

"I give the Holocaust Special Category Status. I do not loot death camps for good crack. They are the emblem of evil to me. They have changed the nature of the human race. As such, they keep the Troubles in their place."

"No . . ." Estrin considered. (The man is reading about bottle collecting. He skips all the articles to do with politics. Someone calls through the mike; he keeps his head down. They rap a coin on the glass and he pretends not to hear. His shift is almost over. Pretty soon they go away. He doesn't feel bad.) "I don't think the Holocaust changes anything. In my experience, people treat each other like shit all over the world. I suppose they always have. If there's such a thing as evil, it's definitely in Northern Ireland."

"Do you realize—" Farrell leaned forward. "The Nazis gassed one man *every four seconds*?"

"Yes, Farrell—" Estrin rubbed her forehead.

"*Every four seconds!*"

She stopped trying to get through. He was rocking back and forth, with his hands between his knees. Fat tears blobbed down the deep lines by his nose. Mucus spidered slowly from his nostrils to the carpet. *Every four seconds* repeated itself about that often. He was sobbing.

It was a maudlin display that gradually eased the angles Estrin had assumed in her seat, not because he was so winningly disturbed by the fate of his Jewish fellowman, but because he was making a fool of himself. She moved to the couch and put her arm around his shoulder. He crumpled against her and draped around her neck; 155 pounds or no, with Estrin tiny herself now, he was heavy. She reached for a napkin and wiped his nose. She supported his weight as best she could and sifted the curls of his hair. She would never have guessed that tonight of all nights one more time she would end up comforting Farrell O'Phelan. But in acting like an inconceivable idiot, Farrell broke her heart. She made herself forgive him for embarrassing her. Lord, he was drunker than she'd ever seen him. And there he was trailing snot on her favorite shirt, still apparently convinced he was crying over Nazi concentration camps.

(The RUC man has gone home. There is no one in the pillbox. The heater is off. The wind sings through the slats of the microphone.)

That forgiveness was the most she could wring from herself, the bit of succor, water from stone. She had to slip herself out from under his arms and scuttle to the loo. There she shat out all the salmon and green beans and baby corn. It was going to take some doing to get back to food. But at least she didn't vomit, and it had been so long since she'd moved her bowels that she rather enjoyed the experience.

When Estrin returned Farrell was sniveling into the sofa, between sobs asleep. She studied him at ten paces. After what he'd admitted tonight, she had every right to kick him out. No sane, self-respecting woman would sleep with a man after an evening like this. But he was in no condition to throw on the whims of the world. Besides, eviction would take too much energy. And how many nights were left, really. Would there even be more than one.

She kissed him between the eyes. "Why don't we go to bed."

He straightened and wiped his face, glancing around as if remembering where he was. He looked at Estrin with a funny surprise, as if this were the first time all night he'd noticed she was there. "But you wanted to talk to me about something, you said."

"Let's wait it."

"No, no. Go ahead. I've nattered all night."

Estrin looked away. "I need money."

"How much?"

"A lot, I—I'm leaving, Farrell. Sooner than I thought. I guess I will go to Armenia. I won't have time to sell the house. So I need enough for an airline ticket. Probably three, four hundred pounds."

"Oh, aye." He rustled through his pockets. "Whatever you need. I'll write you a check." The signature was so indecipherable she wondered if the bank would honor it.

Estrin dragged Farrell in a fireman's carry up the stairs, impressed that after all that fasting those thigh muscles still rallied round when she asked.

Farrell went right to sleep, curled on the far side of the bed in his usual position, hands sandwiched under his genitals. Estrin lay straight on the other, staring up, awake. She would at least have liked him to have noticed that she'd dropped so much weight—not to appreciate how svelte she was, but to say, "You're much too thin," and sternly force eggs on her in the morning. She could live without his admiration, but she longed for his concern.

Finally she slept, never so much as brushing his arm. And there was no chance of wrangling over eggs at breakfast, for when she woke around nine he was gone.

"Well, well," Estrin said to the ceiling. "Happy birthday."

23

What Is So Bloodcurdling about a Swallow in Your Kitchen?

"You stood me up."

Indeed, the room appeared an overnight Miss Havisham's house from *Great Expectations*: the freesia had withdrawn; the assortment lacked a single chocolate; the champagne bucket, its water tepid, rested in a white ring. Amid a profusion of utensils and curlicued china at table, the peaks of napkins had folded.

Farrell collapsed into the sofa. Plumped pillows sprayed cool air refreshingly up his neck with a smell of cotton and furniture polish. "I gather Angus didn't call?"

"You see about you the detritus of drunken revelry? The glasses smashed on the wall, the tattered tissues of popped crackers? Shoes on the stair, nylons trailing from seat cushions? Perhaps it's the telltale snoring overhead, or maybe just the weary but satisfied gleam in my eye that gives away the whole wild, glorious celebration."

Farrell did not know where the notion originated that women were not aggressive. In his experience, any one of them would fill out a pillaging Viking horde to its considerable advantage. "I'm sorry, I decided it was best I renege. Now that the election is over, there is no further need for us to see each other again."

"Pardon?"

It's interesting how when you say something unpleasant people will physically not hear you. "I am ending this relationship."

"I don't believe this!"

Farrell sighed. The third version in twelve hours, he was quite bored with this story. "I can't say that's of any consequence. You've time." Farrell's gaze toured the room, patiently waiting for her reaction to proceed to Phase Two.

"You mean you've just—used me!"

Two! "Yes," he encouraged, as with a quick student. "Mercilessly."

"To keep me from—"

"That's right."

"You are a—a—"

"This is the local consensus."

"You forget, I—I could wreck you and Angus both!"

"No, I'm afraid not." Farrell picked a bit of shrimp shell from underneath a nail. "Rumor won't slay Angus now, not after he's absconded with *my* referendum. And I've plenty evidence that you and I have rolled in our share of hay. Remember where you are, my poppet: you merely end up looking like a whore. Of all of us it's your name needs protecting. As for me, give yourself more credit. You bolster my reputation."

"Along with a whole harem of others, I suppose?"

"There is," he continued with a measured, imperturbable softness that must have enraged her, "one other woman. Whom I have also treated abominably, I fear. I intend to make it up to her, or try. Though I believe it would be kinder if I avoided women altogether. I don't seem to be good for them."

"I could tell Angus."

"My dear, he already knows. He is not jumping for joy. But he will eventually realize I saved his arse. Besides, what can he do, sic the UVF on my taxi? He's a statesman. Or, after all this fuss, refuse to accept the office of Secretary of State, for revenge? Because I tried to warn you long ago: Angus has his eye on the Nobel like a big, sticky sweet Mommy has promised him. He wants credit for sorting out this Province far more than he wants you, or to flummox an uppity Taig who nicks his mistress—one of them. And he will do a good job here. We will be irrelevant."

Looking at the tight, stringy woman across from him, Farrell felt a first moment of tenderness. Roisin St. Clair had felt irrelevant her whole life. It hadn't been easy—while her renowned Republican father got shot in his bed and her two brothers ran guns from the South before getting lifted, Roisin was writing poetry. Her mother never let her forget it, either. How often in this last year Farrell had heard the woman spout after a dose up the road: *Of course it's Roisin markets when the arthritis gets bad, Roisin who's sent to buy fruit for the lads, who does their bloody laundry, all so Ma can troop up in a Provy bus to the Kesh and bring packages and weep every freaking visiting day, and all I ever hear about is Mark and Lalor, Mark and Lalor and the Struggle. Struggle! If anything is irrelevant, it's the Struggle! The real struggle is, Mama, look, I've published another book; remember me, I'm your daughter. The real struggle is, Angus, look at me, I'm thirty-seven and I do want a family, you bastard, what are you going to do?* Then, thought Farrell, suffering doesn't always ennoble. Sometimes it makes you petty. Hadn't the insights Roisin occasioned routinely been this cruel? Why, now the real struggle must be in this sitting room, in not reaching out and wringing his own neck.

"But you said we might have a child—" she choked.

"I lied. Children don't apply to me."

"And a wee house in Ardara where I could write . . ."

"The whole there's-a-place-for-us I filched from *West Side Story*. You shouldn't read so much, Roisin, most of my material is from films. Myself, I haven't had the concentration to finish a book in ten years."

"Not even mine."

"Least of all yours. Oh, I dandered through them, mind you. Research." Farrell wondered if he should stop himself. But the astounding credulity she'd displayed for months now inflamed him. He was offended she hadn't found him out. Like all his previous successes, this coup embarrassed him. Any victory Farrell had ever won merely exposed the contest as bogus, his opponents as cardboard; had he ever had a proper game in his life? Anyway, he wanted to hurt her, badly. He would teach her not to let men walk on her by walking harder than any man ever. She would think twice the next time some gobshite asked her for a jar in Kelly's Bar and straight off put his hand on her shoulder.

Of course, he would teach her nothing, so it was only for the mental exercise that he went on. "If I were you," he advised her genuinely, "I would get married. Soon. To someone a bit older. Catholic, to make it easier, not because of your beliefs. He should be neither handsome nor accomplished. Make him well enough off. He'll be grateful for a reasonably pretty woman, and impressed by your poetry because it's in print. He will not only give you a child but go through ordeals of doctors, thermometers, and funny positions to conceive. Most of all, he should be a bore. But he will never be bored with you, he'll be fascinated. You can have your scenes. You can hide in bed for days, and he will shut the door softly behind you on his way to work, work so dull you can't even remember what your own husband does for a living. And he'll buy you that house in Ardara, if that's what it takes to find out you don't want it.

"That is what you need. Because if you don't heed my advice, you'll end up one of those birdlike women nipping sherry at 11 a.m. Face it, you've not many vaulting Heathcliff affairs left in you. And frankly, you're no good at it. You avail yourself and demand nothing back. Whether Tom and Gerry like it, this is still a capitalist society, where you're worth the price you ask. A diamond is worth five hundred quid not because it's lovely but because it *costs* five hundred quid. And you sell for a song, my pigeon." Funny, that was the first time he'd used the dubious endearment out loud.

Fleeing to Whitewells for a shower, he did not manage to avoid one more of the ugly revelations Roisin could trigger: that it was hardly on to maintain to yourself that you are not the kind of person who does what you are actually doing.

Estrin cleaned the kitchen, then fixed herself coffee with two-thirds milk. She hefted out her neglected Truffle Cake, heavy for such a puck of a thing, to dollop a slab with cream. Unlike the salmon, the cake tasted fantastic. She finished it effortlessly, and had a small second piece.

On her next cup of coffee, Estrin studied the check, with its poor mangled scrawl, newly co-signed with a chocolate fingerprint. He'd made it out for five hundred pounds; it would more than cover a shuttle ticket and an abortion. She'd mail the remainder to Whitewells.

She put it down. Picked up the phone. While she knew you could buy a shuttle ticket at the airport, Estrin called a travel agent and talked for several minutes, scribbling. Then she made one more call, fidgeting when the ringing went on so long. But of course, she realized when the woman's voice croaked over the distance, it was five in the morning there.

"Mother—?"

It's amazing how a parent can burst into tears from a dead sleep.

". . . In Belfast. —No, wait . . . No, let him sleep, just listen. Mother—? Mother! I'm coming home."

With two bombs in the city center after election results, Angus moved quickly to curtail what incidents he could. Much violence and the British would lose their confidence that, unlike Sunningdale, a MacBride coalition could prevail. Maximum finking was in order. There was no better place to start than the RIPs. The Provos would play prima donna, print out letter-quality preconditions for talks, and invite *The Guardian*. The Rips were flattered, and happily agreed to a breakfast meeting without press as long as Angus was buying.

This was the first Republican paramilitary philandering he had done without working through Farrell, and while Angus had sponsored a few public definitions of *scum* himself, he did find the contact exhilarating. They were not such different people as himself—at least they did something about what they wanted without agonizing over whether every little move would get a Sunday-school Good Samaritan prize. A gruff, inarticulate rabble, they had not yet learned to waste your time with talk; amazing the concrete bargaining they got done in less than an hour. City Hall would fork out a flat fee if Rips refrained from planting bombs for the season, in the same way a government will pay farmers not to plant crops. Sure they didn't trust him, but he didn't trust them either, and there was a cleanliness to that. Otherwise they seemed intrigued to like him; the meeting was good crack. Angus intimated that being in with the powers that be is never all that painful.

"Where does O'Phelan fall?"

"Aye, isn't that forever the question."

"He's with you, like?"

"O'Phelan has never been with anyone but himself."

"You wouldn't want him, like—"

"Och no," Angus assured them. "Mr. Morality, so desperate for our admiration, he's too perfect. And how would you replace him? Since for all his fingers on the pulse, the whole Six Counties—" MacBride smiled ingratiatingly. "You boys, the Provies, the Prods—we've all got him sussed. The kid's an egomaniac and transparent as hell. That's the sort to have about. The Great Manipulator's been skippered himself more times than he'd care to know. Don't you worry now, O'Phelan's something between harmless and handy. A safer creature never walked the earth. We've all puzzled how the ghett could survive this long, well, that's how: by being everybody's patsy." MacBride's only dissatisfaction with this speech was that O'Phelan wasn't around to hear it. "On the other hand . . ." he ventured. "I'm curious. You consider yourselves more or less sectarian?"

Their leader, a stranger from Newry, smiled. "Well. The dwarfs are for the dwarfs."

"Sorry?"

"Skip it. Of course, no one likes the word *sectarian*. But everyone has their people here. We do not, ideologically, object to having your own people."

"I'm wondering, see, about your policy on mixed relationships."

"We're old-fashioned on that point. A bit down on them, so we are. Why, positively hos-tile."

"Because O'Phelan seems to have a hot and heavy arrangement with a young Protestant lass. Sure you don't approve?"

"We bleeding well don't."

"I don't exactly approve myself," said Angus. "This business of having your people—well, it is important to maintain coherent cultural identities, isn't it?"

"What's her name?"

"I don't recall. Oddly enough, she lives off the Falls."

"Right queer."

"More injurious mixing. Perhaps—espionage."

"I know the lass," said a man in beige who'd said little and didn't seem very important. "Springfield Road."

"At any rate," said Angus, "it's a well-known carry-on. I thought, if we're going to do business—and preserve the integrity of our two traditions—it's consorting might be made an example of."

His eyes met the man's in beige, who said nothing. Of course, *Protestant* carried meaning only within the strict confines of Northern Ireland; the religion of a foreigner was moot. So it was funny, though they both knew the girl, that neither of them mentioned she was American.

*   *   *

Roisin sat. She ate another chocolate. The morning felt—familiar. She was doing something wrong. She'd been doing something wrong for a while.

She didn't cry. She would later. She'd cry a lot. Roisin liked to cry. It was the only time she felt completely herself, in a state of perfect disappointment. She was never too sure about the poetry, but crying, it was one thing she knew she did well. Roisin cried with confidence.

She moped to the scullery and considered throwing out the poached salmon. She unwrapped the aluminum: Christine did a beautiful job. It would keep Roisin in dinners for a week. She slipped the fish in the icebox.

She lay down on the sofa. And it was no use. After over an hour, she still couldn't hate him. In fact, she couldn't squeeze out one drop of ordinary dislike. Why, she'd never had trouble out and out despising Angus MacBride—one of the man's more appealing qualities. But her pictures of Farrell O'Phelan continued to tinge amber. No matter what he did to other people, Farrell would always appear the tragic one. It had something to do with the perpetually lachrymose expression on his face, which, no matter how lively at times, seemed the mask of keeping up a good front, as if he knew of something dreadful about to happen but was keeping it to himself for your sake.

She tried to work up a good you'll-be-sorry. Why, she'd be internationally anthologized, awarded prizes in London at six-course banquets in satin dresses, and he would read about her—no, look in the window—be invited—sit with her—hold her hand . . . Och, he would only wish her well in her career, politely. And in Roisin's most malicious moments she could not trump up any more bleak an ambition than that he remain as unhappy as he already was.

Desultorily, she removed her pearls, a present. She proceeded to collect all his gifts from around the house and pile them by the truffles. The hillock spangled; he had well-heeled taste. She could not keep such shining reminders of perfidy about her person. There was no choice but to expunge her life of any trace of the man, photos (*Fortnights?*), letters (he hadn't written any), and these trinkets here would go clanging in the bin.

She fingered a gold band, and at length clasped it around her wrist. She stared into her plastic fake fire. Well. It was a lovely watch.

If she couldn't dislike him or even toss his gifts, what was she supposed to do, add him to her Christmas card list? Roisin rehearsed his limpid sorrowing across a table; his repeated dithering over her "exquisite ankle bones," in his desperation to find a single one of her attributes attractive; their tandem savaging of Angus MacBride, and the one aspect of her company that even in retrospect he enjoyed; and upstairs, hands where she dare not even put her own when he was clearly thinking of *one other woman, whom I have also treated abominably, I fear*—

No, this version did not add up. She had seen a look in his eye, and in Roisin's experience there are forms of lying that are flat out impossible. He was finishing their relationship all right. But it was so obvious! The passion, he couldn't take it. The poor kid was scared witless. She knew Farrell by now. He had to be on top, in control, and his feelings for her had grown too overpowering. She remembered how cruel he had been that morning, and saw he'd been fighting himself. A sad figure in the end. Roisin was flattered. He could only have afforded to stay with her if his emotions had been modest. It was perfect proof that she had won him that he had fled.

Not long ago, Estrin had been up in the attic with Robin at Linen Hall and asked him idly for a book about birds. She had checked the index for *S*'s. Sure enough, Farrell was correct: the swallow takes off in its youth and remains in the air for up to four years, until finally it mates, nests, and rears its young. What Farrell failed to mention, however, is that the swallow does not settle down with a two-car garage popping Cheez Doodles. Once the offspring are old enough, the parent lifts on wing once more, wending its way through storm clouds of quelea in Botswana, squealing to trekkers in the Himalayas, surveying the Chilean elections from a safe half mile, swooping once more through the cupola of Ulster's City Hall, sweeping over the domes of Jerusalem's Old City, curling up against the Coral Reef outside Manila, where they still serve Estrin Lancaster's famous ceviche. Swallows could take off again.

Estrin pulled out only one suitcase, since her most important chattel was already packed, and had been for two months or more. For Estrin's mind was working in a way that made her suspect it hardly ever did that; what use was thinking if it didn't change anything, and for once Estrin's opinions had consequences: like that your finest moments are rarely sought but more often thrust upon you; or that sometimes "altruism" was not rescuing Armenians but raising one child right.

Because it was true that Farrell was browning inside, but the seeds remained gold in him, as Tarja knew. Estrin had panned one from his river of sweat in Whitewells, and she would secrete the nugget home, slipped far up inside, the way wives smuggled messages from Long Kesh. She would sneak the best of the country through customs undeclared. He could not be trusted with his own treasure. He had to be wrested from himself, and she had pickpocketed the shining spiral, the 44-carat corkscrew. For once, like it or not, Farrell O'Phelan had given himself away.

The shower hadn't done him much good, since after a certain age there's a kind of clean you can't get.

Still, something happened. It was the same kind of happening that had struck him for a while now: nothing you could point to, nothing you could tell. Farrell chose his dark pinstripe and red tie, just what he'd worn when they met. Bounding from Whitewells, he was filled with a wild, irrational urgency.

Two blocks down Castle Street, he suddenly doubled back to his bank. Lunchtime, an appalling queue. "An emergency." He strode straight to the teller. "I wish to stop payment on a check. This number here. —No, I have no idea how much it was for, I was poleaxed. —I don't care if you have to ring every bank in this city, and post office besides. I am one of your largest depositors, and if that check is honored I will have your job."

Back on Castle Street, the queue for cabs was worse than the bank, and guarded by enough spud-wielding binners he'd best not jump rank. With the stop-payment, he could afford the walk. A miracle he remembered about the check, as the whole evening dreeped so slowly to his head.

—I'm in love with you—

She'd never said that before. Christ, and what did he say back? He'd declared as much himself plenty of times, but that was cheap, and she knew it was cheap—damn it to hell, what did he say—

Tomorrow is my birthday.

That's today. Today, and he'd nothing to give her. Bollocks! It wouldn't do to show up empty-handed. Once more, he turned about-face and ran to Anderson McAuley's. Farrell stood paralyzed in the middle of the first floor. Why, he'd never bought Estrin anything—except that Soviet book, and that was no present, it was a dare. Now she was taking him up on it. While at Roisin's he'd always arrived with some bauble in tow. Och, for her anything glossy and expensive had done the job. But agitating past colognes, scarves, garish jewelry, Farrell felt crazy—rubbish! None of the clothes looked like anything the Swallow would wear, and as for objects, he suddenly felt he didn't know her so well, or he maybe knew too well she'd despise all of them. Raving in the mindless grabby sea of Christmas shoppers, Farrell chose blindly, reasoning the main thing was to get her something, even if he had to apologize it was wick.

Move, you eejit, it's already afternoon. This wasn't the plan. On waking to that first grim gray, head tolling, the girl so far away and so tiny, and those first spits of the evening sputtering in, he had groaned and set himself off to finish the squalid little project he'd started, with every intention of returning before she woke. But with geriatric taxis, Roisin, Whitewells, it was too late and there was a poor chance of that. Again up fucking Castle Street, over the motorway, getting some looks now since you saw precious few pinstripes skeltering past Divis Flats.

Up the road, however, he slowed a tad, for he had so rarely felt this impelled toward any woman, and so rarely felt this driven to apologize—really apologize, and not to Roisin, who in some ineffable way asked for it or deserved it, but to Estrin, who did not—that he wanted to savor the trip. And so, as memories sometimes came to him that would prove connected only if he indulged them a complete rerun, he recalled up the Falls not the story of his last bomb disposal on the roof of Whitewells, told often, but the very first disposal, told seldom, even to himself.

Since the only sport for a sot is where he hoovers his jar, in the mid-seventies Farrell made a point of frequenting Orange bars— joyriding for drinkers. A dicey business, and Farrell didn't hunch obscurely over his pint, either, but often sang, told Republican jokes—maybe his very brashness kept him safe. He was lucky, but not this time.

Farrell retreated to the bog of Union Jackie's when one of the local Presbyterians was getting suspicious; Farrell had failed to rattle off the right grammar school. In the next stall some joker was shitting his guts out, and Farrell waited till after the flush to slip out. He had in mind gliding out of the bar unnoticed; while the unnoticed part went easily enough, the door part did not.

For outside the loo, three things struck him as queer: the whole bar was deserted, even by the publican; there was a young man he recognized, frantically rattling the front door; and the boy was unquestionably from Ballymurphy.

"It's a poor wee Taig who has gone astray," Farrell sang behind him, and the boy shot six feet. "Not to worry, I'm on an intelligence-gathering mission myself," he lisped in the Catholic's ear. "Haven't found any."

"The door," said the McGuckian boy.

"What about it?"

"It's locked. From the outside, like."

Farrell tried it himself, and sure enough, it was one of those thief-proof locks which with the nib down only turned with a key. "Find the barman—"

"He's away," said McGuckian miserably.

"Aye, with the lot. Why?"

"There's a bomb scare."

"What?" said a woman stepping from the ladies'.

"They didn't clear the bogs."

The trio checked for other exits, but there was only the one door; the phone was out of order. Farrell—sozzled, needless to say—cheered them that spending the night with an open bar could only be so desperate. For, "Sure it's a hoax."

"It's not," said McGuckian.

"Bloody hell, if you were in the bog, how do you even know it's a bomb scare?"

Drunk people are slow. McGuckian, now the color of the Province's distinctively flavorless and thin vanilla soft serve, nodded unhappily at his own bookbag.

"Why, you dirty wee skitter, ye," said the woman.

"Well, turn it off!"

"You don't just turn off a bomb, you gombeen."

"I don't care what you call it, make it stop! The door is bleeding locked!"

"I don't know how!" McGuckian wailed.

"What kind of terrorist are you?" accused the woman.

"I just delivered it. I don't know the first frig about bombs. I haven't even looked inside."

"Look, then," said Farrell.

"I'll not touch it, sure I won't. I'm getting out of here."

They tried the windows, which were grated and too small to crawl through anyway. McGuckian kept returning to the front door, as if his fairy godmother should have arrived by now to unlock it. "Would you stop rattling that thing?" Farrell requested.

"Where are the police?" the woman demanded.

"They're out *protecting* our part of town," said Farrell.

"You're—!"

"Oh, aye. Light out for a jar in your local and what do you get but two Taigs and a bomb. We're *everywhere*." He leered, and later wondered if it was because of the drink he was the only one of the three that hadn't driven well round the twist in ten minutes' time. McGuckian was obsessed with the door, and the lady kept insisting, "The RUC will be by in a jot, surely—" when McGuckian confessed that they had only five minutes left on the TPU, the lady claimed she could hear Land Rovers. McGuckian returned to the window grate, but its opulent riveting was a regular monument to Protestant paranoia. How often in Belfast you were trapped by your own defenses.

"If we would all just sit tight and wait for the constabulary—"

"Madame," Farrell interrupted, long aggravated by the sort of permanent child that cannot conceive of a situation where Mommy or Daddy or the Nice Policeman will not come rescue you. Farrell himself was at the height of his anarchism and only took pleasure in the view that bad things happened to good people and there was no one to turn to. "The RUC is undoubtedly cordoning off this whole area for blocks, they do not know we are here, they are too far away to hear either McGuckian's fruitless scraping or your optimistic bleat, so sod off, please. The bomb squad will not necessarily arrive at our convenience."

But while the lady trusted to the RUC, Farrell's trust in nothing was as helpless. So it was a large corner indeed he took around the bar to advance on the bookbag, for Farrell didn't believe in anyone's capacity to affect anything—Farrell was a fatalist, a cynic, and a drunk. Neither did Farrell believe in heroes, least of all in becoming one. He had gladly watched his city self-destruct to reflect his own degradation, and the next day would have read about the decimation of Union Jackie's with only a smile if he hadn't found himself locked smack in the middle of the dive that night.

That was not exactly what turned the key, wanting to save his own skin. For Farrell the bookbag was positively opportune. Six years into Talisker, he could certainly stand a break from his own good time. Tarja's flight to Finland was just long enough ago that the story had changed, and instead of his having driven her away, she had capriciously abandoned her new husband. Those were the days he weaved across the M1 screaming, "Come and get me!" at rush hour, cars swerving to shoulders, horns wailing forlorn farewells; at last a lowly bookbag had answered his call. But while he didn't know the McGuckian kid well, his mother was a peach, who had persistently defended the Peace People even after Betty's mink coat; and though this other bird here was delightful as a dose of salts, when she exclaimed, "But I have five children!" he conceded there were a few people out there for whom she was more than a girn.

"My father," announced Farrell as he unstrapped the flap, "is an electrician," which may have bolstered their confidence, though hardly his own. Farrell's role in the family was, among others, Mechanical Incompetent—recording an LP, he would press Play and Rewind; "helping" with tea, he could never sort out whether the round beater went into the left or right jack of the mixer, in an allergic reaction to domesticity that in its most inflamed state would become Inability to Boil Water. All willful idiocy, for when he looked down at the bomb—Farrell's bomb, not his father's, Farrell's first bomb—it was a logical business to follow the wires and what would connect with where when the timer arm reached this point, logic far cruder than chess or even the resourceful scavenging required to score one more wee whiskey when shy of ready quid. Though he had every right to be frightened, when he reached down with a pair of nail clippers, Farrell felt only exhilarated and his hand was dead steady. It was his first taste of immortality, and of faith: that it was indeed possible to affect matters. So when piece by piece, with the other two cowering in the corners with their hands over their heads, he separated the elements of the device, it was by far the best round he'd ever seen stretched out across a bar. *Bits*. With the bomb asunder, Farrell fused.

The woman threw her arms around his neck and burst into tears. McGuckian was immediately released into the impending implosion of his life without the bomb, for now the inevitable arrival of the army did not strike him as salvation. Farrell reached behind the bar for the Jameson's 1780 and poured them each a large, proprietary short.

"*Slainte.*" He touched the lady's glass.

"Slanty." And though she seemed a right tight old Prod, she stood on tiptoe and kissed him smack on the mouth.

There was a flight out of London tonight; she could fly standby this time of year, for she very much hoped to give some of Farrell's check back, all of it in time—she didn't want his money.

The suitcase full, Estrin paused to focus: no, she hadn't time to clear out of here for good. And maybe not the inclination. Frankly, while she needed a mother now—inside and out, both mothers—she was not intent on settling in Philadelphia so much as anywhere longer than a year and a half. She had a good start on this town, and it wasn't out of the question. She loved Belfast, Robin, Malcolm; whether or not the power-sharing initiative flew, she'd like to follow what happened here, to finish a story she'd started. There was just one problem, and perhaps he could be avoided. Better to decide later, and plan at least one trip back to sort out the house and motorcycle.

This resolved, she unpacked the Guinness glasses and yesterday's *Irish News*, which had suddenly seemed rare. She straightened up and took out the garbage. Estrin eyed the house for a moment: with those curtains, a few plants, an Oriental rug, the sitting room would be lovely. And though it had been absurd to install good windows in this neighborhood, she hadn't been able to resist puttying in the leaded stained glass in the front door, and one pane on the second floor where it poppled the stairway late afternoons with red and gold.

Estrin munched leftover prawns: protein. She wondered what damage she might have done the foetus fasting; remarkable she hadn't miscarried. Must be Farrell's child: it thrived on suffering.

Estrin popped vitamins with another glass of milk, and was

about to dash out to cash that check before the banks closed when there was a knock on the door. She glanced out the curtains to make sure it wasn't a certain someone, but kicked herself when it was only a DHL courier; why expect him, hadn't she learned her lesson yet? How much work it would take to keep from hoping: now, that was discipline. Then, you did not transform overnight, though it was a nice, literary idea.

"What on earth?"

"From a Mr. O'Phelan, miss."

"Good Christ. He remembered my birthday."

"Your birthday, is it?"

"Aye," said Estrin.

"Many happy returns!" The deliveryman waved and darted to his van, whose engine was still running.

She tried not to be excited, easy enough when she opened the carton. It was one of those presents that hurt you not by being cheap, just *wrong*. The ungainly gift expressed too well what she suspected all along: that all those dinners in 44 he hadn't been listening; that when he scanned her bookshelves at breakfast, peered at photos, picked up bits of her past, he had actually been thinking about the problems of representing minority interests in a democratic system. For no one who had truly paid attention to Estrin Lancaster for half an hour would have launched out and retrieved this—this—*object*.

It was a large music box in the form of a cottage, white with lurid green shutters. It was plastic. On top crouched, of all things, a *leprechaun*. Get out of here! Gift-shop merchandise, obviously for tourists, a category she should have earned herself out of by now. Farrell O'Phelan, what was going on in your head?

Out of a sick curiosity she wound the box up. It tinkled "When Irish Eyes Are Smiling," hardly "their song," except in the sense that they both despised it.

Somewhere into the second verse Estrin turned sharply; the smirking leprechaun hit an off note.

* * *

No escapade had ever quite equaled Union Jackie's. Drunken, unbidden, it was still the one disposal that made him happy. Farrell had always considered happiness beneath him; further, an ambition he morally disapproved of. Yet the few times he had been happy—he didn't know what else you called it—the sensation wasn't of a pink tuxedo shirt with ruffles, colored lights with reindeer, but of a plain white button-down, with starch; a single street lamp in fog. He had always conceived of happiness as frilly, trivial, distracted, but he was forced to admit, buoying round the corner to Springfield Road, that what he detested was failed happiness, fake happiness, that he'd simply gotten happiness and misery confused.

Sweeping into Clonard, Farrell warned himself to hold back. Practically, he didn't know if he could live with a woman again. He shouldn't underestimate his privacy, his obstreperousness; however eager he might now feel, the generosity would fade. So he would not arrive with any proposition on his tongue, but with a private hologram in his head:

She has been in the Soviet Union a month. She already knew how to travel; finally she has learned to return. Teaching English on these regular sojourns has improved her Russian; she has taught him a few words. Her *r*'s trill the back of his neck.

How absurd to end up in this neighborhood.

But the house is gorgeous. The door is freshly painted, the planter budding—let's say it is not quite spring. At the gate, his eyes pinwheel; he likes this moment before he sees her as much as the moment itself.

Inside, he finds she has already bought flowers. From global warming, the daffodils have bloomed in premature profusion; on sale at every newsstand for 50 p a bunch, and she must have bought five pounds' worth: mantels and sideboards are aflame. She has run out of vases and stuffed the last bouquets in jam jars.

She hasn't heard him come in. "Amazing Grace" winds to the front room on a scent of tarragon. She has a pretty voice; he heard it once in a singsong at the Green Door, though she'd stopped singing when he walked in the club: accurate, though slight, a bit breathy; sweet like her face, but not as wary. Christ, what was so bloodcurdling about a swallow in your kitchen? And he had faced so many of his fears—phone calls to strangers, girls with their clothes off—why could he not confront this last one? *Tarja!* Angus always thought the marriage a leg pull, but Farrell's biggest secret was that the wedding had been real. Why else would he have turned tail in mortal terror after only two weeks?

Seeing her face, he notes she has filled out, just a bit, losing edges. Now that she is no longer weight lifting, her body is not quite so hard. But she still runs when she travels, down long Leningrad boulevards, and in Belfast the two of them play a lot of squash. For some reason his asthma has virtually disappeared. At squash, she beats him. He doesn't like this one bit.

She kisses him, but fast; he would teach her to say hello properly. But she is boiling with Soviet politics: the rise of the right, the threat of backlash against Gorbachev, the return of anti-Semitism. Dinner is terrific, but they don't pay it much attention. For Farrell, too, has stories to tell, having just returned himself from—

Do not say Armagh, Fermanagh. Do not even say Cork. What is your work? This is a gilt-framed picture where you limn what you like. Do you want to work? Yes! Do you care about anyone but yourself? He would like to find out. He would work to find out. Surely all those taxis to Derry were not simply panaceas for the fact that his mother never held his hand.

All right, in lieu of the more original, South Africa. Not because the North is "solved," but because it doesn't want to be and you cannot force contentment on a belligerent people. He would leave them to their festering and seek conflict with substance. He is a fine negotiator, and his Irishness lends him suitable neutrality. He is useful. The homelands make him cry. Yesterday he had tea with Tutu. The man is astonishingly short.

Because can it be so much more deadly dull to spend an evening with a woman in your pantry than with a *Fortnight* in your hotel? Why did it seem the dispatch of all adventure if at the end of the day a pretty motorcyclist rubbed your head? Wasn't the irony of bomb disposal that even death defiance became ordinary, for wasn't every thrill, over time, destined to feel the way anything that happens to you always feels? Though a Saracen mumbled by, he had seen so many of them for the last twenty years that it could have been a Ford Cordova. Farrell looked at the clouds instead and decided he had not paid enough attention to weather. He couldn't tell if the day was about to turn floral or foul; while the army bored him, the sky infused with suspense; adventure was an attitude.

But anything Farrell had ever learned, in Union Jackie's, on Whitewells' roof, with a gun to his temple in Newry, had been taken back. Clutching the bag from Anderson McAuley, with its drooping silver earrings when Estrin's ears weren't even pierced, was to be no exception. For epiphanies are lies, luring you with the illusion that the truth can be won in seconds, while anything worth knowing takes the whole of your life to earn. It was this revelation which bloomed in his colon as he spotted 133: that there was no making up for things, that you couldn't go back and revise, that you had led your life limping from one bitter barb to the next unkind accusation, and that was the sum of it. There was no redemption, no transformation, no second chance, and anything you ever did understand would explode through your thick skull only because it was too late.

Epilogue:
Boredom as Moral Achievement

Farrell hadn't returned home at Christmas for fifteen years, and in '73 he'd been squiffed and called his mother a cow and knocked over the Christmas tree. Since then his family sent him some little token through Constance every year, which he promptly threw in the bin. He'd hardly replied in kind, either; *I am like this*. Being *like this*, he nearly killed his poor mother by showing up that morning on her doorstep bundled with packages. His sisters fell so over themselves that their gratitude backfired, and instead of making him feel the loving brother, he felt a shite. His mother, that leathery item, cried. At least his da was surly as ever, jabbing from his armchair: All very well now, but hasn't Farrell been absent like for more Christmases than we care to count, and why dither especially over the one member of the family that hasn't shown them a shred of loyalty his entire adult life? The man had a point.

Children have short memories, however, and when the two girls unwrapped his meter-high stuffed hippos, Uncle Farrell's previous boycott of their existence was forgotten. Farrell felt a bit sheepish, for the animals were seventy-five quid each, and shamed the hand puppets and wooden puzzle of the thirty-two counties from their parents.

He made it well into the unwrapping carry-on before his asthma started up (amazing, bingo); as usual, it provided him the excuse to go, for Farrell feared that in one rash morning he was about to undo fifteen years of dedicated neglect; he could already feel their expectations for next Christmas breathing down his neck. He cut out before the meal.

In the long walk from Glengormley, the Cave Hill gloomed beside him, assuming that commonly weary aspect of Irish countryside—washed, ragged, overdescribed. Too many writers had scribbled about these hillsides—an unremarkable, wind-beaten land, exhausted by metaphor, every poet's bloody mother. The poor island couldn't take it, depleted by the obsessions of son on son, soil planted with the same crop year after year, a too-tattered wasteground to bear the raking of so much neurosis; the tufts of its gorse scrabbled in the breeze like torn hair.

He made the house by mid-afternoon. Funny, he was halfway there before he realized where he was headed.

Farrell stood before the gate, once more off its hinges, and toed a bit of broken footpath, clasping his hands; would have taken off his hat but wasn't wearing one. He had that formal feeling like minutes of memorial silence after Enniskillen through which children giggled and shuffled and opened their eyes. He felt like one such child. Even at his own ceremony, his instinct was to defile it.

Though he recognized the odd corner of new molding, a face of freshly painted plaster, a few sticks of varnished table legs, otherwise the place looked basically the way it had when she'd moved in. Well, there it was: you built it up; you tore it down.

What the human race had been doing from the year dot. Just now he had no opinion about the cycle either; or even about the vicious-looking boys breaking up Estrin's four-legged Victorian bathtub with lead pipes. Pipes she'd never connected, anyway—that tub had never held more than paint cans, so why get sentimental? And better not to cross the lads. No more than twelve, but could put a nail bomb together quicker than any thirty-two-county puzzle. And he was not so ghoulish as to shoo them off and scavenge for earplugs, pink pebbles, leftovers of salmon steak.

No matter where he looked he had no opinions. It was quite wonderful. He was left with impassive interestedness. No one looked more attractive than anyone else. The army helicopter overhead could have been a magpie, the big Gerry Adams mural a billboard for Harp. Most of all, when he looked at 133 he could summon neither anger nor remorse. An event had simply: occurred.

Or had it? Well, there wasn't much to do; he hadn't planned anything mawkish, wreath-laying or prayer. Still, he had hoped the return would kick something in, and it wasn't working. Last week he'd phoned in a dinner reservation, and had to ring back. Sorry, that's only a table for one. He knew himself, of course—this was delay rather than denial. The bomb hadn't gone off yet. It might never.

The visit hadn't taken long. Farrell shook himself and moved on, with a quirk of a smile—he'd warned her not to put in those windows.

"You sorry article." Constance had laid her hand on his cheek. "All these years you've told the rest of the world to stay out of your business. We've stayed out. You've had your privacy. And now you can't get shed of it."

"Do you want me to confide in you or not?"

"Aye. But you might have better come to me before it was past time I could give you advice."

"I detest advice. And nothing could have happened otherwise. But I must say," he'd considered more gently, "it's a queer business to fall in love with a woman only after she's dead."

Now that had sounded poignant enough, but walking back from Springfield Road to the comforting anonymity of his hotel room, Farrell conceded the conceit, one more of his high-flown romantic declarations which cost him so little; for he might more accurately have said, "Isn't it cushy to fall in love with a woman when she's dead? How little it requires of you." Because what made him feel worst was not feeling all that bad, really. He had liked telling the story. Why, Constance was the one who cried. He liked having a murdered lover; it fit. *My swallow*, he confessed that night, *I am so much more a swine than you imagined. Do I have an easier time talking to you dead?* Farrell had experienced a failure of adjacency his whole life. He was one of those infants born allergic to everything, whom women poked and waved at from the other side of his plastic tent.

Estrin herself had touched on it with Shearhoon, that one of the great taboos of mourning is admitting how little you feel— what he hadn't told Constance, dreaded telling himself. Then, there are other things to do besides feel, aren't there? Grief never filled a calendar. And he wasn't about to kill himself, not over a girl. Farrell lived beside people. Some of them fell away. If he ever committed suicide, it would have no relation to anyone but would only be a gesture of purified self-loathing.

Farrell wasn't much of a fantasist, but there was one story he preferred to the murdered-girlfriend, and occasionally he indulged a rewrite: where Farrell, say, skips Anderson McAuley and arrives at 133, just after DHL. He recognizes straight off there is something wrong with the delivery and orders Estrin from the house. Rolling up his sleeves, a fork in one hand and a spackling knife in the other, he feels the old acuity return. With seconds to go, our hero prizes the detonator from its explosive, which he carts out back at arm's length like bad meat. Well after the dirty work is done, the ATOs arrive, impressed; Lieutenant Pim introduces "the mad genius" to the squad—

Is it at this point or a little earlier that Farrell starts laughing?

Moreover, Farrell rehearsed his caprice of tea and Gorbachev on her birthday. He nudged himself. What would have happened even a day or two later, *really?* He knew this dance: what came after the one step forward? What were the chances that an old dog of forty-four would learn a new jig?

On the other hand, he witnessed two tiny aberrant behaviors. The old dog of 44 kept a matchbox from that restaurant in his pocket. Though he didn't smoke or light burners, Farrell switched it from suit to suit with his keys. Second, he kept the Phillips screwdriver she had left at Whitewells on his desk. Cleaned his nails with it once in a while, but otherwise Farrell was no Mr. Fix-It. He challenged himself to toss the tool in the bin, irritated with totemism, the morbid souvenir. But something else always came up, the phone rang . . . And he would twist mean little holes in the wood with its tip while Constance informed him of canceled appointments.

It was Farrell who had to contact Estrin's parents. The father got confused. "She wrote us it wasn't as bad as they said," he objected. "She said she was safer than in Philadelphia."

"That depends on who your friends are," said Farrell. "And where is safe?"

Estrin might have been the source of quite a row in the States if her father hadn't Gordon Wilsoned the story; and in America forgiveness only makes the C section. Still, he wondered if she'd be pleased, for once, to make good copy; he should send clippings to her brother in Allentown. Finally something happened to you, my swallow. Wasn't that the sure cure for negaphobia? Afraid you don't exist? Behold, you do not. Relax.

Much as he'd have liked to Throw Himself into His Work, in the months following his Border Poll the violence was positively festive, and moved to the mainland again. Britain got cold feet. Thatcher decided the turnout was marginal enough to ignore, and as the season of good cheer persisted through March and April, Westminster did nothing, zero, zip. At best the army shot a few more Provos in iffy circumstances. But they did not withdraw so much as a rusty M-16, a single nineteen-year-old private with the flu. Not a move to schedule assembly elections, not a peep of the Phase Twos, Threes, and Fours Farrell had negotiated to the footnote all year. Himself, Farrell got escorted to shabbier London bistros by lowlier civil servants; demoted from dinner to lunch, he was well on his way to coffee—instant, with whitener—by the time he got the message. So before they started Farrell-whoing him off the steps of Parliament, he stopped shuttling to England altogether. If the British were talking, it was to someone else. Rumor had it "Molehill" was trying to arrange a Provisional cease-fire—*again*—

Surprisingly, he couldn't be arsed about the results of the referendum. Like everyone else on this island, he cared about winning all right, but he did not care what he won. A kind of irrationality, that. To work so hard for something for the work, not for the something. *Motion toward; inability to arrive*—Farrell thought these phrases and even wrote articles with them, but it was only a naming; they did not change what he was like.

"And so the nationalist entrancement with *aspiration*," he dictated to Constance: "an advance to victory, oblivious to both the prize and the means by which it is secured—" an ugly combination, for you are left only with appetite, like MacBride, voracious discontent. Once you are no longer hungry and you still move on to your third biscuit, you will finish the package and ravage the cupboards for more; you are Estrin Lancaster buying knickers until they tumble over the top of her basket; you are Farrell O'Phelan on his third bottle asking for the wine list. When you are doing the wrong thing, you can do it indefinitely. Twenty years was nothing.

Besides, the whole idea of "power sharing" was rubbish. You chose your sides, or not even. That's why Ulster so captivated international imagination, a paradigm: you couldn't share power. One group had it, one didn't. As for sides, you were stuck. Like it or not, Farrell was a Northern Irish Catholic. Estrin was a dead American. It was all over at the start. You could fight, aye, but you couldn't fight the fighting, because then you still were. Everything whole Farrell ever understood used the same word a number of times. This made for lousy prose, and the articles he sent *Fortnight* were rejected.

Fine. Farrell wouldn't have read them himself. Farrell was bored. He began to realize, for example, the reason he bought ten papers was that otherwise he wouldn't read one. To discriminate was to eliminate the lot. For this wasn't the old impatient, irascible boredom, stimulating, edgy. This boredom ached through his bones like a permanent dose of the cold. Not the subtlest or most perverse observation about the North could tickle a hair on his head. A monument of a boredom, it amounted to a moral achievement.

The one glorious side to the Border Poll fizzle was perfect revenge on Angus MacBride. The British didn't replace Tom King exactly, but fobbed Angus off on a second-in-command spot. Instead of a Nobel lecture tour, Angus opened aerobics rooms in leisure centers, spoke to the Northern Ireland Agoraphobia Society about the joys of the out-of-doors, made guest appearances at Overeaters Anonymous and the Dog Training Club, and MC'ed the Motor Trade Ball. He accumulated all the perks of high office: free vegetarian cooking classes, junkets to Newtownards, matinee tickets to *Sinbad and the Pirates*. Angus knew he'd had it when that spring he was approached for an interview by Eddie McIlwaine.

Not long after that, the *Sunday World* broke the story that MacBride was philandering, and with a Catholic—not even Roisin, another one. Funnily enough, the rumor did no apparent damage to MacBride's standing in the UUU. It turns out everyone pretty much knew he was a rascal, and preferred him that way.

Farrell had dreaded running into Roisin, and of course eventually he did and she was snuffy. But nothing happened. He was a little insulted she didn't seem more upset.

Still, in a world where the Zambian government shoots over

a hundred people for complaining about the price of mealie meal, Farrell's insincere handholding was so terrible? Give over.

In April, tinkering with his emotions as once he had with bombs, Farrell returned for the first and only time to the Green Door. Littered with the odd layabout that afternoon, the club would crowd at night—Duff and Estrin had improved its reputation, for nothing picked up business like a renowned fatality or two. Habitually, Farrell scanned for Shearhoon anyway, who once occluded a good eight-bottle stretch of bar.

Instead, he found Clive Barclay, who had assumed Duff's old stool, and seemed to be working on the breadth as well— his bum now spread down the sides of his seat like icing on a cake. Farrell asked how the thesis was coming, but Clive only enthused about having joined the staff poker game at Linen Hall. Clive "let" Farrell buy him a drink, and Farrell inquired when the student was headed back to Iowa.

"Och . . ." Clive clouded. "The work's taking a wee bit longer than I thought, like."

Farrell clapped him on the shoulder. "Maybe you should stick around. You're beginning to fit right in."

"Aye, you fancy?" Clive beamed.

"What'll it be?"

Malcolm was growing up fast, nearly tall as Farrell himself, and, by the terse sound of that voice, already getting hard.

Farrell ordered Ballygowan, and didn't bother to drink it. "I thought you'd be off to America by now. You're about that age. Packing?"

"I've thought about it," he said, wiping under the plastic bullets briskly. "But Est said I should stay. She said someone's to tend to this country. That when you start leaving you keep leaving and it takes too much of your time. Better to say put, she says, so you don't have to keep buying dish drainers." He smiled, a little.

"Or corkscrews," Farrell remembered. "But plugging to stay put doesn't sound like the lady's line."

"You were hardly underfoot those last few weeks. Estrin started saying different things. Estrin changed. You didn't notice."

"Maybe I didn't want her to change."

"Maybe you didn't care fuck-all."

The hostility made Farrell feel more comfortable. "Best not to comment on affairs of which you know so splendidly little."

"Hardly. Of the two of us and ignorance, I'd say yous take the prize."

Farrell's fist closed; he felt the same unadmirable desire to crush the boy as he had when they played chess. "Meaning?"

Malcolm's chin rose high. "Like, did you know she was pregnant?"

Farrell didn't move.

"Right," said Malcolm, going back to drying glasses. "I didn't think so."

This time there was no poking at himself or plunking himself before bombed-out houses to rouse some meager reaction. He couldn't talk for a week. He couldn't buy newspapers. Why, he couldn't even drink.

And so began a different Farrell O'Phelan: he read novels; he rang his mother. He minded his nieces when their mother left for Dublin, and was surprised to enjoy the girls, their invention and easy affection. He insisted Constance work nine to five, and stopped asking her to buy his sheets.

Whitewells took a downturn as (inconceivably) the Europa enjoyed a vogue with journalists; in fact, his concern had run in the red for some time, so Farrell's more expensive eccentricities were forced to go. Belt tightening refreshed him, actually, like losing weight. It seems many of his idiosyncrasies were decorative. When he swept his own floor the sky didn't fall down, and it didn't take very much time. What had that cleaning girl been doing eight hours a week? With the demise of Whitewells he could no longer afford the taxis zigzagging the Province, the blind rampages on suits. So Farrell economized on his character.

While he missed the extravagance of earlier incarnations, Farrell was beginning to see his life as less a point traveling a line than as an object, present at once: the rabble-rouser of Talisker inhabited the same man reading in his chair. Rising for another cup of hot water, he was at once on the burning barricades, swaying off the overturned bus. As you have ever been, so you remain, and Farrell found the whole crowd in his cup: not just the severe pinstripe magician edging a dowel from the jaws of a clothespin, but also the lonely Queen's freshman with bad skin, or the fourteen-year-old with a fanatic regimen of visiting the elderly, scratching frantic pages about the nature of goodness till 5 a.m., until one day his mother could no more rouse her son than the dead and left him to sleep through to evening, to wake and take sugar in his tea, lumps and lumps with biscuits, gluttonously, like a real child. These languid nights, after a bit of bad TV, Farrell would reach over and sweep the shock of bright blond hair from the face of a beautiful but fragile five-year-old, almost girlish and so often in bed, staring out the window as the other boys played Kick the Tin and his mother brought stirabout, the smell sickening and thick as it mixed with the air already steamy with pans of friar's balsam for his lungs. At last Farrell forgave them all, maybe conceding for the first time they were the same person.

In the same way, too, he still had Estrin, though this was the hardest bit to put over—for while you might always have what you ever had, do you ever have what you never had, quite?

And he repudiated drink. In his abstinence, the habit shrank to an unimpressive dependency, a sad compulsive guzzling, such an obvious substitute for something else, if there was anything else. To think you could salve the grief of existence by putting something in your mouth. Pub crawlers appeared no wiser than their mothers, convinced the answer to bereavement was tea. Bars became anthropological curiosities, crowds gathering every night behind long boards and running pints of drugged liquid through their bodies straight from Margaret Mead.

However, to be shut from pub life was not sweet, for while teetotaling revealed the myth of drink, what wasn't myth at the end of the day? If you took every fancy away, you were left with a huddle of animals rutting and snuffling in the dark, or less: chemicals seething and subsiding on a speck. Farrell had always cherished his pictures of raw ugly nothingness as recherché, but now these visions felt ordinary, nihilism a resort and a cheat, a lack of imagination. He did not care for the planet undressed. He was willing to spin a yarn about the place to keep it cozy. Farrell had studied enough metaphysics at Queen's to know that after all that maybe-we're-not-really-here, maybe-green-is-blue, trees falling silent in faraway forests, you were left with just as much illusion as ever. You had to give yourself permission to tell yourself a story, because you were going to tell one anyway. Certainly the most deluded of Farrell's sort were the ones who thought they lived on specks, bare truth, who stared the gaping maw in the gob—the ones convinced they'd no religion. Farrell's Catholicism might have lapsed, but there was always some fairy tale to take its place—if not Jesus, Connolly, Bobby Sands, Bobby Fischer, or even Farrell O'Phelan, a myth he had told and retold himself until it rang comfortingly familiar as the Three Bears: *Farrell O'Phelan doesn't check*.

So Farrell rounded the last chapter of his tale with an old man who cried a lot. Oh, still dry, astute, and certainly better read than the days he liquored up on British Air. But the most sentimental of films would set him off, *Houdini*; or little girls on swing sets, the sun through the mists on Lough Neagh . . . He wouldn't trust himself in public anymore, for he couldn't fight the tears when they came. And he would abandon grandiose altruism that was really just a cover for egomania in favor of ordinary niceness. He would keep minding his nieces, and they would come to adore him. (Well, they already did.) He would not tackle apartheid in South Africa, but record tapes of Thomas Hardy for the blind. He would forget the Chilean elections, but remember birthdays. He would volunteer for a soup kitchen and humbly learn to dice carrots, take his turn at the reception center at the Maze, selling Cadbury's at cost to distraught prisoners' wives, help dyslexics learn to read . . .

In all, it was like an OD on Quiet Life that lasted exactly six months. At the start of the seventh, celebrated by a car bomb just two doors down from his house that was surely meant for him, Farrell tinkled through the broken glass to his closet and pulled down the creaky case, with its broom handle sections, fishing hooks, and gnarled paper clips. The leather was dusty and the lines stiff, but the tools were in order. The finishing touch, he slipped Estrin's Phillips into an empty sleeve, pleased the kit lacked one. He pulled out his expansive canvas bag that fit snugly under a seat. He rested the case in its bottom, and on top piled two shirts, Y-fronts, a sturdy stack of quid. Whitewells had sold way under value, but then Farrell had always considered irresponsible or even downright feebleminded financial affairs a point of personal pride. Ceremonially, at 10 a.m. he cracked a fresh fifth of Talisker and poured a hardy double, tucking the remains of the bottle in his bag. After all, if drink was a sham, they deserved each other—like any good relationship, they had found each other out. Pausing at the door, he enjoyed leaving the house with all its windows smashed, the cool air coming and going through each well-appointed room with all the presumption of a Communist overthrow. Swinging his carry-on down the walk, he ducked into his waiting taxi, and on to Burma.

Glossary of Troublesome Terms

(AUTHOR'S NOTE:)

The Bleeding Heart is a work of fiction set within a real political context. While presumably a novelist is answerable to a different sort of truth, too often the mixing of the invented and the actual can result in ordinary bad information and does readers a disservice. I would clarify, then, that the following are my own embellishments: the Green Door; Union Jackie's; the Rest in Pieces, not to be confused with "legitimate" paramilitaries; and three organizations: the III, the UUU, and the YYY. Best not visit Belfast hoping to check into Farrell's hotel; Whitewells rests on the corner where the Metropole once stood, an opulent Edwardian hotel razed some time ago. Furthermore, the Border Poll Farrell and Angus organize at the end of 1988 has not been held since 1973; the conference held to marshal its support, the election itself, and its subsequent fallout are all fictional.

That said, the remaining events referred to in *The Bleeding Heart* would have taken place more or less as described, from late 1987 through 1988. Since the intricacies of Northern Ireland are daunting for anyone who simply wants to put his feet up and have a good read, I have included this small glossary to illuminate unfamiliar references. No glossary can substitute for an astute exegesis of Irish politics, but that would require another book, or books, and plenty of authors out there—perhaps too many— have taken that project on board. A Monarch Notes, then, of the North:

ANGLO-IRISH AGREEMENT: An international treaty of potentially little importance whose endurance has been ensured and whose significance has been multiplied by its opponents' determination to get rid of it.

Signed by London and Dublin in 1985, the agreement granted the Republic of Ireland a hazy consultative role in Northern Irish affairs, symbolized by the establishment of a Dublin secretariat in Maryfield, of suburban Belfast—a small toe in the door indeed, but seen by many Unionists as a first step toward a united Ireland. Protestant resistance to the agreement has been both exhaustive and exhausted, though big banners like LISBURN SAYS NO still tatter on public buildings. Meanwhile, the poor Southerners at Maryfield are hustled in under heavy guard for a week at a time, with very little to do. They issue the odd atrocity denouncement like everyone else. They can't leave the building for their own security. There is nothing to drink. They play a lot of cards.

BOLLOCKS: A mess; a confusion; a disaster. Widely applicable to all aspects of politics in the North, but most aptly to its source, the original partition of Ireland.

In 1920, Britain granted its Irish colony independence—almost. The northern six counties, predominantly Protestant, were exempted from the Catholic Free State, remaining in the United Kingdom as they preferred. The border between the North and the South was understood to be temporary. Britain planned to sort out this bollocks later, much the way people who dress in a hurry will safety-pin a torn shirt and promise themselves to sew the seam properly when they've time. They never have time. Ireland is still put together with a safety pin.

BORDER POLL: A referendum mandated every ten years to determine whether the people of Northern Ireland wish to remain in the United Kingdom, and in what form; when first held in 1973, boycotted by most Catholics. As the poll was effectively meaningless, in 1983 no one bothered.

CATHOLIC: A.k.a., *Taig, Fenian Bastard*. Associated with the color green. By Protestant accord, two-faced and dangerous. Attends "Mass" instead of "church services," and while these two ceremonies involve the exact same rituals on Sunday, "church" is civilized, "Mass" is superstitious. Can be found in profusion in the Republic of Ireland and in the Northern counties of Fermanagh, Armagh, and southern Tyrone; in *West Belfast*, a byword for the Catholic ghetto despite the fact that *the Shankill*, a byword for the Protestant ghetto, is smack in the western part of the city. The *Falls Road*, a main artery leading from the center of town to the west, is not a street but a quagmire of treachery— many is the Protestant never to have driven there. While academics have fought to establish some obscure link between the Northern sense of "Catholic" and the Church of Rome, when you come upon the two sects in a punch-up they are rarely arguing over the Reformation.

CIVIL RIGHTS MOVEMENT: Seemingly innocuous demonstrations for justice with unprecedented consequences.

Catholics have long been stifled in Ireland—disenfranchised, dispossessed, leasing land at high rents that once belonged to them. At one time no Catholic was legally allowed to own a horse worth more than five pounds, and if you met a Catholic on the road with any horse, you could give him five pounds and take the animal away. In those days, even to sing about Ireland was punishable by flogging. Perhaps down South they are still oppressed, after independence, by their own Church and by something about the essential nature of this island: it is heavy, the air is close. Up North, however, the oppression has been by no means atmospheric. Election boundaries have been gerrymandered, housing and employment inequably distributed to keep Protestants, if marginally, better off.

While more flagrant discrimination had eased up by the late sixties, improving matters somewhat often inspires people to improve them a lot. The *Northern Ireland Civil Rights Association* (NICRA) was formed in 1967, the more radical *People's Democracy* (PD) in 1968. Inspired by Martin Luther King, Jr., in the United States, the "niggers" of Northern Ireland took to the streets. In newsreels of these marches, it is hard to distinguish the Protestant hecklers from the police, since they are both hitting Catholics over the head. Embarrassed by footage broadcast all over the world, Britain finally took notice and in 1969 sent the army to the North to protect the minority. Along with so many "temporary" arrangements like partition itself, the army is still there.

The civil rights movement initiated the process by which Northern Ireland went to hell. Parts of Derry and Belfast took on the lawless free-for-all aspect of the American Wild West, beginning a tit for tat whereby, whoever started it, rare is the family on either side today who does not harbor a vendetta, and a legitimate one. The IRA, in 1968 a few ancients with rusted Smith & Wessons from an abortive anti-border campaign in the fifties, revived to defend the minority against Orange hoodlums; its ranks swelled with normal, indignant people. Protestants responded with paramilitaries of their own. The civil rights campaign rapidly evolved into a Nationalist one, since apparently Catholics would be treated decently only if they joined their co-religionists in the South. The army became a force of imperialism, and with the arrival of the Brits, the IRA no longer needed the Prods. Two enemies only confuse matters.

CRACK: A good time had by all, as in *McBride is good crack*, or *Last night was good crack*. Last night was always good crack. A word you get very tired of. Confusing for Americans.

DIRECT RULE: When in 1972 Secretary of State Brian Faulkner refused to hand over the powers of security to Britain, Westminster took over not only security but everything else. *Stormont Castle*, the seat of the Protestant-controlled parliament and itself a magnificent if somewhat ludicrous Greek classical building, is now little used, except for the offices of British ministers and the odd swish dinner. Under Direct Rule, Northern Ireland has no government. While the Province limps by with city councils—festive carnivals of sectarian mudslinging—they control little more than admission rates for local leisure centers.

HUNGER STRIKES: In 1981, Republican prisoners in the H-blocks of the Maze prison (SEE LONG KESH) went on hunger strike for the Five Demands, a list of privileges which more or less reinstated the POW status they had had before 1976, after which political terrorists were thrown in with *Ordinary Decent Criminals*, or ODCs. Margaret Thatcher remained either firm or inflexible, unintimidated or coldhearted, depending on your point of view. Ten men died. The hunger strikes polarized the North into two alien universes: while women keened and banged bin lids and thousands took to the streets in West Belfast, the Protestants made Slimmer of the Year jokes. And though the strikes officially failed, all five demands have now been instituted across the board in UK prisons, and ten emaciated corpses did successfully stir both local and international sympathy for the Republican cause.

INTERNMENT: The curious democratic practice of imprisonment without charge. Actively employed 1971–76 but to this date still on the statute books of Britain's emergency powers, internment was exercised largely on Catholics. Consequently, internment recruited more young men to the IRA than any amount of Republican propaganda could ever have done. The IRA has found British reaction to Northern violence infinitely useful. They need never strain resources to achieve an obligingly amplified effect.

IRISH REPUBLICAN ARMY (IRA): Or, as if they were simply good-natured if mischievous fellows, *the lads*. Not to be confused with modern liberation movements—the ANC, the PLO—the IRA is an ancient, venerated institution. That the Republic owes its independence to the ructions of the same violent fringe helps explain why its relationship to the IRA's current incarnation remains ambivalent.

Like all Nationalist cadres, the IRA aims to dissolve partition (see UNITED IRELAND). However, *the* IRA is a misnomer. At the moment, the Provisional IRA (the *PIRA*, or the *Provos*) have the upper hand; their formal policy of targeting only members of the security forces has not prevented repeated civilian casualties, often Catholic. The Official IRA (The *Officials*, or *Stickies*) has repudiated violence and become the *Workers Party*, a minor but dogged Marxist crew who probably despise the Provos with more vitriol than any other group in the Province. Otherwise, the *Irish National Liberation Army* (INLA) of the *Irish Republican Socialist Party* (IRSP, mispronounced the *Irps*, and now virtually extinct) and the *Irish People's Liberation Army* (IPLO) function as lesser competing companies.

LONG KESH: The old name of the prison outside of Belfast, home of the 1981 hunger strikes. While the prison was renamed *the Maze* some time ago, all diehard Republicans will persist in visiting their relatives in *the Kesh*; to visit the Maze is to risk conveying Protestant sympathies. There is no neutral way to refer to this place; to use any name is also to choose your side.

Only one of several opportunities to trip people's switches in ordinary conversation, for language in the North is landmined. In any pub you are faced with referring to *security forces* or *the Brits*; *terrorism* or the *Armed Struggle*, and you are best off choosing these words carefully in different parts of town. Even *Northern Ireland* conveys too much legitimacy to a Republican, who would prefer the ungainly the *Six Counties*, the *Twenty-six Counties* for the Republic, or, though outdated since 1937, the *Free State*. *Ulster* is a Protestant favorite. The *North* and the *South* remain the safest, most nonpartisan terms; "The North *of* Ireland," halfway between neutral and Nationalist, is not very brave. *Londonderry* is pointedly Unionist, *Derry* Nationalist, though the fact is just about everyone calls the town Derry informally because it's shorter.

LOYALIST: (See also: U-WORDS.)

The loyalty implied is to the United Kingdom. *Loyalist* is a slightly more passionate word for *Unionist*, suggesting more emotion and less thought. While he is capable of getting sentimental over "God Save the Queen," the Loyalist's fervor is rooted less in dedication to the Crown than in revulsion at a united Ireland. Like his Nationalist counterpart, the Loyalist feels victimized— for though Protestants in the North outnumber Catholics two to one, many perceive the IRA's intentions as genocidal. Unlike the IRA, which has an international reputation, Loyalist paramilitaries are something of a joke butt. As Britain has usurped the role of the Catholic nemesis, Loyalists feel irrelevant. They would love to defend their culture, if they could only figure out what it is. But British as a Loyalist will claim to be, when he visits England he will be treated, ironically, as an Irishman; as a foreigner. Consequently, the Loyalist feels lost—for apparently Britain has no more interest in the fate of Ulster Protestants than she has in its Catholics. Abandoned by everyone and with no comparable NORAID advocates in the States, Loyalists are suspicious of strangers and reluctant to give interviews. Orange propaganda is poorly produced, sometimes even ungrammatical. Where in Catholic ghettos the street murals are brilliantly drafted, Loyalist murals are childlike; especially the white horses of King William tend to look awkward. Their ballads are painfully colored by Irish traditional music. Their clubs are dark and small. Where Republicans attend IRA funerals in plain clothes, behind a lone piper, dignified black flags whipping on lampposts, Loyalist pageants are anachronistic, swinging with banners, tassels, and fringe, full marching bands; women will wrap themselves in Union Jacks, men parade with maces, in bowler hats and orange sashes. A Loyalist, in short, is a heartbreaker.

MINORITY: A way of thinking that puts one at an advantage, as in "Catholics are a minority in the North," or "Protestants are a minority in the whole of Ireland."

NATIONALIST: (See also: REPUBLICAN, SINN FEIN, and UNITED IRELAND.)

Any person or party that wishes to see Ireland a political whole, which some see as a simple geographic inevitability. Most Catholics are Nationalists, but not all Catholics are Nationalists, nor are all Nationalists Catholic . . . For an attraction of the North is its bollocks of political allegiances—the inadequacy of its categories, the uncooperative way its citizens will not necessarily slot themselves into neat pigeonholes for the convenience of your comprehension. Furthermore, neither do all Nationalists support the IRA. Foremost of these constitutional constituencies is the *Social Democratic and Labour Party* (SDLP), which represents the majority of Northern Catholics and hopes to arrange a thirty-two-county republic by political means. While there are many degrees of tacit or queasy support for the Provisionals in the Catholic community which give rise to Protestant mistrust, the average Nationalist has no use for them, and one can find the same aversion to Republican violence on the Falls Road as on the Shankill.

PLANTATION: The generous if admittedly easy gesture of giving away something that doesn't belong to you. Refers specifically to Britain's award nearly four hundred years ago of a large portion of confiscated Catholic farmland to Scots Presbyterians. "Plantation" sowed the seeds of a psychology which crops up to the present day: a Protestant population that feels guilty and besieged, sometimes rightfully fearful of a resentful Catholic peasantry, themselves robbed, shafted, and determined to get their island back. For while the Protestants have been there longer than the Pilgrims in America, they are still considered interlopers in Ireland.

POWER SHARING: A political framework first attempted in 1973, when a new Northern Ireland Executive was formed with the *Sunningdale Agreement*. In 1974, however, the Protestant *Ulster Workers' Council* (UWC) declared a general strike, barricading streets to cut off supplies of petrol, milk, bread. As a result, the Executive collapsed, though there are those who believe that had Britain held her ground Northern Ireland would not be where it is today. While Sunningdale is cited as proof that power sharing cannot work, recent opinion polls show that a devolved (semi-independent) power-sharing government would be acceptable to the majority of both the Protestant and Catholic communities.

PROTESTANT: A.k.a., *Prod, Orangie, Orange Bastard, Black Bastard, Bastard.* In Catholic mythology, dour, intransigent, bigoted, and rich. Not only more a political than a religious term—Ulstermen are prone to identify with Carson over Calvin—but, like "Catholic," bordering on the racial; for while Prods and Taigs are highly inbred and indistinguishable in face, mannerism, language, each can be convinced that if he ventures up the other's street he will be recognized. Since neighborhoods are small and cliquish, it is more likely the problem that he won't be.

RECONCILIATION GROUPS: A whole clatter of organizations established to fight factionalism which have become, functionally, one more faction.

Notably, the *Peace People*. In response to a family's sidewalk massacre in an auto chase between the army and the IRA, this protest group catapulted to international fame in a matter of months, until its leaders, Betty Williams and Mairead Corrigan, won the Nobel Peace Prize. Many in the Province were mortified when the women did not donate their prize money back to the movement but kept it for themselves. Scandal and organizational infighting put the Peace People's feet promptly back on the ground.

There are others: *Corrymeela*, the *Columbanus Community*, all sleeve-tugging—Why can't we all be friends? "A little wet," it's been said. "Their mothers didn't wipe them." On the whole, the North's relationship to these sorry ecumenists is condescending.

A political equivalent of the reconciliation group, the *Alliance Party* bids for the nonsectarian vote. Disdain for this coalition runs similarly high. Like the SDLP, the Alliance is smeared as middle-class: self-interested, twee.

REPUBLICAN: (See also: SINN FÉIN; UNITED IRELAND.)

Nationalist and then some—a Republican considers himself a socialist, and probably supports the IRA. Republicans regard themselves as defenders of an endangered culture and will often speak Irish among themselves; though as virtually no one in the North has been raised speaking it, Gaelic functions largely as a secret code. Republicans can lay claim not only to an Irishness far more alive in the North than in the Republic, but to a surprisingly old-fashioned Marxism; though dog-eared, an ideology of any kind gives their reasoning a bit more backbone than blind Loyalist flag-waving. Most Republican journalism, like *An Phoblacht*, is articulate. The propaganda is sophisticated, down to the graphics and quality of paper. Republican leaders seem impressively well educated, because they have spent a long time in prison, where there is plenty of time to read.

SINN FÉIN: Pronounced *shin fane*. Irish for "Ourselves Alone."

A legal political party that openly supports the IRA, Sinn

Feín took its first big bite of the Nationalist electorate during the 1981 hunger strikes, when, near death, Bobby Sands won a by-election on its ticket. Once Thatcher let an MP starve, Sinn Feín was here to stay. Sinners (pronounced *shinners*, though the spelling tingles), to the consternation of Unionists, who do not understand how this happened to them, sit on city councils, and run for Parliament.

Contrary to the image of the rough and ready IRA man, Sinn Feín president Gerry Adams sports a trim, natty beard and smokes a pipe. He is lucid, presentable, sharp. He leans back in his chair and makes jokes. He is a gentleman. Elected MP for West Belfast, Adams could not take his seat in Westminster even if he wished to—MP or not, he is under a restraining order and cannot set foot in mainland Britain.

In 1988 Britain censored from the airways Sinn Feín and like organizations that advocate violence. As a result, BBC viewers are now confronted with clips of Adams speaking while a broadcaster reads what the president is saying in a voice-over. Only during elections can Sinners speak with their own voices, at which time one hears from Adams quite a lot. Predictably, not letting Sinn Feín get good publicity has been good publicity for Sinn Feín.

TROUBLES WRITER: A known subspecies in the North, almost always of foreign extraction. Compulsively Romeo-and-Juliets his characters across the sectarian divide. Arrives in two varieties: the Weekend Troubles Writer will typically fly into Belfast for a few days to suss out his setting, return home, and get everything wrong. Type two, the Infatuated Troubles Writer, will stay for much longer, and often returns more than once. Embraces his new home Where Everyone Is So Alive with embarrassing enthusiasm. Will often remain in the North well beyond the point where everyone is quite bored with him. Frequently composes his Serious Novel *in situ*. Prefers Yeats in the title. Gets everything wrong, with feeling.

U-WORDS: The *OUP, UUP, PUP,* or any other acronym inclusive of the letter *U*—standing for *Unionist* or *Ulster*; either indicates an unweaning desire to remain in the gradually sagging bosom of Britannia. Of these, the most rabid is the *DUP*, led by Ian Paisley, an imposing Presbyterian minister with his own church, from whose pulpit he thunders against "the whore of Rome." In his unabashedly sectarian politics lurks a funny respectability: the honest-bigot syndrome.

Some U-words are more pernicious than others. The *Ulster Defense Association* (UDA), their illegal offshoot the *Ulster Freedom Fighters* (UFF), and the *Ulster Volunteer Force* (UVF) constitute the Protestant equivalent of the IRA. Their idea of a canny political statement runs to random assassination: classically Orange gunmen clump into a Catholic neighborhood and shoot *anybody*. Protestant paramilitaries do not kill very many people, though this is probably less because they are restrained than because they are not any good at it.

The *Ulster Defense Regiment* (UDR) is a locally recruited part-time arm of the British Army and dead Protestant—sometimes literally. The *Royal Ulster Constabulary* (RUC) is the largely Protestant local police. Prods nearly to the man, still the UDR and RUC imagine they wheel impartially through the Province to protect each side from slaughtering the other. It doesn't work.

ULSTER: Common Orange reference to the North, "Ulster" is a malaprop: the old Irish county of Ulster included Donegal, now part of the South—and Donegal is in the (lower-case) north . . . Once more, like "West Belfast," the inconveniences of geography are subsumed by the cruder requirements of politics.

UNITED IRELAND: A hypothetical nation in which there are no more problems and all the citizenry thrive in justice and tranquillity. Metaphorically: happiness. Historically: what has never been. Mythologically: *at the end of the day*, a phrase Northerners use compulsively, a time and place where all conflict will be resolved and there will be no more armies, and therefore an eventuality that every faction in Northern Ireland has a vested interest in preventing at all costs.

About the author

About the book

Insights,
Interviews
& More . . .

Read on

Meet Lionel Shriver

LIONEL SHRIVER'S NOVELS include
Big Brother, the National Book Award
finalist *So Much for That*, the *New York
Times* bestseller *The Post-Birthday
World*, and the international bestseller
We Need to Talk About Kevin (which
was made into a feature film starring
Tilda Swinton and John C. Reilly),
winner of the Orange Prize in 2005.
Her story "Kilifi Creek" won the BBC
National Short Story Award in 2014.
Her journalism has appeared in *The
Guardian*, *The New York Times*, *The
Wall Street Journal*, *The Economist*, and
many other publications. Shriver was
educated at Barnard College (BA) and
Columbia University (MFA). She has
lived in Nairobi, Bangkok, and Belfast,
and currently lives in London and
Brooklyn, New York. ◡

Teatime in London
Why I Spurn My Gerry Adams Mugs for the Cups from the John Harvard Library

THOUGH I'VE NEVER SEEN IT excerpted elsewhere, this novel's epigraph, from Ernest Hemingway's *Islands in the Stream*, is one of my favorite quotations. Were I not to prefer cremation, I'd be pleased for that passage to be inscribed on my tombstone.

For in my young adulthood, I surely qualified as one of those "intelligent people" going around "making themselves and everyone else miserable"—emphasis on the former. As a novelist, too, I believed that I gleaned my most valuable material from my own wretchedness. I harvested dejection like a crop. Should my life ever grow perky and pink, I feared I would have no more legitimate "experiences," no fervor to drive midnight rants at the keyboard, no meaty melancholy to chew on, and nothing to say.

Veneration of affliction isn't only a penchant of writers. Younger people of a certain stripe—ambitious, hungry, greedy in a good way—can be prone to perceive contentment as a threat and as a trap. Surely getting too satisfied and too comfortable means you don't go anywhere or do anything, and condemns you to blindly accepting the status quo. Having heart, living life profoundly, ▶

Teatime in London *(continued)*

must involve angst, anger, anguish, and despair. Happiness is for suckers.

If through my twenties I largely equated happiness with placidity, stasis, and idiocy, by the time I turned thirty and began this manuscript I had begun to question my elevation of suffering. Petty, pointless suffering, too, as the self-inflicted sort always is. I fasted for weeks at a time, to no particular purpose beyond seeing if I could do it. (If the experience was marginally interesting, I learned what there was to learn, and you will never again catch me going for days on end powered only by coffee in lieu of a worldwide famine.) I undertook cross-country cycling trips of thousands of miles, churning a hundred miles a day in often ghastly weather. (Ever wonder what controls where the wind blows? Apparently it switches to the exact opposite direction of wherever Lionel Shriver's bicycle is pointed.) I forced myself to decamp to foreign countries when secretly I preferred to stay home. Worst of all, I fell in love with the wrong men—men who didn't love me back, or who could at least be relied upon to make me miserable in those rare instances that I failed to do the job myself.

Ordinary Decent Criminals is both a consequence and an examination of these predilections. The novel is about people, in or out of Northern Ireland, who require troubles with a lower-case *T*—to feel important, stimulated, vital. Accordingly, it is also about people who are leery of love, which menaces the edgy, fractious life of discord with its soft, pillowy goo, and entices the adventurer with respite, ease, and the hellish repose of staying in one place. For the restless and willful, love offers weakness, enslavement, and sloth. Love, like happiness, is for suckers.

To set this novel where it belonged— a city where everyone adulated suffering— I moved to Belfast in 1987, with the intention of staying about nine months. The fact that I would be based in Belfast for the next twelve years helps to validate an aphorism coined in this very novel: *the temporary becomes the permanent.* To call those years formative is an understatement. Ensconced in the attic flat of a ramshackle Victorian manse, I apprenticed myself to the so-called Troubles, effectively earning an ad hoc doctorate in conflict studies. I don't regret any of the time I lived in Northern Ireland. I don't regret leaving, either.

Ordinary Decent Criminals was the product of my first couple of years in that town. I arrived with few preconceptions. Presbyterian by upbringing but aggressively lapsed, I harbored no natural allegiance to Protestants. Politically, I was a blank canvas. Both paramilitary extremes soon inspired an aversion, though the Protestant loyalists' crude, undereducated bumbling tended to trigger a loathing intermingled with pity. By contrast, the slick PR, ▶

Teatime in London *(continued)*

dissembling, and hypocrisy of IRA-supporting, Catholic-in-name-if-not-in-creed Republicans rapidly aroused a deeper and more perfectly untempered disgust. It irked me that back in the United States the IRA was regarded as liberal, left-wing, whereas in fact the organization was wildly illiberal—nationalistic, right-wing—and peopled by bullies and thugs, some of whom I met, none of whom I liked.

A word on the title. In general, titles either come to me effortlessly right away, or they're hard work, often up until the very last minute. Having gone through rubbish titles by the dozen, when the novel was about to press I settled in desperation on *The Bleeding Heart*, which I meant to scan as sardonic. It didn't. It sounded sappy. *The Bleeding Heart* is the worst title I have ever concocted in my life. My capacity to make such a grievous mistake—one that cost me in sales, and understandably gave reviewers a bad attitude from the get-go—humbles me to this day. I conditioned the UK foreign rights contract on permission to rename the book *Ordinary Decent Criminals*, then a real official term in Northern prisons, believe it or not, and a title with which I'm still pleased.

Now, I remained in Belfast many years after this novel's publication. The longer I stayed in Ulster—a nomenclatural giveaway that my sympathies eventually canted toward moderate unionists, who constituted a majority in the province, and wished for the North to remain in the United Kingdom—the more broadly my disgust spread to just about everybody. Though the touch paper of the conflict was a Catholic civil rights movement, by the time I arrived the Troubles had degenerated to an inconsequential feud over whether a tiny territory the size of Connecticut, with the population of Philadelphia, would remain in one democratic country in the European Union or join another democratic country in the European Union. It wasn't about civil rights. It was about nothing.

Which is not to say that nothing was at stake. In addition to the appalling waste of nearly 3,500 lives, the Troubles were a crucial test case of whether terrorism works. The short answer is yes. Terrorism won no end of social, economic, and political concessions for both sides of this ugly tit for tat— particularly for the IRA. Because *Ordinary Decent Criminals* had not fully explored this moral hazard, I was moved to write *The New Republic* in 1999—which, though set on a fictional peninsula of Portugal and about a purely fictional terrorist group, qualifies as this novel's sequel.

Just as I relied on self-imposed torment to feel alive, to feel like myself, to know who I was, to regard my life as compelling, the Northern Irish came to rely on bombs bursting in air for exactly these same certainties. For generations, ▶

Teatime in London *(continued)*

the conflict provided all and sundry with a ready-made identity and a perverse local pride. Disproportionate international attention that, as an American, I myself lavished on this sordid squabble only reinforced the dependency. Yet don't imagine that locals were grateful for the outside world's concern, or touched by foreign focus on the niggling details of their provincial problems. As a New Yorker, I never assumed my neighbors in South Belfast would give two hoots about the MTA, MOMA, or the Mets. By contrast, they took it as a given that I would find the fine historical distinctions between the Provisional IRA, the INLA, and the IRSP absolutely fascinating.

Since the conflict was officially—if not, alas, altogether in practice—brought to an end by the Good Friday Agreement in 1998, the Northern Irish have been forced to go cold turkey. In the dénouement since, citizens of every political stripe have gone through a protracted withdrawal from the crack highs of assassinations, riots, and car bombs. Northerners have had to reconstruct not just busted up buildings, but who they are.

Because my concluding "Glossary of Troublesome Terms" was included in the original text and is thus part of the novel, I have resisted updating it. Any references to the present in that dictionary allude to circa 1990. Much has happened since. Most notably, Northern Ireland has gradually accommodated itself to normal life. Despite a handful of retrograde holdouts, locals are decreasingly likely to define themselves by whom they revile and what grievances they bear. Sure, some Prods will still get irked that the region's license plates alone in the UK do not picture the Union Jack. But Ulster is now largely a land of property bubbles, cancer-charity fund drives, and disputes over water charges. (I find it salutary that the nationally popular 2013–14 BBC series *The Fall* was set in Belfast, yet the plot about a serial killer was wholly unrelated to Troubles politics.) Frankly, it's a lovely place to live.

For my own part, soon after quitting Belfast for London, I became strangely repulsed by the totems of a conflict that had once seemed so captivating. I stashed away the paramilitary posters from both sides that had festooned my Victorian flat with dry mockery; they remain in Tate Gallery tubes in the cellar, irremediably curled. For my afternoon tea, I spurn my extensive collection of Troubles mugs— emblazoned with self-important portraits of Gerry Adams, or a tongue-in-cheek cartoon of gun-toting "Reservoir Prods" in dark glasses— preferring the pleasantly anodyne cups with matching china spoons from the John Harvard Library in Southwark. On my several trips back to my old home, I've never been tempted to seek out the barbed-wired Peace Line, slip into Sinn Fein headquarters, or locate ▶

another Orange Order march. I stop in the secondhand shops on Balmoral Avenue. I stroll through the Botanical Gardens, or repeat my ritual run along the Lagan Towpath. I visit my dentist.

Thus what was initially written as a contemporary tale has mercifully foreshortened into an historical novel. Yet as the era in which *Ordinary Decent Criminals* was set recedes, the book itself becomes only more broadly pertinent, more allegorical. The tension the book explores is eternal: between a thirst for excitement, meaning, energy, purpose, passion, camaraderie, and high drama— all fostered by friction, by war and other forms of peril—and a yearning for peace, tranquility, rest, calm, stillness, safety, self-possession, harmony, and simple joy (embodied in this novel by "The House in Castlecaulfield"). Anyone drawn, say, to fighting in Syria would still wrestle with those opposing inclinations.

I do think the implicit parallel this book makes between the addiction to political upheaval and an addiction to romantic upheaval is sound. The same kind of person who tosses petrol bombs at barricades throws plates at home. Learning to settle into a place where not much happens and people basically get along requires the same spiritual maturity as a successful long-term marriage.

Latterly, I myself am unabashedly happy, and if that makes me dull, I can live with it. The arc I have travelled has doubtless been governed by age. Younger, like my protagonist Estrin Lancaster and her bête noire Farrell O'Phelan, I enjoyed a greater appetite for turmoil, in my environs and in my personal life. In my latter fifties, I enjoy a greater appetite for serenity. But I don't believe that's purely due to having calcified into a stodgy old fart. The cherishing of serenity feels like—dare I say it—wisdom.

I no longer regard happiness as a threat, or as a trap. Happiness is an achievement—"more exciting than any other thing, with the promise of as great intensity as sorrow" to those of us who are, however briefly, blessed with the sensation. Contentment is also a skill, and the folks who have mastered it tend to make superior company. If what you require for exhilaration is peril, life entails peril by its nature, since at any moment it can be snuffed out. Contentment is not the threat; illness, physical decay, penury, human malice, a host of planetary calamities like floods, earthquakes, and drought— *those* are threats. Even as a writer, I needn't harvest my own misery for material. The rest of the world festively obliges with a superabundance of suffering, and all I need do for material is look out the window.

There's peril galore. We're not going to run out. So if, between putting out fires and reporting for chemotherapy, you manage a glass of wine, an engaging book, and a hand to hold, good for you.

Lionel Shriver, 2015 ∾

Have You Read?
More from
Lionel Shriver

BIG BROTHER

When Pandora picks up her older brother Edison at the Iowa airport, she doesn't recognize him. In the four years since she last saw him, the once slim, hip New York jazz pianist has gained hundreds of pounds. What happened? And it's not just the weight. Edison breaks her husband Fletcher's handcrafted furniture, makes overkill breakfasts for the family, and entices her stepson not only to forgo college but to drop out of high school. After Edison has more than overstayed his welcome, Fletcher delivers his wife an ultimatum: it's him or me. But which loyalty is paramount, that of a wife or a sister? For without Pandora's support, surely Edison will eat himself into an early grave.

Rich with Shriver's distinctive wit and ferocious energy, *Big Brother* is about fat—an issue both social and excruciatingly personal. It asks just how much we are obligated to help members of our families, and whether it's ever possible to save loved ones from themselves.

"(A) delicious, highly readable novel . . . (which) raises challenging questions

about how much a loving person can give to another without sacrificing his or her own well-being."
—*People,* People Pick (4 stars)

"Shriver's talents are many: She's especially skilled at playing with readers's reflexes for sympathy and revulsion, never letting us get too comfortable with whatever firm understanding we think we have of a character."   —*Washington Post*

THE NEW REPUBLIC

Ostracized as a kid, Edgar Kellogg has always yearned to be popular. A disgruntled New York corporate lawyer, he's more than ready to leave his lucrative career for the excitement and uncertainty of journalism. When he's offered the post of foreign correspondent in a Portuguese backwater that has sprouted a homegrown terrorist movement, Edgar recognizes the disappeared larger-than-life reporter he's been sent to replace, Barrington Saddler, as exactly the outsize character he longs to emulate. Infuriatingly, all his fellow journalists cannot stop talking about their beloved "Bear," who is no longer lighting up their work lives.

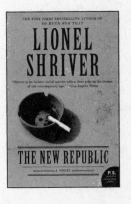

Yet all is not as it appears. *Os Soldados Ousados de Barba*—"The Daring Soldiers of Barba"—have been blowing up the rest of the world for years in order to win independence for a province so dismal, backward, and windblown that you couldn't give the rat hole away. So why, with Barrington vanished, do terrorist incidents claimed by the "SOB" suddenly dry up?

A droll, playful novel, *The New Republic* addresses weighty issues like terrorism with the deft, tongue-in-cheek touch that is vintage Shriver. It also presses the more intimate question: What makes particular people so magnetic, while the rest of us inspire a shrug? What's their secret? And in the end, who has the better life—the admired, or the admirer?

"It takes guts to write a satire about terrorism—and Lionel Shriver has guts. . . . Shriver is an incisive social satirist with a clear grip on the ironies of our contemporary age . . . [Her] take on journalism and international politics is wry, insightful, and just over the top enough to be fun."   —*Los Angeles Times*

SO MUCH FOR THAT

Shep Knacker has long saved for "the Afterlife," an idyllic retreat in the Third World where his nest egg can last forever. Exasperated that his wife, Glynis, has concocted endless excuses why it's never the right time to go, Shep finally announces he's leaving for a Tanzanian island, with or without her. Yet Glynis has some news of her own: she's deathly ill. Shep numbly puts his dream aside, while his nest egg is steadily devastated by staggering bills that their health insurance only partially covers.

Astonishingly, illness not only strains their marriage but saves it.

From acclaimed *New York Times* bestselling author Lionel Shriver comes a searing, ruthlessly honest novel. Brimming with unexpected tenderness and dry humor, it presses the question: How much is one life worth?

"Powerful. . . . Wrenching. . . . Once again Lionel Shriver has stomped into the middle of a pressing national debate with a great ordeal of a novel that's impossible to ignore. . . . If Jodi Picoult has her finger on the zeitgeist, Shriver has her hands around its throat."
　　　　　—Ron Charles, *Washington Post*

"A visceral and deeply affecting story, a story about how illness affects people's relationships and how their efforts to grapple with mortality reshape the arcs of their lives. . . . [Shriver's] understanding of her people is so intimate, so unsentimental . . . it lofts these characters permanently into the reader's imagination."
　　　　　—Michiko Kakutani, *New York Times*

THE POST-BIRTHDAY WORLD

American children's book illustrator Irina McGovern enjoys a secure, settled life in London with her smart, loyal, disciplined partner, Lawrence—until the night she finds herself inexplicably drawn to kissing another man, a passionate, extravagant, top-ranked snooker player. Two competing alternate futures hinge on this single kiss, as Irina's decision—to surrender to temptation or to preserve her seemingly safe partnership with Lawrence—will have momentous consequences for her career, her friendships and familial relationships, and the texture of her daily life.

"A layered and unflinching portrait of infidelity. . . . Shriver pulls off a tremendous feat of characterization. . . . Better yet, the author is more interested in raising questions about love and fidelity than in pat moralizing. Readers will wonder which choice was best for Irina, but Shriver masterfully confounds any attempt to arrive at a sure answer."
—*Kirkus Reviews* (starred review)

WE NEED TO TALK ABOUT KEVIN

Eva never really wanted to be a mother—and certainly not the mother of the malicious boy who murdered seven of his fellow high school students, a cafeteria worker, and a much-adored teacher who had tried to befriend him, all two days before his sixteenth birthday. Now, two years later, it is time for her to come to terms with marriage, career, family, parenthood, and Kevin's horrific rampage in a series of startlingly direct correspondences with her estranged husband, Franklin. Uneasy with the sacrifices and social demotion of motherhood from the start, Eva fears that her alarming dislike for her own son may be responsible for driving him so nihilistically off the rails.

"Sometimes searing . . . impossible to put down . . . brutally honest. . . . Who, in the end, needs to talk about Kevin? Maybe we all do." —*Boston Globe*

DOUBLE FAULT

Tennis has been Willy Novinsky's one love ever since she first picked up a racquet at the age of four. A middle-ranked pro at twenty-three, she's met her match in Eric Oberdorf, a low-ranked, untested Princeton grad who also intends to make his mark on the international tennis circuit. Eric becomes Willy's first passion off the court, and eventually they marry. But while wedded life begins well, full-tilt

competition soon puts a strain on
their relationship—and an unexpected
accident sends driven and gifted Willy
sliding irrevocably toward resentment,
tragedy, and despair.

From acclaimed author Lionel Shriver
comes a brilliant and unflinching novel
about the devastating cost of prizing
achievement over love.

"Shriver shows in a masterstroke
why character is fate and how sport
reveals it."
—*New York Times Book Review*

"A brilliant tale of doomed love. . . . This
is not a novel about tennis or rivalry; it's
about love, marriage, and the balance of
power in relationships. . . . *Double Fault*
is a compelling and playfully ironic take
on the sex wars, blistering with . . .
brilliant writing and caustic language."
—*The Observer* (London)

A PERFECTLY GOOD FAMILY

Following the death of her worthy liberal
parents, Corlis McCrea moves back
into her family's grand Reconstruction
mansion in North Carolina, willed to all
three siblings. Her timid younger brother
has never left home. When her bullying
black-sheep older brother moves into
"his" house as well, it's war.

Each heir wants the house. Yet to buy
the other out, two siblings must team
against one. Just as in girlhood, Corlis
is torn between allying with the decent

but fearful youngest and the iconoclastic eldest, who covets his legacy to destroy it. *A Perfectly Good Family* is a stunning examination of inheritance, literal and psychological: what we take from our parents, what we discard, and what we are stuck with, like it or not.

"Often funny and always intelligent, this is a sharply observed history of the redoubtable McCrea family, shot through with sardonic wit and black comedy."   —*The Independent*

GAME CONTROL

Eleanor Merritt, a do-gooding American family-planning worker, was drawn to Kenya to improve the lot of the poor. Unnervingly, she finds herself falling in love with the beguiling Calvin Piper, despite (or perhaps because of) his misanthropic theories about population control and the future of the human race. Surely, Calvin whispers seductively in Eleanor's ear, if the poor are a responsibility, they are also an imposition.

Set against the vivid backdrop of shambolic modern-day Africa—a continent now primarily populated with wildlife of the two-legged sort—Lionel Shriver's *Game Control* is a wry, grimly comic tale of bad ideas and good intentions. With a deft, droll touch, Shriver highlights the hypocrisy of lofty intellectuals who would "save" humanity but who don't like people.

Have You Read? *(continued)*

"One of the best works of fiction about Africa I've ever read." —Amanda Craig, *New Statesman* (London)

CHECKER AND THE DERAILLEURS

Beautiful and charismatic, nineteen-year-old Checker Secretti is the most gifted drummer that the club-goers of Astoria, Queens, have ever heard. When he plays, conundrums seem to solve themselves, brilliant thoughts spring to mind, and couples fall in love. The members of his band, The Derailleurs, are passionately devoted to their guiding spirit, as are all who fall under Checker's spell. But when another drummer, Eaton Striker, hears the prodigy play, he is pulled inexorably into Checker's orbit by a powerful combination of admiration and envy. Soon The Derailleurs, too, are torn apart by latent jealousies that Eaton does his utmost to bring alive.

"Nothing if not lyrical, both in the internal assonances of its sentences . . . and in sentiment. It is fairy tale as well as theology, a domestic adventure story featuring wisdom."   —*The New Yorker*

Gray Kaiser, at fifty-nine a world-renowned anthropologist, seemingly invincible—and untouchable—returns to the site of her first great triumph in Kenya to make a documentary. She is accompanied by her faithful assistant, Errol McEchern, who has loved her from afar for years. When Raphael Sarasola, a sexy young graduate assistant assigned to Gray's project, arrives on the scene, Gray is captivated and, before Errol's amazed and injured eyes, falls head over heels in love. As Errol watches the progress of their affair with jealous fascination, Raphael's true nature is revealed—but only after his subtle, cruel, and calculating manipulations of Gray reduce this proud and fierce woman to miserable dependence.

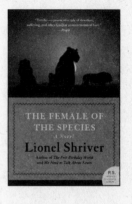

"Stunning . . . wide in its horizons, interesting in its insights, and satisfying in its conclusions."
—*Philadelphia Inquirer*